CALF

CALF

a novel

ANDREA KLEINE

SOFT SKULL PRESS

"You're a Grand Old Flag," song lyrics by George M. Cohan, 1906
The Wonderful Wizard of Oz, book by L. Frank Baum,1899, George M. Hill Company
"My Country 'Tis of Thee," song lyrics by Samuel Francis Smith, 1831

Library of Congress Cataloging-in-Publication Data

Kleine, Andrea, 1970-
Calf : A Novel / Andrea Kleine.
pages cm
1. Hinckley, John W.—Fiction. 2. Socialites—Fiction.
3. Washington (D.C.)—Fiction. 4. Biographical fiction. I. Title.
PS3611.L454C35 2015
813'.6—dc23
2015009332

ISBN: 978-1-59376-655-9

Cover design by Faceout Studios
Interior design by Elyse Strongin, Neuwirth & Associates, Inc.

Soft Skull Press
New York, NY

www.softskull.com

FOR MY SISTER AND MY BROTHER

Although a work of fiction, this novel is inspired by two converging events: John Hinckley Jr.'s attempted assassination of Ronald Reagan, and Leslie deVeau's murder of her ten-year-old daughter. Both events took place in Washington, DC, between 1981–1982. Hinckley and deVeau, both found not guilty by reason of insanity, later became lovers while patients at St. Elizabeths Hospital. DeVeau's daughter was my friend. She was killed on the eve of my twelfth birthday party.

"Well, boys, your troubles are over now; mine have just begun."

—ABRAHAM LINCOLN,
leaving for the White House in 1860

PART ONE

HAIL TO THE REDSKINS

* * *

Tammy's mother liked to tell people that her daughter was conceived the day Neil Armstrong walked on the moon and was born nine months later when word got out that the Beatles had officially broken up. Tammy didn't exactly understand that story, nor the part about "It's a good thing I didn't go to Woodstock." Tammy was born in 1970 so it was easy for her to keep track of how old she was. She would be eleven in 1981. She would be twelve in 1982. In 1988 she would be eighteen, and in the year 2000 she would be thirty. On December 7, 1980, one month after Reagan appeared on the cover of *Time* magazine with the caption, "A fresh start," Tammy was ten and a half years old and the contents of her life were packed into boxes filling a U-Haul truck and her mother's station wagon with the faded green-and-white "Re-Elect Carter/Mondale" bumper sticker on its rear end.

Tammy used to live outside Washington, DC, on the Virginia side. Now she was going to live inside the city, inside the Beltway, on the edge of a nice neighborhood called Friendship Heights. Tammy could tell the new house was on the edge because it was so close to the big street, Wisconsin Avenue, where a Sears department store took up the entire block, and a department store clearly marked the border of something.

The new house had flat green carpeting on the first floor like a miniature golf course. Tammy's mother didn't like carpeting because Steffi had asthma and carpets attract dust and dust causes asthma. Steffi had to sleep with rubber sheets under her regular sheets because of dust, although Tammy liked to tell people it was really because Steffi wet the bed. Tammy's mother and Nick pulled up the mossy carpet and rolled it across the floor until it was just a dusty gray tube. They carried it on their shoulders, out the back door, and dumped it in the alley.

The new house was old. Tammy and Steffi had new bedrooms connected by a separator door. The separator door had windows and looked like a door that led to the outside. The smaller room used to be a terrace and the previous owner had converted it. Tammy was two years older than Steffi so she got first choice of the new rooms. Tammy's bed and dresser were already moved into the bigger room when she realized that Steffi would have to walk through her room in order to get in or out of the smaller room and that it was going to be annoying. Tammy knew it was too late to switch and she wished she had figured that out beforehand.

The new house was full of roaches. Tammy killed three in her bedroom while unpacking boxes of books.

Now that their mother had a job again, Tammy and Steffi were each given a key to wear on a string around their necks. Their mother decided they didn't need a baby-sitter anymore; the girls could take care of themselves. No one would be home when they got out of school, so their mother and Nick made lots of rules. They were not allowed to watch TV during the day. They were never allowed to watch TV in the living room, which was reserved for adults only. They had another TV in a separate kids' room in the back of the house. Tammy's and Steffi's keys were to the back door; the front door lock was too complicated for them. Tammy and Steffi would have to walk Hugh to his preschool in the mornings and baby-sit him in the afternoons. They would switch turns every other day and whose turn it was would be written down on the dry-marker board in the kitchen.

The next morning Steffi was sick. She was always sick. Sometimes she faked it and sometimes she really was sick. She always had a lot of missed days marked off on her report card. Steffi was lying on the sofa in the living room watching *I Love Lucy* reruns. If someone was sick, they were allowed to watch TV during the day, and in the living room.

At the new school Tammy waited on a plastic turquoise-colored chair in the office while her mother filled out forms and corrected the confused secretary about her last name, which was different from Tammy's last name. Her mother had first changed it when she married Tammy's dad. Then they got divorced in 1975, when Tammy was five and Steffi was three, and her mother changed it back to her maiden name. Then she married Nick about a year later in 1976, when Tammy was six and Steffi was four, and changed it to Nick's last name. This confused everybody and she got mail with all sorts of names on it.

Tammy thought December was a really dumb time to start a new school. She thought it was a better idea to take the rest of the year off and start fresh in January. Her mother said, "It doesn't work that way," but she didn't give a real answer. So Tammy sat in the school office, like a kid who had gotten in trouble, while her mother registered her for the fifth grade and Steffi for the third grade. Hugh was only four years old. His feet didn't reach the floor. He swung them back and forth between the silver chair legs as he chewed on the brown string that was supposed to tie the hood of his coat under his chin. Hugh was named after someone in Nick's family whom Tammy had never met. His last name was also different from Tammy's.

Tammy put it together that they had to sell the old house because of the divorce. Before they moved, Tammy had accidentally picked up the phone while her mother was talking to her dad. She knew she wasn't supposed to eavesdrop, but she cupped her hand over the mouthpiece and listened anyway. Her dad said something like, "Look, hon, I let it slide for a long time because of the girls. But it's been almost four years. You married the guy. Enough's enough."

When they were done in the office, the school secretary walked Tammy down the hall to her new classroom. The fifth-grade teacher, Mrs. William, was old, maybe not as old as a grandmother, but definitely older than a mother. She had short, curly hair, the kind that had been set in curlers overnight. Yellow cutout construction-paper ribbons were taped to the windowpanes and on a sectioned-off corner of the blackboard were written the words "The Hostages – Day 400." Mrs. William rummaged around in her desk drawer and handed Tammy a question-naire. Tammy looked down at the purple mimeographed handwriting and realized everyone in the class was staring at her. She got that shaky feeling she usually got right before she had to throw up.

My name is _____

Please call me _____

Things I like: _____

Things I hate: _____

This year in school _____

For a moment, Tammy felt a sense of comfort because she recognized the questionnaire from the book *Are You There God? It's Me, Margaret*, which she had read over the summer. She had read almost all of the Judy Blume books, except *Forever*, the sex book. She wondered for a second if this was a pop quiz to see if she had read the book. Maybe she was supposed to fill in the same answers as Margaret and say she hated religious holidays. Or maybe it was just the teacher's way of proving she knew what kids read.

Tammy forgot to write in cursive the way you were supposed to on all official school papers once you were past the third grade. She couldn't think of anything to write for "This year in school," so she wrote what Margaret wrote in the book: "I want to have fun." It wasn't exactly copying because Tammy wanted to have fun too. Besides, she wasn't 100 percent sure if she was supposed to write her own answers or what was in the book, and she didn't want to start off in the new school with a bunch of wrong answers. She added "the smell of rain" to her likes, just to cover her bases. She handed her completed questionnaire back to Mrs. William who motioned for Tammy to take an empty desk. Before Tammy got her butt in the chair, the teacher started reading her answers out loud to everyone in class.

My name is Tammy

Please call me Tammy

Things I like: to read, draw, salami, the smell of rain

Things I hate: my sister, my brother, cleaning my room

This year in school I want to have fun

"She likes salami," one boy said, wiggling his eyebrows at her. "Big, fat salami." Another one said, "Rain smells like cat piss." And a boy wearing a T-shirt that said, *I'm not a tourist, I live here! Washington, DC*, started cracking up. Mrs. William didn't hear them. She wrote the date, December 8, 1980, on the blackboard and changed the chalked 400 to 401 in the hostage square. Then everyone stood up and faced the flag perched in the corner and began to recite the Pledge of Allegiance. After "with liberty and justice for all" a skinny boy sat down at the piano and the class launched into a rowdy round of "You're a Grand Old Flag" with a few extra beats added on.

> *You're a grand old flag,*
> *You're a high-flying flag,*
> *And forever in peace may you wave.*
> *Rah! Rah! Rah!*

It was the row of all boys who started the *Rah! Rah!* add-ons with their fists raised, punching the air. When the song was over, Tammy was about to sit back down, but Mrs. William said that since the Redskins had won their game on Sunday against the San Diego Chargers, they would sing "Hail to the Redskins." Tammy didn't know the words so she just stood there while everyone else sang the song, which sounded a lot like "You're a Grand Old Flag." Mrs. William explained that they sang that song whenever the Redskins won, and sometimes they sang it even if they lost, if the class thought they had played a good game.

There was no cafeteria like there had been in Tammy's old school. Here all the kids ate at their desks during lunchtime without teacher supervision. The boy wearing the *I'm not a tourist* shirt and another boy wearing a *Solidarność* T-shirt stuffed lunchmeat into Tammy's thermos mug.

"Ignore him, he's gross," said the girl sitting next to Tammy. She picked out the lunchmeat, now soaked with red Kool-Aid, and flung it back across the aisle. The boys ducked out of the way of the flying bologna and it landed on the floor with a wet smack.

"I'm Gretchen," the girl said. She was wearing jeans and a striped sweater and her long hair was clipped back with ribbon barrettes. Tammy thought she was the prettiest girl in class even though she had braces. Gretchen scooted her chair up to Tammy's desk and gave her the dirt on everyone in class. Gretchen said she was the smartest girl in the fifth grade. Tammy was about to ask her how she knew that when Gretchen cut in and said that she always scores way above grade level on standardized tests. "And besides that," Gretchen said, "it's just known."

Gretchen gestured around the room with her sandwich. Monique was the tallest girl in class. She was half Korean and half something else and almost as smart as Gretchen, and also lived on the same block as Gretchen. Heather was the second tallest girl. She had curly hair and big bones. It was rumored that she had gotten her period in the fourth grade. Someone said she brought maxi pads to school in a brown paper bag so it looked like part of her lunch, and that one time she didn't have any pads so she wadded up toilet paper and stuck it in her underwear. She lived practically next door to school and her backyard ran up against the schoolyard fence. Olga was Russian. She wore panty hose and spoke with an accent. Gretchen thought she was held back a grade because she was Russian. Nobody in class liked her.

During the recess period after lunch Tammy's class had to play Circle Dodge. They started out with half of the kids inside the circle and half on the outside. Once someone on the inside got hit, they had to move to the outside. It was better in the beginning when there were lots of people in the middle of the circle and everyone bonded together and there was a chance you could hide behind someone. If you were one of only a few people left, it became personal. They were going to get you.

Olga was terrorized during the game. Gretchen started off a chant of "Down-with Russ-sha, down-with Russ-sha" until Olga left the circle in tears. Once she was gone the chant changed to "U-S-A, U-S-A, U-S-A." The teachers smoked cigarettes a safe distance away and did nothing about it.

After the bell rang at three o'clock, Tammy picked Hugh up from his day care, which was right next door to her school and used the same playground. When she got there Hugh was wearing a blue shower cap on his head. The woman at the day care gave Tammy a note in an envelope and said to give it to her parents. Tammy knew what it meant. It meant Hugh had lice. He had come home from day care this way several times before. Tammy's mother would make all three kids go through the delousing treatment of sitting with insecticide on their heads while a kitchen timer ticked away twenty minutes of metallic clicks. Meanwhile, everything was thrown into the laundry and washed with insecticide detergent. What couldn't be thrown in the wash was sprayed. The whole house would smell of gross chemicals. Tammy's mother would be forced to call the other mothers and tell them her kids had lice and that they should check their kids because they played together. The other mothers would react with "Oh no, not my child" and not check. Then everyone would get reinfected.

The day-care woman looked at Tammy like she didn't think Tammy was old enough to be in charge of her own brother. People were always giving Tammy looks like that. It wasn't that Tammy looked young for her age, but she always found herself getting those kind of looks, usually when her mother or Nick asked her to do something like return meat to the grocery store without a receipt, or explain to a teacher that they tore up some school form because what they did for a living and how much money they made wasn't any of the school's business. But today Tammy knew the look meant she was gross. It wasn't a good thing for Hugh to get lice on his first day of day care. The woman probably thought he had it beforehand. She probably thought Tammy had it too.

"Let's go," Tammy said and tugged on Hugh's sleeve to get them out of there.

When they got outside Tammy tried to put Hugh's hood over the shower cap so no one from her school would see it, but Hugh squirmed away from her and wouldn't let her tie the string under his chin and Tammy didn't want to touch Hugh's head and get his lice. She led Hugh around the long way, behind the Sears department store and away from the kids in her class hanging out in front of the school.

It was drizzling when they got to the first intersection. A minute later it was raining. Tammy and Hugh didn't have any umbrellas or raincoats because they hadn't been unpacked yet.

"Why did we move?" Hugh asked. He hadn't said anything since Tammy picked him up. Now he pulled his hood over his head because of the rain.

"I think because of the divorce," Tammy said.

"What was the divorce?"

"When Mom was married to my dad."

"Do you think we'll move back?" Hugh asked. Tammy had to stop every ten steps or so and let him catch up because his legs were so short. She also had to wait for him at every intersection and hold his hand.

"Probably not," she said. "We have to live here now."

"Why?"

"I don't know. We just have to."

They found their way back to their new house, which was on the corner of Bemis and 43rd Streets according to the map Tammy's mother had made for her showing the way home from school. When they got to their corner, Nick was coming out of the front door. He and her mother had taken the day off from work to unpack and run errands. Tammy told Hugh to play in the yard. Nick heard her and yelled, "Why are you telling him to play outside? It's raining! Are you crazy?" Tammy didn't want to say anything because she was afraid it would make Nick yell more. But Nick was glaring at her and waiting for an answer. "I don't know," she said, looking at the mud squishing around her sneakers. Nick said, "Go inside before you both get sick," and walked over to the car.

Tammy used her key to unlock the back door. Steffi was still on the couch in her pajamas, still watching TV. She looked up at Tammy with a tired expression, which meant, "I'm sick, you have to be nice to me."

Tammy went upstairs and knocked on her mother's door. Her mother didn't yell as much as Nick. Her mother was smart. She used to want to be a lawyer. She went to law school for half a year, but then she met Tammy's dad and got pregnant with Tammy. Tammy once asked her why she never became a lawyer. Her mother said it was too much. Now she worked as a legal secretary.

"Yes?"

Her mother was lying back on the rainbow bedspread wearing jeans and a sweatshirt that were both once dark blue but now had faded to a purplish gray. Tammy knew her mother wore a bra to work, but as soon as she came home she took it off along with her skirt and panty hose, like a girl version of Mister Rogers. She was on the phone and hooked the receiver on her shoulder as she waited for Tammy to say something.

"Hugh's day care said to give you this."

Her mother's expression didn't change. They had just moved and her mother had been filling out forms all week. Tammy had to be more specific.

"He had a shower cap on his head when I went to pick him up."

Her mother quickly said, "I'll call you back," into the phone and hung up. She didn't let Tammy sit on her bed or stand anywhere near it. She pushed her out of the room, down the hall, and into the bathroom. Under the bright light by the sink, she rolled up her sleeves and picked through Tammy's hair. She made a few noises, the kind of noises she made when she had to fish a spoon out of the drain or remove a splinter—things she found gross. At their old house they lived next door to a woman who said she was a vegetarian because she didn't like blood. She made the same noises whenever she had to get out a Band-Aid.

"Yeah, there they are."

She washed her hands.

"Stay here."

She walked downstairs and Tammy heard Steffi say, "What?!" and start to whine. Then Hugh started to cry. He cried at anything. They both trudged up the stairs as her mother came back into the bathroom.

"We'll wash your hair first since you're already here."

Her mother helped Tammy take off her shirt and transfer it to a shopping bag. Then Tammy stood topless in front of the sink as her mother dunked her head with water and lathered her hair with the gross-smelling lice shampoo.

Tammy wiped the water that stung the corners of her eyes and told her mother that Nick yelled a lot. Her mother said Tammy shouldn't do things to set him off. Like what? Tammy asked. Her mother said like being smart and talking back. That just sets him off and you know it. Tammy said everything sets him off. And her mother said that's just how he is. He had been in Vietnam and he had seen some things. Tammy told her there wasn't a war on now. And besides that, he wasn't really a soldier, he was in communications. Her mother said that even though Nick wasn't on the front lines, he was still *in* the army, and he was still stationed *in* Vietnam. Tammy's mother told her she would understand when she was older. That was her response to anything she didn't want to explain.

Tammy told her mother she really didn't like Nick. Tammy started to cry a little when she said that, but her mother didn't notice because Tammy's tears blended with the sink water running down her face. Tammy sniffed water up her nose and tried to breathe normally. She tried to be nice about it and say she thought Nick was okay as a person, but she didn't like living with him and she didn't like him trying to be a father. Her mother said, I'm sorry you feel that way, but you'll have to get used to him. She said Steffi didn't have a problem, and he was her brother's father. Tammy said she wasn't going to get used to him and she wasn't going to like him. Her mother said she had to because they were married. Tammy said she and Dad were married before they got divorced. Why didn't she just divorce Nick?

Her mother didn't say anything. She flicked the water off her hands, set the kitchen timer for twenty minutes, and told Tammy to wait in the bathroom. Tammy sat there on the edge of the tub. Topless, wet, and cold.

She sat there and shivered for twenty metal ticks.

THE NEXT MORNING, Nick had the TV on in the living room and Steffi was watching it with him. They never watched TV in the mornings, unless someone was sick or unless it was Saturday when they were allowed to watch cartoons in the kids' TV room until eleven. Sometimes they listened to the kitchen radio in the morning, but that was it. Nick wanted to watch TV because John Lennon had been shot the night before and this was the first he'd heard about it. Tammy didn't know he liked John Lennon so much, but Nick stood there in front of the TV and didn't eat any breakfast. Tammy thought for a moment that he might actually cry because he covered his mouth with his fist and scrunched his eyebrows up, and when her mother asked him a question, he shrugged and didn't say anything. Steffi reached up and held his hand. Tammy didn't understand why they were so upset about someone they didn't know.

"You're going to be late," Tammy's mother said, and rubbed Nick's back. That was what she did when she thought someone was sad.

"Yeah," Nick said. "God." He coughed a few times into his fist and shrugged his shoulders. He turned to Tammy and said, "That's history, right there," and then picked up his coat and walked out the door without saying good-bye.

Tammy went back up to her room and got her Polaroid camera, which she had unpacked the night before. If Nick thought it was that important, maybe she should take a picture of it. Maybe Nick would want to keep it. She tromped back downstairs with her camera and aimed it at the TV. The camera spat out the greeny-gray photo and Tammy held it carefully by the edges so she wouldn't mess up the developing. Tammy's mother told the kids to hurry up because she was going to lock the front door behind them. Tammy wanted to see the picture come out, but her mother said she would have to wait. It will be there when you get home, she said.

THIS IS REAGAN COUNTRY

* ❧ *

The bus dropped Jeffrey Hackney off in front of the duck pond marking the entrance to the circle. It was called a duck pond, although there were no ducks. The homeowners' association, where his mother served as assistant secretary, didn't want people swimming in it. Jeffrey and his parents lived in the house at the far dead end of the neatly paved suburban enclave. Every place they had ever lived looked the same. Their address always had Cul de Sac or Circle or Court in it. They never lived on a simple Street or Avenue or even a Place. One time, for a year, they had lived on a Way. They moved around a lot when Jeffrey was a kid while his father set up businesses, little franchise colonies stretching from Kansas to Texas, KC to Big D. Each suburban neighborhood was shaped like a tentacle curling over small, sloping, artificial hills. Postwar Utopia planners had it worked out so that people could walk everywhere, mothers could push their strollers down black asphalt paths trimmed with daffodils all the way to the grocery store. No one ever did that. They drove everywhere.

Jeffrey carried with him extra copies of the *Dallas Morning News* and the *Fort Worth Star-Telegram*, and also pages of the *New York Times* photocopied from the college library. Two days after John Lennon had been shot dead on the street while Yoko screamed hysterically, it was still front-page news, although today the coverage was to be continued in the B section and it didn't begin on the top half of the front page, but on the bottom. Still, the front page was the front page. A lot of the photos had stupid captions such as "The Day the Music Died." The little Jimmy Olsens at the newspapers didn't even know that wasn't a Beatles song.

The papers flapped under Jeffrey's arm as he headed up to the house, which commanded the circle from the far side. They were back in a circle now. Neighborhood boys played kick the can in the street, although it really wasn't a street, it was more like a parking lot that no one parked in with little extra villi sprouting off as driveways. If someone did park on the asphalt circle, inevitably a neighbor would drop by with a friendly knock and say, "Hey, pal, you know you parked in the circle? Just wondering when you were going to move it."

Jeffrey skirted the edge of the blacktop to avoid the boys; he knew what they were like. They were the types who would try to hit him with a baseball on purpose and then say, oh, I'm sorry, mister. Really. It flew right out of my hands. Although Jeffrey was older than those boys, they weren't afraid of him. One time they hit him with a Wiffle ball and Jeffrey didn't look up. Just kept walking, bangs hanging in his face, stomach lumbering under his jacket. The boys started in with their "I'm sorry, mister" routine and Jeffrey refused to glance at them. That pissed the boys off and they pelted him a couple more times with the plastic ball. His mother had taught him to ignore people who teased him. Real men don't pick fights, she said. One must turn the other cheek, just as Jesus did. Jeffrey didn't turn his other cheek; he kept the same one aimed at the boys.

"Is that you, Jeffrey?" his mother rang out before he had both feet in the door. He had tried to sneak in quietly. The house was built with the front door on its own landing, a suspended foyer with one staircase leading up to the living room and the other leading down to the den and his bedroom. He was usually good at slipping in, but he was caught this time.

"Jeffrey?"

He glanced up at the living room where skinny metal prison bars cordoned off the staircase and kept people from plummeting to the front door. His mother was perched on the edge of the sofa surrounded by a couple of other ladies in suntanned panty hose. A plate of deviled eggs lay on the coffee table.

"Jeffrey, come up and say hello."

His mother was trying to be nice. She knew he didn't like company. When his parents threw a dinner party he preferred to fake an illness and stay in his room. His high school guidance counselor had told his parents that Jeffrey had problems with *socialization*. Since then, his mother was always on his case about coming to say hello.

"I just need to go to my room for a second," Jeffrey said and backed out down the stairs. He overheard his mother say, ". . . very shy," and, ". . . very upset about that musician shooting," followed by her friends' overly understanding, "Ohhh."

Last year, when he started college, he wanted to reinvent himself as Jeff. Jeffrey Hackney sounded redundant. He liked Jeff. Jeff Hack. That sounded good. Macho. Jeff Hack. Don't fuck with me. He began to write Jeff on his papers and on the first day of the semester when they had to go around and introduce themselves, something he loathed and would often skip the first class to avoid, he said, "I'm Jeff." He hated those get-to-know-you classes, everyone sitting in a circle like duck, duck, goose until slowly it came around to him. He would practice saying, "I'm Jeff," in his head, but when it was finally his turn, he would say it stupidly, with a need to clear his throat, or not loud enough so that some jerk would say, "What? I didn't catch that."

Jeffrey placed the newspapers on his desk to be cut out later and pasted with rubber cement into a memorial scrapbook. He leaned back on his single bed with its corduroy cover and strategically positioned his feet so his shoe soles hung over the edge. He folded his hands across his middle and stared at the ceiling. He hoped his mother's friends weren't staying for dinner. If they were, he expected his mother would be down with a quiet knock on his door and she'd ask him to come to the table. If they weren't, he would hear the ladies walking carefully down the first set of stairs in their sensible pumps and the front door would open and close a couple of times. He imagined it would take the same amount of time, probably half an hour. He could stare for half an hour. He could stare for much longer.

A few months ago, he had cut an advertisement out of the paper for the Columbia School of Broadcasting. *A career in radio broadcasting or sound engineering!* He thought that might be interesting. Maybe he could get free records, giveaways, that sort of thing. Radio stations were always giving away free stuff. He imagined he could clean up pretty well. But then there was the downside of having to deal with deejays and their annoyingly loud voices. Even with someone dead they were making it all about them, all about the time they met John Lennon backstage. They probably *did* meet him, but they were so drunk or stoned they don't really remember, and they don't want to admit it now that he's dead. Deejays were always telling stupid jokes on the air. They were probably that way in real life too. Probably lots of jokes around the station. Jeffrey imagined he would be the brunt of a lot of jokes, so he threw out the ad. He didn't think he could handle it. He needed something where people wouldn't bother him.

He heard someone coming down the second set of stairs. Here we go, he thought. The ladies are staying. The dainty knock on the door.

"Jeffrey?"

Jeffrey curled up using his thighs to barricade his face and protect him from whatever was coming through the door. He hadn't taken off his coat yet. It was an old army coat. Lots of college kids wore them even though they had never been in the army.

The doorknob slowly turned in place.

"Sweetie?"

His mother poked her frosted head into the room. Jeffrey didn't move. He was good at playing dead. As a kid, he would often pretend to be asleep in the car so that when they got home someone would carry him inside, undress him, and put him to bed.

"Honey, are you okay?"

"Not feeling well," he replied without moving. He said it half-muffled into the corduroy cover and he drooled a little bit when he said it.

"What's the matter?"

"Stomach."

"Do you have to go to the bathroom?"

This was her standard response to everything. His mother thought nothing could cure someone like a good shit. It was how she kept her girlish figure, she confided to her friends. She carried chewable ex-lax in her purse and fumbled around for them after lunch, brow furrowed, as though she were looking for a lost bobby pin. Then she would pop a tab in her mouth, zip up her bag, and emerge refreshed, knowing refreshment was on the way.

His mother sat gingerly on the edge of his bed. She put a motherly hand on his leg and looked at him with her concerned, constipated eyes.

"It's not that," Jeffrey said.

"What is it, sweetie?"

"I just don't feel well."

"Can you tell me a little more what it is?"

"No. Not really."

His mother paused. She stopped rubbing his leg. He could tell she was giving in. She usually didn't give him a hard time with this routine. She was a sucker for this—the sick routine. He never had to put a thermometer to a light bulb or clam his face in a hot blanket. If he said he was sick, she simply believed him.

"Do you want me to bring you some ginger ale?"

Done. He was free.

"Not right now. Maybe later."

"Okay, sweetie."

She gave him one more pat for the road and left. It was almost too easy.

Using the least amount of effort, only one arm and one leg, Jeffrey crawled off the bed. He put on his *Double Fantasy* record, plugged his headphones into the hi-fi, and resituated himself on the bed cover. The curly wire bounced and stretched across the moat from his ears to the wooden TV stand he used for his turntable. His ears felt warm and cushioned inside the headphones' black donut padding. He imagined himself listening along in a private recording studio.

It bothered Jeffrey having the ladies in the house. He cherished the hours when his mother was out in the afternoon and he had the whole place to himself. He would often stay in his parents' room, lying on the big, flat bed, watching the room darken as the afternoon sun descended behind the manicured suburban hillside. He didn't know what attracted him to his parents' bedroom; he supposed because it was the room in which he spent the least amount of time. His older brother's room was kept exactly the way he had it in high school, before he moved on to college, the great job, and the bachelor pad. It was decorated with a collection of beer cans on wooden shelves, half a dozen model airplanes, and photos of girls in short shorts—Farrah Fawcett slowly unzipping a halter top. Typical. His brother was a typical guy. A winner, his father would say. Jeffrey used to snoop around in there, but there wasn't anything interesting.

His sister's room was something out of a dollhouse. She came home every now and then from the big college back East. Her room had a canopy bed piled high with snow-white teddy bears. Girl stuff.

Jeffrey was the only interesting person in the family. Everyone else was boring. They might be winners, but they wouldn't amount to much.

An hour or so later, his mother was back with her soft knock on the door.

"Jeffrey?"

She opened the door a crack. She must have had a good dump, because the look on her face, although not completely gone, had settled into a relaxed sagginess.

"Are you sure you don't want something to eat?"

"No."

"Not even some soup? I could heat you up a can of soup."

"No, I'm okay."

Unfortunately, this wasn't enough to satisfy her tonight. He supposed he could agree to a can of soup and then pour it down the toilet, but he hated bringing food into the bathroom. That was something his brother would do. He would get up from the table and head to the bathroom still chewing his last bite of food.

After waiting the requisite thinking minute by the door, she moved forward into his space, smoothed out a spot on his bedspread, and took a seat. Jeffrey pulled off the headphones. They reclamped above his head and he could still hear the tinny music playing softly.

"Jeffrey . . ." she began in a voice that said, I have to tell you something, I really care about you, but this is difficult to say. "Your father and I love you very much. We're very worried about you. You've missed so many classes and your father . . ."

The mention of his father made Jeffrey recoil. He curled into a fetal position with his cheek squished against the pillow. Jeffrey had stopped going to classes, that's what had brought up this most recent spate of criticism. His father had called him a dropout, which Jeffrey didn't think was true. If he were a dropout, he had to officially *drop* out, fill out a form or something. All Jeffrey had done was stop going to classes. He still went to the college campus. He still ate lunch in the cafeteria. He still drank coffee in the student commons at the corner table near the bathroom. He still went to the library and listened to old 78s on headphones in a cubicle. He did all the normal things; he just wasn't going to classes.

In fact, everything was going fine until his father burst into his room one night waving a piece of paper like a maniac. The college had sent a letter concerned about Jeffrey's lengthy absence. If it weren't due to a medical condition, for which they required a doctor's note, they would be forced to place him on academic probation.

If he couldn't hack it in school, he would have to get a job and pay some rent to his mother. This was his father's brilliant idea. Or that's it. You're out on your own. That was his father. Mr. Sensible. Mr. Businessman. Mr. Successful. Vietnam was in the hands of the Communists, the ayatollah was holding hostages, the Soviets could nuke if they wanted, and Lennon was shot dead. The world was fucked up and his father, Mr. Capitalist Crusader, was out there raking in the dough.

What Jeffrey really wanted to do was paint. Or play rhythm guitar. Or write. Maybe writing was better because he had lots of ideas for stories. He hated the painting class he had taken his freshman year of college. He walked in on the first day and a naked woman was standing in the middle of the room. She was naked and smoking a cigarette and talking to one of the other students. Jeffrey stood there, frozen, holding on to his art supplies. He felt himself starting to get hard. She had a good ass, if a little big, and a decent pair of tits. Someone motioned for him to sign in and sit down. He took a seat holding his large sketchpad in front of his pants. No chances.

The worst thing about the art class was that every so often they had "crit" days. Everyone had to put up a drawing or painting on the wall and the teacher would lead the students around the room to critique the work. The teacher was an asshole, full of himself. That's what Jeffrey told his parents when he brought home a C for the class. How could anyone get a C in a painting class? his father wanted to know. That's the kind of class you take for fun, to round things out. It's supposed to be an easy A. But that upset Jeffrey even more. No one thought Vincent van Gogh was any good either, he said to his father as he fled to his room; he had to cut off his ear before anyone discovered him. The art teacher thought of himself as a brain surgeon leading his med students around. As if he were doing something important.

So Jeffrey started getting sick on crit days.

Which is why he thought maybe writing might be his ticket.

With writing he could be alone.

How hard could it be? he thought. You type out your story, mail it to a magazine. Not so bad. He didn't imagine there was much money in poetry. Actually, he couldn't even think of any living poet now that John was dead. Yoko, maybe, if you could call her that. He supposed the most dough was in Hollywood writing screenplays. That was probably easy money. How hard could it be? Most of the movies he saw were pretty lousy or they were all exactly the same.

"Jeffrey, we'd like you to see this doctor. We think he could help you."

Jeffrey stared blankly at his mother.

"I'm not *that* sick," he said, trying to remain as unemotional as possible while he studied her face. His father had put her up to something. He only had to figure out what it was and lure her back to his side.

"I'm not talking about Dr. Jameson. This is a different doctor. He's a . . . you know, he's a psychiatrist. A specialist."

Something fluttered in Jeffrey's chest. His mother had remained seated in profile on his bed for her little speech, but now she lifted her droopy cheeks upward and turned to face him. He could tell it was one of her fake smiles because she didn't separate her lips. She raised her cheeks up to scrunch out her eyes and held them there. Jeffrey thought she did it more to blur her vision. With her cheeks bulging up and her fake lashes batting down, he wondered how she could see anything at all.

When she turned toward him Jeffrey hissed his breath out between his teeth. He had to retain some kind of control.

"You want me to see a shrink?" Jeffrey managed to keep his voice steady, although it took quite a lot of effort. He couldn't show he was angry or it would be used against him.

"He's a *doctor*. We think he could help you. I know you've been having such a tough time since your sister moved away, and you don't seem to have made any friends since you started college. And now these problems at school . . . your father and I are just very worried about you."

"I'm fine." If he stuck to only a few words it was easier.

"We all know you're a bright boy. Your father doesn't see any motivation coming from you and that makes him worried about your future.

It doesn't mean he doesn't love you. We both love you very much. And Jeffrey—"here she reached out to put a hand on his leg. It fell just below his knee, locking him to the bed. "I know you're very shy."

Now she was overly mouthing her words and lowering her voice, ashamed of the big secret she was dutifully carrying on her wiry shoulders.

"I'm shy too." Now the hand flew back to her chest. "It's just something you have to work through and it can take a long time. Before I met your father, I was very, very shy. I hardly talked to anyone. And now look: I have a wonderful family, it's easy for me to make friends, and I enjoy my life. It turns out, it wasn't that hard. You just have to put your mind to it."

She was deteriorating into stock phrases. She probably picked up the lingo from one of those pop-psychology books—*When I Say No, I Feel Guilty*; *I'm OK—You're OK*—or something equally idiotic.

"I think this doctor might be able to help you. Make it easier on you. Your father researched him. He has very good credentials."

His father was all about credentials.

His mother proceeded to list them: where he went to school, what kind of degrees he held, which boards he sat on, which charities he gave to, whom he played golf with, blah, blah, blah, blah, blah.

"Fine," Jeffrey said. He wasn't interested in the detailed résumé.

"You'll go?" his mother seemed surprised.

"Yeah."

"Oh good." She paused. She obviously hadn't planned her speech this far along. "Good. I think he could help you."

"Okay."

His mother smoothed out her skirt and stood up.

"I'll tell your father to make the appointment. And Jeffrey, I worry about you getting sick so much of the time. You know, honey? I want you to make an effort to take better care of yourself."

"Uh-huh."

"Because Jesus only gave you one body."

Usually it was God, but today it was Jesus.

"Now, I found this for you." She pulled out a magazine clipping. "My friend Harriet had a lot of success with it. I thought maybe you could give it a try."

He took the paper shakily with his uncoordinated left hand and held it in front of his face, blocking his view of her. It was some gimmicky diet. He guessed that his mother, even though she said, "All my children are beautiful," thought he was fat. Even though "Everyone was beautiful in the eyes of the Lord," Jesus thought he was fat too.

"I could put it up on the refrigerator and we could both do it. It could be something we do together."

His mother, with her bony back, didn't need to lose any weight. She merely liked to try things she cut out of magazines. He knew it wouldn't last. Half a grapefruit, six ounces of cottage cheese, Special K with skim milk—no one could live on that for long. And for a snack, a quarter-cup of raisins, four celery sticks with peanut butter, two low-salt pretzels, or six more ounces of cottage cheese.

"All right," he said.

He handed her back the paper and she folded it into neat little squares. She was happy. Her mission was accomplished.

"I'll bring you down some soup."

She came back down ten minutes later carrying a plastic TV tray with a bowl of chicken consommé and a handful of scattered saltines. It was only then that Jeffrey peeled himself off the bed. He slurped a spoonful of the metallic-tasting broth in her presence to make her happy. When she left, he emptied the bowl into the avocado plant on his windowsill and returned to his bed.

John Lennon was dead dead dead.

How is it, he wondered, that a nobody, from Hawaii of all places, can step out of the blue one night and shoot you cold? Right in front of your house. Right in front of your Japanese wife. Just as you were recording a new album.

THREE DAYS LATER, Jeffrey was sitting in the waiting room of Dr. Gans. It resembled a regular doctor's or dentist's office, except instead of reading material about the telltale signs of heart disease or the Great American Smokeout, there were pamphlets on troubled teens and communication styles: *Why don't you understand what I am trying to tell you?*, *Making a marriage work!*, *Kids today—ten reasons why your teen may turn to drugs*. And last, but not least: *Why me?*

A couple emerged from the inner office and paused at the reception-ist's window. The guy was saying something like, "Next time you feel like you can't cope, you come to me and say, 'I can't cope,' and I'll say back to you, 'Yes you can. You can cope and I can help you. It's a *together* thing.'"

His wife nodded. She had obviously been crying, and she didn't look too happy that her husband was saying this stuff in the middle of the waiting room. He kept saying, "We can cope, we can cope *together*," over and over again, trying to sell her on the *together* thing. Or maybe he was trying to convince himself, because he kept saying it as he flipped open his checkbook to pay the receptionist.

The door leading to the office opened and a man stuck his head into the waiting room.

"Mr. Hackney?"

The man, whom Jeffrey assumed was the reputable Dr. Gans, Jewish Tonto of Dallas, Texas, kept one hand on the doorknob as he leaned his skinny body into the trepid waiting area. Jeffrey rose without saying anything and followed him to the inner sanctum.

Dr. Gans led Jeffrey to a small room and closed the door behind them. There was a desk, a chair, and a couch. The shrink sat on the chair; Jeffrey sat on the couch. On every possible table surface stood a box of tissues. These people are just like my mother, Jeffrey thought, except for them it's tears instead of shit: one good cry and you're all better.

Jeffrey crossed his legs like a girl, knee on top of knee. He never did feel comfortable with the manly ankle-to-knee, open-leg cross, or the wide-knees spread, the way men sat on the bus taking up as much room as possible.

"So, Jeffrey," the shrink started off, "can you tell me what brings you here today?"

Jeffrey didn't answer. The *Romper Room* attitude was insulting.

The shrink let the silence sit for a moment before breaking it.

"Can you tell me why you made an appointment?"

"My parents made the appointment."

"Right. You're right. Why do you think they asked you to come?"

Jeffrey shrugged.

"How are you doing in school?"

Jeffrey shrugged again. The shrink obviously knew the answers to his own questions.

"Well, Jeffrey, when your parents called me, they sounded very concerned about you. They were worried that you were dropping out of college, that you couldn't find a job, that you didn't have any goals for yourself . . ." The shrink planted several pauses in his speech where he raised his eyebrows expectantly. But Jeffrey was the master of immobility. He kept his breathing small and shallow and blinked as little as possible.

The shrink took a long, deep breath at the beginning of each new sentence.

"They also tell me you have a hard time making friends, that you spend a lot of time alone in your room."

The shrink kept a yellow legal pad balanced on his knee. On his desk, a mini tape recorder stood vertically on its end. Jeffrey hadn't noticed it before. He watched the rectangular recorder closely and saw the white plastic wheels turning around inside. The shrink was recording him. Jeffrey didn't remember the shrink turning on the recorder or popping in a tape. Perhaps the "we can cope" couple was also on this tape. One nervous wreck bleeding into the next. Jeffrey imagined the shrink going home and playing back the tape, probably as he fucked his wife.

"I have friends," Jeffrey said.

"Can you tell me about them?"

Jeffrey could see the shrink reaching for his pencil and then stopping himself. He was trying to be casual about everything, but he was such a phony.

"Right now I mostly spend time with my girlfriend."

"What's her name?"

"Pam," Jeffrey said. He didn't really like the name Pam. It was the name of a girl who had lived next door to him when he was seven. It was simple. "Her name's really Pamela, but everybody calls her Pam."

"Where'd you meet Pam?"

"At school."

"Was she in one of your classes?"

"Not exactly. . . . She was in one of my classes, but she's not a student."

"Oh?"

"Yeah, I was taking an art class and she was the model. You know, we drew her. They call it 'life drawing.'"

"So, that's how you met."

"Yeah. A lot of guys in class would try and pick her up, you know, because of the situation, but she would mostly ignore them. Our teacher had us put our drawings up on the wall one day and I put up a picture of her. I had drawn just her face. She has a beautiful face and long hair. Everyone else had these body drawings that were really ugly. But Pam actually came up to me and told me she liked my drawing. So I gave it to her. That's how we met."

"Interesting."

"I guess."

"She probably respected you for not objectifying her like the other fellows."

"I guess."

"Have your parents met Pam?"

"No. Pam's kind of embarrassed about . . . her job. She doesn't feel right meeting them. She wants to get a different job and then she'll feel more comfortable."

"I see."

"She doesn't think my parents would approve. Pam's had a hard life. She left home when she was sixteen because her stepfather was coming on to her. She went to live with her brother so she could finish high school. Now she's only doing this job so she can save money to move to California. She wants to be an actress. And she could be a really good actress. She's incredibly pretty. She did one of her speeches that she memorized for me and it was really something. I think she has a lot of talent. I think she could be famous if someone gives her a shot at it."

"She sounds like a nice girl."

The shrink was buying this hook, line, and sinker.

"Tell me," the shrink started up again, "what do you plan to do when Pam moves to California?"

"Oh, I'm going with her."

"You are?"

"Yeah, Pam and I have it all planned out. She's going to be an actress and I'm going to be a screenwriter and a songwriter. My parents don't know about it. I haven't told them yet. But when it's closer to the time we're going, then I'll let them know. Because, my mother, she worries about every little thing. And she would just worry. If I wait until we're about to go, she'll have less time to worry."

"I can understand your reasoning, but do you perhaps think that your mother might have a different reaction? She made this appointment because she was worried that you didn't have a plan for what to do with your life, and now you tell me you do have a plan. Perhaps telling her would relieve her of some of this worry."

The shrink liked to use the word "perhaps."

"Maybe," Jeffrey said. He could tell the shrink wanted to hear that he was right.

"Could you consider telling her?"

"It's just that Pam asked me not to, on account of the nature of her job."

"Could you talk to Pam about it?"

"Yeah, I guess I could."

"Okay." The shrink stood up.

The tape recorder clicked itself off.

The shrink told Jeffrey he was going to see if his mother was in the waiting area. Jeffrey was left alone for a moment to relish in his achievement. Maybe he could be a writer after all.

The shrink escorted Jeffrey's mother into the room. For the next appointment, the shrink wanted to talk to Jeffrey and his mother together. Jeffrey's mother nodded, her fingers clenching her purse as if its enclosures contained a potentially embarrassing emotion. She looked over at Jeffrey and Jeffrey stuck out his hand and bid the shrink good-bye.

I can play the game too, he thought.

As his mother drove him home, Jeffrey noticed the twittering on her face, which usually meant she was thinking of something to say and just the right way to say it.

"You don't have to tell me what you discussed with Dr. Gans," she said as they turned at the duck pond and entered the circle. "But if you ever want to, I'm here to listen."

The last part sounded like she picked it up verbatim from some women's magazine, some true-life, heart-to-heart story buried in the back pages of *Good Housekeeping*.

Jeffrey was disappointed when she pulled the car into the driveway. It meant she wasn't just dropping him off at home before going to run errands; she would probably be puttering around the house all day. She was home more and more these days. It must be off-season for all her ladies' groups.

When he got to his room, Jeffrey pulled his guitar case out from under his bed. The case was black and clean. He didn't cover it with stickers the way other people did in an effort to look cool. He thought a guitar and its case should be pristine. It was the same thing with books. He didn't like it when people underlined sentences and wrote in the margins. Whenever he opened up a library book like that, he had to immediately return it. He couldn't even have it around.

He clicked open the case and pulled out the guitar. In one uninterrupted motion, he laid back on his bed with the guitar lying flat across his wide middle. He held on to the neck with one hand and let the rest of his limbs go limp. The guitar rode up and down on his soft stomach as he breathed in and out. Jeffrey enjoyed its gentle weight resting on his body. He felt no need to strum when he was already receiving pleasure.

His mother's clacking heels on the floor upstairs brought him, reluctantly, back to reality. He rolled himself up to a sitting position with the guitar propped sideways on his thighs. Jeffrey hunched forward and let the instrument support his weight. In Jeffrey's private universe, he was a lonely movie hero searching for comfort, for a life that didn't ask anything of him, but provided for him, loved him, and didn't bother him and didn't ask him to give anything up. Jeffrey felt small. Jeffrey wanted to reserve as much of Jeffrey as possible for himself. The shrink presented a quandary: it would buy him some time, but eventually his parents would want to see results, and Jeffrey knew that at the end of the series of prescribed visits, he would have no results to give. He would have to stay one step ahead of the game.

Perhaps, Jeffrey thought, my lie is worth living.

JEFFREY REACHED ACROSS the table for a second pork chop and a second helping of mashed potatoes. His father looked up from his plate, noticed the transaction, and paused his mechanical chewing long enough to speak.

"Don't you think you've had your fill?"

Jeffrey froze with the spoon hovering between the serving dish and his plate. It bobbled above an uncovered sliver of wood that shined from his mother's daily wipe-downs with Pledge.

"It seems to me you've had your fill."

Jeffrey dropped the spoon back into the large bowl, letting it land with a wet plop.

"He's a growing boy," his mother said quietly.

"He's growing more sideways than up. And he's no boy. He's a man. When I was his age . . ."

And here Jeffrey dropped out. He was an expert at it. He didn't even need to take LSD, he could just flip the magic switch inside his head and his father's voice would be tuned out. He usually replaced him with a Beatles song. Some nights he went through entire albums in his head.

But he was still hungry.

His mother was harder to block out.

"I just don't believe in denying someone food if they're hungry. You can't just say, 'Don't eat.' You have to be organized about it and start a diet. Otherwise, it's not healthy."

His mother would have to back this up with a magazine article if his father was in an arguing mood.

The black plastic spoon handle was pointing at Jeffrey, calling him back to the dim dinner-table universe. It was a microphone beckoning him to sing. It was whispering, "Show time!"

"I have an announcement," Jeffrey said demurely into the plastic mic.

His mother looked at him and nodded encouragingly. She probably thinks I got a job, he thought. His father rolled his eyes and kept on eating.

"I'm moving out."

Although it hadn't yet materialized on his face, Jeffrey felt a beam start to glow inside his soft chest.

"Did you get the job at the club?" his mother asked. He had interviewed for a kitchen job at their country club where his dad played golf with business cronies. It was eons ago and he never heard back. When he went in and filled out an application, the other kitchen workers looked embarrassed for him. He was crossing a line. Just as some kitchen guy with tattoos and a hair net would never be allowed to play golf at the club, Jeffrey would never be allowed to work in the kitchen. He learned his place. He was better than that.

His father chewed, waiting for an answer.

"I'm moving to California."

Jeffrey could see his mother's throat tighten in a panic. His father stopped chewing but didn't swallow. Jeffrey imagined his father's food melting into liquid and mixing with saliva in the pocket of his cheek.

"What do you plan to do out there?" his father asked.

"I plan to move out there to live."

"But what do you plan to *do*? Do you even have a plan?"

"My girlfriend, Pam—"

"You have a girlfriend?" His mother was turning to putty.

"My girlfriend Pam is going to be an actress and I am going to try and break into the music business."

"Break into the music business doing what?" His father was a hard sell.

"Writing songs. Writing songs for movies and TV shows."

"What makes you think you can do that?"

"Every TV show has a song. Somebody's got to write them."

"Don't you think they hire professionals to do that? Do you know anyone who does that?"

"He certainly does know a lot about music," his mother piped in trying to defend him. "He has all those records. And the guitar."

"I thought you were interested in painting."

"I can do both."

"No, you can't. You need to focus on one thing. That's your problem. When something gets too hard for you, you switch to something else. You never get good at any one thing. It's about commitment, Jeffrey. You made a commitment to go to college and now you've reneged on that. Do you think Jesus kept changing his mind about what he believed in? No, he held fast. He made other people come over to his side, to his beliefs. That was his attitude."

His father shoveled another forkful of food and dumped it in his mouth. Jesus ate this way too.

"And who's this girl?" he asked.

"She's my girlfriend."

"Where'd you meet her?"

"At school. I told Dr. Gans about her."

"You can tell Dr. Gans about her but you can't talk to us? Does Dr. Gans know about your big plans?"

Jeffrey knew that the best answer was no answer. Keep them guessing then spill it all.

"I thought it would be best to tell you in person, as opposed to just leaving you a note."

It worked. His parents looked truly shocked.

His mother was about to cry. She asked Jeffrey what he was going to live on until he found work. He told her he still had some Christmas money left and a savings bond from Grandma. That worked too. His mother knew it wasn't much. Jeffrey saw the tear buds sprout from the corners of her eyes, as though the skin of her face had stretched to its limits and began to bleed tears.

"Where are you going to live?" his mother asked as tears dribbled down into the napkin on her lap.

"We're staying with some friends of Pam until we get our own place."

"Your mother and I would like to meet this girl before you take off across the country with her."

"She already left. She's out there already. She left a couple days ago." That was a good one, he thought, fast and smooth.

"When is this migration taking place?" His father was agreeing a little too easily, Jeffrey thought. It was as though he wanted him gone.

"Saturday."

Jeffrey hadn't really decided on a date before that moment. Part of him wanted to say, "Tomorrow," for dramatic effect, but he thought it might be too over-the-top. Saturday gave them three days to adjust.

Jeffrey didn't want to say anything more. He was looking for a way to end the conversation. His father solved this for him. He placed both palms flat on the table and stood up, pushing out his chair with the backs of his knees. He looked at Jeffrey and walked away from the table.

ON SATURDAY, JEFFREY'S mother drove him to the airport. His father had gone into the office to catch up on paperwork but left a greeting card on the breakfast table that said: "I appreciate the risk you are taking to move your life forward. I wish you luck. Work hard. Love, Dad." It was a typical note from his father. Jeffrey got similar ones on his birthday.

His mother kept circling, looking for a place to park, growing more and more anxious. On the third sweep, Jeffrey asked her to let him off at the curb with the red caps. Jeffrey got out and pulled his guitar and suitcase from the trunk. When he walked around to her window to say good-bye, Jeffrey knew she had been crying. She had snuck in a quick tissue wipe when he removed his luggage and now her makeup was smeared from left to right. She had enough time to wipe her eyes, but not enough to check her face in the rearview mirror.

She put on a big I'm-proud-of-you face. She looked like a doll that was melting in the sun.

"Here, Jeffrey," she said and reached for her purse. She pulled out a white envelope from the bank and pressed it into his hand. "It's a little something to help you until you get on your feet. Put it somewhere safe."

"Thanks."

"And I'd like to meet this girlfriend of yours. I'm glad she's from around here. That way you can visit together."

"Okay."

He leaned in and gave her a hug. He didn't like to get too mushy in public, but he figured he owed it to her for the bankroll.

As Jeffrey walked into the airport terminal, the sliding glass doors magically parted to let him in. Welcome, they said, the world is yours.

Jeffrey thought he could go anywhere.

THE GAME OF LIFE

* * *

After New Year's, Tammy and Steffi visited their dad for the first time since they moved to the DC house. They went to his apartment and he made dinner—Howard Johnson's fried clams from a box and frozen Tater Tots he heated up on a cookie sheet in the oven. Tammy thought they were both quite good dipped in ketchup. Tammy and Steffi spent the night on his living room floor in sleeping bags they had brought from home. The next morning he took them out to a restaurant for breakfast. Tammy and Steffi ordered waffles with strawberries and whipped cream on top. It was like eating dessert, but technically it was breakfast.

It took longer for their dad to drive them home than it used to. It used to be that if they left his apartment when one TV program was over, but before they showed scenes for next week, they could get home in time for the next show or maybe only miss the opening theme song. Now it took about an hour, or fifty-five minutes to be exact. It might be even longer since they started from the Waffle House and not from their dad's apartment. When they got to Bemis Street, Tammy's dad didn't shut off the car and get out, he just turned around in his seat and said, "Okay, bye," as he reached back to give them a kiss. Tammy and Steffi didn't get out of the car right away because they were waiting for him to park. After a minute, Tammy realized he wasn't going to get out, walk them to the door, and talk for a few minutes with their mother. Tammy pulled on the handle and got out of the car; Steffi followed her, scooching across the seat, her skirt dragging up over her tights. They walked up the steps to the front porch and their dad drove off.

Kids in DC got Reagan's inauguration off from school in January 1981. Tammy asked her mother if they could go to the parade, but she said no. Tammy asked why not, and her mother said, because I didn't vote for him and it's too cold. She said she never understood why they had that parade in January when it's freezing outside. Tammy said the New Year's Day parade is in January and her mother said that's different because it's in California and it's warm all the time there. The next day back in Mrs. William's classroom, they took down the yellow construction-paper ribbons that were taped to the windowpanes. The hostages in Iran were released on Inauguration Day.

Tammy and Steffi and Hugh settled into a walking-to-school routine. After their mother and Nick left for work, the three of them would sit on the front porch steps and wait for the other neighborhood kids, the ones who lived farther away from school and deeper in the nice neighborhood, to make it to their house. Gretchen and Monique lived on the same block of 46th Street as Steffi's friend Kirin; Tammy and Steffi lived closer to school on the corner of 43rd. Monique didn't walk to school because she took gymnastics in the morning, but Gretchen and Kirin would hook up with Tammy, Steffi, and Hugh at 43rd Street and walk the rest of the way with them.

Gretchen thought it was cool that there were no grown-ups at Tammy's house during the day. She didn't care that Tammy had to baby-sit Hugh after school half the time or that they weren't allowed to watch TV in the living room. Gretchen said, "At least you have some privacy and your mom's not snooping around all the time."

In Steffi's room there was a big closet that didn't have any doors and an old three-drawer dresser was shoved inside and took up most of the space. Steffi and Kirin would stand on top of the dresser and sing songs to the radio, using a hairbrush as a microphone, and Gretchen and Tammy would pretend to be deejays. "That was Juice Newton's 'Queen of Hearts'!" "I'm Kasey Kasem." "And I'm Wolfman Jack." "You're listening to Q107—Capitol Rock!"

Tammy didn't really like playing with Steffi and her friends because they were younger than her and not as mature. Gretchen didn't seem to mind. Tammy thought maybe it was because Gretchen was an only child and she didn't get that having a younger sister and half brother was annoying. But when Steffi and Kirin started lining up stuffed animals to play "school," Gretchen agreed with Tammy that the game was stupid, and she and Tammy stopped hanging out with them, stopped waiting for them after school, and kept the separator door between the bedrooms shut.

Steffi and Kirin were more annoying than average third graders because they liked to show off and pretend they were smarter than Tammy and Gretchen. It made them crazy that Tammy and Gretchen kept the separator door shut and didn't hang out with them anymore because they had no one to make fun of and embarrass and rope into one of their stupid games. They finally came up with something a few weeks later. Tammy and Gretchen came home from school and heard footsteps running across the upstairs hallway. When they got up to Tammy's room, Steffi and Kirin peeked at them through the window of the separator door and burst out laughing.

"Oh," Steffi said, "it was just you."

Tammy ignored them and asked Gretchen if she wanted to do homework in her bedroom or downstairs at the dinner table. She could hear Steffi and Kirin whisper something to each other because they were right on the other side of the separator door. They giggled quietly for a moment and then slowly turned the knob.

Steffi was pink and puffy from laughing. She still had a tiny blue mark in her cheek where she once accidentally stabbed herself with a pencil. The doctor had said it would work its way out, but it was still there.

Kirin took a deep breath and held it, smiling.

"Do you want to see something?" Kirin asked.

"What?"

"Do you want to see it or not?"

"What is it?"

"First you have to tell us *if* you want to see it," Steffi said.

Steffi always said idiotic things like that.

"How am I supposed to know if I want to see it if I don't know what it is?"

"Because we won't show it to you if you don't say you want to see it."

Tammy didn't say anything. She tried to ignore Steffi. Steffi was just trying to embarrass her in front of Gretchen.

Kirin looked back and forth at Tammy and Steffi like a dog waiting to see what was going to happen. She wore her bright blonde hair in two ponytails on either side of her head. This also made her look like a puppy with floppy ears. And she had a goofy expression. She had big blue eyes that were too shiny and her mouth was always trying to suppress a grin. Tammy didn't have a dog, but she knew this was what they were like.

Gretchen plopped down on Tammy's bed, opened her math book, and muttered, "Whatever," without looking up.

"Fine," Tammy said, figuring it was the only way to get rid of them.

Kirin's eyes bugged out and she and Steffi ran down the hall. When they came back they stood in front of Tammy's bed hiding something behind Steffi's back.

"Look!"

Steffi thrust her hands in front of Tammy.

They were pictures. Pictures of her mother and Nick. Naked. There were a couple of her mother totally naked sprawled out against their rainbow bedspread on the floor of their bedroom. There was one of Nick lying on the rainbow bedspread, his legs stretched out and his feet crossed at the ankles. There were five or six in all. The last one was of Nick. It was Nick totally naked taking a picture of himself in a mirror. The mirror was on the back of the closet door in their bedroom. He was standing sideways, one hand holding on to his penis, holding it straight up, big and stiff. He had his head turned to face the mirror and his other hand held up the camera in front of his face.

Tammy heard the bed creak as Gretchen stood up and looked over her shoulder. Gretchen half snorted and half laughed and said, "Oh my God," but Tammy didn't say anything and she didn't look at Gretchen. She couldn't stop looking at the pictures. She kept flipping through them, stopping on the last one of Nick. This time she noticed he was wearing socks. And his watch. He looked like a skinny robot. His arms and legs were like sticks from a stick figure and the camera covered his face like a mask. She could still see his hair. And underneath the camera it looked like he was smiling. Tammy couldn't quite see his mouth, but it looked like he was smiling. Like he was proud of himself. Or he knew something he wasn't going to tell you. Two little balls of light had hit the mirror and bounced off. That was from the flash. Tammy knew it was. She knew because it was her camera.

That's what made her keep staring at the last picture. She could tell when Steffi first handed her the photos that they were from a Polaroid camera because of the black back and the white frame with the thick part on the bottom. Tammy knew they were Polaroids, but she didn't get it until she saw Nick standing there with his penis in one hand and her camera in the other.

Tammy didn't want to mention the camera part to Gretchen. She was too scared to think that her mother and Nick had used her camera. How did they get it? Had they snuck into her room in the middle of the night while she was asleep? Tammy kept the camera on the shelf above her desk, but she didn't want to look at it right now to see how many pictures were left. She didn't want to draw Gretchen's attention to it. Gretchen might tell Monique or someone. She might tell someone else. And it was gross. There was something gross about it. About them using her camera. Had they bought their own film for it? Tammy wanted to know. It was expensive. Almost six dollars. It was expensive because it was Polaroid and you didn't have to pay for developing. Tammy didn't even take that many pictures herself because it was so expensive and she had to pay for it out of her allowance. It was like they had stolen from her. They had done it once before. Tammy kept her savings in a tin peanut brittle can leftover from when she was a Campfire Girl in the third grade. Once she had come home and her peanut brittle can was on the wrong shelf, and when she looked inside, ten dollars was missing. She had saved up almost thirteen. Tammy ran hysterically to her mother and said they had been robbed. Her mother said they hadn't been robbed. She and Nick had taken the ten dollars because they needed gas money. Tammy cried and said they didn't even ask her. "If you keep this up," Nick said, "you're not going to get it back."

"Where'd you get this?" Tammy asked.

Steffi and Kirin skipped down the hall, past Hugh's room where he was quietly playing with Legos, and Tammy and Gretchen followed them into her mother's and Nick's bedroom.

Nick had an old dresser he had owned before he lived with them. It was short and fat and painted dark blue, but it had been painted other colors before that and on the edges you could see little scrapes of green and orange. Steffi unlatched the top part from where it sat up on a diagonal and lowered it down so it looked like an old-fashioned desk.

On top was a bowl of change, some shoe polish, and a jar of Vaseline. In the hutch part there were narrow shelves on either side and in the center was a tiny door, like the door to a mouse's house. Steffi opened the mouse door and there were even tinier shelves inside and one skinny drawer on the bottom. Steffi pulled the skinny drawer open and in it were Nick's silver dog tags on a chain with his name, SCHRANKER, NICHOLAS P., stamped on them.

"In there," Steffi said.

Tammy put the pictures in the drawer. Steffi turned them over.

"They were like that," she said.

Then Steffi showed Tammy and Gretchen something else. She pulled out a white handkerchief that was stuffed in one of the little shelves and reached her pink stubby hand way in the back. She dragged something forward along the wood and when she pulled out her hand she was holding Nick's gun gently between her fingers. Nick had shown it to Tammy and Steffi when he first moved in. He said under no circumstances were they allowed to touch it. If they touched it at all, he would know and they would get in big trouble. He went through the same long speech adults always give kids in school about how a gun is not a toy, blah, blah, blah, like kids are stupid. He said he would've thrown the gun away since there were kids in the house now, but it had belonged to a buddy of his who had died in Vietnam, and it was the only thing he had to help him remember his friend.

Steffi and Kirin smiled at Tammy and Gretchen and their eyes twinkled like they were really proud of themselves. Nick hadn't told Tammy and Steffi where he kept the gun; Steffi and Kirin had found it on their own. Steffi didn't even slide it all the way out of the shelf. She didn't even say a word. She just pulled it out halfway, enough so Tammy and Gretchen could see it, then slid it back in place and stuffed the handkerchief in front of it. She backtracked her way out of the desk, closing the drawer, shutting the mouse door, and flipping the desk part back up. She turned the brass latch that held it together and then she and Kirin scampered downstairs to make Kool-Aid.

Gretchen said she had to go home.

Tammy went back into her room alone and pulled her Polaroid camera down from the shelf above her desk. She had only taken two pictures since she moved to DC—one of her dad and one on the day after

John Lennon died when she tried to take a picture of the TV news, but it came out all blurry.

There were ten pictures in a packet of film. Tammy turned the camera over and looked at the tiny window that tells how many pictures are left.

Only two.

Tammy wanted to yell, but her throat clenched up and silenced her. They had used her camera without asking. They hadn't even replaced her film. They had just left it like that. And now Tammy couldn't ask for it back or she would get in trouble. They would know she and Steffi had been snooping in their room and they would know she and Steffi had seen the pictures. And now Gretchen knew about it too. The whole thing was gross. Tammy was mad that she had slept through them sneaking into her room. They must have snuck in twice: once to take the camera, and once to put it back. And Tammy had slept through the whole thing. Now Tammy would never get her film back. She would have to live with only two pictures left. They probably thought they could use it since they had given her the camera as a present. They should have never given her the camera. She should have saved up for a long time and bought it herself. Tammy guessed they didn't think of it as stealing.

Tammy thought she should hide her camera. Who knew if they would do it again? Although they probably wouldn't if there were only two pictures left. But still, Tammy thought she should hide it. She opened her closet door and put the camera on a shelf behind her sleeping bag. The closet was at the foot of her bed. If they tried to come in and take it while she was asleep, she would definitely wake up.

Steffi and Kirin were watching TV in the adults-only living room, being really obvious about breaking the rules. Tammy didn't want to sit in the downstairs, off-limits living room with the two of them and she didn't want to stay upstairs with the naked pictures. She didn't want to sit in the stupid kids' TV room, which was full of Hugh's stupid toys. She wished there was a place she could go where she could be alone and where no one would bother her and no one would make fun of her. Sometimes when they got the Sunday paper, Tammy would flip through the back of *Parade* magazine where they had ads for sleep-away camps and boarding schools. Tammy thought it would be nice to go to boarding school and sleep there and have a built-in set of friends. She had once cut out an ad for a summer camp and asked her mother if she could go. Her mother had looked at the small square of paper and said, "I don't think so, Tammy. I don't think it's your type of place." When Tammy said it was, her mother said, "I'm sorry, I know you think it is, but it's not."

GRETCHEN WAS HAVING a birthday party and she was inviting boys. Tammy hadn't been to a party with boys since she was a little kid, and even then it was usually only one boy or somebody's brother. She decided not to tell her mother and Nick about the boys because she wasn't sure what they would say and she didn't want them to say she couldn't go.

Gretchen was actually having two birthday parties, one the day before her birthday and a slumber party on her actual birthday. The one the day before her birthday was the one with boys. It was also a dress-up party, Gretchen said. Tammy decided to dress up as a hobo for the party. She tied a bandana to a stick and wore an old polka-dot shirt of Nick's, his army boots, and his old army jacket, which was green and had *Schranker* written on the chest pocket.

Tammy drew on her face with a black eyeliner pencil to make it look like she had a beard. Then she clomped down the stairs in the combat boots to see if her mother or Nick would drive her to the party. She knew they probably wouldn't. They would say it's close enough for her to walk. They didn't care if it was dark out or if she was scared or if at school they told kids not to stand too close to the curb while they were waiting for the light to change because a girl from the Catholic junior high got pushed into a car and kidnapped.

Her mother and Nick were watching TV in the adults-only living room. When Tammy made it to the bottom step, her mother glanced over and opened her mouth to say something, but nothing came out. Finally she laughed a little bit and said, "What are you doing?"

"I'm going to Gretchen's. Can you drive me?"

Tammy braced herself for the usual "You can walk" from Nick. Her mother let out another laugh, kind of like a hiccup, and said, "That's tomorrow. Gretchen's party is tomorrow." Tammy said, "No, it's tonight, the dress-up party is tonight, and the sleepover is tomorrow."

Tammy's mother looked up at Nick, smiled and nodded, and it looked like the two of them were communicating with ESP. Nick shrugged his shoulders and exhaled heavily into his mustache.

"I'll just walk, I guess," Tammy said. She knew she shouldn't have asked for a ride. She knew they were nicer if she didn't ask them for anything. She put on her coat, even though she was already wearing the army coat. She didn't want to get in trouble for not wearing a coat.

"Tammy," her mother said, "you told us she was having a birthday party."

"Yeah?"

"You only told us about one party."

"No I didn't." Her mother and Nick always did this. They always claimed Tammy didn't tell them something when she did. Or they claimed she waited too long, until the last minute, which she didn't. They often gave permission for something and then forgot about it and said, no, they didn't give permission for that, they would never give permission for that, Tammy just wanted them to give permission for that and so she heard what she wanted to hear, but they didn't actually say it. Tammy never bought that excuse, but they said it in such a way she couldn't argue with them without getting into more trouble. Tammy knew she was pretty smart. Sure, she forgot stuff, just like everyone forgot stuff sometimes, but she never thought she heard something that wasn't said just because she wanted to hear it.

"Tammy, all you told us was that she was having a birthday party."

"No I didn't. I said there was a dress-up party tonight with everyone from school and she's having a slumber party tomorrow."

"That's not what you told us."

"Yes it is."

"You told us it was tomorrow," Nick butted in. "You didn't give us all the information. You weren't specific."

"Yes I was!"

"Tammy!" Nick didn't exactly yell, but he raised his pointer finger at the same time as his eyebrows, which translated into a "watch it." A "watch it" translated into a "shut up or you're in big trouble." Tammy felt her bottom lip start to tremble the way Hugh's did when he was about to cry. Hugh's lip did that all the time, but Tammy knew it looked ridiculous on someone like herself who was almost eleven years old.

"Tammy," her mother put on a Nice Mom voice, "I'm sorry, but we've had a misunderstanding. Unfortunately, Nick and I are going out tonight and you're going to have to stay here."

"What!?"

"I'm sorry, but you weren't specific about all the parties. Nick and I have tickets. We already paid for them."

Tammy felt this was so unfair. She wanted to yell that to them, but she knew she would just dig herself in deeper. They were always doing stuff like this and Tammy had to go along with it or she would get in trouble for simply having an opinion that was different from theirs.

Tammy knew she should just shut up, but she couldn't help herself.

"Why can't Steffi watch Hugh?"

When her mother and Nick went out at night, Tammy and Steffi were both in charge of watching Hugh. Tammy was older, but she wasn't officially the one in charge. Hugh rarely did what Tammy told him to. He paid more attention to Steffi because she was nicer and babied him. He was supposed to go to bed earlier than Tammy and Steffi, but when Tammy told him to go to bed he would say, "You're not the boss."

Her mother said Tammy was the oldest and she needed to be home. Tammy thought this was dumb because it wasn't like she was in charge of Steffi, and Steffi watched Hugh in the afternoons by herself all the time. Nick yelled in, "That's not the point, Tammy!" Her mother said she was sorry about the misunderstanding, but sometimes things like this happen and you just have to deal with them.

Tammy stomped upstairs to her room. She stomped on purpose and she hoped the combat boots left marks.

She flopped onto her bed and started reading *Deenie* by Judy Blume about a girl who wants to be a model, but she gets scoliosis. Tammy's mother used to come up to her room and sit on the edge of her bed after they had an argument and now she never did. Lots of times Tammy felt a need to talk to her, but she never got her alone for long without someone barging in and interrupting them. When Nick came along, her mother started acting more and more like him. Tammy didn't notice it when Nick first moved in. She was younger then and she just kind of went along with things.

Steffi and Kirin ran through Tammy's room. Kirin had been hanging out since after school and stayed over for dinner because Friday was pizza night. Sometimes it felt like Kirin was over twenty-four hours a day.

Steffi turned on her clock radio to Q107.

"Turn your damn radio down," Tammy said.

"I'm allowed to play it and you shouldn't curse," Steffi said. She was always so pleased with herself. It was just like when they had to get dressed up for something and Steffi would put on some perfect frilly dress that matched her pink puffy cheeks. Tammy hated dressing up. She hated wearing dresses. Last year her mother had bought her a pants suit to wear to a funeral, but Tammy didn't like wearing that either. It itched.

"Turn it down, goddamn it!" Tammy was yelling now. She had stuck her face into the window of the separator door. There was a pane of glass missing and she yelled right through it.

"Shut up!" Steffi said.

"She has to turn it up because you're yelling so loud," Kirin piped in. Kirin had the same smarty-pants attitude.

"I have to yell because your radio's so goddamn loud!"

"You certainly like to say 'goddamn,'" Kirin said.

Steffi and Kirin took the mustard-colored blanket off of Steffi's bed and held it up over the separator door so that it blocked the window. Kirin got Scotch tape from Steffi's desk and they started taping it in place. It was hard for them to do. The blanket kept falling down and it was hard to hold it up with tape.

"You're not allowed to do this," Tammy said as her view slowly turned into a wall of yellow lint.

"Yes I am," Steffi said.

"No you're not."

"Nobody said I couldn't and you can't say whether I can or not."

Tammy started yelling. She didn't know what. She was just yelling at them. Steffi dragged her desk chair over to tape the upper corners of the blanket to the separator door window. The next thing Tammy knew, Nick was in her room.

"She's blocking the window," Tammy complained.

"You don't need to be looking in her room all the time," Nick said with his finger in her face. He had a thick mustache and his eyebrows ran together underneath the long bangs that hung down over his forehead. "You're not too old to be spanked," he said in a low voice so that only Tammy could hear it.

Nick turned to Steffi and said her friend had to leave. They weren't allowed to have friends over at night if no grown-ups were home. To top it all off, Nick said he would give Kirin a ride.

Tammy shut herself in the bathroom. It was the only place she could be alone. She sat down on the bath rug and stared at the hexagon tiles on the floor. Near the pipe where the heat came up, the tiles were starting to crumble away. A few were cracked and the cracked part was coming up. Sometimes they left little dust bits on the bath rug, which was an ugly green bath rug—the same color green as the coffee table that Nick had from before he lived with them, and the same color green as his army jacket that Tammy was still wearing. They had a lot of things in that color green. One of the boys in Tammy's class had pointed to the green Tupperware container full of tuna noodle casserole she had brought on potluck day and called it shit green. He told everyone she made shit-green casserole. Only Mrs. William ate it.

After Tammy heard the front door shut, she left the bathroom and went downstairs to the kids' TV room. The TV in there was big and old. Nick had it before he lived with them. It had a thick black line that ran along the bottom of the screen when it was turned on. Tammy and Steffi thought this was because Nick had dropped it when they moved. Tammy was secretly saving up her money to buy her own TV to watch in her room—just a small one, probably black and white—that way she could watch whatever she wanted. She could even watch TV in bed.

In the kids' TV room, there were two discarded armchairs that looked like giant cubes with seat cushions cut out. The chairs used to be in the living room before they got the shit-brown couch. Tammy always sat on the left, and Steffi always sat on the right. The chairs were pushed together and jutting out from Tammy's chair was a red bench with a vinyl-cushioned top. The seat of the bench lifted up and it was full of dress-up clothes, old things their mother didn't wear anymore: frilly see-through nightgowns, bridesmaid dresses, and high-heeled shoes covered in gold foil. Hugh would sit on top of the bench, or he would lie on top so he could see the TV. When Tammy came downstairs, Steffi and Hugh were already watching some boring show. Hugh was sitting in Tammy's chair, but he moved to the bench when Tammy came in. Even Steffi wouldn't back him up if he tried to claim Tammy's chair.

"It's not Halloween, silly," Steffi said.

"Shut up," Tammy said, but she mumbled it and her heart wasn't into it. Steffi probably didn't hear it. It was a wasted "shut up."

Tammy was looking at the screen, not really paying attention. She was slumped way down in her chair with her torso parallel to the floor and her head propped up just enough to see the TV. Her arms were folded across her chest covering up the *Schranker* tag on her jacket. Her knees reached far out in front of her body and she thought she could probably touch the TV with her foot. She lifted up her left combat boot and placed it squarely on the screen.

"Stop it," Steffi said.

Tammy dropped her foot to the floor. She lifted up her right leg, the one that was closer to Steffi, and put her foot in the middle of the screen.

"Stop it," Steffi said. "Move your foot."

Tammy walked her foot, heel-toe-heel-toe, wiggling it across the screen until it was even more on Steffi's side.

"Move your foot," Steffi said.

"I am moving it."

"Move it *off* the TV."

Tammy was enjoying the fact that there was no one home for Steffi to run complaining to. That's when Tammy got the idea. Why should she stay here? She should just go to Gretchen's and be back before her mother and Nick got home. Steffi might tell, but she might not. She might want to save it and use it later to get something out of Tammy that she really wanted. There might be something she wanted Tammy to do and she'd say, do this for me or I'll tell about Gretchen's party. If Steffi were smart, that's what she'd do.

Tammy let her combat boot slide to the floor. It made a squeaking sound along the screen and she thought it might leave a black mark like a bike does when it skids to a stop, but it didn't. She got out of her chair and clomped to the back door. She didn't bother getting her coat; she thought, why should she since no one would know, and she walked out.

Steffi opened the back door while Tammy was still on the steps.

"Where are you going?"

"To Gretchen's."

"You can't. You have to stay here."

"I'll be back later."

"Tammy, you can't go!"

When Tammy made it out of the yard, she turned and walked to the corner of 43rd Street. She looked back and saw Steffi and Hugh standing in the doorway. They looked like black cutout silhouettes, one tall, one short, because the light from the TV room was shining behind them. Steffi yelled out, "You can't go! You're not allowed to do this!" but Tammy didn't care about what she was not allowed to do. She wanted to do something as if she had no sister or brother at all. She crossed 43rd Street and heard Hugh call out, "Tammy, come back!" in his little high-pitched voice. He even gave one last, "Tam-meeeeee!" that sounded as though it could break a wine glass like the singer on the "Is it live, or is it Memorex?" cassette-tape commercial. Tammy didn't turn around. She was sick of being stuck with them.

Tammy rang Gretchen's bell and Gretchen's mom answered the door. She didn't say anything at first and Tammy wondered if she was mad because Tammy was late.

"Hi, Tammy, I didn't recognize you for a second," she said as she held the door open. "Come on in."

Gretchen's mom walked her through the living room where a couple of other moms were sitting on the couch drinking wine and eating cheese and crackers. Tammy didn't know mothers were invited too. Gretchen hadn't mentioned anything about it and there was nothing about it on the invitations Gretchen handed out at school. Maybe only these mothers were invited and Tammy's mother wasn't.

"Everyone's downstairs," Gretchen's mom said.

Tammy walked down to the basement rec room. Gretchen was there, along with Heather and Monique, and Kenny, Colin, and Josh from class. Kenny wore a suit jacket with a bowtie and a top hat. Other then that, no one else was wearing a costume.

"What are you supposed to be?" Kenny asked.

"A hobo."

"You mean a bum?" he said laughing. "You came to the party as a bum? Oh man!"

Gretchen was staring at Tammy. The girls were dressed up, but they weren't wearing costumes. They were wearing skirts. Monique scrunched her eyes at Tammy and whispered something to Gretchen like, "What is she wearing?"

Gretchen's mom came down with a plate of little triangle-shaped sandwiches. When she left, Heather suggested they play Seven Minutes in Heaven. They would draw names out of a hat, one for boys and one for girls, and then they would go into the laundry closet and turn off the light for seven minutes. Tammy got Colin the piano player. Gretchen got Josh, but Tammy thought she rigged it. Everyone knew Gretchen liked him. Heather probably came up with the whole thing so that Gretchen could go into the closet with him. Tammy asked what they were supposed to do in there and Kenny said, "Suck face."

Gretchen and Josh went in first. When they came out, Gretchen didn't say anything, but she was obviously trying to hide a smile. Then it was Tammy's and Colin's turn. Gretchen and Heather led them into the laundry closet and switched off the light. It was pitch black in there since it was in the basement. Tammy reached out her hands to feel her way around. All she felt was the dryer and the ironing board. She brushed against something, she thought it was Colin's hand, and they found each other in the dark. Tammy thought maybe he would try and kiss her, but he kept reaching out with his hands until he found the pull string and switched on the light.

"Are you supposed to do that?" Tammy asked.

"I don't know."

Colin hopped up on the dryer to sit. Tammy didn't know what to do now. Colin kept looking at his digital watch that ticked off time in nanoseconds. At one point he looked up at Tammy. She tried to smile at him. Maybe it would turn out that he liked her and he would send her notes in class. Tammy thought she was a little pretty, she wasn't into makeup or dresses or anything, but she wasn't fat or ugly.

Colin gave her a weird look. Then he looked back at his watch.

"Seven minutes," he said and slid off the dryer. He put one hand on the doorknob, switched off the light with the other, then opened the door and walked out.

"Did you suck face?"

"I don't want to kiss a bum!" Colin said and all the boys laughed really hard.

Tammy wasn't sure if she was supposed to laugh with them or shrug it off and pretend like she didn't want to kiss him either. She wasn't sure if she was supposed to like boys or think they were gross. She thought Gretchen was her friend, but Gretchen was looking at Tammy as if she didn't like her. Tammy felt like everyone could see everything that was wrong with her. It was as though she had farted in class, and everyone had heard it, and there was nothing she could do about it and no one was going to stick up for her and say, no, she didn't fart, it was just her sneaker rubbing against the floor.

Tammy said she had to go. She wanted to get out of there before they did a second round in the closet and someone else didn't want to kiss her. She thought someone might ask why she had to leave so early, but no one did.

"Are you leaving, Tammy?" Gretchen's mom asked when Tammy headed through the living room to the front door. "Do you need to call your parents to come pick you up?"

"No," Tammy said. "I'm going to walk."

"Oh no," another mom perked up. She was actually Kirin's mom. "No, no, you can't walk home in the dark."

Tammy walked home in the dark all the time. And all Tammy wanted to do now was walk out the door and go home. But now she had to make something up. She couldn't call home for a ride because no one was there. Even if her mother and Nick were home, they probably wouldn't come pick her up. They just didn't do it unless it was really late or really far. Tammy couldn't tell the group of mothers that this was normal because Kirin's mom thought it was dangerous. And then they would all think she was weird.

"You can use the phone in the kitchen Tammy," Gretchen's mom said.

Tammy looked over to the kitchen and could see the phone perched on the wall by the window. She could pretend to call home and say no one answered, but then they would ask why. She could say it was busy, but then they would tell her to wait. She could pretend to talk on the phone and make up a story about how they had to rush out somewhere. They had to take Steffi or Hugh to the doctor or something like that. It was hard to decide what to do.

"You know what?" said Kirin's mom, standing up. "I'll drive her home."

"Are you sure, Valerie?" Gretchen's mom asked.

"Sure I'm sure," she said. "Come on, Tammy."

Valerie's car was parked right outside because she and Kirin lived next door to Gretchen. Tammy got into the front seat and bucked the seatbelt across the army jacket. Valerie didn't wear a seatbelt.

"Okay," Valerie said. "Where to?"

Tammy thought maybe she was joking. She had picked up Kirin from Tammy's house dozens of times. But Valerie didn't say anything, so Tammy gave her the address. Valerie just sat there staring out the window. Maybe she was pulling some long practical joke, but it was taking a long time to get to the funny part.

Kirin's mom finally looked over at Tammy. "I'm sorry," she said. "I'm sorry. I'll drive you home, Tammy. I said I would."

"You don't have to," Tammy said. "I'm allowed to walk."

"No, I'm just a little nervous. I was in a car accident a little while ago and I'm just a little nervous about cars still." She looked over at Tammy. "But we're not going to get into an accident. Don't worry." She released the emergency brake and turned the car into the street.

Valerie came to a complete stop at every stop sign. Tammy's mother and Nick usually just slowed down and checked to see if anyone was coming and then kept going.

"I'm sorry no one else wore a costume," Valerie said. "That wasn't very nice of them."

"It's okay," Tammy said.

"It's more fun to wear costumes. It doesn't have to be Halloween. You can dress up whenever you want. It's good for your imagination. Like on *Mister Rogers* you can take the train to Imagination Land."

It was called the Neighborhood of Make-Believe, and it was a trolley, not a train, but Tammy didn't feel like correcting Valerie. Hugh watched *Mister Rogers* sometimes, but Tammy was way too old for that show and she hadn't watched in years.

"It's hard growing up," Valerie said. "No one wants to talk about anything anymore. Everyone just wants to get ahead. It can be very lonely."

"Can we turn on the radio?" Tammy asked. She felt awkward talking to Valerie. If Steffi or Kirin were in the car it would be different. But it was very weird to be talking to a younger kid's mom for no reason.

"Yeah, sure. We can turn on the radio. Sure." She reached down and turned the knob. They were in the middle of a song. Valerie knew the words and she sang along with the chorus at the ending.

"That was sad," Valerie said. "When he died. John Lennon. From the Beatles. That was sad."

"My stepfather was sad about it," Tammy said.

"Last nail in the coffin of the sixties. That's what they said."

Everyone was always bringing up the sixties, but Tammy wasn't alive then so she usually found the conversation boring.

Valerie turned to Tammy. "Can I ask you a question?"

"Okay," Tammy said.

"When you walk to school, with Steffi and Kirin, you follow all the rules, right? You don't talk to strangers, you walk straight to school, you're careful crossing the street . . . things like that?"

Tammy understood now why Valerie acted so funny. She was an overprotective mother. That's what Tammy's mother called some of her friends' mothers who wouldn't let them come over in the afternoon if no adults were home. "She has an overprotective mother," Tammy's mother said to try and make her feel better. "It's not your friend's fault."

Valerie stopped at the stop sign on the corner of Bemis and 43rd Streets. She looked over at Tammy, waiting for an answer.

"Yes," Tammy said. She knew it was the answer an overprotective mother wanted to hear.

Tammy got out of the car and walked around to the back of the house. Valerie followed her in the car and waited until she climbed the back steps, fished out her key from under her hobo shirt, and let herself in.

Steffi was in the TV room just as she was when Tammy had left. Hugh wasn't there; Steffi must've gotten him to go to bed somehow. Steffi looked over at Tammy and then back at the TV. She was sitting up straight with her hands on her knee-socked knees as though she were playing the part of someone watching TV. It was like she was faking watching TV. Steffi kept her eyes glued to the screen. She had a perfectly blank expression on her face. Tammy knew Steffi was up to something, but decided she didn't care what, and walked past her into the kitchen.

Her mother and Nick were sitting on the couch in the living room watching TV. Nick stood up as soon as he saw her.

"Where've you been?" He walked up to her, put his hands in his pockets, and stooped over so he could look her in the eye. Tammy didn't say anything back and he gave her a sharp "Huh?" trying to get her to say something.

Tammy didn't speak. She stared at the floorboards between her combat boots and the toes of Nick's brown shoes.

"Did you go to the party after we said you couldn't?"

There was no way Nick could prove anything. She could say she'd been sitting on the back porch and they just hadn't noticed her. That would technically still count as being home, even though she wasn't inside. That would still count as being on the property. But for some reason, Tammy thought if she told the truth, that it would be okay. That she wouldn't be punished. After all, her mother and Nick were the ones who got the dates mixed up. And it's always better to tell the truth. If Tammy told the truth they would realize she was a good person. Even if she did something bad, they would realize she was at least trying to be good.

"Yes," Tammy said in a very small voice.

Nick yanked his hand out of his pocket and smacked the wall right by the side of Tammy's head. He hit it so hard the red wall-mounted phone jumped out of its holder and fell to the kitchen floor. Tammy jerked a little when he did it, but she didn't yell out or make any sort of sound. Her mother stood up and Tammy thought she might be coming to her rescue and was going to tell Nick to stop hitting things. But her mother only stood there, not even very close by, while Nick started yelling about how irresponsible Tammy was, how selfish she was, how she only thought about herself, and how she was going to have to learn that she doesn't always get what she wants in life. But most of all Tammy had to learn about *responsibility*. She was the oldest and she had the most responsibility. When there was a break in his yelling speech, Tammy stuck in a tiny "Okay," but Nick cut her off and said, "No, it's not okay. It's not okay to leave your brother and sister alone at night. What if something happened?"

"Like what?" Tammy didn't say this to be smart. She really wanted to know, like what? What could happen?

"TAMMY!" Nick shouted. Tammy thought he was going to shout something more, or maybe actually spank her. She hadn't been spanked since the fourth grade. Or maybe the third. It had definitely been a year. She thought it was over. Once when she was eight, he told her to turn off the TV, and then he spanked her hard across the butt. She was reaching to turn it off when he spanked her. Tammy asked him why he did that and he said she wasn't turning it off fast enough.

Nick took a deep inhale through his nose that sucked up some of his mustache hairs and said, "Go to your room."

Tammy trudged past her mother and Nick. When she put her first foot on the stairs she tripped on the boots again and said, "Shit," under her breath. She said it quietly and no one heard her.

"Tammy," her mother called after her, "think about what could've happened if Steffi had had an asthma attack. Hugh wouldn't have known what to do or how to call an ambulance. She could've died."

Tammy kept clomping up the stairs and didn't answer anything back. She had never heard of anyone dying from an asthma attack before, but she supposed it could happen since Steffi did have to go to the emergency room sometimes. And so what if Steffi did die? Life would be easier if she did. No one would be walking through Tammy's room all the time. And she could spread out and use both rooms and keep the separator door open.

Her mother and Nick came upstairs a few minutes later and told Tammy they had decided on a punishment for her. Tammy had forgotten about a punishment because usually they gave it right away, they usually yelled out, no dessert, no TV, you're grounded, or something like that. She knew "go to your room" was not a real punishment, it was just something they said when they couldn't think of anything else.

They stood in the doorway to Tammy's room and said that Tammy's punishment would be watching Hugh next week—*every day*. Her days and Steffi's days. Tammy said that was unfair. Why should Steffi get something for free? It wasn't as if Steffi had done something super good. They said that it wasn't fair to Steffi that Tammy left her alone with Hugh. They thought this was an appropriate punishment. Oh, and she wasn't allowed to go the slumber party tomorrow either. Then they shut the door and went back downstairs.

Tammy wanted to break something, but she had been sent to her room and she didn't want to mess up any of her own stuff. She didn't feel like reading so there was nothing left for her to do but go to bed. She got into bed without washing off her makeup beard because the last thing in the world she wanted to do was to walk into the hallway and see any of them. She preferred to get into bed, close her eyes, and pretend that since she couldn't see anyone, no one could see her.

TAMMY AND STEFFI spent the weekend of Spring Break at their dad's apartment. It was also Tammy's eleventh birthday. Tammy had wanted to have a party at home, but most of her friends were away because it was Spring Break. Tammy was a little upset about it, but her mother said, "I'm sure your dad will have something special planned." When they got to their dad's apartment, a lady was sitting on the couch reading a magazine. Tammy and Steffi asked who she was, and their dad said, "That's Cindy. She's a friend of mine." Tammy and Steffi didn't know their dad had friends. When they had visited him before, no one else was ever there. Tammy thought maybe they were dating, but her dad said "friend"; he didn't say "girlfriend."

They drove to King's Dominion amusement park near Richmond and stopped at a McDonald's for lunch. Cindy wore lipstick and it left a red mark on her straw. At King's Dominion, Tammy and her dad waited in line for the roller coasters while Cindy bought Steffi cotton candy and sat on a bench. When it was getting late, their dad said they had time for just one more ride. Tammy and Steffi wanted to go on the log flume, but Cindy said, "I'd rather not get my hair wet and be soaked for the whole ride home," so they ended up going to the house of mirrors, which Tammy thought was boring because all she had to do was look at the floor and she could figure out where the mirrors were. Tammy was the first one out.

Cindy rode with them all the way back to DC. Before Tammy and Steffi got out of the car, Cindy handed each of the girls a little present. Steffi got barrettes and Tammy got lip gloss. "I want us to be friends," Cindy said.

AWAY TO THE WEST

*   ❖   *

Los Angeles made Jeffrey's head hurt. He felt like an alien from another galaxy and the Earth dwellers' strange eyes, hidden behind sunglasses, were biologically unable to see him.

In the perky afternoon sun, Jeffrey squinted and slogged along the sidewalk inlaid with stars back to his grimy YMCA room. He had picked up "the trades," as he heard the girls in the Laundromat call them. The trades were the local papers that listed auditions and the go-ings-on of show biz. He flipped through the cheap newsprint pages looking at notices for models, girls next door (some nudity required), college preppies, mobsters, and fat people. In art class the instructor always tried to be nice and say the fat model was Rubenesque, but what he really meant was she was fat, and usually, very fat.

The ads for writers were tucked away in a separate box entitled "Script Search." Most of them were for comedy writers. The rest were for writing teams, someone looking to collaborate. Jeffrey knew it was probably some jerk looking for a partner to do all the work for him before he walked away with all the credit. That kind of thing happened all the time in Hollywood. People were out to suck you dry, Jeffrey thought, and it wasn't just your money they were after. They wanted your brain as well.

Jeffrey spent his days alone in his dingy Y room, but unlike his room at home, he felt anxious about doing so. He felt there was only a set number of hours he was allowed to remain indoors. His sister once told him about the youth hostel in London where she had stayed while on her senior class trip. She and her friends were locked out every day after breakfast and they couldn't come back until five o'clock. She didn't care. "You don't go to London to sit in a room," she said.

But here in Los Angeles, surrounded by walls of chipped paint and ensphered by a saggy mattress, Jeffrey read through his paperback novels too quickly. He didn't get good transistor radio reception. He had to make trips to the bathroom across the hall when nobody was looking. He would listen for several minutes at his door to be absolutely sure the coast was clear. The one good thing about the place was that the cinder-block walls and linoleum floors echoed everything. Jeffrey could hear the reverbs of footsteps shuffling down the long corridor, and every slam of every door.

It was okay, he tried to tell himself, that he spent so much time alone in his room. He was a writer. That's what writers do. He had been working on an idea for a movie based on his life story. It was about a young guy, like himself, who begins to travel through time. Everyone at his high school thinks he's a geek, but he has the ability to travel into the future and see what his classmates become when they grow up. They all turn out to be losers and phonies. This gives his character the confidence to ignore their stupid jokes at school and he is able to convince the girl he likes not to marry the idiot football player because he will turn out to be a beer-drinking, alcoholic wife abuser. The Jeffrey-based character turns out to be a rich songwriter who reunites the Beatles and is loved by millions of fans around the world. Maybe it was a hokey ending, but that's the kind of ending most movies have.

Jeffrey heard the bathroom door slam and footsteps plod down the hall. He pushed the newspapers aside, got up from his bed, and listened at the door until the walker rounded the corner. Then he gently turned the doorknob and stepped into the hallway. The walker hadn't gone around the corner; he was standing outside a door near the stairwell. A black guy. The place was full of them. They walked around in bathrobes with nothing underneath and no shoes. This guy was looking for his key in the folds of his towel. His bathrobe was brown, a few shades lighter than his chocolate skin.

Jeffrey didn't want to move. He didn't want to draw attention to himself. He didn't want this guy looking at him. He didn't know how long he stood there until the guy finally found his key and unlocked his door, allowing Jeffrey to slip across the linoleum threshold.

The Y bathroom was divided in two by a shoulder-high cement wall, one side had a row of toilet stalls and the other, three shower cubicles. The sink in there was a strange construction. It had two circular levels, looked like a gigantic, beige wedding cake, and took up most of the room. The first time Jeffrey saw it, he had no idea how it worked. He wasn't even sure if it was a sink, he thought it might be some sort of industrial-sized piece of janitorial equipment. Jeffrey was perplexed by the structure until he watched someone step on a hose that ran in a circle under the sink and water shot out of the top tier and washed away in the bottom. Jeffrey wondered if it used to be a public fountain and the Y obtained it for free thinking it would work well as a sink. It could accommodate a lot of people at the same time. Jeffrey imagined prisons probably had the same sort of thing. It probably kept inmates from un-screwing the faucets and using them as weapons.

Jeffrey walked over to the behemoth beige sink, stepped on the hose, and held his hands under the lukewarm spray. He didn't use the tiny bars of soap balanced on the edge of the upper level. He didn't like sharing soap. It was a mystery to him why no one else felt the same way. Why would you want to use something that someone else had rubbed between their dirty hands right after they came out of the toilet? Jeffrey thought. Why would you want to use the same bar of soap in the shower that someone else had rubbed all over their naked body? Up their ass, even?

Jeffrey stepped off the hose and shook the excess water off his hands. That's when he noticed the tiny black hairs sitting at the bottom of the basin. Tiny, black, very black, curly hairs. Sitting there. Refusing to be washed down the drain. Jeffrey's stomach somersaulted and his tongue swelled up in the back of his throat. He took a step backward not wanting to get too close. One of those things could jump out and get on him. That fucker, he thought, what did he do? Rinse his dick off in the sink? Doesn't he know how to use a shower? Doesn't he at least have the decency to rinse out the sink?

Though he usually checked the hallway before dashing back to his room, Jeffrey bolted from the bathroom, knocking the door open with his shoulder. He rushed into his room and sat on the edge of the bed. A shaky feeling coursed through his blood, as though he had skipped breakfast, the most important meal of the day. He couldn't be here in this place meant for losers and outcasts and nobodies. Didn't they realize how great he was? Nobody gave him a chance. It wasn't his fault he didn't have connections or parents who believed in him and encouraged him and sent him to Juilliard, who stayed up all night stuffing his picture into envelopes addressed to casting people and film directors. He was a star, a genius. Didn't they see that someday he would win the Academy Award and the Nobel Prize and his book would have a shiny gold medal stuck on the front cover? People would want his autograph. People would chase him down in the street. He'd have to wear dark glasses the whole time, maybe even a disguise, maybe even have to hire a bodyguard. He might get kidnapped and held for ransom by crazy hippie radicals fighting for a lost political cause. Couldn't anyone see this? Were they going to let him waste away in this shithole? Were they going to let a talent like his just die?

He started to hyperventilate. He needed some air. He had to leave.

Jeffrey bounded down the stairs and pushed his way out the front door onto the super bright radioactive sidewalk. He walked at a fast pace, swinging his arms wildly, until he reached a bus stop and collapsed onto the bench. He was sweaty and out of breath. He put his head in his shaking hands and the weight of his skull helped quiet them down. He closed his eyes and focused on the blackness. Slowly, his breathing returned to normal, and he no longer had to consciously think about forcing his body to function.

Behind his palms, he opened his eyes and adjusted to the strips of light filtering through his flesh. He separated his fingers a little wider and stared at the black tar of the road, the cars whizzing by, the scorched palm trees lining the opposite sidewalk, and the building slowly coming into focus across the street.

Los Angeles Public Library.

Jeffrey glided through the glass door into quiet puttering and cool air-conditioning. It was a modern building made of polished steel and filled with sleek, wooden shelves. Jeffrey liked it instantly. He walked up to the information desk and asked the short, ruffle-bloused librarian for a library card.

"You need to fill out this form."

Jeffrey picked up the pen attached to the clipboard by a piece of old string and filled out the page with tiny block letters. He pushed the board back across the desk.

"And I'll need to see some ID with proof of address."

Jeffrey opened his wallet and pulled out his Texas non-driver state-issued ID card. After he had taken the DMV road test three times and failed, he had given up and settled for this useless piece of laminate in order to get into rated-R movies. The librarian looked at it and frowned.

"I'm sorry, this is from out of state."

"I just moved here."

"I need something that shows your local address. Utility bill, bank book, pay stub, anything like that."

"I literally just got here. I'm staying at the YMCA while I apartment hunt."

"I could accept a payment receipt from the Y until you get yourself set up."

"I don't have that with me right now."

"Well, I'll keep your form on file and you can come back when you have it."

I must be a bum, Jeffrey thought, if they won't even give me a library card.

Jeffrey turned around and left without another word to the frumpy librarian. He walked out of the glass library and back onto the street. As he stumbled down the sidewalk, he thought he must be the only guy in LA without a car.

IT WAS DARK when Jeffrey headed back to the Y carrying a paper bag of food: bread, peanut butter, grape jelly, and a package of vanilla wafers. They weren't allowed to cook at the Y so he had to make do. Plus he didn't have the cash to spend on restaurant meals. When he walked in, a few guys were slouching in the lobby common room watching TV on brown, cracked-leather couches. Jeffrey noticed some trades lying on a table. He casually flipped through the pages, observing several square holes where acting notices had been cut out. He wondered which of these guys were actors trying their luck with stars in their eyes. They probably wouldn't make it, unless they were really good looking or really ordinary looking. That's the kind of actor that makes it in Hollywood. Doesn't really have anything to do with talent. Jeffrey'd hate to be the one to break it to these guys; most of them would probably end up in porn films. Hey, at least they'd be making money.

Without asking whose it was, Jeffrey folded the paper and tucked it under his arm. He headed up the stairs to his room where he continued to read while munching on a sandwich. He came across a listing that caught his eye:

— WANTED —

Singer-songwriters

TV contract in development with major studio

Looking for all types: rock, pop, Billy Joel, Blondie, Smokey, disco

YOU COULD BE THE NEXT MUSIC SENSATION!

Open call, Tues. starting @ 9 a.m.

With a razor blade, Jeffrey carefully drew a box around the listing and lifted the square off the page.

JEFFREY WALKED UP to the impressively tall office building with tinted glass doors. As he extended his arms forward to the metal handle, a security guard stopped him.

"Where you going, pal?"

Jeffrey's fingers hesitated, suddenly immobile, a few inches from the bar.

"Who you going to see?"

"I'm dropping off some music samples."

"Line's around there," the guard gestured with his thumb.

The line stretched along the side of the building almost to the corner. Jeffrey was surprised there were this many songwriters in Hollywood.

Jeffrey made his way to the end of the line passing black doo-wop singers harmonizing in a group with matching hats, a bunch of guys slinging guitars, and lots of girls all done up, hair, makeup, dress, like they were going out on a Saturday night. A lot of them were doing singing exercises, singing mah-may-mee-mo-moo like they were cows climbing over a hill. There was even some skinny guy wearing makeup and carrying an electric keyboard.

Jeffrey took his place in line behind a husband-and-wife team. They were rehearsing dance moves as they whispered song lyrics. At one point they turned to each other, pointed their fingers, and nodded in unison. Then they smiled in unison, faced forward, and raised their arms for a big finish.

All these people are idiots, Jeffrey thought. Stupid. Fools. Jeffrey kept his hands in the pockets of his army jacket. In one pocket he had a cassette he made of his songs; he also had an envelope of his lyrics in his breast pocket and a John Lennon pin on his lapel. He looked serious, like a serious musician. Jeffrey thought all these people were amateurish, dressing up and embarrassing themselves by dancing on the sidewalk. They were all phonies. They don't even care about music. They just want to be movie stars.

Every now and then the starry-eyed hopefuls shuffled forward about four feet. Word came down the line that they were letting people upstairs ten at a time. A group of girls stood directly behind Jeffrey. He couldn't tell if they were a singing group or if they were just friends who were each here separately but came as a group.

"I've done pretty well since I got here. I haven't gotten anything, but I've gotten called back for a lot of stuff and I was just accepted into this workshop that you have to audition for. It's really hard to get into."

"My manager thinks I might have better luck in New York since I'm a strong singer. But I don't want to only do plays. The pay sucks. You can't live on that. And the same thing over and over, night after night. Frankly, I'd rather do a Vegas show."

"I got offered a part in a play, but it's out of town. I don't know what to do. I mean, should I take it? I feel like I just got here. I don't want to just get here and then have to go out of town to do some play that no one is going to see and then come back and be in the same position I was in before where nobody knows who I am. You know?"

"I know. It's all about who you know."

"You just have to get to know as many people as you can."

"Or as many people as possible have to know who you are."

"You know what would just suck? Turning thirty and not having gotten anywhere. Because by then you're too old to play young parts and you're too young to play old parts. That's when it's time to marry the first rich guy you meet."

"Definitely."

"It wouldn't be so bad if you actually had a good run for a while. Then it would be a life-change thing. You could marry some rich guy and pick and choose your projects. Do guest spots, that sort of thing."

The girls bantered on about how the best thing was to get a guest spot on *Love Boat* or *Fantasy Island*.

Jeffrey thought they had no class.

The line shuffled forward and Jeffrey estimated there would be one more shuffle before he made it inside.

The girls suddenly let out tiny squeals of "Oh my God, oh my God, oh my God!" A thin, smartly dressed woman was walking down the street toward them. Jeffrey didn't know who it was because she wore a large brimmed hat and pink sunglasses balanced on her delicate nose. One of the girls jumped out of the line and went up to her. She walked backward in front of the woman and gushed about how much she admired her, what an inspiration, she loved her last film, she wanted to model her career just like hers. The woman, who Jeffrey gathered must be a movie star although he didn't recognize her, smiled a gentle, lipsticked smile and asked the girl if she wanted an autograph.

"Oh, yeah!"

The girl searched her pocketbook for a pen, but she didn't have one. She ran back to her friends, but stupidly, none of them had one either.

"Mister, do you have a pen?"

The girl wore her hair in long ponytails on either side of her head like Marcia Brady in the early days. Her eyes were wide and green and desperate. Her career was in his hands. It all rested on his pen.

"Sure," he said. He pulled out a pen and offered it to her with his hand wrapped around the ink tip, the same considerate way one is supposed to pass a pair of scissors.

"Thanks!" she said and bounded back to the movie star.

She returned to her friends who gushed over the signature, which was written across the girl's own picture. She held it up to her face, like a mask, and moved her head from side to side. The girls agreed it was a sign that she would one day be as famous as the movie star.

The security guard ushered Jeffrey and the girls inside the lobby. Marcia Brady still hadn't returned the pen. Jeffrey kept glancing back trying to catch her attention. He met her eyes once, but she grinned and turned away. She noticed him again and whispered to her friend who focused her beady, disgusted glare on him. They've forgotten all about me, Jeffrey thought. They didn't even bother with a "thank you." They probably forgot it was me who loaned them the pen and now they think I'm some sort of creep. Jeffrey thought all would be rectified because they were right after him in line. They would hear his tape and change their tune. They would be asking for his autograph. He would be someone to know.

The elevator arrived and ten of them crowded in. The husband-and-wife team had quieted down; they were taking deep breaths, in through the nose, out through the mouth. The doors opened on the seventh floor.

Lucky, Jeffrey thought.

They stepped into an ordinary office hallway and again they lined up along a wall. A tall, thin guy wearing a woman's blouse was working his way down the line with a Polaroid camera. When he got to Jeffrey he pointed the camera right in his face.

"Smile!" he said and popped the flash before Jeffrey got the chance.

"Write your name on the bottom," he said, handing the blank photo to Jeffrey and proceeding down the line.

"Excuse me," Jeffrey said to the girl behind him. She turned her head just as her picture was being taken.

"What? Oh no! Can you do another one?"

"Sorry, one per customer."

The girl glared at Jeffrey.

"I'm sorry, I need my pen back."

The girl scowled at him and turned back to her friends. She made a big deal of demonstrating how she waited for the flash to go off before asking her friend for the pen. They all looked at Jeffrey like he was crazy.

The pen was passed back to him.

As his face slowly appeared on the filmy surface, Jeffrey wrote "Jeff Hack" on the white border. He would use that as his professional name. Everybody in show business used a different name.

When he finished, he offered the pen back to the girls.

"Here you go," he said. He was met with angry stares. "So you can write your name."

"I got one from someone else. Thanks."

The girls turned their backs to him and tightened their huddle. They didn't need him anymore.

It was the same deal up here, the same shuffling and waiting.

The Polaroid guy sashayed back up the line.

"If you're asked to stay, be prepared to dance."

He repeated it about every five people. Jeffrey thought it was a joke.

When Jeffrey was the third person from the front of the line, the Polaroid guy collected his picture and opened the door just enough to get his wispy body through the crack.

A few minutes later, four people came out of the room. The Polaroid guy opened the door and said the next four people, Jeffrey included, could come in.

Inside was a large empty office. There was a long table where two men and a woman sat smoking cigarettes and sifting through piles of papers and photos. The Polaroid guy went up to the table and laid the four snapshots out for them.

Jeffrey didn't know how this was going to work. He didn't know if there was yet another room where he would have a meeting with someone one-on-one. Right now he just followed along. The four contestants lined up, standing up very straight, in a row, facing the table. They didn't say anything. They waited to be spoken to.

The table people mulled over the photographs.

"Chuck and Diane," they called out.

The married couple took a deep breath and stepped forward. This is like going to see the wizard, Jeffrey thought.

"What've you got for us today?"

The husband gave a brief introduction, lathering on the charm. Then he and his wife took their places at opposite ends of the room and began a Broadway-style number walking toward each other, step by step, until they met in the middle, and then moved through the dance routine Jeffrey had seen them rehearse outside. They did their big finish, belting out the last note, holding their final pose, arms raised triumphantly in the air, until one of the table people said, "Great, thanks" without any shred of emotion. Chuck and Diane kept their perfect poise and walked back to their place next to Jeffrey.

"Caroline?"

This was one of the pen girls. Marcia Brady's friend.

Caroline stepped forward and gave a cheery, "Hi!"

"What have you got for us, Caroline?"

"I'd like to do a song that I wrote. I have a tape here with the music, if you have a player . . ."

They had one on the table. Caroline popped in her tape and scurried back to take her position.

Piano music drifted out of the tape player. It was a slow song and the table looked bored. They stopped her before the second verse.

"That's all we have time for right now."

Caroline covered up her disappointment with a cheery "Okay!" She walked over to the table, ejected her cassette, and returned to Jeffrey's side.

Jeffrey's heart was pounding in his chest. He felt his legs go numb and he doubted their ability to hold him up. He swallowed repeatedly in an attempt to water his throat. He knew he was next. He wanted to step forward on his own and not wait for them to call out his name. His hand felt sweaty wrapped around the cassette case in his pocket, but he didn't want to let go and wipe it off. The plastic case was the only thing anchoring him to the earth. Without it, his numb legs might lift off the floor like a hot air balloon.

"And . . . Jeff."

Jeffrey swallowed the excess saliva in his mouth and stepped forward.

"What've you got for us today?"

Jeffrey pulled out his tape and offered it to the table.

"Going to sing along?" one of them asked and popped open the tape player, exposing the naked little knobs.

Jeffrey placed his tape in the machine feeling his hand shake uncontrollably the whole time.

"Just uh . . ." he let his hair fall in his face as a protective measure, "going to play it."

Jeffrey pressed the PLAY tab down and took a couple of steps back. Guitar music and his soft voice flowed out of the machine. One of the table guys tried to turn the volume up. Jeffrey had recorded it in his Y room and the noise from the hallway and the street down below could be heard in the background.

The lone woman at the table stared at him quizzically.

"Are you not going to sing?" she asked.

"I made the tape," Jeffrey said. He kept his eyes on the machine, watching the wheels slowly turn and wondering for a second if he could hypnotize himself.

Jeffrey dug the envelope out of his breast pocket.

"Here are the lyrics if you want to follow along."

"But, you're not going to sing for us right now?"

The guy sitting by the recorder pressed STOP.

"No, I . . . didn't bring my guitar."

"Could you do something a cappella?"

"I thought you wanted samples. That's why I made the tape."

The woman smiled at him. He thought maybe she understood.

"Could you give us just a little something?"

Jeffrey didn't know what to do. He stood there staring at his cassette frozen in the tape player window. The woman smiled again.

"I can tell you're not a show biz type," she said softly, "but we have a lot of work for studio singers. It could be good work for someone like you. If you could just give us a little something. Anything really."

The table men weren't looking at him anymore. One of them leaned over to the woman and said, "Let's move on." The woman looked at Jeffrey. He could tell she was deciding whether or not to give up on him.

"What would you like?" Jeffrey asked.

"Anything. Sing a few lines from your favorite pop song, or any musical you've been in. Anything you know."

Jeffrey's mind went blank.

"I'm having trouble thinking of something."

"How about 'My Country, 'Tis Of Thee'? Everyone knows that. You sang it every day in school."

Jeffrey knew the song, he just didn't know how to begin. He decided to do what everyone else did. He walked into the middle of the room. He took a deep breath and began singing. Problem was, he started too high. By the time he got to *land where my father died*, his voice cracked. He looked at the table to see if they noticed. The woman was mouthing the words along with him: *land of the pilgrim's pride, from e-e-vry mountainside—*

"Big finish," one of the men said jokingly. The other one cracked up. "Le-et freedom ring."

Jeffrey stood still for a moment.

"Thanks."

Jeffrey walked back to his place between Chuck and Caroline the pen girl.

"Okay, thank you, we'll be in touch."

The group gave a cheery, cacophonous "Thank you" and walked toward the door. Jeffrey realized his tape was still in the player and headed back to retrieve it. He pressed EJECT, but then remembered his father saying always to leave a card. Jeffrey didn't have a card.

"You know what? Keep it."

He took out the tape and hastily wrote his name and address on the label. He placed it on the table next to his Polaroid. Then he followed Chuck and Diane out of the room and down the stairs. They were asked to use the stairs on their way out to keep the elevators free.

Jeffrey felt upbeat. It didn't matter that he had to sing a corny patriotic song. Now they had his tape. They'd figure it out. It was all set. No one else had a tape. Even Caroline the pen girl got stopped halfway through. They didn't let her finish, even though she was an okay singer; not great. They let Jeffrey finish and now they had his demo. This is how it happens. This is how people get their start. He was on his way.

Dear Jeffrey,

I hope sunny California is treating you well. The weather we've been having here is just awful. Rain, rain, rain. You probably have a suntan by now.

How are things in the music business? Don't be discouraged if it's hard at first. Your father had to knock on a lot of doors to get his business started, and a lot of doors got slammed in his face! He used to come home feeling rejected, just like you. You two are more alike than you think.

Have you found a job yet? I know it's hard. You do have restaurant experience and there are a lot of restaurants in Hollywood. Fancy ones too, where you might make extra money in tips. Maybe even wait on movie stars and get to see what they have for dinner.

I worry that you haven't written us yet. Please drop me a quick note and let me know you're okay. You know how I worry. You left in such a rush and didn't tell us anything about your plans. We had no idea you wanted to move. Your father worries that this was a hasty idea and you didn't think it through. I want you to know that a lot of people try and fail, and there's no shame in that. It takes some people longer than others to figure out their path in life. Remember Jesus was rejected at first too.

How is Pam? I realize we never got a chance to meet her before you left. Maybe we could have her over for dinner at Easter. You will be coming home for Easter, I hope?

Most of all, Jeffrey, I miss you. The house is very empty and quiet with you gone (not that you were loud!). I hope that you are doing well and that your dreams really do come true.

All my love,
Mother.

Jeffrey let the note fall back into its folded shape. He was planning on waiting a little longer before writing to his parents. He wanted to draw it out as long as possible, figuring that would make them more and more anxious. It was always best when he came back from the dead. He had seen a television movie where a family was trying to get their daughter out of a cult. They got her home once, but she tricked them and ran back to the ashram. Years went by, and they had basically given her up for dead, when out of the blue she showed up on their doorstep looking like a completely different person, like a bum off the street. Everyone hugged and cried and lived happily ever after and they never bothered her again. Sometimes Jeffrey thought about joining a cult. They would take care of him, house him, and feed him. Of course, they'd be trying to cram Jesus or Krishna or something like it down his throat and he'd probably have to wear some kooky outfit while he passed out pamphlets on the street corner. Too many people. In the end, Jeffrey thought a cult would probably be like any other job.

He had to change his plans because of a different letter that was slid under his door. The Y was limiting his stay. He could stay longer if he was a student or employed, but Jeffrey was neither. He would have to move on and, preferably, up. He was too good for this shithole. Jeffrey wanted his own apartment, but he was running low on funds. Anyone else with parents like his would have his own apartment, or at the very least, a decent efficiency unit. Jeffrey suspected someone had given his parents the advice of "tough love." Throw him in the water and he'll learn how to swim.

Jeffrey sat up and made his way over to the desk. He was good at writing letters.

Dear Mom and Dad,

Greetings from California! I apologize for not having written before, but it took a while to get my bearings straight. The Y is very basic, but generally okay, with the exception of a few shady characters. For the most part, nobody bothers me. Pam has been staying with friends of hers who have an extra room. She lives in a house full of aspiring actresses. They joke that they live in a sorority house. One of her roommates actually landed a part in a TV commercial.

As for me, the music business has started off well. I was recently hand-picked at an audition for new musical talent. They are reviewing my materials and are interested in working with me. They said at first it would probably be studio work, playing backup for someone famous who is recording a new album, but that would only be temporary until my own career gets off the ground.

I've been looking around for a good job because eventually Pam and I would like to get our own place. The job market is tough because all the out-of-work actors take up most of the restaurant jobs, but I'm still looking! I spend most of my days looking for jobs and "making the rounds," as they say out here, which means dropping off demo tapes to people in record company offices. I made my own demo tapes on my tape recorder in my room. They're not very good quality. I'll have to get one professionally done soon.

Sorry about the rain. It's been nothing but sun out here. In fact, everyone wears sunglasses every day!

Love,
Jeffrey

Jeffrey folded the letter and stuffed it in an envelope. He tore off an American flag stamp from the roll his mother had tucked in his bag right before he left. Letter in hand, he walked downstairs to the lobby and dropped it in the outgoing mailbox. Then he turned around, went back up to his room, and took out another sheet of paper.

Dear Mom and Dad,

I don't know if you've sent any letters recently. You may have and I didn't get them. The reason for that is I've been kicked out of the Y. It's a long story and not my fault. I came home last week to find my room had been broken into. Everything was gone, my money, my tape recorder, even some of my clothes! Strangely the only thing they didn't take was my guitar. Although I was shocked, I was not surprised considering the shady types that hung around the Y. I think it was probably one of my not-so-friendly neighbors. After that, I couldn't pay the rent on the room and was kicked out.

On the same day, Pam and I had a big fight and she told me she had met a new guy, a director, and that she and I were history. It was right after our last supper that I came home to my ransacked room. I didn't really have a chance to make any new friends out here because I was so busy looking for a job, so I had nowhere to go. I'm ashamed to admit it, but I've basically been living on the street for the past three days. I clean myself up at the public library in the morning and get some breakfast out of garbage cans. I am really at my lowest low. Also, the company that wanted to start me as a studio musician now says they don't need me. And on top of that, they never returned my demo cassette. I can't make any new ones because the tape recorder is gone.

I hate to ask this because it was my dream to make it out here on my own, but I think this qualifies as an emergency. Could you please send me some money? The one smart thing I did do was to get a post office box, so you can send it there instead of the Y. I feel like such a failure for asking. I know I've let you down more than once. Right now I wish I'd never come out here, but I'd feel like an even bigger failure if I gave up.

I'd call, but I don't have a dime to my name.

Love,
Jeffrey

Jeffrey folded this letter up and sealed it in an envelope. He would need to wait a few days before sending it. Maybe a week.

JEFFREY OPENED THE sliding patio door to the Sunrise Motel office. Two old ladies were behind the counter, knitting or crocheting or doing some other kind of old-lady craft. The TV was blaring game shows, *Family Feud* or *Wheel of Fortune* or *The Price Is Right, come on down!* One of the grannies turned around when Jeffrey walked in and put down her needles, the other one decided to buy a vowel. Jeffrey registered, obtained a key, and was told the pool was closed right now because it was being drained.

As he climbed the steps to his second-level room, he noticed a woman standing under the stairs. She had one hand on her hip and a cigarette dangling from the other a few inches above her naked thigh. She was facing the parking lot and didn't seem to be waiting for anyone inside. She was tall, black, and wearing a short skirt and a halter top. It wasn't until he was halfway up the stairs and peeking down at her through the slats between the steps that Jeffrey realized she was a prostitute. Probably the whole place was full of them. He wondered if the two office ladies knew or if they just assumed that was the fashion girls were wearing today. Or the office ladies could be madams and the whole place could be some kind of operation.

Jeffrey's room was decorated with a dark blue worn-out carpet, a dark blue worn-out double bed, and a TV molded onto a white pedestal stand, which was the only thing in the room capable of reflecting light. He walked over to the window to close the dark blue worn-out drapes. Outside in the parking lot, he saw the black girl lean into the window of a red car. Jeffrey thought it must be customary to examine a prostitute's tits before you hire her. This was LA, you have to audition for everything. A moment later she opened the passenger door and got in. The car did a three-point turn and exited the lot.

Although he liked the Sunrise, Jeffrey didn't feel as secure as he did at the Y. He felt the motel was on the edge of something. It was a place not many people knew about, a place someone came to only when he was lost and desperate and forgotten, a place someone came to only if he wanted to disappear. Maybe that's what unnerved Jeffrey about it—the thought that he, too, might begin to vanish.

It was dark when Jeffrey ventured out of his room and onto the second-floor balcony to make his way to the soda machine. He bought two bottles of Coke and tried to hold one of them in his armpit in order to unlock his door. The shock of the cold glass against his skin caused him to shiver and the bottle fell to the ground, smashing open on the concrete. The soda spread out, darkening the doorstep, and fizzled away. Jeffrey panicked and thought about cleaning it up, but then who would know it was his mess? He could slip back into his room and pretend he didn't know anything about it. That's what they had maids for anyway.

As he turned his key in the lock, another door opened and a teenage girl stepped out onto the balcony. She wore high-heeled sandals and had long blonde hair that fell straight down to her tits, strapped in a tube top. She would have been a knockout, but her nose was a little too odd and a little too long. She was a little too skinny and her collarbone stuck out below her shoulders like it was too big for her body. She walked toward Jeffrey and he stood there with his door cracked open, unable to move.

"Popped your pop, huh?" she said as she stepped over the tide of fizz. Jeffrey stared after her. She's another one, he thought.

She turned to go down the stairs to the parking lot, stepping carefully in her precarious shoes. As she disappeared down the stairwell, she raised her eyes and looked up at him through her long blonde bangs. Jeffrey felt the lips of his tightly controlled mouth begin to part as her head bounced down and out of view.

Jeffrey retreated into his room and gently closed the door. He waited there, crouched in the shadow, ear pressed to the dark blue wooden door. He was close enough to the wall so that no one would see him if they glanced in the window. They would think no one was home. Only the spilt soda marking his door could give him away. Jeffrey waited for a car to drive off with the blonde girl inside, but he didn't hear anything. It was as if she had walked down the stairs and out of life.

The other conclusion Jeffrey came to was that she could be staying here as well. They could be neighbors.

Quietly, Jeffrey opened his door, tiptoed out onto the soda-stained cement, and looked over the railing. He couldn't see anything directly underneath him, only the wash of light from the street-level walkway. He inched over to the stairwell where he could peer down through the slats in the steps. She was still there. She was sitting on the fence that separated the parking lot from the first-floor rooms. He looked directly down at the part in her hair, a line drawn down the center of her scalp with black roots poking through the blonde. She was smoking a cigarette and playing with her shoe. She lifted her leg halfway up to the railing and flapped her foot trying to loosen her sandal. Then she wiggled her foot back in place and tapped the toe of her shoe on the ground for good measure. She moved her legs with the laziness of someone lounging on the beach. Her days were long with nothing much to do but lie around.

Jeffrey wanted to walk down and strike up a conversation, but he decided to wait. She was almost too perfect like this. And besides, he thought, she probably doesn't get that much time to herself. He left her there, dangling her legs, dreaming she had a pool in which to dip them, and he quietly returned to his room. He felt as though he had made a friend.

JEFFREY THOUGHT THE best way to see a movie was alone, during the day, during the week. He hated going at night when people went on dates. He hated the fact that people went to the movies not to watch, but to make out or get in the mood for sex. His brother once told him how a girl had let him stick his hand down her pants during a movie and how one time he and his buddies went to a porno film and the whole place was sticky and stained from guys jerking off in the seats. Jeffrey tried to show no reaction when his brother told him that kind of stuff. He knew that the whole point of those stories was to embarrass him and he didn't want to give his brother the satisfaction. His brother won at everything else, why give him that as well?

Jeffrey enjoyed being alone in the large dark room. He liked the decaying grandeur of the old Hollywood Boulevard theaters—the Egyptian and the El Capitan. He shied away from Grauman's Chinese across the street. Too many tourists. He didn't like worrying about getting a good seat during the crowded weekends, sharing an armrest with some stranger, or sitting behind some girl flicking her hair over her seatback and into his space. He liked the comfort of emptiness around him, of no one bothering him, of no one looking at him funny.

On his way back to the Sunrise, Jeffrey stopped in a 7-Eleven and bought a pack of cigarettes. He didn't smoke. It was all part of his plan. Later that night he kept the TV volume low and his window cracked. Finally, as midnight approached, he heard the door down the hall open and the familiar click-clack of high-heeled sandals. Jeffrey reached over and shut off the TV.

The sandals clicked down the stairs.

When the noise stopped, Jeffrey put on his jacket, with his cigarettes already placed in the pocket, and carefully opened the door.

He had it all planned out. He walked to the railing in front of his door. He rested his forearms on the metal bar and leaned out, pretending he was enjoying the night air, but really he was scanning the parking lot below. Once he was satisfied the coast was clear, he reached into his pocket and pulled out his pack of cigarettes. He smacked the package against the palm of his hand a couple times as he had seen his sister do. He wasn't sure what purpose it served, but his sister always did it methodically with every new pack. Then he pulled out a single cigarette and stuck it in the corner of his mouth.

He went through the motions of his plan as if there were an audience watching him. I'm like Romeo on the balcony, he thought, remembering the awkward Shakespeare scenes they had to act out in high school English class. Then he remembered that it was Juliet on the balcony and Romeo down below. It was backward, but he thought it was okay.

He patted down his pockets pretending to look for a lighter. He purposefully didn't buy one at the 7-Eleven, and he left the free matches on the counter. He thought it would be too over-the-top to say something out loud like "Oh no, I don't seem to have a light." Instead, he tried to act as natural as possible; he held the cigarette in place with his teeth and walked over to the stairs. He knew he should do this without pausing to look down. If anything, he should walk quickly.

As he approached the stairwell he couldn't see for sure if she was there or not. He decided to continue according to plan, hoping that maybe she was still there but only slightly out of view.

He saw her when he got to the bottom of the stairs. She wasn't leaning on the fence; she was sitting opposite the stairs on the ground with her knees bent up by her chest and her back to the wall. He could see her white underwear shining between her thighs because her skirt was so short. The tiny little patch of white cotton glowed in the dark. He felt a little strange looking down on her like that. He wished she would stand up.

She peered at him through the blonde hair hanging in her face.

"Hey, Pop," she said.

Jeffrey was immobile. He forgot his lines. He finally managed to squeeze out a barely audible "Hi." He was thankful that she was already smoking.

"Do you have a light?" he asked.

The girl crawled forward and pushed herself to her feet. When she stood up, she was taller than Jeffrey. It was the shoes.

She passed her cigarette to Jeffrey. Jeffrey had never done this before. He carefully held her burning end to his virgin cigarette and sucked in. Slowly, a little ring of black started to form and it began to smoke on its own. He didn't want to give the cigarette back to her, the fiery stub with her lipstick print, but she dipped her fingers in and lifted it away from him. She took a puff on it for good measure, to reinforce the fact that it was hers.

Jeffrey didn't know what to do next so he just said, "Thanks." Lucky for him, the girl was bored.

"You staying here?" she asked.

"Yeah."

"You from outta town?"

"Yeah."

She gave him a half smile.

"You don't look like an actor."

"No. I'm a writer."

"You write for the movies?"

"No, I'm working on a book. I'm also a . . . I write songs."

"Oh yeah. You look like you could be a rock star."

Jeffrey's entire face began to beam. No one had ever said anything like that to him before. This girl was the one person in the entire universe who got him.

"Thanks."

"Yeah, you look like you could be one of the Beatles."

"Really?"

"Yeah, I'm not sure which one though."

She sat back down on the ground and stretched her skinny legs out in front of her. The soles of her sandals almost reached Jeffrey's toes. She tilted her head to the side and studied him for a moment.

"I wouldn't say you look exactly like John Lennon, but you look like you could be a John Lennon type. Do you know what I mean?"

Jeffrey was melting in the dark under the motel's neon *Vacancy* light.

"Thanks. He's my idol."

"Oh really?"

"Yeah. I mean, he's my songwriting idol. Or, *was*."

"Yeah, I get it."

Headlights passed over them as a car entered the parking lot. The girl got up and crushed her cigarette under the wood supporting her bare toes. Jeffrey was worried she might get away.

"Hey . . . do you . . . want to . . . go get a cup of coffee sometime?"

"That's my friend who's giving me a ride," she said walking out into the black.

"My name's Jeff."

"Have a good night, Jeff."

"I'm staying upstairs."

"I know. See ya."

She slipped into the car; her blonde hair was the only thing visible behind the glass.

Jeffrey couldn't sleep that night. He stayed up waiting to hear if the car returned. He wasn't sure if it did or it didn't because he couldn't be 100 percent sure he hadn't fallen asleep for a few seconds here and there. He didn't take a shower the next day and he didn't flush the toilet. He didn't do anything that would block out sounds from the parking lot. He told the maid who came by that he wasn't feeling well and asked her not to clean his room. He spent the entire day listening.

That evening, as he continued to listen, he thought if for some strange reason he had missed her coming back, that she would surely scrape her sandals across the balcony the same way she had done the previous night. By this time, Jeffrey had moved a chair next to the window. He didn't read. He sat there all evening catatonically listening. As the clock crept toward midnight, he wondered if it was him that was keeping her locked up. Maybe she was waiting to hear him before she would come out. He should've figured that out earlier.

He left his room and nervously walked down the stairs. The girl was nowhere to be seen. Jeffrey already had his excuse worked out. He headed over to the motel office where there was an automatic coffee machine. When he stepped inside, the two old ladies were watching Johnny Carson and practicing their needlecrafts. Jeffrey deposited his coins into the coffee machine and watched the paper cup forced down by a strong spray of brown water. He pulled the cup out from the compartment and quickly drank it. He put in a coin for another round and waited again for the spray to finish. With his second cup, he walked over to the ladies. He politely waited for a commercial break before getting their attention.

"Oh hello!" one of them said. She had sparkles on her face. They were constructing a Fourth of July display of glittery fireworks and knitted flags. A couple of modern-day Betsy Rosses. Was it July already, Jeffrey wondered? Or was the craftwork for Memorial Day at the end of the merry, merry month of May?

"I was wondering," Jeffrey said putting his elbow on the counter the way men do in the movies when they are trying to project casualness, "have either of you seen that young blonde girl around today?"

"What girl?"

"Um, kinda thin, with long blonde hair and shoes that make her seem tall."

"Oh no, I don't know any girls like that."

"I think she's staying here."

"Oh no, I don't think we have any single girls staying here."

"Except for us!" the other one chimed in.

"Are you sure? I've talked to her here a couple of times. It seemed like she was staying here."

"She was probably visiting someone. A lot of people stay here when they are visiting someone in town. Maybe she was visiting someone who was visiting."

Jeffrey nodded and started to back out of the office. He decided these two women were crazy.

"Hey, are you an actor?" the sparkled one called after him.

Jeffrey turned around, but didn't say yes or no.

"They're going to be shooting part of a TV show here next week. Could be an opportunity!"

Jeffrey was frightened of the old biddies. The blonde girl had disappeared and they hadn't noticed. The same thing could happen to him. He could vanish and no one would notice. Completely vanish from the Earth, as though he were never here, as if he never mattered.

For some reason, Jeffrey thought about his father. His father was big on deadlines, he always had to buy or sell something by a certain date.

Jeffrey thought maybe that's what he needed. He needed a deadline. Either something was going to happen by a certain date or that was it. He'd have to kill himself. At least he could have some power that way, otherwise it would be a lifetime of not mattering and then the world would decide when his time was up. This way, even if Jeffrey didn't matter, he could at least have some say in his own existence.

Jeffrey didn't leave his room for a week. He called the pizza parlor across the street and convinced the guy that he had hurt his leg. He got the guy to bring a pizza over, even though they usually didn't do deliveries. He did this for five days, ordering one large pizza a day, until the guy said, "Maybe you need a doctor instead of pizza." The day after that, one of ladies knocked on his door and asked how much longer he would be staying. If he didn't pay for last week, and in advance for each additional night, they were going to have to ask him to move on. Jeffrey tried to explain that he was sick. The woman nodded her head. She probably didn't believe him. She'd probably heard it all before.

The blonde girl never came back.

Finally, the ladies came to his door with the big guy who did repairs around the joint. They were sorry, but Jeffrey would have to leave. They hoped he would pack up his things right away so they wouldn't have to get the police involved. Jeffrey gathered his scattered clothes into his suitcase. He started to stack up the empty pizza boxes, but they said not to worry about that. He was just trying to be nice.

Jeffrey stood on the street outside the motel thinking that maybe the girl would show up at the last minute. A bus pulled over and opened its doors. Jeffrey shook his head at the driver. He would give her until the next bus came along and then that would be it. When the second bus came, a car pulled into the motel driveway. Jeffrey turned away from the bus so it wouldn't stop. The car didn't stop either. It was just using the parking lot to make a U-turn.

When the third bus came, Jeffrey climbed aboard and rode out to the airport. He called his parents collect from a pay phone and made up a story about being robbed on the street at gunpoint. They said they would call in a ticket and it would be waiting for him at the counter. In the men's room, Jeffrey threw away all of his possessions except for his guitar and a few cassettes. He pushed the tape recorder into the metal trashcan, remembering that it too was supposed to have been stolen a few weeks ago. He left his empty suitcase in a toilet stall. He threw out his wallet and kept only the last of his money, his non-driver's license, and his Dallas library card.

He stared at himself in the men's room mirror. He looked pale and pasty, as though he had been living alone in a cave for many years.

THE ROAD THROUGH THE FOREST

* * *

Tammy hardly saw any of the girls from school over the summer. Gretchen had gone to a gifted and talented day camp and wasn't around much. Plus she had swim practice, she had gone to a beach house, and she had visited her grandparents. Gretchen seemed busier over the summer than she was during the school year. Tammy and Steffi would sometimes drag Hugh to the indoor pool at the public high school, but their mother and Nick said whoever was in charge of Hugh that day would have to stay with him in the baby pool. Tammy and Steffi would tell Hugh that he had to put on his swimsuit before they left because they couldn't go with him into the boys' changing room. In the summer they were left alone all day.

Tammy didn't belong to any swim team or summer camp. She and Steffi were supposed to visit their dad at some point, but their mother said, "It hasn't been decided yet."

Gretchen finally called Tammy during the last week of summer vacation. She said she was having an end-of-summer swim party at the Promenade Swim Club, and did Tammy want to come? The Promenade was a private club. Gretchen was on the swim team there. Steffi went there a lot with Kirin. Kirin was also on the swim team. Tammy's family didn't belong to the Promenade.

Tammy wanted a new bathing suit. The strap on her old one had come off and was held together with a safety pin. Her mother didn't want to buy Tammy a new suit because she said that summer was over now and she didn't really need one. She said that if she bought Tammy a new suit now, she would just outgrow it by next summer. She didn't want to spend money on two suits. "It's not practical," she said. "It's a waste of money." Tammy asked again and her mother said no. She said Tammy should just wear her old suit and they would get a new one next June. She said that if Tammy wanted a new suit so badly she could use her allowance to buy one.

Tammy decided that's what she would do. She knew her mother didn't think it was a good idea. That's why her mother said it—so Tammy would tell her that she didn't want to use her own money, and then her mother would say, well then, you'll have to wait until next summer.

Tammy wasn't sure how much bathing suits cost, but she took twelve dollars out of her peanut brittle can. She was pretty sure it wouldn't be that much. She decided to go shopping the next morning because she wasn't sure if her mother could take her that night. And Nick didn't like things coming up at the last minute. It pushed his buttons.

It was Tammy's day to watch Hugh so she dragged him along on the long walk to the Maza Gallerie mall. Hugh demanded they take rests and sometimes he would sit down on the sidewalk even though Tammy told him he wasn't allowed to. When they got to the mall someone was handing out free balloons. Tammy got one for Hugh and tied it to his wrist.

This was the same mall where Tammy's mother had taken her to return a pair of sneakers that fell apart two days after they bought them. It was actually Tammy's fault. She had been riding her bike and put her shoe down to stop and skidded forward a little bit on her toe. The rubber sole peeled right off. Tammy walked home kicking her foot forward to slap the rubber out.

Tammy didn't tell her mother about the bike. She said it just happened. Tammy didn't know why her mother had to drag her back to that store too. She could've just gotten the same pair of shoes in the same size. But her mother said no, Tammy had to come, because each pair of shoes was different and you should try them on. And, her mother said, Tammy couldn't get the same kind of shoes because that brand wasn't any good if they were going to fall apart so easily. They should last until you grew out of them. Her mother took the shoes up to the register and explained the whole story. The salesmen wore suits. They examined the shoes like detectives. They said this shouldn't have happened. This was a good brand. Was her daughter doing something different? Playing rough? Tammy looked at the floor. The salesmen bought the story. Tammy's mother insisted they measure her foot again. Tammy put her foot on the metal plate and stood up. She was barefoot because the only other pair of shoes she had were sandals. The salesman brought out a box of footie stockings for her to wear while trying on the shoes. Her mother said to make sure they were a little loose otherwise there would be no room for socks.

Tammy and Hugh went into a department store to the Young Miss section and Tammy looked through racks of one-piece suits. She saw the bathing suit that Gretchen had worn at the end-of-the-year pool party when school got out. It was dark blue with tiny pink stripes. It had a skinny pink belt that went around the waist, but you could take it off if you wanted. Tammy loved that bathing suit. It was cool. In the next rack, she saw another version of the suit. It was white with skinny blue stripes and a light blue belt. Tammy took it into the dressing room and tried it on. She thought it looked good. It was on sale for seven dollars plus tax.

Tammy was a little worried that Gretchen would be mad. But she thought, why? It wasn't the exact same suit as hers. It was a different color. And Tammy decided she wouldn't wear the belt with it. When she got home, she took the belt off and used her school scissors to cut off the little belt loops on the side.

Gretchen's pool party was on Labor Day, so neither Tammy nor Steffi had to watch Hugh because their mother and Nick were home all day. When Tammy got to Gretchen's house, the other girls were waiting on the front steps for Gretchen's mom to drive them to the Promenade. "Josie's driving us," Gretchen said. Gretchen had started calling her mother "Josie" because she thought it sounded more grown up. The girls all piled into her station wagon. Tammy climbed into the wayback. She thought they would all cram in there together, but Gretchen and Heather slid into the backseat and Monique sat up front because she was the tallest and she said the carpeting in the wayback itched her legs. Tammy felt like an idiot. She was going to get out and squeeze into the backseat, but Gretchen yelled out, "Josie, let's go!" and her mom shut the back hatch.

When Gretchen's mom got in the car, she put her keys in the steering wheel, but the car wouldn't start. Gretchen didn't understand at first and kept saying, "Josie, let's go," in a bitchy tone. Her mom said, "I'm trying, but it's not turning over." Gretchen folded her arms across her chest and slumped back in her seat. Her mom kept turning the key but nothing happened. Then she would count to five in between tries. But nothing happened still.

"Aren't you supposed to look under the hood?" That was Heather.

"Right," said Gretchen's mom. She got out of the car and walked around to the hood. She lifted it up and stood there with her hands on her hips.

"What's the problem?" Gretchen asked. Gretchen was always impatient. She was always mean to her mom like that. It was the same way after one of Gretchen's slumber parties when her mom told all the girls to eat breakfast outside on the picnic table in the backyard. Gretchen didn't want to. She said she hated eating outside because bugs would get in her food. And sure enough, a leaf fell onto Gretchen's plate and she made a big deal about it. Tammy had seen a tiny green caterpillar creep along the rim of her Styrofoam plate, but she just flicked it away.

"Well, what is it, Josie?" Gretchen asked.

"I think it's the battery."

Her mom closed the hood. She told them she needed to get a jump from someone and that she was going to ask a neighbor.

Tammy and the girls watched Gretchen's mom walk across the front lawn and across the front lawn next door. Gretchen's mom had long skinny legs and long tan-colored hair. She wore tan-colored shorts. She looked like she was all one color. The girls watched her disappear between the shrubs that surrounded the next-door neighbor's front door. Gretchen moaned that this was taking forever.

Gretchen's mom called over from across the lawns. She was standing in the grass next door and waving to them. Everyone got out of the car. No one opened up the back to let Tammy out so she had to climb over the backseat. Gretchen's mom was standing in front of Kirin's house. The front door was open and Kirin's mom was standing inside. She was wearing big sunglasses and a turtleneck shirt even though it was practically ninety degrees. Tammy had been reading a book where the main character's older sister wore a turtleneck in the middle of summer to cover up hickeys. Gretchen's mom said that they were going to borrow Kirin's mom's car.

"What happened to getting a jump?" Gretchen asked.

"Oh, it's kind of complicated and neither of us are sure how to do it."

"So Valerie's just letting you borrow her car?"

"That's right. Why don't you thank Valerie for saving your swim party? Otherwise we'd be all washed up!"

Gretchen's mom laughed at her own joke. No one else thought it was that funny.

Kirin and Steffi popped out from the front door. They were carrying huge beach towels slung over their shoulders. Steffi was wearing one of Kirin's bathing suits and a pair of shorts. They trotted over to Kirin's car and waited to be let in. They were coming along.

Gretchen's mom explained that Valerie wasn't feeling well, so she didn't mind them borrowing the car. And it was a good idea to bring Kirin and Steffi along so she could get some rest. Tammy was mad. This was so typical of Steffi. She was always trying to come along and butt in on Tammy's friends.

Gretchen's mom unlocked the car and Kirin and Steffi piled in to the wayback.

"One more person needs to get in the wayback for us all to fit," Josie announced.

"Same seats," Gretchen said. "Tammy, you were in the wayback before."

At the Promenade, Tammy and her friends talked in the changing room about the fact that their new teacher, Mrs. Perkins, was supposed to be tough, much tougher than Mrs. William, who really wasn't that tough. Tammy took off her shorts and stuffed them in her bag. She tried not to look at anyone although she wanted to see what their bodies looked like. Heather already wore a bra. Monique didn't, but she was starting to get breasts. They puffed out of her chest like cookies baking in the oven. Tammy tried to keep her back to everyone while she pulled on her suit, but Gretchen was watching her.

"One tit's bigger than the other."

She meant nipples. One of Tammy's nipples was bigger than the other. One was puffed out and the other was flat. They weren't always like that, just sometimes. Tammy knew they were supposed to match.

"I guess they'll even out," Gretchen said. "I've heard of that happening when things develop unevenly."

Tammy didn't know what she was supposed to say. She pretended to be looking for something in her bag so Gretchen would forget about it.

When Tammy emerged from the bathroom wearing her new bathing suit, Gretchen squinted at her. She didn't say anything and she ignored Tammy until the two of them were left alone on the lounge chairs.

"How come you got that suit?"

"It's not the same as yours."

"Yes it is."

"No it's not. It's a different color."

"It's so dumb of you. I can't believe you did it on purpose."

"I didn't do it on purpose."

"You already saw my suit. So you already knew what it looked like when you bought it. And you bought the same one."

"It's a different color."

"It doesn't matter."

"And I don't wear the belt. I cut off the belt loops because I didn't like it. It made it look like an exercise suit."

Gretchen scowled and got up from chair, which left lines on the backs of her thighs, and jumped into the pool.

Tammy felt weird without anyone to talk to on the chairs, so she went to the pool too. As she lowered herself in down the ladder, she heard Gretchen and Monique squeal in high-pitched voices:

"It looks like an exercise suit!"

Tammy jumped down the rest of the way. She dipped her head backward into the water, holding her nose, to slick her hair out of her face. When she un-squinted her eyes, Gretchen and Monique had swum to the deep end.

Steffi and Kirin didn't bother Tammy at the pool. She hardly saw them. When they were getting ready to leave, Steffi and Kirin were already standing by the car slurping ice cream bars on sticks.

"What's wrong with your mom?" Tammy asked Kirin.

"She had an accident," Kirin said between slurps.

"What kind of accident?"

"Just an accident. Accidents happen, nobody plans them, that's why they're called accidents." Kirin said it very fast, like she had it memorized.

It was probably something her mother told her to tell people, the same way Tammy's mother told her if anyone called after school to say, "My mother can't come to the phone right now," instead of saying no one's at home.

When they got back to Gretchen's block, Kirin and Steffi ran out of the car and disappeared into Kirin's house. The other girls trampled across Gretchen's lawn and waited for her mother to unlock the front door.

"Gretchen, why don't you run over to Valerie's and give these back to her," Josie said holding out the car keys.

"No way," Gretchen said.

"I think it would be a nice gesture since she loaned us the car."

"She loaned *you* the car. I can't drive."

"Gretchen—"

"I'm not going over there. She's too weird."

"Sometimes when people aren't feeling well, they act weird," Gretchen's mom said. Tammy could tell she was trying not to cause a scene. "It doesn't mean they're weird."

Gretchen didn't say anything to her mother right then, but she looked like she was really mad.

Josie finally unlocked the door.

"I'm taking a shower," Gretchen said as she headed up the stairs. "Someone else can use the shower in my mom's room." Heather called dibs on the other shower. Monique said she would run home across the street, take a shower, and come back.

"That's a nice suit, Tammy."

Tammy was suddenly alone with Gretchen's mom wearing only a bathing suit. She wasn't sure if that was normal or not. She wasn't sure if Gretchen's mom had noticed that Tammy had the same suit as Gretchen.

"It looks pretty on you," she said.

Tammy didn't know what to say. She thought Gretchen's mom was just being nice because Tammy was stuck with no one to talk to.

"I'll take the keys back to Valerie's if you want," Tammy said.

"Oh thanks," Gretchen's mom said and slid them across the kitchen counter to Tammy.

Tammy cut across the grass of the front lawns and headed to Valerie's front door. She rang the doorbell and Kirin and Steffi opened up.

"Can I help you?" Kirin asked like she and Steffi were playing a game and pretending they didn't know who Tammy was. It was the kind of thing younger kids did and thought was really funny.

"I'm supposed to give these car keys to your mom," Tammy said.

"Kirin, Kirin," her mom called from the living room. She walked slowly over to the door. "You're not supposed to open the door to strangers."

"It's not a stranger, it's Steffi's sister," Kirin said.

"I don't want you opening the door by yourself."

"Well, that's silly," Kirin said and walked away from the door.

"I was just giving back the car keys," Tammy said. Kirin's mom nodded and shut the door.

Tammy still had the car keys. Neither Kirin nor Valerie had taken them back. She rang the doorbell again, but only the dog came to peek through the window by the front door. Maybe they were playing a game of not answering the door, Tammy thought, probably because they know it's me and now they've decided to be annoying about it. Tammy could keep on ringing the doorbell, but Valerie would probably get mad about it. She didn't want to take the keys back to Gretchen's because then Josie would be mad. There was nothing Tammy could do without someone getting mad at her.

She decided to leave the keys on Valerie's front steps. They weren't house keys, so it wasn't like someone could find the keys and break in to her house and steal things. And no one would be able to see the keys from the sidewalk so no one would steal her car. But as soon as Valerie stepped outside her house, she would see them. She couldn't miss them. And who's to say that Tammy didn't give them back and Valerie didn't accidentally drop them there?

Tammy put the keys on the top step and walked back to Gretchen's house. Now it was only Gretchen who could be mad at her. If Tammy changed out of her bathing suit before Gretchen got out of the shower, then hopefully Gretchen would forget about it.

ON THE FIRST day of sixth grade, Tammy sat on the front steps of her house with Steffi and Hugh and waited for Gretchen and Kirin to hook up with them. Steffi got impatient sitting on the steps, walked out to the sidewalk, and looked down Bemis Street to see if they were coming. Hugh sat next to Tammy and squeezed his Incredible Hulk lunchbox between his knees making the tin sides pop in and out. Hugh was starting kindergarten so Tammy and Steffi would only have to walk him to school and not the extra distance to the preschool. It would make things easier.

Steffi called out, "They're here! Let's go!" Steffi was very excited about the first day of school and had spent the night before organizing her pencil case and school bag.

Steffi and Kirin walked a few steps ahead of Tammy and Gretchen. They were both wearing skirts and knee socks, but Kirin wore clogs and Steffi wore sneakers, which looked dumb with a skirt. Tammy and Gretchen wore jeans. Hugh wore jeans too, but nobody cared what a kindergartener wore to school.

Gretchen slowed down her walking pace so that she and Tammy were a little farther behind Kirin and Steffi and out of earshot. She told Tammy that Monique had gotten her period over the summer. Gretchen and Tammy still hadn't gotten theirs. "It's probably because we're skinny," Gretchen said. The two of them thought maybe that was it, since Monique and Heather had both gotten theirs and they were both a little fat. Tammy could tell the rules for the sixth grade were going to be different. In the fifth grade it wasn't cool for a girl to have her period. Now it seemed like it was okay. Gretchen didn't mention wearing a bra to school and Tammy couldn't tell if she was wearing one or not. Tammy figured Gretchen would tell her when she should start wearing one.

Sixth grade with Mrs. Perkins was basically the same as fifth grade with Mrs. William, except that Olga the Russian girl didn't come back. Mrs. Perkins was much tougher; she would pick up a chair and drop it on the floor if she thought the class wasn't paying attention. The sixth-grade class was invited to visit the Soviet embassy school as part of a special social studies program. The Soviet kids had to wear plain blue uniforms and Red Pioneer scarves. Whenever someone walked into the classroom, all the Soviet kids stood up. Gretchen said that was because they were Communists. All they had for lunch was a slice of bread with a single slice of lunchmeat on it and a small can of apple juice, and they ate standing up. As Tammy and Gretchen walked out of the lunchroom, they saw the cafeteria workers pouring leftover apple juice from the cans into large jugs. Gretchen thought this was gross—what were they going to do, drink it? Monique told the Soviet girls that they had no freedom. The Soviet girls told the Americans it was stupid that they had to pay for medical care and a college education. They said in Russia a loaf of bread only costs ten cents and here it's a dollar. The second time they visited the Soviet school, lunch was a large piece of cake and a little individual container of ice cream.

THE MUSIC TEACHER announced that the school was going to do a play and there were going to be auditions. The school never had a music teacher before the sixth grade and they never had a play before either. The music teacher said the school play was going to be *The Wizard of Oz*. Everyone was going to be involved. If they didn't have a regular part, they would be in the chorus. If they didn't want to do that, they would be behind the scenes. Tammy didn't understand why the music teacher was having auditions if she already had it all figured out.

Mrs. Perkins was very excited about the play idea and made the sixth graders practice their auditions in class. There were mimeographed sheets with speeches for each character. Everyone wanted to be Dorothy or the Scarecrow. When Mrs. Perkins asked Tammy which character she wanted to audition for, Tammy said, "The Witch." Tammy thought that would be a cool choice and that way she wouldn't have to sing any songs.

The auditions were held upstairs in the music room during a special class with the fifth and sixth grades together. When you auditioned, you went to the front of the room and said your memorized speech. So far, no one else was doing the Witch speech.

The music teacher called Tammy's name.

Tammy stood in front of the class. The music teacher didn't say anything, so Tammy decided to start. She shivered as if someone had dumped a bucket of water on her head.

"See what you have done! In a minute I shall melt away."

Tammy waited a little bit for the space where Dorothy would say something back, and then she went on as though Dorothy had said her line.

"Didn't you know water would be the end of me?"

Again, Tammy waited in silence and said the Dorothy line to herself inside her head. Then she melted by slowly crouching down to the floor.

"Well, in a few minutes I shall be all melted, and you will have the castle to yourself. I have been wicked in my day, but I never thought a little girl like you would ever be able to melt me and end my wicked deeds. Look out—here I go!"

Tammy squatted down and curled up in a ball on the floor with her cheek on the speckled linoleum. She couldn't see anything in the classroom because her hair fell in front of her face like a curtain. She waited there for the music teacher to say something.

"Is she dead yet?" Kenny called out from the back of the room.

"Okay. Good job," the music teacher said.

Tammy got up off the floor and took her seat. She didn't know if the music teacher liked her audition or not. The music teacher said "good job" to everyone.

"Did you lick the floor when you melted?" Kenny was sitting right behind her. "Did you? Did you? I don't want to suck face with someone who eats off the floor. Gross!"

"She's a shrinky dink!" someone else said.

People always acted this way in music class because no one was afraid of the music teacher. They never did this with Mrs. Perkins. If they acted up in class, Mrs. Perkins would drop a stack of textbooks on the floor that would make everyone gasp and look up. The music teacher was dumb and nobody liked her.

The next week in music class, the music teacher had written who had what parts on the blackboard.

Gretchen was Dorothy.

Colin was the Scarecrow.

Monique was the Tin Man.

Josh was the Lion.

Kenny was the King of the Winged Monkeys.

And Tammy was the Witch.

When Tammy got home from school, Steffi told her that the whole fourth-grade class was going to be the chorus. They were going to sing all the songs and wear green shirts that said *OZ*. Tammy told her she didn't care. Tammy said the songs were stupid and the OZ shirts looked like baby bibs and the whole reason she wanted to be the Witch was because the Witch didn't sing any songs. Steffi tried to say that Tammy felt that way because she wasn't a good singer, which wasn't true. Steffi was just saying that to be mean in her Miss Know It All way.

At dinner, Tammy's mother said she had an announcement. Tammy and Steffi already knew she was going out of town on Friday and that they would be left with Nick. Now she said that Nick had to go out of town too. It had something to do with his job. Tammy and Steffi looked at each other. They didn't know exactly what this meant. They baby-sat themselves whenever their mother and Nick went out somewhere at night. They were used to that. But they had never been left alone overnight before.

Steffi piped up and said that she was going to spend the night at Kirin's. Kirin had invited her to sleep over, so they didn't have to worry about her. That was typical Steffi. She was going to stick Tammy with baby-sitting Hugh. Steffi didn't care about anyone else and she didn't like getting stuck having to do anything extra. That's why she got sick and had asthma all the time, so she didn't have to do anything.

Tammy's mother said she was going to ask a friend of hers at work if she could stay over with the kids. Tammy knew this was not going to be good. Her mother and Nick were terrible at picking baby-sitters. They were always weird, like Mrs. Brown who ate all their ice cream. Or once they had a boy baby-sitter who washed their faces before bed by rubbing a bar of soap all over without any water. Or the skinny woman who made them kneel down and say prayers even though they didn't say prayers in their house. When Tammy asked her why they had to do that, she said so God won't send you to Hell when you die.

Steffi was always weaseling out of things. She always had something up her sleeve, and if for some reason she didn't, she could always get sick. Now Steffi was leaving Tammy in the lurch overnight and Tammy would have to think of something so she wouldn't get stuck with their stupid brother.

Nothing was decided at that meal. Tammy's mother and Nick gave them one of those lines like "When you need to know, you'll know." That meant they didn't know. It was the same as when Tammy asked, "What's for dinner?" and they answered back, "Food." That meant they didn't know.

The next day Tammy's mother and Nick told them they had spoken to Kirin's mother and that all three of them would spend the night at

Kirin's house. Tammy couldn't believe this. She couldn't believe that she was being forced to spend the night at a friend of her sister's. A fourth grader. It was embarrassing. Hugh didn't say anything. He didn't care and he probably didn't get it. This was totally unfair.

"What happened to your friend from work?" Tammy asked.

"She had weekend plans," her mother said.

"Like what?"

"She had plans!" Nick yelled in. "It's all been settled!"

Tammy shut up because if she didn't, he would start in with no TV, no dessert, and whatever else he could think of.

This sucked.

Tammy was so embarrassed she didn't mention it to anyone at school on Friday. Her biggest worry was that Gretchen and Monique both lived on the same block as Kirin and they might see her over there. Tammy thought maybe she could sneak by and make a point of not going outside.

Nick had left for his trip early in the day. When Tammy's mother came home from work she told the kids to pack their overnight gear and she would drive them to Kirin's. Tammy didn't know why they had to go over there so soon. Couldn't they wait until it was time to go to bed and then go over? But her mother said no, it doesn't work that way.

When her mother parked the car in front of Kirin's house, Tammy immediately got out and walked quickly to the front door so that she was hidden between the two big bushes on either side of the porch. Tammy's mother took a long time walking over. She walked so slowly, swinging her purse on her wrist, and then acted as if she didn't know where the doorbell was.

Kirin answered the door and let them in. Valerie walked over from the kitchen with a big goofy smile on her face. She looked like a stretched-out version of Kirin. She probably didn't want them there and was just putting on a show to make them feel better.

When Tammy's mother left, Valerie asked, "Who wants pizza for dinner?"

Kirin and Steffi started jumping up and down, holding hands, and acting younger than they were. They were chanting, "Pizza! Pizza! Pizza!" like crazy.

Everyone went into the kitchen and Valerie gave the kids orange sodas. Then she asked what kind of pizza they wanted.

"Extra cheese!" Kirin said.

"Yes, extra cheese!" Steffi piped in.

"Nothing else?" Valerie asked.

"Nope!" they said together.

When Tammy's family ordered pizza at home they always got it with everything. Even with anchovies, because Nick liked them. Tammy and Steffi thought they were too salty, but Nick said they could pick them off. That's what they always got. They never got plain cheese pizza. Tammy had never even thought about what she would want on her ideal pizza. Steffi was breaking the rules, but there was no way she would get caught, and she wasn't really breaking the rules since this was someone else's house. Tammy was a little mad at Steffi for figuring that out.

Kirin's mom ate with them. She was one of those mothers who tried to pretend she was a kid too. Tammy thought those mothers were kind of fake. After all, they weren't kids. It was like they were trying too hard to be cool and they really weren't.

The cool thing about Kirin's house was that there really were no rules. Kirin fed Pudding the dog her pizza crusts. They could have a second soda if they wanted. They could have a second ice cream bar if they wanted. They could watch whatever they wanted on TV—*cable* TV—and they weren't banished to a kids' TV room. Those were all cool things. The weird thing was it was just weird. Tammy felt like she couldn't relax.

Kirin's mom thought it would be fun for all of the kids to sleep together in the guest room. Kirin dug out her sleeping bag and laid it on the floor next to Steffi's. Then the four of them rearranged themselves in a circle with their heads in the center, as if there were a campfire on the floor. They watched TV in the dark and the giant HBO letters spun around against a starry background.

There was some movie on about Vietnam called *The Deer Hunter*. Ten minutes into it Kirin stood up and switched off the TV.

"This is boring."

She and Steffi walked out of the room. Tammy would've preferred to watch *Grease* on the laser disc player, but she didn't know how it worked. She followed Steffi and Kirin across the hall into Kirin's bedroom.

"Let's play a game," Kirin said as she bounced onto her bed. "I know!"

She dipped her head over the side and rummaged around under her bed. Then she wiggled a little farther and did a somersault onto the floor.

"Tada!"

She opened up her closet door and pulled out a bunch of board games—Sorry!, Monopoly, and The Game of Life—and brought them over to her bed. Then she went back and squatted on the closet floor and pulled out a see-through Tupperware container with a lid on it. Inside was a pale liquid that looked like pee. Kirin opened it and drank some. She passed it to Steffi who drank some too.

"What is it?" Tammy asked as Steffi handed it to her.

"Just drink it, silly."

Tammy drank some. It tasted bad. Like rotten apple juice.

"What is it?"

"It's wine," said Steffi.

"You're not supposed to drink that."

Kirin and Steffi each took another gulp. "It makes silly things sillier. It makes you feel better," Kirin said. "It's kind of like medicine," Steffi said. They took one more drink each before Kirin snapped the lid back on and stowed the container back in the closet.

"Do you want to hear a spooky story?" Kirin asked.

"Yes!" Steffi said. She was enjoying this whole thing because it made her feel like she was in charge.

Tammy didn't like scary stories or scary movies, but she didn't want to seem like a chicken when she was the oldest one there. She ignored them and walked back to the TV guest room. Just because she had to spend the night there didn't mean she had to hang out with them.

"Well, for one thing, this house is haunted!" Kirin said. She and Steffi followed Tammy like annoying little gnats that won't leave you alone. They plopped down onto their sleeping bags. "Not haunted with ghosts," Kirin said, "but with angels."

Tammy didn't believe stuff like that. A ghost she might actually believe. After Tammy saw The Amityville Horror, she stopped going down into the basement of her house. She no longer liked to hang up her coat in the closet that led down to the basement. If she had to do it, she waited until someone else was home and then she did it really fast. But angels were like fairies and Kirin was obviously making this up.

"There's no such thing," Tammy said.

"Yes there is."

"No there's not."

"Yes there is. There are haunting angels. I know because my mom says so. She's seen them and sometimes they talk to her."

"Your mom's just saying that. It's not really true. It's like Santa Claus or the Tooth Fairy. They're not really real, adults just pretend they're real so they don't hurt your feelings."

"My mom sees them. They don't talk to me, they only talk to her."

"You probably still believe in the Easter Bunny too."

"No, I don't. That's made up by candy companies."

"Well, your stupid angel ghosts are made up too."

"Why are you being mean?" That was Steffi putting on her goody-two-shoes voice.

"Shut up," Tammy said.

"This is my house and you can't tell her to shut up," Kirin said.

Hugh wasn't paying attention. He was tracing the designs of his Superman sleeping bag with two fingers, making them walk like the legs of a little person around the giant red S.

"Then ask your mom. I won't believe you until she says so, and she better not be pretending little kids' stuff, because I can tell when grown-ups do that."

Kirin stood up on her skinny legs sticking out from her cow-jumping-over-the-moon nightgown. She padded her way out of the room and they heard her yell, "Mommy!" down the hall. Tammy could hear them talking in another room. Then Kirin came back and said, "She says it's true."

"Yeah, but I didn't hear her say it."

"She just went and asked her!" Steffi said.

"I couldn't hear what she said. How am I supposed to know?"

"I just asked her and she said they're real," Kirin said.

"Maybe that's something she just tells you. It doesn't mean they're really real."

"You're just being mean. You really are the Wicked Witch."

"Well you're just two dumb fourth graders in the chorus wearing stupid Oz bibs. You wear bibs because you're babies and you'll probably drool on yourselves when you sing."

There was a silence while Kirin and Steffi thought about what to say back. Pudding the dog wandered in the room and sat down by Kirin.

"My dog thinks you're dumb."

"Fuck you, you're both dumb."

Kirin and Steffi looked shocked that Tammy said that to them. Steffi knew that Tammy said "fuck" at home when they were alone, but it was another thing to say it at somebody else's house. It was like saying it at school. She wasn't supposed to do it.

Kirin stood up again on her twiggy legs and marched out of the room. Pudding scampered after her.

"Why do you have to ruin everything?" Steffi whispered to Tammy. "You always have to go and get in trouble for nothing. Just because you're mad about something you have to go and be mean to everybody."

Tammy ignored her. She was pissed that she was stuck here with the two of them and her brother. She was in the sixth grade. Next year she would be in junior high. She was too old to be forced into hanging around with younger kids.

Kirin returned with her mother and dog. Kirin had a big know-it-all smile on her face.

"Tammy wants to ask you something," Kirin said.

Tammy hated being put on the spot like that. It made her look stupid. This was probably all some big joke. She looked down at her sleeping bag and pulled at the strap that connected the green canvas outside to the plaid flannel inside. It used to be Nick's before he lived with them. Tammy hoped that by not looking at Kirin and her mother, they would eventually go away.

"Yes?" Valerie asked.

Tammy looked up at her. Valerie had a funny look on her face and her eyes were glassy and watery. Tammy knew that look. It meant she'd been crying and was trying to cover it up. She was wearing a long see-through nightgown and Tammy could see her boobs right through it. She hadn't put a bathrobe on over it. Maybe she thought Tammy had something serious to ask her.

"Nothing," Tammy said.

Kirin wasn't going to let her off so easily. Little kids were like that. If they thought they could win something over on a big kid, they milked it for all it was worth. Steffi did that all the time.

"She wants to know about the angel ghosts. She doesn't believe they're real," Kirin said, swinging her mom's arm back and forth in the doorway.

Her mom didn't say anything. She stood there thinking about something else and not paying attention.

"Maaa-uhhmm!" Kirin whined.

"What?"

"The angel ghosts!"

"What about them?"

"They're real, right?"

Her mom looked around the room and she looked very scared. Tammy couldn't tell if she was putting them on or not. Usually people's dads would do that, tell ghost stories to freak kids out and then laugh and say it was all a joke.

"You should go to sleep now," she said, but she didn't turn out the lights. "Do you want a story?"

"Okay," Kirin said in a cheery voice. Valerie walked in and sat on the couch. Kirin and Steffi laid on their stomachs with their chins propped up on their fists, kicking their legs backward into the air. Tammy was too old for bedtime stories. She would've preferred to read. She had brought the book *Island of the Blue Dolphins* in her overnight bag and she was near the end. It was about an Indian girl who was left alone on an island when her tribe moved away. She was sailing away on a boat with her tribe, but she dove into the water to save her brother who was accidentally left behind. Then her brother died and she made friends with a wild dog. Tammy was near the end so she knew the Indian girl would get rescued soon.

"Tell the angel ghost story," Kirin said.

"No," Tammy said.

"Yes, tell it!" Steffi said.

"You'll scare him," Tammy said quietly and motioned to Hugh.

"He's already asleep!"

"No he's not," Tammy said. "Are you asleep?" She said it loudly, on purpose, to wake him up.

"Wha—" he said in a high-pitched sleepy voice. He rolled away from them and curled up into a ball.

"Okay, I'll tell you the story," Valerie said. She took one of the couch pillows and hugged it to her chest. "Once upon a time, there was a very rich man and a very poor, but very pretty woman. The woman was happy when the man asked her to marry him because her mother always said it's just as easy to fall in love with a rich man as it is a poor man. So they got married and went looking for their dream house. They looked and they looked, but they couldn't find a house they really liked. Finally, they went to see a real estate agent. She was an old woman who used to be a teacher, but she got fired for being so mean to the kids. She took a set of keys off the rack and said, 'I'll take you to your dream house.'

"She took them to a big house on the edge of town near the woods that had a Century 21 For Sale sign in the front yard. There were big gardens all around the house and that made the pretty wife very happy. She liked flowers and she liked to go for long walks in the woods. The rich husband liked it because it had good parking and a two-car garage. The house had six bedrooms and six bathrooms and a rec room with a ping-pong table. The strange thing was, the people who had lived there before had left all of their furniture.

"'Oh that,' the real estate agent said. 'The former owners had to leave in a hurry. The husband got an offer out of town and they were getting all new furniture anyway so they decided to leave it. It comes with the house. It's a package deal.'

"All of a sudden, a little girl popped out. The husband and wife asked the real estate agent who she was. 'Oh her,' the real estate agent said. 'She is the daughter of the former owners. They didn't allow children in their new apartment building and they were going to have another baby anyway, so they decided to leave her. She comes with the house. It's a package deal.'

"There were a lot creaking noises as the couple walked around. The real estate agent said, 'Oh that, that's just the wind. That's what you get from living near the woods. It's part of the package deal.'

"Even with all the strange things, the couple decided to buy the house because they liked it so much. They stuck a "sold" sticker on the Century 21 sign in the front lawn. They moved in and put down new carpeting. They kept some of the old furniture and sold the rest in a yard sale. They kept the little girl and named her Katie. And everything was normal for a little while.

"But what they didn't know was that the house was haunted and that everyone who had ever lived in the house before them had died a mysterious death. The real estate agent knew this and she purposefully showed the house to people she didn't like just to be mean.

"Then one day while the husband was at work and little Katie was taking a nap, the pretty wife decided to go for a walk in the woods. She walked out of the backyard and followed the path into the woods. She walked deeper and deeper into the woods until the air was cold and she couldn't see the house anymore. Then it got very, very quiet. So quiet that she could hear her own heart beating in her chest. She got a shiver up her spine and she felt like someone, or some*thing*, was watching her. She got scared and started wheezing, like she was having an asthma attack. She let out a scream, but nobody heard her because she was so far away and little Katie was asleep.

"Later, the husband came home from work and his wife wasn't around. He went up to little Katie's room and she was still lying in her bed asleep. He tried to wake her, but she wouldn't wake up. She wasn't dead, but she was in a coma and couldn't wake up. The husband called the police. The police officers came, but they couldn't start a search until morning because it was too dark.

"Finally, the next morning, they found the wife in the woods. She had been killed, but they didn't know how. Her hair had turned totally white, and her eyes were totally white, and her skin was extra white. She had seen something that had frightened her to death. When the police were carrying her out of the woods on a stretcher, they noticed some blood coming out of her chest. They unzipped her jacket and saw there was a big bloody hole where her heart should be. Then they took her hand out of her pocket and saw that she was holding her own heart in her hand. She had ripped out her own heart."

Valerie took a long pause, indicating that this was the end of the story.

"That wasn't the angel ghost story," Kirin said quietly. Tammy turned and looked at Kirin. She was curled up tightly on her sleeping bag facing away from everybody. "I don't like that story," she said.

Steffi looked across the circle at Tammy. She had her "I'm sad" look on. She looked at Tammy to see what she thought.

"What happened to the little girl?" Tammy asked Valerie.

"They moved out and she had to go into a special hospital until she woke up."

"What about the real estate agent?"

"She . . . sold the house to the next people she didn't like."

"So people keep dying there over and over again and no one figures it out?"

"I suppose so," Valerie said. "Time for bed now." She stood up and turned off the light. "Good night," she said.

No one else said anything. There was nothing left to do but go to bed.

Tammy crawled to the end of her sleeping bag and wiggled her way in. When she rolled over onto her side she looked out into the hallway and saw Kirin's mom still standing there. She hadn't gone back to her room. She was standing there in the dark. She looked scary because the light from the street outside shone through Kirin's bedroom window and lit her up from behind. Her white see-through nightgown glowed like a lantern. If there really were angel ghosts, this is how they must look.

There was an awkward feeling in Tammy's stomach as if she had accidentally seen someone naked and it was hard to look away. The only thing she could think to do was to ask Kirin to close the door.

"Why?"

"You're not supposed to sleep with the door open. In case of fire." Tammy knew this from a TV show where they explained what to do in case of emergencies. You weren't supposed to sleep with the door open, you were supposed to feel the door first with your hand to see if it was hot. If there was an earthquake, you were supposed to brace yourself in a doorjamb. And you were supposed to have an emergency family evacuation plan and have a meeting point outside on the corner. If you were at school and the Russians sent over a missile, you were supposed to get under your desk. There were fallout signs at school leading to the basement, but no one ever went down there.

Kirin kicked the door closed with her foot.

Tammy stared up at the ceiling. Valerie's story reminded Tammy of when she asked her mother if Nick actually loved Tammy and Steffi, even though they weren't his kids. Her mother said, "He loved me and he knew it was a package deal," but she didn't say yes. She didn't have to, because Tammy knew Nick didn't love her. He loved Hugh because Hugh was actually his kid. He probably loved Steffi because she was nice and cute. But there really wasn't anything lovable about Tammy. She wasn't nice and she wasn't cute. She got in trouble a lot, she yelled, and she cursed. She got good grades, but she didn't like school. She didn't like her sister or her brother, and she didn't like Nick. She thought her mother was okay, but her mother was always siding with Nick and Steffi. Her mother never took Tammy's side and if she could get rid of Tammy, she probably would. Without Tammy her life would be a whole lot easier and nicer. Tammy just reminded her of Dad.

Tammy thought it must be nice to be an only child like Kirin and have your own room without a separator door and not have to baby-sit your brother after school. She hated sleeping over here and being treated like a little kid.

The next morning when Tammy woke up she was alone, surrounded by flat sleeping bags. She got up and wandered downstairs, not really sure what to do with herself in someone else's house.

Kirin, Steffi, and Hugh were already dressed and eating cereal in the kitchen. The choices were Fruit Loops, Frosted Flakes, or Honeycomb. They never had this at home. They weren't allowed to have sugary cereal. They didn't even have regular non-sugary cereal like Cheerios or Rice Krispies. It was always generic brand cereals called Crispy Rice and Toasty O's.

"Hi, sleepyhead!" Steffi said.

Tammy glared at her and chose Frosted Flakes.

Kirin's mom was standing by the window smoking a cigarette.

"Do you want to go swimming?" Kirin asked.

"No," Tammy said without looking up from her bowl.

"Why not?"

"Because I don't."

"That's not a real reason."

"Well, I don't want to and I didn't bring my suit."

"We could stop by your house and you could run in and get it."

"I don't want to."

"Why not?"

"BECAUSE I DON'T!" Tammy yelled.

Kirin's eyes bugged out. Steffi put on her "I'm hurt" look and squinted her eyes to force herself to cry. Hugh looked at Tammy with his spoon in midair, needing permission to take another bite. Tammy sat very still because she had forgotten she was in someone else's house and she was supposed to behave and not yell.

Kirin's mom didn't say anything. Tammy slowly turned around in her seat and looked at her. She hadn't moved an inch. She was still staring out the window. Her cigarette had burned almost all the way down to her fingers. There was a long piece of ash that tilted down toward the floor and then dripped off and fell into the sink. She still didn't move.

Tammy slowly turned back around and smiled at Steffi. Kirin opened her mouthful of chewed Fruit Loops and stuck out her tongue at Tammy.

THE COUNCIL WITH THE DOCTOR

* * *

Jeffrey sat on the shrink's couch next to his mother; his father sat in a separate chair facing the shrink. The shrink had his legs crossed like a girl and was reading aloud from a paper Jeffrey had written. The shrink liked to give homework assignments, one of which was to write an autobiography—the life of Jeffrey Hackney up until now. Jeffrey enjoyed writing it and embellished very little. He thought it best, under these circumstances, to be as pathetic as possible.

The thing Jeffrey didn't like was the shrink reading it aloud to his parents. It made him sick to his stomach. He didn't want to look at them, although he was curious about their reaction. He chose instead to stare at the orange carpet and count the niblets of yarn as they faded from maroon to brown in some semblance of a sunset. He had to concentrate on something to keep his face blank because he could feel his father look over at him from time to time. His father had assumed one of his serious listening poses: legs crossed, ankle over opposite knee, chin in hand, elbow balanced on the armrest. He slowly rotated back and forth in the office-style chair like a pendulum swinging, ticking off time. The rest of his body didn't move, his eyes remained fixed on the white sheet of college-ruled notebook paper in the shrink's hand. Every now and then his eyes would dart over at Jeffrey, but he still kept time in his chair on wheels.

Jeffrey counted bumps in the carpet, calculating the distance between chair legs and air vents and electrical outlets. When he needed a break he sang a Beatles song in his head. He was halfway through *The White Album* when the shrink laid the paper on his desk and they all shifted in their seats, unsure of what the next act would bring. His mother unclasped her hands and hooked them together horizontally with curled fingers, like a yin-yang symbol. She had learned this in church choir as the proper way to hold one's hands while singing.

Jeffrey looked up. Everyone was looking back at him.

"Jeffrey," the shrink began, "how does it feel having your autobiography read to your parents?"

"Nervous."

"Do you feel relieved to have it out in the open, off your chest?"

"I don't know."

"How does it feel now, with it all over and done?"

"The same, kind of."

Jeffrey's father lifted his ankle off his knee and planted his foot flat on the floor. He took a deep inhale, which meant he was about to say something, hand down his proclamation, like God to Moses the Shrink, and have the session wrapped up. Jeffrey gave Dr. Gans credit for spotting it and shushing his father with a slightly raised hand.

"Do you have some inclination as to what your parents are feeling right now?"

It was almost too easy, Jeffrey thought. This was his cue to look over at them with eyes on the verge of tears and tell them how afraid he was that they might be ashamed of him. But Jeffrey already knew what they thought. His father wasn't so much ashamed of him as he was looking for a way to get rid of him. Jeffrey wasn't a son, but an employee, someone his father wanted to fire without having to hand over a severance package.

"I don't know," Jeffrey said, playing the middle.

"What kind of autobiography do you think would please them?"

Jeffrey went back to the carpet niblets.

"I don't know. One where I was rich and famous. More like my brother and sister."

"Are either your brother or sister rich and famous?"

"No."

Jeffrey's father leaned back in his chair. It was killing him not being able to say anything, but those were the rules of the session. They had to listen and not interrupt.

"What do you think your parents want from you for the immediate future?"

"Get a job. Move out."

"Or you could finish school," his mother said and, quickly catching herself, uttered an embarrassed, "Sorry."

"Don't those seem like rather attainable goals? School, a job, your own apartment. Don't they seem much easier to achieve than becoming rich and famous?"

"I guess."

"Should we make that our focus in these sessions?"

"Sure."

The shrink nodded, satisfied with himself. The four of them got up, shook hands all around, and shuffled through the waiting room full of unhappy hopefuls looking to be told what to do with their lives.

When they got home, his father took out a pen and drew a circle around a day in next month's calendar.

"One month. Nothing gets done without a deadline, Jeffrey. One month to find a job and look for your own place. We can help you out with a deposit on the apartment, but that's it. If you had balls enough to pick up and move to California, you have balls enough to knock on doors for a job."

Jeffrey's mother bit her bottom lip and curled it into her mouth. She didn't like the word "balls" being bantered about her kitchen. She peeled back the tin foil covering her CorningWare and placed the dish delicately in the oven.

His father, thusly satisfied, disappeared into his room to pray, or as he called it, his one-on-one time with the Lord.

Jeffrey's mother began chatting about how school was still an option even though his father mostly talked about job, job, job. You could get a better job if you have a better education. Plus you'd meet people. It's important to meet people. I don't really know what kind of people you would meet working in a restaurant. Maybe you could try the club again. They have lots of young people working there. Maybe your father could talk to someone. . . . She chattered on and on like this. She liked talking to Jeffrey because Jeffrey let her ramble and he didn't talk back.

In between her meal preparations and talking to herself, she plunked two white tablets and a glass of water down in front of Jeffrey. Jeffrey stared at the medication prescribed by the shrink for treatment of a nervous condition. His mother had forgotten that Jeffrey had taken his pills before the appointment. She was slipping up because he usually took them right before dinner, but tonight they were having dinner late because of their after-work family session. The two miniature white eyeballs looked up at him from the table. They jiggled on the vinyl kitchen tablecloth as his mother walked back and forth from oven to fridge. They jiggled like a giant pair of tiny tits for a skinny white female insect, some slutty mini creature performing a disembodied striptease on the edge of a flat world.

Jeffrey licked two fingertips and placed them on top of the pills. They stuck to his skin as he lifted them up and dropped them in his mouth. Double your pleasure, double your fun.

His mother kept on chattering as she wandered in and out, setting the table, folding paper napkins into irregular triangles, filling up amber glasses with white milk. Jeffrey felt as though he was sliding into a deep bath, maybe one filled with mud or warm Jell-O. He let his head rest against the rubbery kitchen wallpaper and set sail for a distant land in which he had no worries and no cares.

PART TWO

FRIENDSHIP HEIGHTS

＊ ◇ ＊

Josie pulled her head out of the oven, which she had been attempting to clean, and was startled to see a pair of bare legs she did not recognize. She jerked upright, banging her head on the oven ceiling, and found Valerie standing before her in the kitchen doorway.

"How'd you get in?" Josie asked. "Did I leave the door open?" She felt around the crown of her head to see if she had picked up any grease. There was a patch that seemed damp, but when she removed her fingers they were clean.

Valerie didn't answer the question. If Josie thought about it, it was the type of thing Valerie might do, just kind of wander in somewhere, ignoring "employees only" signs or closed doors. But Josie was embarrassed about being caught doing something so mundane. Although Josie didn't have a job, she didn't consider herself a housewife. It was passé to consider one's self a housewife, she thought, although she didn't feel comfortable with the refrigerator magnet her husband had given her as a joke present that said, "All mothers are working mothers." She knew he meant well by it, but it didn't feel like enough.

"I wanted to give this back to you," Valerie said and, smiling, extended a book to Josie.

"Oh, did you finish it already?" Josie asked.

"No, I just don't have time to read it."

"Oh." Josie was disappointed. She had lent the book to Valerie in the hopes that she would read it and maybe they would talk about it and start a book group that met once a month. Josie had to start somewhere, so she started with Val.

"I'm sorry," Val said.

"That's okay."

"I should've knocked. I'm disturbing you."

"No, no," Josie said. Josie wasn't disturbed. Cleaning an oven that didn't really need cleaning was disturbed. Cleaning an oven when one should be trying to get back into one's thesis research was disturbed.

"And this was yours too," Valerie handed over a patterned shawl. Josie didn't recognize it at first and didn't automatically move to take it from Valerie's hands. A minute must have ticked by before Josie realized the shawl had once belonged to her.

"Wow," Josie said, "I forgot about this."

"I know. I'm sorry I kept it so long."

"Didn't I . . ." It all was coming back to Josie now. "Didn't I give this to you? I think I did." Josie remembered it now. She had given the shawl to Valerie ages ago, when she was pregnant with Kirin and it was wintertime. For some reason it was always cold in Valerie's house at night; Carl had a thing about the heating bill. Josie suggested Valerie adjust the thermostat, but she declined. "It upsets him," she said. And so Josie brought over the shawl. Josie had no qualms about giving it away. It never did suit her. It was black with large roses sprawled over it and stringy fringe. She had seen a woman in grad school with the same one artfully draped on her shoulders and Josie thought she should have one too. She thought that was what a progressive, intellectual, thinking woman would wear. It wasn't too sixties, but it said something. It said, "I care," and, "I think about the world."

Josie never could find a way to wear it. It was always getting in her way or catching on something, and she felt uncomfortably dramatic swinging it across her chest and over one shoulder. She brought it over to Valerie's thinking it would be the perfect thing to wrap around one's self when pregnant. Funny though, Josie thought, that I never wore it when I was pregnant.

She had meant for Valerie to keep it, but Valerie was giving it back so thoughtfully, as if it meant something important to her to have remembered about the shawl and to now be giving it back.

Josie took the shawl and placed it on her kitchen counter where it deflated next to the can of oven cleaner.

Valerie looked relieved. Her face looked shiny. Her hair was long and loose and could use a brushing. Josie thought she might have lost weight. How is it, Josie thought, that I am thirty-eight and getting wider, cottage cheese thighs, and Valerie is the same age and is losing weight?

Valerie was still smiling like she wanted a gold star for bringing back the book and the shawl. Maybe Josie should give her something else to hold on to for a little while and then give back.

"You know, she has a new book out," Josie said. "Maybe we could read that together."

"That's okay," Valerie said. "I have to pick up Kirin. I was just cleaning up and going through some things. There's a lot to do."

"I'll bet," Josie said.

The front door opened and closed without warning, which usually meant it was Gretchen returning home from school. Without even a "Hi, Mom," she disappeared up the stairs and into her bedroom.

"Gretchen?" Josie called after her. A faint television laugh track greeted her in return.

"I should go," Valerie said quietly. She left through Josie's back door and walked lightly through the yard on her way to the alley. Josie didn't notice until Valerie was at the back gate that she was barefoot.

The television laughed at Josie from above the ceiling. Josie looked up. This is getting ridiculous, she thought.

Josie knocked on Gretchen's door and let herself in.

"How about homework?" Josie asked.

"How about it?" Gretchen replied, not looking at her mother.

"How about," Josie said, making it up as she went along, "we have a reading session together. We can spread out on the bed in me and Daddy's room and I can read and you can do homework until Daddy gets home."

"I kind of need to do homework at my desk," Gretchen said as she reached over and switched off the TV. At least I got that much, Josie thought.

"Okay, well, I'll be reading in my room," Josie tried to convince herself it sounded like fun and that she was not, in effect, policing her daughter's television habits.

Josie climbed onto her bed with the book Valerie returned, *Passages* by Gail Sheehy. She had seen the book on several people's shelves but had never read it herself. And, actually, she still hadn't read it. She had skimmed through the chapter about being in your thirties, but when she got to "The Age 35 Survey" and found it wasn't actually a survey that you could fill in, but just another chapter, she began to flip through pages out of order. The tidbits she did consume were mostly about women who decided to strike out on their own and move to Big Sur, and, of course, a few who did move to Big Sur discovered they really didn't like it that much.

Josie shut the book. She was stuck in this room now for another hour and a half. She looked over at her desk perfectly positioned between the two windows. A few months ago, she had reorganized her closet and pulled out the box containing her thesis research, abandoned since her daughter was born. She could finish her thesis and finally have her master's degree. That could open some doors, she thought. But as she sifted through the notes and files, she found herself uninterested. She thumbed through books that used to mean the world to her, only to find herself paying more attention to what was on the radio. She arranged her scholarly materials in neat piles on her bedroom desk and bought a new ribbon for the typewriter, figuring that having these things visible and ready would spark her inspiration. But now months had gone by, and Josie had yet to study or type or call the university about rematriculating.

Josie fought the urge to get under the covers. On her husband's nightstand was Carl Sagan's *Cosmos.* The book about black holes was flattened, pages down, between a lamp and the edge of the stand. Josie reached over and extracted the book. It fanned open and bold letters announced the chapter her husband had barely begun: "The Persistence of Memory." A photograph of a giant humpback whale arching gracefully, headfirst out of the water, glistened from the opposite page. The whale was strangely, majestically vertical. It had managed, despite its mass, and without the assistance of a harpoon or crane, to defy gravity. Josie flipped forward a few pages looking at diagrams of whale song rhythms and remembering very little about the PBS television series. She flipped a few pages further and was confronted by pictures of human brains sitting on a counter like hunks of raw, wet meat. She snapped the book shut and tossed it to her husband's side of the bed. A moment later she realized she hadn't marked his place in the book. She closed her eyes and put it out of her mind.

THE ORDINARY DAY

＊　＊　＊

Valerie awoke from a dream in which she was already awake. She had dreamt she had woken up, gotten out of bed, and started making breakfast. But when she turned to look at the clock on the stove, she realized she was horribly late. It was after ten o'clock. She hadn't woken Kirin. School had already started. Game shows had already begun. There was nothing she could do. She ran back up to her bedroom and discovered a beautiful new closet. She opened the door and flung herself inside. She hit the back wall, which was cushioned in pink satin, and flipped around to watch the door close in her face. There was one little pull light with a Chinese lampshade hanging from the ceiling. She tugged the string, bathed herself in a rosy glow, and as she calmed down, a thought repeated over and over in her mind: You must leave this place. It will soon be too late. There will be no time. There will be no time to reach this safe closet when all the buttons have been pushed and the bombs are on their way. The CIA will surely find you. They know where to look. They know all the hiding places. The same thing happened to your mother. She was caught and forced to disappear.

Valerie woke up.

From her pillow, she gazed forward and saw the reflection of her sleeping body in the vanity mirror across the room. She couldn't quite make out her face. It was early and barely light out. In the mirror she saw the burly form of her husband bending over to pull on socks.

She closed her eyes. She forced herself to dream of a tropical island. She forced a pleasant dream of a beach and sunshine, a simple wooden house with a screened-in porch. Kirin was small and her husband wasn't there. She tried to remember what the beach smelled like.

Valerie opened her eyes again. The room was empty. She hadn't really dreamt the second dream, but she felt more prepared to deal with the first. The one that was giving her the cue:

Today

Today

Today

Today.

She tried not to breathe too deeply.

She got out of bed and walked into the hallway. At the top of the stairs she heard the toaster pop. Her husband's waffles. Or Pop-Tarts. She paused outside Kirin's door. It was today. Maybe Valerie was already gone. Maybe she had already passed away. She had read somewhere that if you dreamed you died, it was quite possible you would die in your sleep. You would wake up dead. This could actually be happening to Valerie. That would be good. That would be an easier plan. She thought that was the plan until she remembered that she had seen herself in the mirror. She was still here.

It didn't matter. This was Today.

She floated down the stairs. Her feet were bare, she hadn't put on slippers, her breath was light. She imagined she was smiling.

Her husband didn't look at her. He was standing up, bent over the counter, reading a business report. She poured him a cup of coffee.

"Kirin's not going to swim practice today."

He didn't respond. Maybe he hadn't heard her. Maybe she hadn't said it.

"She's not feeling well. Better to let her sleep."

He responded with "Okay." She barely heard it. It didn't matter. He didn't need to know. He wouldn't be saved. He wouldn't be a part of it. He didn't matter. She didn't need him.

"I still have to drive the others."

This time the "okay" had a chirpy upswing on the end, as if to say, "Good idea."

But the "okay" was all she needed to lower her eyes and glide out of the room. She floated back up the stairs and got dressed. When she emerged in the hallway again she tried not to look at Kirin's door that was starting to throb with a hum of *soon, soon.* Things had to be done a certain way. She couldn't simply give in or it wouldn't work. That's what happened last time.

As she started back down the stairs, she heard him unlock the front door and walk out of the house. She paused there, on the landing. She heard the car door open and slam shut, and finally the engine started up and her husband drove away. She stayed on the landing as silence stole in and surrounded her. For a second she forgot how to move her body. She glanced down at her feet. Her frosty-pink toenails poked out of her Dr. Scholl's. She always wore them in the morning even though they made it slightly difficult to drive. She stared down at her toenails and commanded her feet to move, which they did, step by step, down the stairs.

She opened the front door and walked out into the pearly-gray, early light, still awkward on her wooden feet. There were already a few children leaning against her car. They were, for the most part, unhappy. For the most part, this was not their idea, early-morning swimming before school. Tuesdays and Thursdays were her days. She drove the children to the Promenade Swim Club and another mother picked them up.

One of them said hi to her between bites of a sandwich made of peanut butter and toast. Valerie thought she had used up all the words she was going to say today, so she only nodded back. She opened the car doors for the children and they slid silently into the backseat. At the end of the block she saw another child approaching with his familiar posture: towel draped over one shoulder, sneakers dragging on the pavement. He walked down the middle of the street instead of the sidewalk. Valerie always told him this was dangerous, a car could hit him. Today she said nothing and he didn't notice.

Last always was Gretchen. Valerie got in the car and honked the horn. Gretchen would not emerge from her house otherwise. She lived the closest, but she was always the last one out.

Gretchen sat next to Valerie in the front seat. She always managed to sit up front. She was smart. She intimidated Valerie. In two or three years she would start sleeping with her friends' husbands. She was the type. And in the end they would all blame the men for being weak. No one would blame Gretchen.

"Can I turn on the radio?"

Valerie turned to Gretchen and looked at her through her sunglasses. Valerie didn't really need sunglasses this early in the morning, but she needed protection. She knew that's why movie stars wore sunglasses all the time—because they were tired of people trying to look them in the eye. It gave them a sense of power to be a little bit invisible.

I could kill her, Valerie thought, I could crash the whole car and still make it back home in time.

Gretchen, always cranky in the morning, cocked her head and opened her eyes wider waiting for an answer.

Valerie smiled and turned back to the road.

Gretchen took that as a yes and flipped on the radio. She adjusted it to Q107. *The Q*, all the children sang along, *the Q zoo in the morning!*

It wasn't until Valerie turned into the driveway of the Promenade that a voice from the backseat asked where Kirin was. Valerie knew she would have to speak. She tried to calm herself. Be as economical as possible.

"Sick."

One word. Only one.

The children slithered out of the car like little lizards breaking out of their eggs. They gave her a few "byes" and "okays" and one "see ya." They trudged toward the pool house and didn't look back. Their day was ordinary.

THE MOVIE

* * *

Jeffrey thought it had a good opening. Prison bars sliding across his face. You weren't sure if they were opening or shutting, it had something to do with the direction they were moving. You were surprised when the bars slid away and nothing was blocking the guy's face. The guy takes a step forward and looks around. Cut to a wide shot. The guy steps outside into a prison parking lot. He's carrying a brown paper grocery bag full of his belongings from when he was arrested. He did his time and now he's cast back into the world.

He doesn't say much, this guy, but you get the feeling something is bugging him.

A car pulls up and some straight-arrow suburban guy in a golf shirt rolls down the window. It's a nice car. Expensive. European. We learn that this is his brother. The brother is all friendly, but he has a nervous way about him and he's holding on to everything. He grips the steering wheel tightly. He adjusts the radio himself. He leans over, gets some-thing out of the glove compartment, and shoves the door shut. He's into his stuff. Our hero's been up the river for three years and his brother doesn't touch him at all.

They drive to the brother's house; our hero is staying there until he gets settled. The wife isn't too happy about this. The house is nice, but it's full of messy kid stuff. The wife is pissed off that she ever had kids because it makes her less sexy and she's not sure if she'll ever get her figure back.

His brother shows him to his room. It's not a room, really; it's part of the garage that's been sectioned off with cheap wood paneling and an old car carpet thrown on the cement floor. No window. Our hero knew what they were thinking: he's just been in prison; this is probably a step up for him.

We soon learn that our hero did time for the brother. It had something to do with a business embezzlement, a break-in, an inside job, and a loan shark—your typical crime movie stuff. The details of it weren't important. It was more about the fact that our hero kept his mouth shut and took the rap so that his brother could stay with the wife and kiddies. He did the right thing. Three years. Age twenty-one to twenty-four.

One night, it's fucking hot and he can't stand being cooped up in his festering swamp of a room. He lifts up the garage door, ducks underneath, and walks out to sit on the curb. His brother's house is in one of those ultra-modern suburban developments with wide white sidewalks and curvy roads. The curb itself isn't a real curb, it's a modern design as well—it's sloped so that kids can get their bikes in and out of the street without the clumsy bump that could make them wipe out.

He sits down on this slanted curb and a girl comes walking along out of the night. It's strange because no one really walks around here. Even with these big modern sidewalks, they all drive. The girl looks like a teenager, but she's probably a little older. She's walking fast, as if she's worried someone is following her. She's wearing high-heeled shoes that click across the pavement. If she were smart, she'd take them off so she'd stop making so much noise and drawing attention to herself. She's dressed kind of slutty too, definitely not one of the PTA moms.

He's not sure if she's noticed him or not. He tracks her with his eyes and then decides to get up and follow her down the street. Just to make sure she gets home safely. If he doesn't do it, who will?

He trails her by walking along the edge of the grassy front lawns that butt up against the sidewalk, that way he doesn't make any noise. He follows her around one suburban loop and into another. She finally turns up a driveway and pulls her keys out of her purse. He gets a good look at her under her porch lamp as she opens her door and disappears inside. The heavy drapes are closed, covering the sliding glass doors that open onto the front yard. A sliver of light trickles out from underneath the curtains' wavy trim. He could break in there if he wanted. Sliding glass doors are easy.

He stares at her house for a few minutes almost hoping the girl sees him. He wants somebody in this picture-perfect planned community to know he exists.

He walks back to his garage along the sand-colored sidewalk. A car zooms by and stops abruptly. He turns around and the driver looks back at him as the car slowly steamrolls over a speed bump.

He visits the girl during daylight hours. It turns out she is connected to the whole mess with his brother. She's even slept with his brother, but she likes him better. She and our hero, they're alike, she says, because they are both trapped. They have to pretend they love something they really don't. But, she tells him, he is worse than her. He lets them walk all over him and doesn't say a word. She is at least stealing from them behind their backs. When he suggests that he is also getting what he wants behind their backs (because by now they have had sex) she gets mad at him and throws him out and all of a sudden gives him a bunch of women's lib crap. He knows she doesn't mean it, she's just afraid of her own emotions. But she throws a whopper at him when she tells him that he's a coward.

"You think you're tough because you took the rap and kept your mouth shut, but you don't realize what a coward that makes you. You're not a man. You're so weak that you'll let them destroy you just to avoid standing up to them."

He doesn't say anything and she uses it against him.

"You don't say anything for yourself. You don't stand up for yourself. You probably don't even know who you really are."

Then he grabs her and throws her down onto the bed. Her blonde hair splays out against the sheets and he is holding her arms firmly with his hands, the way his brother held on to the steering wheel.

"I know who I am," he says.

"Then prove it. Stop living in silence. Do something. Otherwise it doesn't matter if they kill you or not. You're already dead."

She was a blonde medusa against the white pillowcase, but instead of turning him to stone, she brought him back to life.

It ends with a shootout, brother to brother, on the suburban ghost town's main street. We think our hero is dead, because he's lying on the newly paved tar and he's been shot. His brother is standing over him, the sun behind him, tiny blood spots staining his pink Izod golf shirt. Our hero is writhing in pain, but when he looks up and sees his brother, something changes. It's in his eyes. They're full of something. A knowledge of who he is. He looks into the face of his brother and knows that he is not that man.

A shot goes off and we're not entirely sure what happens, but in the next scene another sliding door opens and our hero is leaving a hospital, his arm in a sling and his old bloodied clothes in a paper bag. He walks out into the parking lot and a convertible pulls up. The girl hops out of the car and runs up to him, throwing her arms around him. He cringes from where she accidentally touches his wound. They joke about it. She drives him home. This time he has been truly set free.

JEFFREY IDENTIFIED WITH this guy. Everybody wanted something from him and all he wanted was to be left alone. He was torn between wanting nobody to notice him and wanting to feel alive. There was no in-between for this guy. There were no everyday pleasures and disappointments. There were no little things that meant a lot. He was either having rough sex with the girl or staring catatonically at the car radio dial in his brother's garage. He was either smoking cigarettes in the darkness of a deserted curb or he was edging his way into a building, gun drawn, ready to step out of a doorway and fire on all the motherfuckers. There was nothing day to day. There was no reason to get up in the morning. The only reason the guy got out of bed was his body betraying him and forcing him back into reality.

Before the shootout with his brother (whom Jeffrey noticed the second time he saw the film was only his half brother) there is a whole cat-and-mouse game with his brother's partners in crime. Guys who wear expensive suits but are only one step up from street-trash thugs. They're the lowlifes from high school who roughed people up. You keep your chin down, your eyes on your books, and walk quickly out of the cafeteria to avoid them. Now they're all grown up and running drugs in and out of the suburbs, getting bake sale moms and church ladies hooked on smack, seducing teenage girls in bad parental situations, girls who become emancipated minors and then fall on hard times. That's what happened to the girl in the picture. She couldn't pay the rent on her place and fell in with these types.

His brother was the perfect front man because he looked so normal. Coach of the fucking soccer team, on the board of the homeowners' association, neighborhood watch, carpooler. Just a guy with a pretty wife and a couple of kids. Fucker. Got his wife hooked as well. She was the nervous type and he had to feed her a steady stream of downers when the coke started making her paranoid.

Jeffrey liked how the movie corroborated everything he knew to be true. That some successful polo-shirt brother wasn't all that hot. That the guy you least expect was actually the good guy, the guy who takes all your bad feelings and evil deeds for you and puts them away so you don't have to worry about them. You don't even have to see them. Then everyone gets greedy and demands that even the receptacle of all their bad thoughts go away. That by doing this, it will be as though the bad thoughts never existed. Well, Jeffrey wasn't going to have it. He wasn't going to be put out with the trash just because people were sick of looking at him, just because he did all this for them and now they were sick of carrying him along, sick of providing decent human things like a roof over his head and a plate at dinner. That was the problem with society: people thought normal people were normal and quiet people were freaks. In reality it was the other way around. Normal people were lying traitors and quiet people were the world's polite saviors.

Nobody got this but Jeffrey.

There was one scene in the movie that made Jeffrey sit up. It was during the cat-and-mouse sequence when our hero has snuck into the bad guys' building. The suit gang's leader and some other thugs were leading the girl down a flight of stairs. It was an industrial-type stairwell painted white with gray steps. They came out of a door and it was Jeffrey looking down at them from the next level up. As they led the girl out, she glanced up and saw him there. She was halfway between panic and arousal. Jeffrey was holding on to his gun with both hands, professional style, pointing down, elbows locked. She had blonde hair. The same as the girl at the Sunrise motel. The same look bouncing carefully down the stairs in high heels. His mother had once gotten dressed up in a long evening gown for a charity dinner at the club and demonstrated how a lady walks down stairs in high heels and a long dress by kicking her leg forward a little bit. This shakes the dress off her shoe and prevents tripping. The girl was doing the same thing, taking her time, pointing her toes forward.

Jeffrey squinted his eyes. It could be the same girl. Maybe the movie producers had cheated her out of her pay and that's why she was living at the motel, or maybe she was just visiting. Maybe she had moved on up and was visiting a friend who was still struggling. That's the kind of girl she was. She didn't abandon everyone she knew before she was famous and pretend like she never knew them.

Jeffrey usually didn't stay for the credits after a movie, he thought they ruined the whole experience and they reminded him that it was just a movie, that it wasn't real. He didn't like seeing the names of all the behind-the-scenes union guys. He didn't want to believe there was a behind the scenes. But he stayed this time to see the girl's real name.

Amber Carrol.

It sounded like a fake Hollywood name, probably her name was Carol Ambers and they switched it around. Carol was an old-fashioned name, a granny with gray hair set in curlers, glasses on a chain around her neck, wearing a brightly patterned dress in an attempt to be funky. Amber Carrol was a nice girl who would sleep with you. Very California. Suntanned.

Jeffrey saw the movie daily, sometimes twice in a row. Then he worried that he was getting spoiled and switched to every other day. That way he really wanted it. It was his reward for having lived through a day of hell in the outside world. His favorite way to see it was to go to the four o'clock show, get the bargain matinee price, settle in, and pop a Valium before the lights went down. The pill gave him a little extra push into the movie world, and the screen that stood between him and the celluloid reality evaporated. When he came out of the theater, it was dark outside, the day had passed, and he felt closer to the next time he would be reunited with Miss Carrol.

Jeffrey wandered home through the early evening setting sun. He had taken to walking on the edge of people's front lawns as he made his way from the bus stop, past the duck pond, to the innermost tentacle of the circle. This evening, after the bus deposited him on a random, side-of-the-road stretch of green a few yards from a gas station (you wouldn't quite call it a corner), he decided to stop at the 7-Eleven for a Slurpee, cola flavored, his favorite because it didn't leave his mouth all cherry red. His mother had him on a perpetual diet. On his way out of the store, he passed by the gumball machines and decided to try his luck. He dropped a coin into the machine and a plastic bubble tumbled down the chute and into his hand. Jeffrey held the tiny bell jar to his eye and sucked the flavored ice through his straw. Inside the bubble was a tiny, pink, bird-like cartoon creature with a white wind-up spoke sticking out of her side.

Jeffrey exited the store and sat down on the bench outside. He twisted the bubble open and took out the bird. She had a goofy expression, eyes wide, beak open in a welcoming grin. She had been stopped in the middle of a sentence. Jeffrey wound her up and set her down carefully on the wooden slat. The bird wobbled and walked a little ways in an irregular line and then tipped over the side of the bench. She fell to the ground landing on her side, gears still turning. When the bird ran out of juice, Jeffrey felt it was safe to pick her up.

The bird still hadn't changed her expression. She still hadn't gotten the words out.

In the movie, our hero catches his little nephews playing in his room. The kids are scared to death, shaking in their Keds. Our hero doesn't say anything because he's not really mad, but the kids mumble a hasty "sorry" and scramble the hell out of there. They leave so quickly that a couple of their toys are left behind. One of them is a stuffed monkey—the kind you wind up and it smashes cymbals together and bobs its head up and down. The monkey permanently has his mouth open with a red felt tongue hanging out. You wind it up and he laughs at you.

Jeffrey thought this little pink bird was a sign. It was trying to tell him something. Even a pink wind-up bird in a plastic gumball machine bubble can have an effect on the world. What the fuck was Jeffrey doing?

Jeffrey slurped the last of his Slurpee and used the spoon end of the straw to get the bits he missed. The last bits were always the worst. The flavor had been sucked out of them and they were little more than plain, watery ice. That's how they get you, Jeffrey thought, they take away the last bit to keep you wanting more.

Jeffrey wanted to come home and find Amber walking out of the shower with a towel wrapped around her middle. Then he would grab her by the shoulders and throw her down on the bed. Thwack! Her wet hair slaps against the clean white sheets. Thwack! Jeffrey loved that moment. She looks a little bit scared, a little bit turned on.

The front door had barely clicked shut behind Jeffery when his father's voice came down from on high.

"Jeffrey?"

Jeffrey paused with one foot on the first step leading downstairs. He kept his eyes focused on his front shoe. He didn't want to be suckered into looking up.

"Yes?"

"Your mother and I would like to speak with you before dinner."

Jeffrey scanned his mind to anticipate the topic.

"Jeffrey?"

"Just let me put my coat down."

He slipped into the safety of his room and perched the bird on the corner of his desk so it would face him when he returned. He hung up his jacket and popped another Valium. Make this easy, easy, easy.

Upstairs, his parents were seated across from each other at the dinner table. There was no food waiting and the table wasn't set. His parents were both sitting in the same position, hands clasped, resting on the table. They probably had a little mumbled prayer together right before this.

Jeffrey took his usual seat. He was tempted to assume the same position as his parents, but he was afraid he might crack up. He could maintain a better gauge of the situation with his hands in his lap.

"Do you know what day it is?" his father asked.

"Thursday."

"Don't be smart."

"Sorry."

His father did one of his eye-lock shots at Jeffrey. His father was good at this, locking his eyes on Jeffrey and forcing him to whimper and cave. His father even managed to stand up from the table still looking at him. Then he purposefully looked away and walked into the kitchen. He came back holding the wall calendar and tossed it on the table.

The magic marker circle stared up at Jeffrey.

"D day," his father said.

Jeffrey was quiet. Think fast, but not too fast.

"What have you got to tell me?"

Stay quiet. Appear ashamed.

"Well?"

"Jeffrey," his mother said, trying to be encouraging. Either that or she was trying to say, "Break it to us gently. Let us help you."

"I don't know."

"Have you found a job?"

"No, but—"

"But?"

"I've been looking, but it's a hard time right now. There aren't any jobs."

"Jeffrey you're an able-bodied young man. You've got a high school diploma, almost two years of college, and you're going to tell me there isn't a job for you anywhere?"

"It's not a good time right now. That's what everyone's been telling me."

"Everyone?"

"Yes. Everyone."

"Have you thought about some of the fast-food places? Burger Chef is always looking for people."

"No."

"Why not?"

"I can't do that."

"Why not?"

"Because, Dad . . . it wouldn't be right. It wouldn't be the right place for me. They only take kids and dropouts."

"I don't think you're in a position right now to have a sense of pride. And that's what you are, Jeffrey. You're a dropout."

His mother opened her mouth to say something in protest.

"That's what he is," his father said, cutting her off. "Let's be honest about the whole situation. We had a deal here for you to find a job and an apartment by the end of business today. Your mother's got dinner waiting and I'm waiting to hear an answer from you, Jeffrey."

Jeffrey paused. He searched for a plan he had not made.

"I was thinking about . . . going back to California. . . . Giving it another try."

His father drew a long breath in through his nose and wiped his forehead with the palm of his hand. Jeffrey could see him reciting some Jesus mantra in his head. He reclasped his hands and reset his gaze.

"Why?" He said it like a bullet, a challenge.

"I learned a lot last time about what not to do. I think I could do it right this time. I've been working on a new demo tape and I think it's really good. And I have a story treatment for a movie I'd like to sell. Based on my novel."

"Jeffrey, your mother and I know you're very . . . artistic. But that's not the point right now. Right now, we need you to focus on the practical so you can stand on your own two feet."

"I want to do it with my music and my writing."

"What you need to do is get a job and work on those things in your spare time. That way you have a base income and if you sell some songs, you'll have extra money. You can do that until the songs start paying for themselves."

"That's not how it works. You have to do it all the time or you'll never get any good."

"What happened to going back to school?" his mother finally managed to get in. She also managed to relieve Jeffrey of his father's eyes for a few seconds before being shot back with "Well?"

"I was thinking that would be my backup plan."

This warranted another wipe of the brow.

"Jeffrey, I don't know what cockamamie way your brain works. We had a deal. A job and an apartment by this date and once again you've let us down. As far as I'm concerned you're scheduled to move out tomorrow. I'm happy to extend it through Monday breakfast so you can make arrangements, but that's it. I suggest you get a good night's sleep and hit the pavement early tomorrow morning. You've got three days. After that, I don't care if you go to California or not. Dismissed!"

With that, his father walked down the hall, into his bedroom, and shut the door. Hopefully, the Lord was available for emergency walk-ins.

His mother smiled meekly and reached across the table to pat Jeffrey's hand.

Plans to make. Plans indeed.

After a dinner with no conversation, Jeffrey retreated to his room. He lay on his bed with his shoes hanging off the end and the bird balanced on his chest. He wound her up and tried to make her waddle across his chest. She could only go a few steps before getting tangled up in his shirt, losing her balance, and falling over, feet still going.

Little thing, Jeffrey thought, she's just like me.

IT WAS THE Sunday paper that saved him. The Entertainment section had a feature article about Amber Carrol and her new movie. She was shooting a political thriller in Washington, DC, in which she plays a secretary working for a senator. The senator is then murdered over a mysterious file that falls into her lap. She joked with the interviewer about how she had to take a typing class for the role. She still wasn't very good, and steno was a killer! But, she joked, at least now I'll have something to fall back on, you know, in case this whole actress thing doesn't work out. There was one scene they just finished shooting where she runs out of the Jefferson Memorial and dives into the Potomac River to get away from the bad guys. I can't tell you how many times we had to shoot that, she said. And that was really *me* diving into the water, not a double! Even more exciting (and a lot dryer!) we all got to meet President Reagan, which was such an honor. I feel a real kinship with him because we're both actors and we both know what it means to have to make it on your own.

The interviewer asked her about her romantic life. Is there a someone special? She smiled and visibly blushed. No, I guess I'm still waiting for Mr. Right to come along and sweep me off my feet. What are you looking for in a Mr. Right? (Giggle.) Well, (smile, small giggle) I guess I'm looking for someone who's kind, someone who understands me and supports me having a career, a good listener, and someone who misses John Lennon just as much as I do.

There was a photo spread featuring stills from her first movie, a silly TV guest spot that gave her a big break, a scene from the new movie with her on the Capitol steps, and a glamour shot with her all made up, smoky eyes, hands digging into the sides of her head messing up her hair. Sexy.

Jeffrey slipped the page out of the Entertainment section. He didn't want to tear it and make any noise.

Later, he was flipping through Words & Ideas, past the book reviews, and lazily through the assortment of ads on the last page.

THE COLUMBIA SCHOOL OF BROADCASTING
Are you ready for an exciting career in radio and broadcasting?
Located in the Washington, DC, metro area!
Start hearing your voice—today!

It was too perfect.

Jeffrey wasn't sure if he believed in guardian angels or not, but something like this always seemed to come through for him. Something always saved him from being kicked into the gutter.

That evening, during their early Sunday dinner, all three Hackneys were quiet. Jeffrey's father was purposefully not saying anything; although several thoughts manifested across his face, he let them all go. He's probably feeling guilty, Jeffrey thought. Well, here's a whopper for you.

"I have a plan."

His father took an aggressive bite of ham mixed with mashed potatoes. Jeffrey hated the way his father ate, mixing his food together. Jeffrey ate his foods separately. His father once chastised him for not cleaning his plate because Jeffrey didn't want to eat the bits of food that ran together. "It's all going to the same place," his father said.

"I want to enroll in the Columbia School of Broadcasting."

"The what?"

"It's a trade school in Washington, DC. They teach you how to do stuff for radio stations."

"Do stuff?"

Jeffrey relished the next word and let it seductively roll off his tongue. "Engineering."

It was a word his father understood.

"I can still leave tomorrow, go to Washington, and get set up before classes start."

"How do you plan on paying for this?"

"I thought school was still an option."

His father didn't like to be beaten.

"We'll discuss it," he said with another forkful.

After dinner, his father read the brochure Jeffrey had snuck out of the public library that afternoon. When he was through, Jeffrey was summoned to the living room.

"I'm taking a chance on you, Jeffrey. I'm taking a risk. This wasn't exactly what we talked about, but I'm impressed that you've finally made a practical decision that matches your interests and I'd like to support that."

Jeffrey waited as his father took a ceremonial deep breath.

"Your mother and I have decided to approve this mission, but we have a few requirements of our own. Number one: Your mother and I will cover the cost of tuition, but you're still going to need to get a part-time job for your incidentals. Number two: I want to get a recommendation from Dr. Gans for someone you can check in with locally. I don't want your mother to worry about your health. And number three: We want to hear from you weekly. You can give us a call and reverse the charges or you can send a letter, but we want to know where you are, where you're staying, and how things are progressing. We don't want this to be like last time when you waited until you were desperate to ask for help. We're your parents and we worry. I know this all sounds rather harsh, but it's only because we love you."

All Jeffrey needed to hear was the yes. The rest of it really didn't matter. It was a variation on the same speech they had perfected through three childhoods. And more importantly, the money flow had been turned back on.

"I suggest you get packing. Dismissed."

Jeffrey about-faced and went to his room.

The next morning, at oh-nine hundred hours, the three Hackneys drove to the bank. Jeffrey's father went inside while he and his mother waited in the car. His father returned after twenty minutes or so and handed Jeffrey an envelope.

"Keep this somewhere safe. Don't let it hang out your back pocket. There are traveler's checks and cash."

Jeffrey peeked into the envelope and the swirly American Express typescript glimmered back at him.

His parents dropped him off at the airport curbside entrance; it would've been too difficult to park. Jeffrey got out and fetched his bags. His mother cranked down the window and Jeffrey stuck his head in to say good-bye.

"Don't worry," Jeffrey said. "I've got it all figured out this time."

CALF

* * *

Valerie pulled her car into the same parking spot in front of her house she had left twenty minutes earlier. She didn't realize the radio was still playing until she shut the engine and was abruptly met by silence. She was light-headed now and buoyant, skimming the earth in her wooden sandals, which, strangely, didn't make any noise clopping against the sidewalk. Someone said, "Morning, Val," but she didn't see who it was. An angel waved back for her.

As she opened the door, the dog jumped up, happy and eager, paws on her mistress's knees. She wanted to go out, and any other morning, that's what they would do. But not today. Pudding would have to be left behind. She couldn't come along. Valerie thought about it for a moment. Kirin loved that dog. But, no, they couldn't. It would give them away. It would be too much.

Valerie placed her hand on the banister and it began. The airy lightness that had gotten her through the carpool suddenly wore off and she was left with crushing weight. Her palm magnetized to the banister's curved wood. It all flooded back to her. All of it. Everything. Her hand stuck to the railing as her thin knees buckled. She mustn't sob or scream. It would wake her. With her free hand Val capped her mouth. She closed her eyes.

It was now or never.

And magically an angel released her hand from the banister and peeled her fingers from her mouth. Both hands were delicately placed on her knees and Valerie began to feel a sense of peace kneeling there, chastely, at the bottom of the stairs. It can all be done. It can all be done.

And it will all be done this time. It will all be done. Not like last time. She won't wake up to a blindness of white. To more pain than she left with. To more existence than she ever imagined possible when all she wanted to do was vanish. To disappear. To get smaller and smaller until she was so small a speck God could flick her away. Into oblivion. Into the comfort of nothingness.

Valerie opened her eyes. She knew she was opening them. It was she who lifted her lids and it didn't hurt. She gazed down at her fingernails resting on her knees, pointing forward to the eggshell-colored carpet. They were showing her which way to go.

Up.

It was time.

It can all be done.

The lightness returned. Her angels helped her to her feet. They told her not to look back at the door. At the people getting into their cars and driving off to work. At the telescopes pointed at her house, watching. They won't be able to see her today. Don't worry about the dog, an angel said as she lured Pudding into the kitchen and put food in her bowl. Don't worry.

Valerie stepped out of her Dr. Scholl's and walked up the stairs.

The door to Kirin's room was melting. The angels told her not to look at it. Not yet. You must take precautions. Valerie obeyed. She turned away from the door and walked to her bedroom.

She knelt down at the side of the bed, the same position she assumed at the bottom of the stairs, and just as before her fingernails pointed the way. She lifted the bed skirt and tugged the slender leather case forward. It was locked like a suitcase with a tiny gold Master Lock linking two zippers together. Valerie backed up on all fours and crawled over to her husband's dresser. She climbed to the top by pulling on the brass drawer handles. She didn't want to stand up just yet.

She peered into the ceramic dish where he kept the cufflinks he rarely wore. Mixed in at the bottom was the gold key. The tiny gold key. So small. It was hard to pick up. Valerie pushed it with the pad of her index finger up to the rim of the dish and set it free. Free from the tyranny of cufflinks. There could be a tiny camera in there. It would be just like her husband to be involved. That was why he never wore those cufflinks.

Valerie turned the dish over and trapped the cufflinks underneath. That would take care of that.

She crawled back over to the case. She felt safe on the floor.

She unlocked the case and lifted the lid.

And there it was.

She picked it up with both hands and laid it on top of the case. She knew it was still loaded. She knew he had come home unlucky last November, and had forgotten to remove the cartridges.

We have to leave you now, the angels said. We can't be here when it happens. But you know what to do.

Valerie nodded and with a very small voice she said, "Yes," aloud.

The angels tiptoed out of the room. Don't worry, it will all be over soon, and we'll be right there to meet you. Good-bye. Good-bye. They waved and dissolved into tiny balls of light.

The clock flicked to 7:11. It was a good time. Something she recognized.

Valerie wrapped her fingers around the slender barrel. It was easy. Just make yourself stand up. You can do it. Just stand up.

She stood up.

She told herself to breathe through her nose. She didn't want to open her mouth. She didn't want to risk the chance of talking herself out of it. She tried to hang on to the feeling of lightness even though the weight of being left alone was beginning to pour over her. It was trying to push her back down to her knees. But she had to stand up. She had to. She couldn't let them win. She wasn't going to let that happen. This was the only way. The only way. She had to do it. She had to save her. She had to.

She turned toward the bedroom door that was still open. The angels had left it open for her. They were nice.

She walked toward the threshold, but stopped herself when she noticed the white phone glaring at her from the nightstand. Had it been watching her the whole time? Valerie felt her heart beat faster. Everything was going wrong. Who put this phone here? Why hadn't the angels taken care of it? Was it looking at her? Were they listening the whole time? They could be on their way. They could know everything already. Time was running out.

She lifted the receiver off the hook. She brought it up to her ear and, just in case anyone was watching, she lightly traced seven numbers on the pad. She could have been an actress. Everyone always said.

She gently laid the receiver on the table perfectly parallel to the phone.

She walked into the hallway in slow motion.

She walked toward the door that was melting.

She noticed it wasn't closed all the way. It looked closed, but it wasn't. This was good because the door appeared too hot to touch.

She nudged it open with the gun.

And there she was.

Kirin.

The golden girl. Asleep in her pigtails. Valerie let her sleep that way. Her little blonde bumpkin.

Please hang up, there appears to be a receiver off the hook . . .

It was so loud. The voice was so loud. She was going to wake up. She couldn't wake up. She had to stay asleep. She had to. That was the best way.

If you'd like to make a call, please hang up and try again . . .

And over and over and—

Valerie stepped into the room. Kirin was curled up under the covers. She had kicked off the blue knitted blanket and was sprawled under a mess of sheets. She was wearing her nightgown with the little jumping cows on it. Their legs reached out in front of them as they sailed over yellow crescent moons.

Please hang up, there appears to be a receiver off the hook . . .

Valerie looked up from the bed and saw Kirin's stuffed animal collection staring back at her with their frozen glass eyes. They looked shocked, as if something had already happened, as if they existed a few moments ahead in the future and already knew what Valerie did next.

Please hang up . . .

It had to be now, it had to be—

Valerie took a few more steps deeper into the sunny bedroom. There was a fight going on in her body between the lightness and the weight, whether she was going to expand or shrink. The angels were fighting for her. She knew they were. They were fighting as hard as they could.

Valerie reached the bed. She wanted to look at Kirin's face, but she remembered the angels had told her not to. Not a good idea. Don't mess it up now. Valerie's shins pressed against the side of the bed. That was good, she thought. That will help hold me up. She pointed the gun at Kirin's back, hovering it a few inches from her nightgown, directly aiming at one of the dancing cows.

Please hang up and try—

The recording cut off and was replaced with a loud pulsing alarm. It was so loud. Stop it. Stop it. Stop. She'll wake up now. Do it now. Now. It has to be done. It has to. You can't stop now. Think of what will happen if you stop. They will take you away. They will take her away. It has to be done. Now.

The alarm was so loud. Valerie no longer knew where it was coming from. She couldn't tell if it was from the phone, the police, or inside her head. She saw her hands beginning to shake. They couldn't focus on the little cow. The barrel danced around. It refused to be quiet. Everything was falling apart.

Now. Now. Now. Now Now Now Now Now Hurry hurry hurry hurry hurry hurry hurry hurry.

And then it happened. She had strength. It was in her fingernails. She saw them and her hands stopped quivering. They pointed at the baby cow and stopped moving. It was going to be okay. She knew what she was doing. And her fingernails guided her, showed her which way to go. She was too far away. An inch was too far away. She pointed the gun closer until it touched the calf's white belly, and then through the calf until it stopped at Kirin's back. And for one second Valerie felt her daughter. The gun moved up and down with her breathing body. Valerie breathed in synch with her. One last time. Then she pulled the trigger.

And the first part was over.

Valerie was on the floor. She was sitting down. The shot had knocked her backward and she had fallen. There was so little time now. There was even less. But the hard part was over, wasn't it? She stood up again.

The calf was bleeding. There was a hole and red was gushing out. The bed was becoming engulfed in liquid. A flood. Valerie thought this was good. It would soon float Kirin away to their island, to their beautiful beach house with salty air. This was good.

Valerie slowly turned the gun around and pointed the barrel at her chest. She stood the gun up on the bed and leaned into it. She tried to reach down to the trigger, but the mattress swallowed it into a sinkhole of sheets. The bed was too soft. She needed to move quickly. She moved the gun onto the floor. She arranged herself again with her chest resting on the barrel. She planted her feet wide and reached down for the trigger.

Her fingernails failed her. She couldn't reach. It was too far.

The phone alarm was getting louder. Make it stop.

It had to work. It had to.

Valerie began to feel desperate. She looked around the room for something to use. The stuffed animals weren't helping. They just stared at her with their hard yellow eyes. Their fixed pupils. They were thinking. She could hear them thinking. She knew they didn't like her. She wanted to tell them to fuck off but the angels had told her not to speak. Where were they? Why weren't they here? Why had they abandoned her?

The phone alarm was making her head throb.

Now now now now now now now now now.

She could do it. She could reach.

She set herself up again, gun standing upright on the floor. She held it in place with the weight of her chest leaning on the barrel, barrel pointed at her heart. Fingernails reaching down. It was still too far.

Valerie moved her right foot in toward the gun. Then somehow she kept her balance as she lifted her left foot up and pressed the trigger with her toes.

The gun went off. Valerie said something as it did, but she couldn't make out what. It sounded like "yes" as the world went black.

Bliss

blissful

blackness

CALF

. . . until her eyes slipped open.

I might have to wait, she thought, I might have to wait. Sometimes this happens.

She was on the floor. She could see blood inking the carpet, a stain slowly spreading out beneath her.

She waited, but nothing happened. She prayed for it to hurry up. Please hurry up.

But it wasn't happening.

It occurred to her that maybe she had missed. That maybe she had tripped and fallen over backward and knocked herself out. Given herself a bump on the head. Maybe she hadn't shot herself at all. That's probably what happened. Probably.

She rolled herself up to sit. Something was wrong, but it wasn't the right kind of wrong. Her shoulder was screaming in pain. Her left arm was limp. It wasn't working anymore. She grabbed the gun with her other hand and used it as a cane to prop herself up. Her head was dizzy. She wasn't feeling well. She needed to finish herself off.

She leaned her chest onto the gun again. It was harder this time. It was harder to stay upright. She didn't think she could do it. She fell over. This couldn't be happening. She crawled over to the wall and sat with her back against it. She pointed the gun at her chest and wiggled her toes into the trigger hole. She sickled her other foot behind the gun handle to hold it in place and pressed down on the trigger with her toes.

It clicked, but nothing happened. She pressed again, and again nothing happened.

NoNoNoNoNoNoNoNoNo.

Valerie started to cry. She had lost. She looked over at the bed. Oh god oh god oh god oh god. Her little girl was floating away. Her baby had drowned.

Valerie crawled up the wall until she was standing on her unsteady feet. She had to get out. She couldn't be in this room. She used the wall for support and made her way to the door. As soon as she set foot back in the hallway, the phone alarm stopped.

She bumped along the hallway wall back to her bedroom. Reality was cruelly rushing back through the quiet din of the day. The silence was smacking her in the face. Her angels were nowhere to be found. They had cut her off. They had tricked her. Valerie caught sight of herself in her dresser mirror. The left side of her body was covered in blood. Her shoulder had been ripped open and her arm, which she could no longer feel, hung heavily at her side.

The leather case was still open. She could try to reload the gun, but she didn't have the slightest idea how. She knew her husband had long since emptied the bathroom of anything more dangerous than nail clippers. He kept the pills under lock and key. He used an electric razor and made her switch to Nair. There was nothing in there and she knew that if she went downstairs some neighbor or postman would see her and want to save her. No, she would have to wait. She would have to wait until all the blood flowed out of her body. She would die. She would just have to wait.

Valerie crawled back into her unmade bed and waited.

Josie tucked her tennis racquet in her armpit and dialed the number again. She was already late. She had a small moment of hope in the silent few seconds after the last button was pushed, but as soon as she gave up and said to herself, "It's still going to be busy," the signal blared in her ear. She hung up the phone, frustrated. She knew Valerie was home because her car was parked outside. Josie tugged her visor cap over her forehead and marched out the front door, pom-poms sticking out of her sneakers giving her an added huff.

Josie walked across the lawn that separated their houses and hopped up onto Valerie's front porch. The least she can do is answer the door, Josie thought, even if she's canceling. She probably isn't even on the phone. She probably took it off the hook and is passed out upstairs with all the curtains drawn.

Josie rang the bell. In the glass next to the door she saw Pudding scamper down the stairs. The dog ran over and scratched at the glass, black eyes opened wide. Valerie probably forgot to walk her. Poor thing needed to go. That was Valerie these days, head in the clouds. Maybe she was having an affair. I'm probably the only one who hasn't had an affair, Josie thought. I wouldn't even know how to go about it.

She gave the bell one more ring. The dog whined pathetically, but Valerie, wherever she was, wasn't moving. So much for tennis doubles.

Josie sighed and slung her racquet over her shoulder. As she turned away, Pudding jumped her paws high up on the glass. Please don't leave me, she seemed to be saying. Poor thing.

Josie walked back to her house and grabbed her sports bag. It was too late to call Meredith, who was bringing her friend visiting from West Berlin. They would just have to rotate singles and complain about how Valerie managed to stay so thin even though she never played anymore. She never swam either. She would just sit by the pool in a lounge chair wearing sunglasses and smoking cigarettes, book opened to the same page all afternoon.

"You know," Meredith said, "she has some problems."

Meredith could play tennis and carry on a bilingual conversation at the same time. Josie had rotated out and Meredith played her friend, who Josie now remembered was Swiss because she and Meredith would give the score in French.

"Like what?" Josie asked from the sidelines.

"You know, nervous problems, she sees that shrink."

Meredith said it the way one might mention how an acquaintance recently had their appendix out. Or maybe a little more than that. Maybe more like someone used to be an alcoholic and that's why they ordered club soda all the time.

Meredith was currently sleeping with a married man, someone in the State Department. It was her vicarious revenge against her husband who left her after having an affair with a Congressional page, a girl still in her teens. Meredith thought the State Department was glamorous. International intrigue. Meredith used to say she would never date a lobbyist or an activist. They would always leave you for someone who believed in them more.

Josie couldn't manage to respond with anything more than, "Oh." She wanted to change the subject, but she couldn't think of anything to ask Meredith's friend and she felt left out because she didn't speak French. She twiddled with the pom-poms on her socks, something she kept telling Gretchen not to do. She was always pulling pom-pom socks out of the dryer with the furry white balls hanging on by a single thread.

"And she had that nervous breakdown a couple years ago. That time Carl told everyone she was in Europe for two months."

People often said "nervous breakdown" as if it were something that happened to everyone sooner or later, the same as a really bad flu or strep throat. Josie wondered if it was more like chicken pox, if you felt safer after you've already had it.

Josie lost her singles game.

Valerie's car was still sitting there when Josie got home. Meredith pulled up at the same time. Josie motioned to Valerie's car. Meredith shrugged.

Josie walked into her kitchen and tossed her tennis things on the table. She dialed Valerie's number one more time, but she knew it would still be busy even before she heard the signal.

Gretchen wandered in, home from school, without saying a word and barely acknowledging Josie's existence. She opened the refrigerator and emerged with a can of Fresca.

"Hey," Josie said, pretending she was her daughter's best friend, "did you see Kirin in school today?"

"I don't know."

Typical, Josie thought. This was all she could get out of Gretchen these days.

"So, you didn't see her?"

"It's not like she's in my class."

True, Josie thought. Maybe I should just let it go. She stared out her window where she could see the back of Valerie's car through the hedges. Maybe I'm making a big deal out of nothing.

The problem was, Josie couldn't stand loose ends. She hated busy signals. She was the kind of person who would keep calling over and over again, but never had the nerve to ask the operator to make an emergency breakthrough. And now she couldn't call again with Gretchen standing right there.

Josie walked outside; she'd give the door another try. Valerie can't sleep forever. And that bell was loud. A good old-fashioned ding-dong.

She rang the bell. Pudding scampered down the stairs, this time faster. She pawed at the glass and her mouth opened as if she were trying to relearn how to bark. When Josie leaned over to ring the bell again, the dog jumped. Please don't go, please don't go, she seemed to be saying. Poor thing. She probably hasn't been out all day.

"She's sick."

Josie spun around. It was one of the carpool boys from the swim team. He peeled a layer of fruit-flavored skin from its plastic wrapper and attacked it with his tongue. His skinny ten-year-old eating habits intimidated Josie. She looked down at her white tennis shoes and by the time she mustered up the first syllable of a response, the boy had walked away.

The dog was still at the door. Josie noticed something on her paw. It looked like blood. The poor thing was hurt.

Josie walked back to her house. Gretchen's ear was glued to the kitchen phone.

"Gretchen?" Josie tried to get her attention, but Gretchen wasn't giving it.

"Gretchen!" Josie resorted to the stern maternal voice that made being thirty-eight years old seem quite severe.

"What? I'm on the phone!"

"Was Kirin at swim practice this morning?"

"I don't know."

"Was she or wasn't she? I'm only asking you to remember something from this morning."

"I don't remember. It was early."

"Did Valerie drive you?"

"Yeah."

"Was Kirin with her?"

Gretchen scowled. She was beaten. A rare victory for Josie.

"No. Valerie said she was sick."

Something could be wrong. Something could be terribly wrong. At the very least, Valerie could be with Kirin at the doctor's and the dog could have gotten in some kind of trouble. Josie was sincerely worried, but she also secretly cherished the excitement. This was as close to adventure as Josie got. After all, she wasn't having sex with men in the State Department or members of the foreign press. She didn't do cocaine and she wasn't campaigning for the ERA or No Nukes. She wasn't a liberal or a radical or a Reaganite. She was normal. And because she was normal, her days were monotonized into everyday disappointments. She got used to them and stopped feeling like her life was slipping away into boredom. She stopped questioning things about the house, her daughter, giving up her career, or restaining the back deck. If this dog was the one iota of adventure Josie was going to get, she was taking it.

Josie walked out of her house, pom-poms still perky, and hiked across the kelly-green front lawns down to Meredith's house. Meredith had a key, Josie remembered her saying once off-handedly. She must have had it since the first nervous breakdown.

Valerie knew she was dying. It was just taking so long, much longer than she imagined. She kept falling asleep, each time hoping she would never wake up. She couldn't feel her arm anymore. It had stopped hurting. Maybe this was how death was, she thought. Maybe one part of your body dies off first and you slowly drop away, piece by piece. As she drifted in and out of consciousness, she awakened with another part of her body gone. The angels were slowly erasing her with giant black crayons. They had such tiny hands. It would take them a while. But they were helping her.

From somewhere else, a doorbell rang.

Valerie instinctively sat up, like a robot whose job it was to answer the door. Her head filled with a thousand little lights and she wavered back and forth before falling down to the bed again. It all rushed back to her. Stupid, stupid, don't get the door. Don't let them know you're here. Don't let them get to you before you're gone.

She heard footsteps and what was left of her body stiffened on the bed. Please don't find me. Please don't find me. Not yet.

The footsteps stopped at her bedroom doorway. She tried not to move. The footsteps weren't walking away. Valerie rolled her eyes to the far corners of their sockets to see who it was. Her neck hurt too much to turn her head.

It was the dog. She was staring up at Valerie, unable to cross the imaginary line into the bedroom. She had been trained that way. Carl didn't want dog hair getting all over their clothes. He had wanted the line to be drawn at the bottom of the stairs, that way the dog wouldn't come upstairs at all. But Valerie had thought that was unfair to Kirin, so the only off-limits room was their bedroom. It had been harder to train her that way.

Pudding stood at the bedroom entrance. Concerned. Worried. She needed to go out. Valerie should have left some newspapers out downstairs, but she didn't think of it.

The doorbell rang again and Pudding hopped away. It rang one more time, and then the noise, finally, ceased.

Pudding came back and stood in the doorway. Whine whine whine. Valerie could hear her wander down the hall and back again. Whine whine whine, some more. Just leave me in peace, dog. Just let me go.

Valerie careened her eyes around again, just to make sure the dog was alone, that she hadn't brought anyone with her. As soon as Valerie met the dog's eyes, Pudding started to whine again. With her one good hand Valerie covered her face. I'm hanging on too much, she thought, I'm looking too much. It's not helping. She had an urge to check the clock, but she thought, no. Don't do it. You'll be like the dog. Painfully aware of minutes not ticking away, time not passing. Who knows how long it might take? She'd heard of people lost in the woods going days without food and water before dying of exposure. She only had until her husband got home. Probably nine o'clock. Maybe ten. There was a meeting tonight. Or a dinner. There was something.

She needed to stop thinking. Thinking was keeping her tied to the Earth. It was causing her to reemerge after the angels had taken such care to erase her.

Her hand slid off of her eyes and rested just under her nose. She thought that without her thumb, her four fingers looked like the feathers of a tiny wing.

An angel took a break from her coloring and wiped her brow.

"How much longer?" Valerie asked.

I don't know, the angel said back. It's hard to tell sometimes.

We're here for you, the other one said. We're doing our best.

"I know. I know you are," Valerie said. "I'm just worried. Maybe I should get up. Maybe Kirin is still here too."

No, don't do that. That's not a good idea.

"Why not?"

Don't worry. She's gone. She's waiting for you. It was fast. In her sleep. The best way.

Valerie felt herself start to cry.

"What if," she said, feeling her face quiver, "what if I don't make it?"

The angels stopped moving their crayons and arrived at a perfect stillness. Then they moved only their eyes and looked at Valerie. They were at a loss for words. They moved close, very close to her face, and peered into her. Valerie thought they might help by smothering her with their wings, but they retreated back to her limbs and looked intently at each other. After a moment, they picked up their crayons and started coloring again, but their hearts weren't into it. They looked as if they were doing it just for show. Just to make her happy.

"If she's gone, could I see her like you?"

The angels squinted at her quizzically. They didn't understand what she meant. She meant that if Kirin were gone, could she see her here, like them. As an angel.

The angels smiled to themselves like she was a child asking an amusingly naïve question. It doesn't work that way, they said.

Valerie was starting to think that maybe they weren't her friends after all. They were turning into nasty little girls. Like the ones Kirin would insist on inviting to her slumber parties. Perhaps they weren't angels after all. They could be spies. Like narcs. Recruited to spy on her because she believed in angels and they looked like angels.

"Prove it," Valerie spat out, surprised at the forcefulness of her lips.

Prove what?

"Prove that you are who you say you are."

Who did we say we were?

They were already giving her the runaround. Valerie was starting to lose it. Maybe they weren't erasing her. Maybe they were sucking everything out of her brain with tiny instruments that looked like crayons. Maybe they were implanting electrodes under her skin. Maybe they made her misfire on purpose. Maybe they will replace her arm with a bionic one that they can control and they'll make her go around killing people. And then, when she is all used up, and they have no more use for her, they will dump her somewhere. A labor camp. Siberia. Some place like that.

She wasn't asking for much. Just a little reassurance.

But the angels weren't talking.

"Who are you?" Valerie whispered.

They didn't hear her. Or they pretended not to.

"Who are you?" she said louder.

Quiet! one of them said, and they started coloring faster, pressing hard into her skin with their waxy crayons.

The doorbell rang again.

Valerie made a noise in her throat. The angels gave her a look. Shut up, they were saying. It's too late now. What are you going to do now? You fucked up. You fucked everything up. Firing with your toe? Who does that? That was a stupid idea.

"You wouldn't help me!"

The doorbell rang again.

Keep it down!

We couldn't help you. We couldn't go in there. You had to. We helped you with everything else. We helped you plan everything. We gave you the idea. We told you today was a good day. We offered you moral support. We were good friends. You only had to do that one little thing by yourself. That one little thing. Everyone has a role in the plan and that was yours. And you fucked it up! Now here we are and we have to clean up this mess. You'll be lucky if you get out of this dead.

Valerie was mad. She felt like calling out to the person at the door, just to spite the little angels.

We know what you're thinking, they said. Don't even try it.

Valerie looked back at them. She hated them. She wanted them to stop. She wanted to die on her own. She wanted, at least, to accomplish something on her own in what was left of her life.

The angels shook their heads. You are no longer in charge, they said.

Valerie started to cry.

Not again, the angels said. Don't be such a baby.

I hate you I hate you I hate you I hate you!

You're so spoiled, one of them said. You think you get everything you want. This is business. It isn't about you.

Valerie felt like she had heard this all before.

If I am going to have to wait, Valerie thought, I want to be alone.

Oh, the angels said, is that it? They dropped their crayons, which disappeared into the puddle of blood.

Should we go away now?

"Yes, go away."

No last requests?

"Just go! Go away! Get out!"

They didn't say anything more. They simply stood up, brushed off their hands, and melted into vapor. And they were gone. They were still watching, but Valerie couldn't see them anymore. She used to think she needed them, but now she realized that she didn't want them around. And she didn't want them where she was going. She would make new friends. She didn't need a beach house full of ghosts.

Her body felt heavy. It'll be soon. The angels were making her hang on. It couldn't take that long to bleed to death. And she was really bleeding. On television it only seemed to take a few minutes, which meant in reality it probably took an hour. She had been here for at least an hour. Valerie glanced over at the clock.

3:59.

The number didn't make sense to her. She didn't recognize it. 3:59. Almost four. Afternoon. She had to put it together. She had to focus in order to think it through. Bed. Nightgown. Morning. Carpool. Pool. 7:11.

She had been lying here all day, still alive. Maybe it took all day. If that were the case, she was more than halfway through. Almost four. She had another five hours. She could surely die by then.

Meredith's flimsy screen door was the only barrier preventing the outside world from entering her house. Josie didn't think it was very safe to leave the front door wide open, but Meredith had a thing for fresh air. Josie once asked her what she would do if some crazy person walked in. "I could handle him," Meredith said.

Josie was uncomfortable with casually sauntering in, so she stood on the porch with her face as close as possible to the wire mesh without touching it. She could see Meredith in the back, talking on the phone. Meredith spotted her and waved her inside.

Meredith was walking around her kitchen with her extra-long phone cord winding through her elbow and a beer in one hand. Meredith liked to drink. She offered Josie a beer, but Josie shook her head. Meredith's kitchen was newly redone with the stove embedded in a sleek island countertop surrounded by Danish designer barstools. The barstools were made from the same blonde wood as her customized cabinets. The renovation was part of her divorce settlement. "You should get a divorce too," Meredith told Josie. "It's fantastic!"

Josie had a difficult time controlling her excitement, which was slowly disintegrating into anxiety, but she waited patiently for Meredith to finish her phone conversation and didn't attempt to interrupt. She knew Meredith was talking to another one of her European friends because her usual American "I know" was punctuated by a German "*Schiesse!*" Meredith pulled out a barstool for Josie. Josie stared at the modern Scandinavian chair. She knew all would be lost if she allowed herself to sit down.

"Mom," came a voice, along with a screen door slam. It was Meredith's son from her first marriage. The kitchen settlement was from the second divorce.

He walked into the kitchen, a basketball balanced on one hip. Meredith didn't miss a beat of her phone conversation. Her son raised his arms and acted like he was going to bash her head with the basketball, then pulled back with a laugh and said, "Psych!"

Meredith tried to wave him away. He took Meredith's beer, drank the rest of it down, and handed it back to her empty. Meredith made a face as he walked out of the room, dribbling the ball against the tiled floor. Josie didn't think it was such a great idea letting underage kids drink alcohol. She brought it up once and Meredith said something like, better here where I can keep an eye on him. Also, Meredith said, he could drink legally in less than a year when he turned eighteen, and when they were in France last summer he drank all the time and it was fine.

Meredith finally hung up the phone with an overacted, exasperated sigh. She opened the refrigerator and pulled out a replacement beer.

"Where were we?" she asked, as if she and Josie had been in the middle of a deep, important talk.

"Do you still have the key to Valerie's?" Josie asked, trying to keep the tone casual.

"I think so. Why? You're worried because she missed tennis?"

"No, it's just . . . well, it's that and her phone's been busy all afternoon and Gretchen says Kirin wasn't in school today."

"Maybe the phone's off the hook and she took Kirin to the doctor."

"Right," Josie said, trying not to let Meredith spoil her fun.

Meredith took a glamorous swig of her beer and shrugged her shoulders as if to say, okay? Problem solved.

"Right," Josie repeated. If she repeated it enough, perhaps she would believe it. "I just rang her bell, and she's still not there."

"I hope it's nothing serious." Meredith had already bought her own story and moved on.

"The dog came to the door both times. I don't think she's been out all day."

"Did you try the back door?"

"No."

"Try the back door. She's probably sitting there in the backyard and didn't hear you. That's where she is whenever I can't find her."

Josie said, "Okay," and turned toward the front door.

"Go around back," Meredith said, indicating the kitchen door. Josie had already retraced one step and now stood half-turned with one foot awkwardly on tiptoe. She hung there for a moment, on the rubber edges of her tennis shoes, between the two entranceways of Meredith's house, before reluctantly doing as she was told.

Josie swung out around the fence that divided the backyards and entered Valerie's property from the alley. Valerie wasn't in the backyard and there wasn't any evidence, such as an ashtray or a half-drunk can of Tab, to indicate she'd recently been there. It looked as though no one had been in the yard for a long time, and to Josie, who tried not to believe in such things, it felt haunted.

She walked up the wooden steps to the deck, pulled the screen door open, and tried the back door. Locked. She gave it a couple jiggles just to make sure. She heard the dog patter through the kitchen and put her paws up on the other side of the Venetian blinds that covered the kitchen door. Josie couldn't see inside and she was slightly spooked by the undulating blinds, though she was certain it was the dog.

Josie stepped back and released the screen door. The braking mechanism kept it from slamming shut by releasing a bit of air. It flew halfway closed and then, as if in slow motion, exhaled until it obediently clicked into place.

Josie tried to peek inside, but all the curtains and blinds were tightly drawn. Valerie used to open them during the day until she found out the family across the street worked for the FBI. Or the CIA. Josie couldn't remember which. Valerie had made such a big deal about it. Josie thought her reaction rather odd since they lived in DC, everyone worked for the government, and they could easily get classified information from Meredith, although Meredith's information usually had to do with which junior senator from the Sunbelt was sleeping with his aide and which one was secretly gay. Not exactly state secrets, but not the type of thing people wanted getting around. Meredith had told Josie a high-level person in the vice president's office had his mistress evicted and sent back to Delaware or Kentucky or wherever because she started blabbing.

The only window without curtains was high up over the sink and Josie was too short to see inside. She dragged over a large potted plant, shoved it against the side of the house, and carefully stepped onto the terra-cotta rim, digging her toes into the dirt. The pom-poms on her heels lifted toward the sun as she peered into the kitchen.

The dog was still at the back door, but when Josie put her hand on the sill, Pudding twitched her head and looked at the window. She padded over to the sink, but didn't know how to get to Josie from six feet below. That's when Josie noticed the floor. The dog had walked over and left dark paw prints across the linoleum.

Josie felt her eyebrows squeeze together and stick there. A prickling sensation crept down her legs. Her eyes darted around the rest of the kitchen, but unlike the jittery queasiness unfurling in her body, it seemed strangely serene. A model kitchen. Clean and undirtied, except for the dog stamping a new pattern onto the floor.

Josie looked back at the dog. Pudding opened her mouth to catch an invisible scrap of food.

Something in Josie wanted to run back to Meredith's. She tried to talk some sense into herself. Meredith would think she was making a big deal about nothing. Gretchen always said that too. "You're such a worrywart, Mom." Josie didn't know what to do in this situation. It was the same feeling she had at her husband's office Christmas party when she saw him put his hand on the bare, spaghetti-strapped shoulder of a young secretary. She didn't know how to interpret it. That night she had gone home and written down a list of all the possible things it could have been. He could have been helping her put on a sweater, or politely brushing off a piece of fuzz, or a fly, she could've been falling backward from too much wine and he had steadied her, or it could've been consoling, she could've been telling him about problems at home.

It was Valerie who sat with Josie as she read the list. But Valerie wasn't listening. She had spaced out and when Josie playfully said, "Earth to Val," it took a few seconds before Valerie rematerialized, and when she did, she didn't have any advice.

"Valerie?"

Pudding turned around and looked up at her.

"Val?"

No response.

Josie tried to lift the little window. She dug her toes deeper into the soil and awkwardly transferred a little more strength into her arms. The window refused to budge. Why am I doing this? she thought. Meredith has a key.

She stepped out of the flowerpot, accidentally tipping it over and spilling black dirt onto the deck. She stood the pot back up and instinctively swept the loose soil together, scooped it up with her hands, and deposited it back into the pot. She started to brush the remaining dirt off the deck with her foot when she wondered what invisible force possessed her to clean. She left the half-swept deck and walked back around into Meredith's yard.

Meredith was on the phone again, switching effortlessly between English and French and peppering the talk with several accentuated mm's when Josie reappeared in her kitchen. Meredith frowned at Josie's formerly pristine white tennis shoes, now covered in dirt and tracking across her Florentine tile.

Josie had to get Meredith off the phone, but she didn't know how to politely interrupt. Meredith was busying herself throwing dinner together, opening and closing the refrigerator, walking to the limits of her long stretchy phone cord. Josie's throat was dry and she felt that if she did speak, her voice would sound embarrassingly laryngitic. She walked over to Meredith and tugged on her sleeve. It felt like a childish thing to do, but Josie was scared and she didn't want her voice to betray her. It was the same reason she didn't go into her own backyard alone at night. Josie was getting that same tightness in her throat that unveiled itself whenever she was unable to keep her fear in check, when she was forced to admit that she was afraid of the dark, and that she was terrified of being alone.

Meredith, annoyed, silently mouthed, "What?"

Josie licked her lips but nothing came out.

Meredith rolled her eyes and made an excuse to get off the phone in overly annunciated English. Then she said, "What?" aloud.

"I think we should go check. With the key."

Meredith put a spaghetti pot under the faucet and flipped on the tap. "Why?" she asked over the running water.

"I looked in the back, and the dog . . . there was some blood, and there were foot prints all over the floor."

"How do you know it was blood?"

"I just think we should go check."

Josie didn't see why Meredith was making this so difficult. Meredith gave another glamorous sigh, picked up her phone, and started dialing. Josie couldn't believe she was going back to her bilingual conversation without missing a beat.

"Maybe you could just give me the key," Josie suggested.

"Let me try calling her first."

It would be Josie's luck for Meredith to get through and have it all be a big misunderstanding.

"Busy," Meredith said and hung up. She stayed there for a moment, standing by the phone, her arms folded across her chest. Josie didn't know why, out of all of their friends, Meredith had this big-sister authority. Josie only wanted the key. She would leave Meredith out of it. This was her thing. A part of her didn't want Meredith involved.

"I would really like to go and check. Then if it's nothing, we can all have a beer and laugh about it. You can make fun of me, and laugh about how uptight I am."

Meredith opened her odds-and-ends drawer and pulled out an old Tupperware container full of keys. She dumped them on the counter and spread them out into a single layer. Valerie's had the yellow tag with a V scratched into it by a ballpoint pen.

"Okay, let's go check. You're giving me a panic attack."

Meredith was holding the key. They walked out the front door.

Meredith immediately turned around.

"Her car's still here?!" she said angrily.

"Yes—"

"You didn't tell me her car was here the whole time!"

"Yes, I did—"

"No, if you had told me that, we wouldn't have had this whole back-and-forth conversation."

Josie now couldn't remember if she had told Meredith about the car or not. She couldn't remember if she had noticed it herself.

"You know what she told me last week?"

"What?"

"She said she was thinking about killing herself."

Meredith was stealing Josie's adventure. It was turning into a Meredith show and somehow Josie's timidity was going to be blamed if anything went wrong.

"Yeah," Meredith said, tossing her hair off her shoulders as they crossed the front lawn. "She joked about almost driving her car off a bridge and said something like, 'It's good weather today for a suicide.'"

Josie had to shut up now. Once Meredith took over, she had to go along with it.

They stood at Valerie's front door and Meredith wiggled the key into the lock. Pudding was there to meet them. She put her paws on Meredith's thighs and left little red flecks on her suntanned skin.

"You see," Josie said.

"Hey, hey, are you bleeding? Are you bleeding, old girl? Huh?" Meredith rubbed the dog behind her ears. Pudding slid down Meredith's legs and stood by the staircase next to an empty pair of Dr. Scholl's sandals.

"Why don't you let her out back?" Meredith said.

No way, Josie thought, I'm not getting relegated to dog duty.

The dog anxiously hopped onto the first step of the carpeted staircase.

"Val?" Josie called out.

"Look," Meredith said pointing to the floor, "is this what you were talking about?"

There were paw prints leading from the stairs around to the back of the house. Josie and Meredith followed the tracks to Valerie's otherwise sparkling-clean kitchen.

"Here ya go," Meredith said, opening the back door to coax Pudding out, "go on."

The dog wasn't moving.

"Go on, now. Outside." Meredith held the screen door open for her.

The dog turned to Josie for support.

Meredith let the screen door close. For some reason, the breaking mechanism didn't catch, and the door unexpectedly banged shut.

"Valerie?" Josie called out again.

"We're in the damn house. We can go check. We don't have to yell." Meredith acted as though Josie were several levels of sophistication beneath her.

Josie walked out of the room. Fuck her, she thought, and she didn't think that very often.

Pudding scampered ahead of Josie and again hopped onto the first step. Come this way, she seemed to be saying.

"I'm going upstairs," Josie called out. She raised one foot and the dog moved with her, keeping an eye on her, hopping up one step at a time.

When Josie reached the landing and turned to face the upstairs hallway, the lips of her mouth parted and an invisible vacuum sucked the air out of her lungs. There was a long smear along the wall, like a modern art painting she didn't quite understand. It was a red, drippy brush stroke and it looked like blood. Josie wasn't sure what propelled her body the rest of the way up the stairs. Her bare knees lifted as if she were a marionette doll with strings attached to her joints. She walked strangely, straight up and down, not using her usual side-side gait. The dog was waiting for her at the top of the stairs. When Josie made it all the way up, she could see that the brush stroke led down the hall to the master bedroom. The dog scurried to the doorway of the room, but she wouldn't go in. Josie followed her down the hall, along the painted trail, a sleepwalker only half-aware that she was moving through space. At the end, in the doorjamb, was a handprint. An ancient marking. Beware.

Josie looked down at the dog before setting foot in the room. Pudding's black eyes seemed more watery than usual and cloudy drips leaked onto her butterscotch face. Josie stood there for a moment as if she too were obeying the imaginary force field that prevented the dog from entering the room.

Then she walked in.

Valerie was there. Lying on the bed. On a bed stained with blood. A lot of blood.

Josie's eyes widened so much that her tightly knit eyebrows finally parted, but her lips refused to separate and she could not speak.

Valerie's eyelids slowly parted.

Josie felt pee running down the insides of her legs.

Josie opened her mouth and desperately gasped for the air that had abandoned her. She made ugly, guttural sounds, her mouth was uncontrollable for several moments, until she finally formed part of a word.

"Meredi—!"

Josie couldn't tell if she was pissing or crying. Everything was wet. She leaned forward and placed her hands on the bloody mattress, and that was wet too.

Valerie was alive. She was a talking piece of flesh from a horror movie. The only thing she said to Josie was, "Go away."

The next thing she knew, Meredith was standing beside her and shoving her out of the way. Josie heard the two of them talking as if they were far, far in the distance, a radio station that was barely coming in.

"Don't tell anyone," Valerie was saying, "just go away and pretend you didn't see anything. It's better. It's better this way. I still have some time. It'll happen. I know it will. I've been waiting all day."

Meredith ran to the bathroom, came back with a towel, and pressed it on Valerie's arm. Josie felt her knees go weak and she plopped onto the floor the way a toddler sits straight down as if pulled by a retracting cord. She put the back of her hand over her eyes and tried to wipe away the image of a decomposing Valerie. Where am I? she thought. This can't be real. This isn't happening. When she opened her eyes she saw a rifle lying in front of her.

"Oh my God! A gun!" It was a stupid thing to say considering the situation, but she wasn't thinking. She kicked it a few inches away and got back on her feet.

"Where's Kirin?" Josie waited a few seconds for an answer. "She wasn't in school."

The muscles around Valerie's mouth twitched.

"Just go," Valerie said. "Go away. It'll be all right. It's getting close. Just forget." She reached over to give Josie a pet.

Meredith noticed the phone on the nightstand with the receiver off the hook. She hung it back up.

"I'm calling you an ambulance."

"No . . . no . . . don't . . . please . . ." Valerie waved her one good hand trying to take it away from Meredith who hung up the phone to calm her down.

Josie backed out of the room. She almost tripped over the dog. She didn't know where she was going.

The dog led her down the hall, back along the trail, to another bedroom and nudged at the door with her snout.

The door opened onto a white carpet mottled with blood. Josie stepped out of the dark hallway and into the brilliant natural light of Kirin's room.

The dog hopped onto the bed and started whining.

Josie looked at the form lying there. More blood. Lots more blood. The form was perfectly still with a giant red bull's-eye on the back. Josie slowly walked around, past a menagerie of stuffed animals piled on a bench, past swim team ribbons pinned to a cork board, past a round globe with bumpy raised mountains and wide blue oceans, to the other side of the bed.

It was Kirin, lying there, still in her cows-jumping-over-the-moon pajamas, lying there, under the covers, being swallowed by blood. Her face was puffy. Her body looked strangely jangled, out of place, limbs blown out of sockets, as though the small girl was simply a bag of bones someone had shaken up and dropped on the bed. Blood was soaked through the front of her pajamas. The little cows had all turned red. They had been slaughtered in their sleep.

Josie reached her wet hand across the gulf that stood between her and the bed. Her fingers shook as they traveled over the sky-blue blanket that lay in a heap on the floor. They danced through the air and landed on Kirin's shoulder.

She was cold.

Josie didn't want to touch the red front of Kirin's pajamas to feel if the girl's heart was still beating. But she had to check. She had to prove that it wasn't real. She let her fingers slide into the crevice of Kirin's neck and felt for a pulse at the jugular. She had learned to do this when she took CPR at the Promenade. She thought it was a good idea at the time. She thought, you never know when you might need it.

Josie didn't feel anything.

Maybe she wasn't doing it right; maybe her hand was shaking too much. She lifted her free hand up to her own neck and felt around for her pulse. She felt it right away, throbbing out of the side of her neck so strongly, she was sure it could be seen from the outside. She moved her finger a little farther under Kirin's jaw line and then removed her hand from her own neck.

The pulse disappeared. She closed her eyes and listened hard. She tried to listen with her fingers. In the blackness behind her eyes, she felt a momentary sense of peace. She thought it was quite possible to fall asleep standing up.

Josie's head tilted toward the floor. In her serene, blissful state, she allowed her eyes to open. When she saw her hand touching the dead child, she opened her mouth and screamed.

Meredith was suddenly in the room. Josie didn't know how she got there. Everything sounded muffled, everything looked hazy. Meredith started screaming. She ran over to the bed and fell onto it with her knees. She waded her way across the bloody sheets and rolled Kirin onto her back. Josie batted Meredith away and straddled Kirin. She placed her hands on the wet spot of her chest and tried to do compressions. She pinched the girl's button nose and puffed air into her mouth. Josie was slowly becoming covered in blood. But she didn't care now. She could have shit smeared on her and she wouldn't care. She had lost control. She didn't know who she was. She certainly wasn't Josie, Meredith's timid tagalong, the bored mother with a decade-old, half-finished master's degree in a useless subject she could scarcely recall. She was now a screaming CPR machine barely capable of counting out ten pumps on the girl's chest.

Meredith pulled Josie off of the girl. Meredith could tell the girl was dead. Josie kicked out at the world as Meredith grabbed her around the waist. Meredith was bigger than she was. Meredith could handle Josie's tantrum.

"What did she do? What did she do? What did—"Josie screamed over and over.

"It was probably an accident," Meredith cooed. "She probably came in here to say good-bye before she killed herself and Kirin got in the way. That's all. She didn't mean it. She didn't mean it to be like this."

Josie jerked herself free from Meredith's grasp and ran back down the hall to Valerie's room.

"WHAT THE FUCK DID YOU DO?" Josie screamed at her.

"Don't be mad. Just go away."

"No! Tell me! What did you do?"

"Don't be mad, Josie. Just go away."

"Are you out of your mind? Did you shoot her on purpose?"

"Just let me die, Josie. Just go away."

Meredith walked back into the room. Valerie craned her eyes to look at her.

"Do you have a cigarette?"

Meredith instinctively pulled one out of her pocket and pressed it in Valerie's good hand. Valerie tried to place it in her mouth but she dropped it and the cigarette rolled between ripples of sheets. Meredith picked it up and stuck it in Valerie's lips. Then she leaned over and lit it for her.

"Thanks," Valerie said with almost a smile.

Josie was sitting on the floor sobbing. She covered her face with her hands and when she lifted her head, her fingers had smeared blood across her cheeks and forehead. Josie was starting to look worse than Valerie.

Valerie lay there with the cigarette pointing out of her mouth parallel to the floor. A mirage of smoke clouded her face.

"YOU KILLED HER ON PURPOSE!" Josie screamed.

Valerie looked at Josie as if she couldn't possibly understand. She looked at her with pity.

"Did you call 911?" Josie asked Meredith. Meredith looked at her confusedly, with her lips pouted like one of her French friends who couldn't come up with the word she wanted to say.

Josie scrambled to her knees and crawled to the nightstand. She stained the receiver with her palm and pointed a long, shaky *E.T.* finger at the touch pad.

"What are you doing, Jo?" Meredith had regained her mastery of the English language, but she looked exhausted. This was enough to wear out even the glamorous, coke-sniffing, ambassador-screwing, diplomat-dinner-party Meredith.

Josie had to catch her breath in order to push a button.

"I'm calling the police."

Meredith reached over and pressed down on the clear plastic nodule that matched the color of her French nail polish.

"Let's think about this. I'm not sure if that's the best idea."

Josie couldn't believe what she was hearing, but something in her instinctively obeyed Meredith. Meredith had the command of a cool teenage baby-sitter who would let you stay up late as long as you didn't tell. Josie thought she was doing the right thing, that for once, being the good girl put her in the lead.

"Let's just wait."

The furrow and lump returned to Josie's face and throat. Wait for what? Valerie obviously needed a doctor. And what were they supposed to do? Bury the girl in the backyard like a dead cat?

"Let's just wait. Give her a little time. See what happens."

Meredith gently pried the phone from Josie's fingers and placed it back on the hook. Josie stared down at her red fingerprints covering the ivory phone. She couldn't look at either of them. She didn't know where she was. She knew she was physically in Valerie's bedroom, in Valerie's house. She had been here before. The three of them would sit on the back porch, sip spiked iced tea, and listen to tales of Meredith's sexploits on the Beltway trail, about how she once took an eighty-dollar taxi back from God knows where in Virginia after a wife walked in on her with her doggy bag from a state dinner. Josie had never cheated on her husband. She never had much to add to the conversation except retelling the same old tales from college. The last time she was in this room was during Valerie's and Carl's Christmas party. She had come up here to use the bathroom and found Valerie sitting on the edge of her bed with an untouched glass of eggnog, staring into the vanity mirror. Josie had stuck her head in the mirror and made a funny face, but Valerie hadn't noticed. She was in another world until Josie spoke her name.

And that's where Josie was now, in another world. A bizarre, twisted, fairytale land. She was a princess condemned to be a slave. She had to work in the evil castle. She had forgotten what her own home was like, what her own family was like, she had forgotten, even, that she had her own thoughts. An evil witch had drugged her and she was obeying. Loving, honoring, and obeying.

But why?

Meredith could read her mind now. That must have been part of the spell. Meredith could be trusted to pull something off. Josie was unfairly maligned as a tattletale, which she wasn't. Her whole life was arranged around being someone she wasn't. Josie never felt the freedom to be who she was. Even Valerie the space cadet had the freedom to lose her mind.

"It's what she wants."

Valerie's eyes peeled open again. She wasn't dead yet. The ash was building on her cigarette. Valerie separated her lips ever so slightly and the cigarette titled out of her mouth and rested on the covers. Josie watched as the waning butt toasted a brown spot on the sheet before extinguishing itself.

Josie had to leave.

She didn't know what possessed her, she just started walking. She kept her eyes on the carpeted floor as she made her way into the hallway and down the stairs, the dog following at her heels. Meredith called after her, but Josie didn't look back. If she looked back, she would lose it again. She would lose all sense of herself. She had to get outside to prove that she still existed, that she too hadn't been obliterated by a shotgun in her sleep.

Meredith followed her halfway down the stairs, calling out, "Josie, wait." Josie flung open the front door and stepped out into the spring sunset. People were coming home from work, parking cars, heading inside. A couple of boys were riding their bikes in circles trying to pop wheelies, which Josie always thought was dangerous. She tried not to look at the boys being boys and all of the other early-evening normalcy, and no one noticed Josie as she trampled off the brick walkway and across the bright green lawn. No one noticed the bloody monster right under their noses, the gory middle-aged girl in blood-drenched tennis clothes and pom-pom socks, with blood staining her white inner thighs as though she had just gotten her period for the first time. No one noticed the war paint smeared on her face. She kept her head down and pointed her invisible antennas forward to guide her home.

Josie clumsily pushed open her front door with both hands, barely noticing the smudges she left behind. She walked into her kitchen observing for the first time how similar the layout was to Valerie's house.

Gretchen was sitting on a stool, talking on the phone, as she flipped through the pages of Josie's *Mademoiselle*. Gretchen didn't really read the magazine, she just liked to flip the pages with a loud snap. She was an odd mix of child and teen, swinging her legs back and forth as she flipped past "Do You Know How to Please Your Man?" questionnaires.

It was in the middle of one of Gretchen's "uh huhs" that Josie entered the kitchen. Gretchen's eyes exploded and she screamed something unintelligible. She dropped the phone and it dangled from the wall mount gently knocking the floor as it bounced up and down on its springy cord. Josie couldn't see her daughter. She didn't quite want to register that she had a daughter. She walked toward the bouncing phone and pulled it up as if she were lifting a dead fish out of the water. She hung up the phone, picked up the receiver again, and this time had control over her alien fingers and was able to punch the three numbers to get the police. She explained in shaky breaths what had happened, and said, "Send an ambulance." She hung up and thought, fuck Valerie. If Josie had to live with life as a punishment, so would she.

Josie looked over at Gretchen who was glued to the opposite wall. Josie opened her arms; she needed a hug. She wasn't the monster here.

Gretchen ran upstairs to her room. Doesn't she realize, Josie thought, that is the worst place to hide.

From very far away, Josie heard the sirens cross the border into the nice neighborhood, turning off the busy Wisconsin Avenue rush-hour traffic and onto the leafy side streets that stretched into Friendship Heights. Josie walked outside and back across the padded grass to Valerie's front porch. She sat down on the concrete steps and waited as the sunset became intensified with swirling red lights. The dog emerged from under a shrub and sat beside her, unable to run away.

YOU'RE INVITED!

WHAT: *Tammy's birthday slumber party!*
WHEN: *Friday, April 9, at 7:00 P.M. (after dinner)*
WHERE: *Tammy's house*
NOTE: *Bring your sleeping bags and overnight gear!*

Tammy didn't want to write "overnight gear" on the invitation—that was her mother's idea. Tammy didn't want to write anything in the note section. She thought "slumber party" made it clear to bring a sleeping bag and pajamas and stuff. But her mother made her write it so people wouldn't think that she was going to provide sleeping bags. She also made Tammy write "after dinner" so people wouldn't be confused. Her mother said they could have cake and snacks, but they couldn't provide dinner for all those people. Tammy had asked if they could order a pizza and her mother said she could have a pizza party or a slumber party, but not both. Tammy opted for a slumber party. Everyone had slumber parties, or sometimes movie parties where they would all go see a movie together, but Tammy knew if she did that, her mother and Nick would make her write "please buy your own ticket," which was embarrassing. Tammy also hated that Nick's birthday was right before hers. The first year he lived with them her mother said, "You two can have a joint birthday and share a cake!" Her mother thought this made them more of a family, more related. Also, Nick's favorite cake was carrot cake, which Tammy did not like. She didn't believe vegetables should be in cake. She hated carrot cake, zucchini cake, and zucchini bread. Everyone was making zucchini bread now and it was gross. Tammy liked yellow cake with white icing and little sugar flowers on top. She just wanted a normal birthday cake.

The day before Tammy's party, her class made plaster masks of their faces in school. One by one the sixth graders went up to Mrs. Perkins and smeared their faces with Vaseline. Then Mrs. Perkins layered on gauze soaked in plaster over their cheeks, foreheads, noses, and lips. They had to keep their mouths shut, breathe through their nostrils, and be very still while it dried, otherwise it would come out cracked.

Someone said that a lady had gotten killed this way. She was letting her plaster mask dry and someone tied her up and stuck cotton balls up her nose so she couldn't breathe. She suffocated to death.

While Tammy's plaster was drying, the only part of her face she could move was her eyes. It was like being underwater. Tammy had a cousin who used to dunk her head in the pool when she visited one summer. He would hold her head underwater and not let her up. When he finally let her come up for air, she would be coughing on chlorine water. Tammy would try and swim away from him, but he would follow her, saying, "Come on, come on, I won't do it again, I promise." Then he would do it again. Every time.

Mrs. Perkins had the kids in an assembly line at the front of the classroom. She would put someone's plaster on and then take someone's plaster off. Everyone who was still drying would shift down the row of chairs. When Mrs. Perkins pulled off Tammy's mask, bits of plaster got stuck in her hair. She was allowed to go to the bathroom to wash it out.

Tammy walked down to the girls' room on the first floor. As she got to the door, she could hear Gretchen and Monique talking inside.

"Are you going to go to her party?"

"I guess."

"She's not allowed to stay up all night."

"They have a computer."

"Yeah, but I bet she's not allowed to use it. Besides, the only game on it is tic-tac-toe. It's pretty boring."

Tammy thought for a second about using the sink in the hall where they washed out paintbrushes, but she decided that was gross. She stood by the door for another second and then walked in.

When they saw her, Gretchen and Monique both smiled and said, "Hi." Tammy could feel Gretchen looking at her as she splashed her face with water and picked the white plaster bits out of her hair.

Gretchen said it was too bad there wouldn't be any boys at Tammy's party. Tammy wondered for a moment if Gretchen had forgotten that she was having a slumber party because boys were never invited to slumber parties. Gretchen said her parents had told her she wasn't allowed to go on dates with boys until she was in high school, which Gretchen thought was way too old. Her parents told her that because Josh and Kenny started stopping over at her house after school. Gretchen said if her mother wasn't home, she'd let them in and they would go down into her basement.

"What would you do?" Tammy asked.

"Suck face," Gretchen said. Now she was looking directly at Tammy with a smirky smile like she knew everything. "You know, French-kiss."

"Both of them?"

"I French-kissed with both of them, but I really only like Josh."

"You like Kenny, don't you?" Monique asked Tammy.

"I guess so."

Monique and Gretchen looked at each other. Tammy couldn't tell if they were giving each other a look or if they were just looking at each other.

Gretchen went on and on about how to French-kiss. She also said that during sex, when a man sticks his penis inside a woman's vagina, he pees a little bit inside, except it's not exactly pee. She also said that once they went over to Heather's house because Heather had developed big boobs already and Kenny and Josh wanted to feel her up.

"And do you know what we found?" Gretchen said with her smirky smile growing bigger.

"What?"

"In her parents' room, in a drawer in the dresser, we found a dildo."

Tammy didn't say anything. Tammy didn't know what a dildo was, but from the way Gretchen said it, Tammy felt that she should.

"You know what a dildo is, right?" Monique asked.

"Yeah," Tammy said, trying to play it cool until she figured it out.

"Heather didn't know what it was," Gretchen went on. "You can tell what it is from the way it looks, but she didn't know exactly what it was or why her mother had one. So Kenny yells out, 'Your mom has a dildo!' and Heather says, 'What's a dildo?' and Kenny goes, 'You use it to practice having sex!'"

There it was and Tammy didn't have to do anything.

"Did you use it?" Tammy asked.

"Eww! Gross!" Monique shrieked.

"No," Gretchen said and she gave Tammy a weird look. "That would be gross."

"I meant Heather," Tammy said, trying to cover her tracks. "What did she do with it?"

"She didn't even touch it. We just put it back in the drawer."

Gretchen was always doing this. She was always digging traps for Tammy to fall into. And Tammy would always fall into them.

That night was Nick's actual birthday. They had London broil for dinner and carrot cake for dessert. Tammy only ate the icing. They had dinner early because her mother and Nick were going out to see a band. Nick got his favorite dinner, a cake, and he got to go out, which was the same as having a party.

Even with their mother and Nick out of the house for the evening, the kids were still forbidden to watch TV in the adults-only living room. They decided it was too risky to do it anyway because one time their mother and Nick came home early and they almost got caught. If their mother and Nick didn't like the band, they would sometimes leave early. So Tammy, Steffi, and Hugh sat in their dingy kids' TV room. It was messy and full of junk: old toys they never played with anymore, old furniture they didn't have a place for, old clothes in garbage bags they were going to give to the Vietnam vets charity.

They were watching *Diff'rent Strokes*, which was okay. Tammy had wanted to watch *Barney Miller*, but Steffi voted against it and she wooed Hugh to vote with her. She was good at doing that. Steffi said she didn't like police shows, even though *Barney Miller* was a comedy. Steffi thought police shows were boring. She got her way and they were watching her show. That's why she made Tammy answer the phone.

In the kitchen, the brick-red phone hung on the wall by the shit-green refrigerator. It had a long cord that always got tangled up. The other phone was in their mother's and Nick's bedroom. This was the only phone the kids were allowed to use.

"Hello?"

"Tammy?"

"Yeah?"

"It's Monique."

"Hi. What's up?"

"Are your parents there?"

"No, they went out."

"Oh."

"What's up?"

"Um, it's about Kirin."

Monique lived down the street from Kirin and Gretchen.

"What about her?"

"Well . . . she's dead."

"Come on!"

"No, she is. She's dead."

Tammy could tell this had Gretchen written all over it. It was some big joke. Monique could always be counted on for a joke.

"Yeah, right."

"No, she is. I'm serious."

Tammy just had to play it cool and prove she wasn't falling for it.

"Oh, come on. Stop joking."

"I'm not joking. I wanted to call you because I know your sister is best friends with her." Someone was talking in the background at her house. "Wait . . . my dad wants to talk to you."

In that instant, when she heard the adult voice of Monique's dad in the distance and the untangling of phone cords several blocks away, the water in Tammy's mouth dried up and her hand holding the red phone went numb. All the blood in her veins and arteries and capillaries drained down toward the floor like pee does when you wet your pants. Monique's dad wouldn't be part of the joke. Monique wasn't joking. She was being serious.

"Wait—what happened? How did she die?"

"I don't know, I don't think I can tell you."

"Tell me."

"I don't know, I don't know if I can, if I'm allowed to say."

"Just tell me."

"Are you sure?"

"Yeah. Tell me."

Tammy could tell Monique was cupping her hand around the mouthpiece so that no one else could hear what she was saying.

"It was her mother," she whispered in a low voice. When Monique whispered she sounded like a woman on a TV commercial selling Chanel Number Five perfume. She always sounded more grown up when she whispered.

Tammy couldn't believe what Monique was saying. What she was saying didn't sound real. Tammy couldn't believe her. She wanted to go back to the joke and say, "Oh, come on! Give me a break!" But she only managed to push out a shaky voice.

"What?"

"It was her mother. Her mother killed her."

"What?"

"Her mother. Her mother killed her. She shot her."

"Why?"

"I don't know. I think it was an accident. Then she tried to shoot herself."

"What?"

"Her mother. First she shot Kirin, then she tried to shoot herself, but she missed. They're taking her to the hospital."

Tammy could hear Monique jangle the phone. Someone had caught her.

"My dad wants to talk to you."

A lump was growing in Tammy's throat, like a piece of hard candy she had accidentally swallowed whole. Monique's dad got on the phone and said something to Tammy, but she couldn't tell what. Monique's dad had come to their school once to talk about careers. He was a professor.

"Tammy?"

"Yeah?"

"Where are your parents? Are they there?"

"No."

"Where are they? Is there a baby-sitter?"

"No."

"You're by yourself?"

"Yeah." It was getting harder and harder to talk. Tammy wanted to get off the phone. She didn't want to be talking to someone else's dad.

"I want you to tell your mother to call me as soon as she gets home. Do you know when they're getting home?"

"Ten thirty or eleven."

"Okay, they can call me whatever time they get home. Doesn't matter how late."

"Okay." The lump in her throat was hurting now. She suddenly had a bad sore throat when even swallowing hurts. Each sound coming out of her mouth ripped off another layer of skin.

"Okay. You can call me back if you need to."

"Okay."

"Okay," he said and hung up the phone.

Tammy put the red phone back on the hook. As soon as it clicked into place, she started screaming.

It wasn't far from the kitchen to the kids' TV room. It was probably less than five steps, but to Tammy, it felt like forever. It felt like she was running through a tunnel in slow motion, or really super fast on fast-forward, but with the tunnel having no end. She could never reach the other side. She kept running and running and the lights and stuff on the walls whizzed by her like laser beams. There is always a part like this in a scary movie when the person knows someone is coming after them. Someone is attacking them from all over and they can't see who it is.

Tammy ran into the kids' TV room like this—screaming and crying and out of control. Like an airplane making a crash landing.

The TV program had changed to *Gimme a Break!*

Tammy was screaming so loudly that Steffi and Hugh jumped out of their seats and onto to the linoleum floor as if the house had suddenly been hit by an earthquake.

Steffi and Hugh started crying. They didn't know what was going on. They were scared because Tammy was screaming and crying so much. They were asking Tammy, "What, what, what is it, tell us?" but she couldn't speak. Tammy couldn't keep her voice from wailing. In between heavy sobs, she managed to push out a question, the last possible possibility that this was some huge joke she had fallen for.

"Was Kirin at school today?" she asked Steffi's pink teary face.

Steffi's saucer eyes searched Tammy's face with an "I don't get it" look.

"No," Steffi said, dragging out the O part so it sounded like a question. This made Tammy cry even more. It was true. It was all true.

Tammy wrapped her arms around her head and hid her face in the crooks of her elbows. She crouched over and rubbed her arms down her body like she was trying to push something off of her. She was like the guy at the end of *Raiders of the Lost Ark* who starts scratching everywhere as though he has a million bugs crawling on him. That's what Tammy felt like. Like there were bugs crawling all over her and she had to get out. She had to get out of her skin. She had to get out of her body. She had to get out of this house. Nothing good had ever happened to her since they moved here. She had thought before that maybe this house was haunted and now she knew it was. She knew there were ghosts all around her and they weren't very nice.

Steffi and Hugh were looking at Tammy like she was crazy. Steffi kept asking, "What's wrong?" but Tammy had already gone. She was still in the kids' TV room on the linoleum floor, which was still sticky from a Kool-Aid spill that happened last week. Steffi and Hugh were there, but Steffi's voice sounded very far away and when Tammy tried to open her eyes, Steffi and Hugh were underwater and Tammy was floating away. She was leaving this world that she always knew was imaginary. She knew these weren't her real parents and this wasn't her real house. When they first moved here she used to think that if she stood in a patch of sunlight on the floor long enough, she would be magically transported back to their old house, Dad would come back and live with them, and everything would be okay again.

Right now it was nighttime. It was dark outside and there were no sun patches.

"Please tell us," Steffi said with a sad and concerned look on her face that under any other circumstances Tammy would have brushed off as phony. But tonight it was real. Tammy knew that she was scaring Steffi and Hugh, and she knew she would have to scare them even more. She would have to tell them.

Tammy looked away from Steffi's pink face with the blue pencil dot still in her cheek. She looked at the sticky cold floor and felt every muscle in her body twist and clench and try to hang on to her bones. She was all alone here. There were no grown-ups. There was no one to come in at the last minute and say, it's okay. It's all right. Mommy's here. There was no one to save her from having to tell Steffi.

Finally Tammy blurted it out.

"She died! She's dead!"

"Who?"

"Kirin! She's dead!"

At the moment when Steffi should have started to cry, she stopped.

"What?"

"Call Monique if you don't believe me! Call Monique's dad!"

Steffi still didn't cry. Or, she didn't cry a mess of snot like Tammy did. Her eyes became watery and little streams of baby-doll tears drizzled down her cheeks.

"But . . . what—?"

"Her mother! Her mother killed her! She shot her with a gun!"

Now Steffi's pink body stiffened. The tears stopped in their slick tracks like tiny, slow-moving slugs.

"Come on!" Tammy said and whipped around, heading back to the kitchen. She picked up the phone and dialed Monique's number. Steffi followed her, not saying anything and not really crying out loud. Hugh followed a few steps behind Steffi.

Tammy got Monique and told her Steffi didn't believe it. Tammy held the phone out to Steffi and the long curly cord bounced between them. Steffi carefully took the phone and sat down on one of the dinner table chairs in a perfect little girl position. She didn't say anything to Monique other than a "yes" or an "okay." She nodded a few times and drizzled more tears. Then without saying good-bye to Monique, she gave the phone back to Tammy.

"Hello?" Tammy said into the phone.

"Yeah, I told her," Monique said.

"Yeah."

"My dad wants to know if your parents are home yet."

"No."

"What?" she said to someone at her house. "I gotta go," she said back to Tammy.

Tammy hung up the phone. Steffi had gone up to her room. Hugh was standing there staring at Tammy like he was waiting for someone to tell him what to do.

"Do I have to go to bed now?" Hugh asked.

"YES!" Tammy yelled. It made Hugh jump back. Tammy didn't want to be mean to him personally, but she was mad and upset and she had to yell at somebody.

Hugh skirted by her, probably afraid that she was going to yell at him again, and ran up the stairs. Tammy sat down on the shit-brown couch in the off-limits living room and didn't follow him.

Tammy decided this was an emergency and she could call her mother and Nick at the number they had left. Her mother and Nick would write the number of where they were going on the dry-marker board next to the refrigerator. Tammy looked over at the board. Nothing was there except for squiggly lines that someone had partially erased. A blue marker was balanced on the edge of the frame like a piece of chalk.

Nothing ever worked when Tammy needed it to.

It didn't matter because Tammy knew the name of the music place. She got the *Washington Post* from the shit-green coffee table, opened up the Style section, and looked at the ads. She saw the name of the music place and called the tiny number that was printed in white against the black background. It was in Alexandria, just across the border in Virginia, and she had to dial a one.

The guy who answered the phone said there weren't assigned seats, people sat wherever they wanted, so he wouldn't know where to look for her mother. He said there were a lot of people and he couldn't go around to all the tables and ask if anyone sitting there was her mother. Tammy tried to describe what she looked like. She said her mother had long brown hair in a ponytail and glasses, and that she was five feet five inches tall. He said it was dark and he couldn't really see anyone from where he was sitting. He said the only thing he could do was make an announcement at intermission. Tammy asked when that would be. He said probably in half an hour.

Tammy hung up. She tried to call Gretchen, but her line was busy.

She went upstairs. She didn't want to be downstairs by herself.

Tammy could hear Steffi crying in her room. Hugh had turned out his light and gone to sleep. Tammy didn't want to go into her room, so she walked down the hall and into her mom and Nick's room. It was usually off-limits, but she figured tonight was an exception.

She tried Gretchen again on the phone in her mother's room, but it was still busy. She decided to call Heather instead. When Heather came to the phone, Tammy told her matter-of-factly what had happened. Tammy wasn't crying anymore. She told Heather like it was no big deal. It was just something that had happened. Kirin's mother had shot her and she was dead. Her mother had also shot herself, but she wasn't dead. She was going to the hospital. Heather seemed shocked but she didn't cry. She reminded Tammy that it was quite possible her mother could die too. Sometimes people got shot and went to the hospital and then they died a couple days later.

Heather asked Tammy if she was sure Kirin was dead or if she was going to the hospital too. Tammy said that, yes, Kirin was definitely dead. That she had died right away. She didn't know this for sure, she just assumed. Heather asked Tammy how many times Kirin was shot. Tammy said, probably five or six if she died right away.

Heather said she would call Monique to see if there was anything new and then she would call back. Tammy said she would try Gretchen again. And then Tammy started to like calling. It was like telling a secret, as if someone had gotten in trouble at school, or someone liked a boy. She liked calling her friends and talking about the fact that Kirin was dead.

A half hour later, she called the music place in Alexandria again and spoke to the same guy. He said he had made an announcement at intermission but no one had responded. He had called out twice over the PA but no one had come up to him. He said maybe her mother had gone to the bathroom during intermission and didn't hear the announcement.

Or maybe she had stepped outside. Or maybe she had left early and would be home soon. Tammy asked him if he could make one more announcement and he said no, he couldn't. He said the band had started playing again and the lights were dark. He couldn't talk on the PA while the band was playing, only in between. Like on the radio, he said. Tammy asked him one more time and she said it was important. He said he couldn't. He could get in trouble. He could lose his job.

Tammy hung up.

She lay down on the double bed. The bedspread was white with a skinny rainbow that arched where your head goes. There were two rainbow stripes on the flat bed part and the pillowcases made the circle part that connected them, except her mother had made the bed wrong and the circle parts didn't match up. They were switched. They looked like pieces of a puzzle that didn't fit, or broken-off bits of donut.

Tammy fell asleep.

She woke up twenty minutes later. Her mother and Nick still weren't home. She wrote them a note.

Dear Mom and Nick,

Kirin is dead. Her mom shot her. Then her mom tried to shoot herself. Her mom is not dead. She went to the hospital. Monique's dad said to call him when you got home. I tried to call you and have someone make an announcement, but you didn't hear it. I went to bed.

♥

Tammy

She wrote it in magic marker and left it under the rainbow.

THE NEXT MORNING Tammy woke up when her mother and Nick walked into her room, through the separator door, and into Steffi's room. They woke Steffi up and told her she didn't have to go to school if she didn't want to, but they thought she should. The weirdest thing was that Nick was crying. He was already dressed in a suit for work. He wasn't crying all the way, but he had a Kleenex folded up into a square and he was dabbing his eyes with it and his mustache was damp and shiny.

Tammy and Steffi got ready for school. Steffi put on jeans and a bright red sweater and brushed her long hair. Tammy said Steffi could borrow her ribbon barrettes if she wanted to. Steffi said okay and Tammy snapped them on for her.

After their mother and Nick left for work, Tammy, Steffi, and Hugh sat on the front porch and waited. This is what they always did. They always waited for Gretchen and Kirin. Tammy had a hard time remembering what had happened yesterday morning. She didn't remember Kirin not being there because Kirin was always there. She sort of remembered Gretchen coming by herself and saying something like Kirin was coming later, or her mother was driving her later, or she was sick. She couldn't remember what it was, but she didn't remember it being anything weird.

The three of them sat there on the porch for almost thirty minutes, until it was ten to nine. It took them that long to figure out Kirin wasn't coming.

"Let's just go," Tammy said.

Steffi and Hugh stood up and followed Tammy. It was the first time since they moved to DC that they walked to school together, just the three of them. When they got to school, the bell was already ringing. The three of them split up and went their separate ways.

In Mrs. Perkins's class, everyone was talking in hushed voices. Everyone knew. Everyone had called everyone last night. Kenny said a news reporter had knocked on his door and asked if he had a picture of Kirin from the school portraits. He said it was going to be on the evening news tonight. Colin said a camera crew had interviewed his parents. Monique said there were lots of cop cars on their block all night. She said she watched the cops from her bedroom window and that Kirin's dad didn't get home until late and he didn't know what was going on. Gretchen came in a few minutes after the bell rang. Her dad had driven her to school.

The class spent the whole morning talking about it. They were supposed to have a vocabulary test, but they didn't have it. The principal came in and talked to them about it too. The kids were given freshly mimeographed memos to take home about a parents' meeting.

During recess they talked about it some more. Someone asked why her mom did it. One of the boys answered, because she was probably psycho. At one point Tammy turned around and looked across the playground. Steffi had turned into a tomato. She was crying out loud and her pink face had turned red and matched her sweater. Tammy left her class group and walked over to her. She put her arm around Steffi and asked if she was okay. Steffi didn't say anything. She just kept crying and shook Tammy's arm off her shoulder. Steffi walked back inside the school. She wasn't supposed to do that during recess. Everyone was supposed to stay outside on the playground. Tammy followed her sister as she walked through the small door that went to the gym. Steffi walked across the wood floor and the big room made her cries echo. She left the gym and walked across the hall to the girls' bathroom. Tammy followed her inside, but Steffi immediately went into a stall and locked the door. Tammy stood by the sinks and waited for her. Steffi stayed in there for the rest of recess.

Tammy hadn't thought about her party all day until Heather asked her about it in the coatroom as they were getting ready to leave. She wanted to know if it was canceled or not. Tammy said she didn't know. Her mother didn't say. Tammy said she would call everybody after school.

That evening, Tammy, Steffi, and their mother watched the five o'clock news. There was a report and they showed Kirin's house with cop cars in front of it. They showed Kirin's mom being lifted out of the house on a stretcher and put in the ambulance. Tammy's mother said she looked different. She didn't look like herself.

Tammy asked her mother if they were still having her birthday party tonight. Her mother blinked a few times and said, "Let me talk about it with Nick."

Tammy pretended to be reading a magazine in the living room while her mother and Nick spoke in the kitchen. They couldn't decide by themselves so they called around to see what the other parents thought was the best thing to do. After a couple of calls, Tammy's mother told her that people seemed to think it was a good idea to have the party tonight as planned. It'll give you kids something to do and take your minds off of it. Plus, it would be good for Steffi. She needs to be around people, her mother said.

Her mother said they could order a pizza for her friends. Tammy thought it was weird that someone had to die in order for her to get a pizza.

Tammy's friends came over, but all they did after the lights were turned out was talk about Kirin and what they saw on the news and how her mother was now in Psychiatrics at the hospital. They wondered if she was going to go to jail or if they would just keep her in the loony bin.

It was 1982. Tammy was now twelve years old. It was like she didn't have a birthday that year.

STALKER

* * *

Jeffrey loved the names of the DC Metro stops: L'Enfant Plaza, Far-ragut North, Smithsonian, Judiciary. They sounded dignified and Eu-ropean. Unlike the names proliferating his parents' suburb: South Shore Square, Elm Tree Court, West End Lane; interchangeable names with no identity, no history. Who makes up those names? Jeffrey wondered. There were definitely guidelines for it somewhere. Pleasantview Drive, Overlook Terrace, Skyline Circle. Names made up to make people feel safe. Sell the prospective home-owning couple the American dream of property values skyrocketing. Buy your small starter house, sell it, buy a bigger house, sell it, buy a golf course. Oak Leaf Avenue, Maple Square, Sycamore Lane. All things nice and green. None of that city grime and crime. You're not bussing our kids! We moved out here to get away from all that. And, of course, the patriotic: Liberty Court, Franklin Place, Washington Way. Doesn't anyone live on a *Street* anymore? That must be someone's job, Jeffrey thought, coming up with names for streets. Probably some civil servant sitting in an energy-efficient, sealed building working for some pseudo-government agency. Was the government in charge of that? Or was it a corporation? Either way, it's the same loser guy sitting in an office with a window he can't open.

Washington was organized. It was elegant. Designed by French archi-tects. A city whose existence was engineered to be the model home of the brave. Division lines sprung out of the Capitol dome separating quadrants, colors, and parties: Northeast, Northwest, Southeast, Southwest. Jeffrey liked the way streets were listed: "Connecticut Avenue, Northwest." It sounded classy. Better than saying "Northwest Connecticut Avenue." Every state had its own avenue. Even Hawaii.

Washington felt like a foreign country.

Jeffrey watched the Metro lights blink on and off indicating a train was approaching. He felt like he was in the movie *2001*, waiting for his moon shuttle to dock. He loved watching the platform's little circles of light begin to pulse. He stayed in the same station for an hour or more watching trains pull in and out along with the light show. DC was a white-granite Emerald City.

Jeffrey splurged on an upscale hotel. He was feeling footloose and fancy and free. He was feeling groovy. His hotel had a lobby decorated with paintings from history books—the Battle of Gettysburg, Ben Franklin flying a kite, the "Give me liberty, or give me death!" speech, and Aaron Burr shooting Alexander Hamilton in a gentlemanly duel. The paintings reminded Jeffrey of children's Bible illustrations: the kind that had Jesus with long, blown-dry hair looking like he just stepped out of a shampoo commercial. Jesus the Breck girl. Jesus healing the sick. Jesus in Heaven with all the children because he loves them so. The meek shall inherit the Earth. Jeffrey took comfort in that.

Jeffrey ambled through the shiny lobby and dropped off his key with the front desk. The clerk asked if he was interested in a free tour of historic Ford's Theater. There's a group leaving right now with a few extra seats. The bus is right outside.

Jeffrey was the only man on the Stars and Stripes chartered coach with the exception of an older Japanese guy sitting with his wife right behind the driver. The bus stopped at several other hotels to pick up passengers, all women, bored wives whose husbands were in town on business. Who knew what the men were doing? They could be arms negotiators or secret operatives reporting in. Except no one was supposed to know they were secret operatives or reporting in. That's why they pretended to be tourists.

At Ford's Theater they watched a slide show of inky illustrations depicting Lincoln getting shot: Lincoln falling over backward in his rocking chair with his hands fluttering around his heart, big fat Mary Todd jumping out of her seat, and John Wilkes Booth making his

getaway. All because they went to see a stupid play. *Our American Cousin.*
A comedy.

The last slides were photos of Shakespeare productions and Nut-
cracker ballets they had at the theater today. After the lights came up, a
woman raised her hand and asked if the theater was named after President Ford.

A tour guide led them through the theater and up the stairs to Lincoln's presidential box. This is where Booth shot him in the head straight
through his stovepipe hat, stabbed the other guy, jumped down onto the
stage, shouted, "Sic semper tyrannis!" and ran off with a broken leg. One
by one the tourists each got to move to the front of the velvet rope and
get a close-up snapshot of Lincoln's rocking chair. Jeffrey imagined it
must have been annoying having Lincoln there rocking back and forth
making creaking sounds when people were trying to watch a show.

The tour group shuffled back downstairs and across the street to the
old boarding house where Lincoln actually died. Four men carried him
over to this cruddy little room where they tried to lay him on the bed,
but he was so tall he didn't fit. He died an uncomfortable death with
his legs hanging off the bed. Jeffrey thought the tour of this dead president was boring. He would have preferred the Booth tour. Actors know
drama. Shimmy down the curtains and run off with Doctor Mudd to die
in a tobacco barn shootout. Give me liberty, or give me death. You can't
make that kind of shit up.

When the tour bus dropped him back at the hotel, Jeffrey could see
the blonde hair shining through the glass-encased lobby. As he walked
in he became hypnotized to the mane of glistening hair, the waterfall
of shimmering yellow light. The blonde left the desk and drifted to the
elevator. Jeffrey followed her sparkly wake several steps behind. The elevator dinged and opened and the blonde stepped in. When she pressed
her button and turned around to face the lobby, Jeffrey caught her eye
for a split second, the time it takes for a single blink, before the elevator
doors were sealed.

Amber Carrol.

She was staying in his hotel.

It was such dumb luck.

Or, no, no, it wasn't luck. Jeffrey didn't believe in luck. He had never
been lucky. He couldn't believe it was a coincidence. It could only be fate.

He had spent the past week trolling tourist traps looking for where she might be filming her movie, and here she was the whole time. Right here.

Jeffrey finally noticed the world bustling around him. It was as if her glorious crown of blonde hair had lit up the entire building, changed all the light bulbs, and turned up the wattage. The place was full of actors. They were sitting in the bar next to the lobby. They weren't famous actors, but Jeffrey recognized them from TV. They were the kind of actors who were always playing the same parts: "Dottering Professor," "Crooked Cop," "Overweight Office Boss," "Nerd with Glasses." They were all over *Love Boat, Fantasy Island,* or the *TV Movie of the Week.* Another group of men sat around a table drinking beer, guts hanging over their belts, tossing back peanuts, bitching about "crew calls" and "prima donnas."

Jeffrey felt his own light bulb glowing inside his body, transforming him into a human firefly. It was too good to be true. It was too unreal. He had walked through the looking glass and into a movie.

He decided to search the hotel for Amber. He had to be subtle about it. He didn't want her to think he was some crazy person off the street. He started waiting by the elevator on different floors. If someone caught him, he had the excuse of "Oh, pardon me, I forgot to push the button." Then he would get off on another floor and start over.

His second strategy was wandering through the hallways with an ice bucket. That way people would get used to seeing him. If anyone came out of their room before Amber appeared, he had a destination: ice machine, end of the hall.

His third strategy was sorting through change by the soda machine. There was one on every floor right next to the ice. It was innocent enough, counting out exact change. That's what he was doing when one of the beer drinkers from the lobby showed up. A fat guy wearing a tie-dyed Deadhead T-shirt with a multitude of colors spilling out of a grinning skull. His hair was long, wet, and combed back into a skinny, snake-like ponytail. Jeffrey couldn't tell if the ponytail was wet from a shower or just greasy, and he didn't want to get close enough to smell the guy.

"Hey, man, you got a nickel for five pennies?" he asked.

Jeffrey handed it over. He had more than enough change. He often bought several sodas a night and threw them out unopened when he got to the next floor.

"Thanks, man."

The ponytail dropped his coins in the machine and punched the Mountain Dew pad with his fist.

"I tell you, this bitch is going to be the end of me."

He pulled his soda out of the machine, peeled off the metal tab, and dropped it in his can.

"This chick takes two-hour lunches and then complains that we're behind schedule. Can you believe that?" He took a slurp of his soda and licked the fringe of his mustache with his bottom lip. "You can't stop the fucking sun from going down, man."

Jeffrey usually didn't like to look at people when they were talking to him, but he felt comfortable with this guy. He was into himself and didn't expect Jeffrey to give much of a response.

"That's something you learn in life. What goes up, must come down. Know what I mean? Sun goes up," he raised his Mountain Dew over his head, "sun comes down." He lowered the can to his gut. "Any kid can figure that out."

He took a giant slurp from his can.

"Do you know how many films I've made?"

Jeffrey shook his head.

"Thirty. Thirty films. Know how many she's made?"

He didn't wait for Jeffrey to answer.

"One. She's made one. This is her second film. It's like she's a two-year-old. You know? She's a baby and I'm a grown-up. I'm drinking beer; she's still on her mother's tit. That's why she's such a fucking prima donna, man. She's a baby. She's never been down. She's only been up. That's the problem with girls like that. They don't get it. They don't get that one minute you're in the penthouse, next thing you're in the dog-house. Or the cathouse. You know, I made a film once with this actress, same as this chick, you know, cute, young, trying to make a big splash. A couple years later I'm out with some buddies and there she is up on the triple-X screen. And let me tell you, that happens a lot. More than you would like to know."

The guy took another swig from his can. Jeffrey plunked his coins into the machine and pressed the Dr Pepper button with his fingertips.

Try and act casual.

"So she's in the penthouse now?" Jeffrey asked as he took a dainty sip.

"Yeah she's in the penthouse. So's the dipshit leading man. There are only two penthouse suites and they took them. Even the director didn't get one. What a fucking pushover."

He gulped the last of his Mountain Dew and then crushed the can into a disc between his palms as he let out an elongated belch.

"Okay. Gotta call the old lady."

He clamped a hand on Jeffrey's shoulder as he headed back down the hall.

"Thanks, man."

Jeffrey waited until he heard the guy disappear into his room before heading to the elevator. When the doors opened, Jeffrey stepped inside still holding on to his Dr Pepper. He pressed the PH button, but it refused to light up. Jeffrey gave it a couple more pokes, but it didn't seem to be working and he began to feel naked standing in the elevator with the doors wide open. It must be a security thing, Jeffrey thought. They can't have just anyone wandering up there. He pressed the button for his own floor and the doors politely covered him from view.

JEFFREY SAT AT the desk in his hotel room and stared down at the blank stationary. He picked up the pencil, with its clean white eraser, and held it ready over the sheet. She was so close and yet there was an evil force keeping them apart, a devil playing mind games with him by keeping her in a parallel universe, just to torture him. But Jeffrey knew how to win. He had seen it plenty of times. True love wins in the end. Beats out the devil. True love conquers all.

He touched the lead to the page and marked the fresh snow.

Dear Amber,

At first I thought meeting you in Hollywood at the Sunrise was a coincidence. We were two strangers on the edge of the world trying to hold on. But now as I look back, you were able to see the real me even then. I saw your movie and of course I thought you were amazing. Every movement of your eyes conveyed total truth. I've seen that movie so many times now. I feel like I'm right there with you. I feel like I'm inside your skin.

I guess that was the second time I saw you (in the movie, not in person). Then the other day when I saw you standing in the lobby I knew it was no

longer a coincidence. How can two people be at the same hotel again on the
opposite side of the country? Isn't that too much of a chance? There must be
something else at work. A force bringing us together because we were meant
to be together.

I want to push something in you to make you light up. I know you know
the real me and I know the real you. I'm waiting for you, but I can't help
loving you already.

Love,

Jeff

P.S. I miss John too.

Jeffrey folded the letter and slipped it into an envelope. He wrote in his best script across the front: "Miss Amber Carrol." Then he put on his jacket and went downstairs. He hadn't slept all night.

When the elevator opened on the lobby level, Jeffrey was surprised at the amount of hubbub. It was just before five thirty a.m. The complimentary, continental breakfast buffet was being demolished by the beer-drinking guys as they gulped coffee out of Styrofoam cups. Jeffrey was expecting an empty lobby and a half-asleep desk clerk who wouldn't remember his face when he dropped off the letter. Now the joint was full of people.

Jeffrey almost didn't get off the elevator, but when it started to shut, he put his arm out to stop it. He felt clammy from lack of sleep and realized he hadn't eaten dinner last night.

Jeffrey walked up to the front desk and pretended to be looking at the street map under the plastic countertop. The desk clerk asked if he needed help. Jeffrey shook his head and followed a random avenue with his index finger. With his other hand he fingered the letter in his breast pocket and slowly tugged it out, millimeter by millimeter, until the envelope fully emerged and lightly stroked his chin. Without anyone seeing, he let the envelope fall into the message box. It touched down and Jeffrey gave it a little push, sliding it between the other letters and folded messages until it was innocently hidden from view. For good measure, he summoned the desk clerk and asked him the best way to the Library of Congress.

As the clerk was explaining the bus route, the pony-tailed soda guy from the night before came up behind him.

"Hey, man," he said, clamping his meaty hand on Jeffrey's shoulder. "Ready to rock and roll?"

He gave Jeffrey a burly one-armed hug and pulled him toward the door. He turned to another beer drinker and said, "Hey, this is the dude who let me bend his ear last night about the old lady." He laughed and gave Jeffrey a few slaps on the back.

"Hey, oh, wait a minute," the soda guy said. He walked over to the buffet table and picked up two donuts.

"One for the baby," he said biting into the first donut and rubbing his potbelly, "and one for the road." He wrapped his second donut in a napkin.

"Let's rock," he said and busted through the lobby doors.

Jeffrey, unused to being welcomed into the masculine fray, followed suit and picked up a jelly donut with a napkin. He climbed aboard the private bus and sat in his own seat across from the soda guy. Jeffrey could play along, help out even, and get closer to Amber.

The bus lurched through the pre-rush-hour streets and most of the guys dozed off or flipped through clipboards of paper. When they arrived at their "location," everyone stumbled out and began unloading black boxes from the luggage compartment. Jeffrey thought lifting them would be bad for his back. He saw other guys sling thick extension cords over their shoulders, so he opted for that as camouflage. They were on the grassy Mall setting up equipment around a park bench, the Washington Monument shimmering behind them through the early-morning mist. We need to hurry, someone said, if we're going to make magic hour. This was countered with, that all depends if Sleeping Beauty wakes up. Someone yelled back, oh yeah, why don't you go and be her Prince Charming?

Finally he saw her. She was marching across the green being chased by a guy with a clipboard and a walkie-talkie. She turned around and yelled at him, "IF YOU EVER FUCKING DO THAT TO ME AGAIN, I'LL HAVE YOU KILLED! DO YOU HEAR ME!"

The group fell silent.

"Who the fuck does she think she is?" one guy said under his breath.

"Maybe that was a rehearsal," someone else said and a chuckle rippled through the group.

Clipboard guy tried to reason with her.

"FUCK YOU!" she screamed and slammed her trailer door shut.

"Good morning, sunshine," soda guy said.

Jeffrey stared at the metal mobile home, the extension cord still hanging from his shoulder.

"Hey man, I think they probably need that over there." Someone was pointing to the park bench. Jeffrey walked over to the guys threading wires through the slats. It looked as if they were rigging dynamite.

"Thanks, man," a guy said as he lifted the wires off Jeffrey's shoulder.

Jeffrey felt naked without them. It was going to take more effort to blend in. He needed a clipboard, or at least a notebook and pencil.

He wandered through the set and made his way to the outskirts where there were four parked trailers. They were marked on the door: "Hair and Makeup," "CIA Informer," "Ted." The last one was marked by a star with simply the letter A.

Jeffrey stood by her thin door and listened. He heard her sobbing inside. His heart went out to her. How could she possibly act under these circumstances when all these people hated her? They were all jealous. They didn't know her. Jeffrey wanted to knock on the door and go inside to comfort her. He wanted to put his arms around her and stroke her soft head like a tiny kitten. He hesitated because this might be part of her process. Maybe she had to cry in the next scene and she was getting into character. On the other hand, she could be truly upset.

Jeffrey needed to write something. He noticed a pile of equipment cases next to a fire hydrant and slowly walked over. There was a clipboard resting on top of a case and Jeffrey plucked it and pulled the pen out from under its metal clasp. He flipped through the pages looking for a blank sheet. Finding none, he took one of the last pages, thinking they probably weren't that important. He turned it over and wrote a quick note.

Don't cry, my little Amber lamb. I am always here for you. If you need me just open the door and let me in. None of these jerks understand you the way I do.
I love you forever. I will protect you.

—Jeff

Jeffrey folded the note in half. He wrote in large block letters, "TO AMBER," across the front so she would know it was for her.

Jeffrey walked over to her trailer door. He took precautions not to step on any twigs or fallen leaves so he wouldn't make any noise. That was something the American Indians were always careful to do. Two suspended metal steps led up to her starred door. Jeffrey kept his feet on the ground. He tried to slide his note under the door, but a piece of rubber blocked it. Instead, he pushed it between the vent openings in the lower half of the door. He tapped it all the way through to the other side and heard it drift to the floor like a paper airplane. He thought he shouldn't be too obvious; he should try to blend in. He walked away from the trailer, listening carefully in case she called out to him.

When Jeffrey heard the trailer door open, he consciously kept one foot moving in front of the other. He needed an extension cord to swing over his shoulder. He needed something, a walkie-talkie or something. He should have held on to that clipboard, but now it was too far away, all the way back by the hydrant. Although, that could be a good excuse. Walk over there and say he forgot his clipboard.

Jeffrey thought he should go for it. He turned and walked a round-about way back to the hydrant. He could see Amber standing on the metal steps holding the note in her hand pressed against her hip. Jeffrey was giddy—something he had written was touching her body.

He was almost at the fire hydrant equipment pile when someone swept in, picked up the clipboard, tucked it under his arm, and quickly walked away. Jeffrey stopped in his tracks. He had lost his alibi. He had lost his point of destination. He decided to walk to the hydrant anyway. When he arrived, he sat sideways to Amber and stared at the ground. This was his perfected surveillance technique: Let your hair fall in your face and then turn your head ever so slightly toward what you want to see. That way you can peer through your hair and no one will know you are looking at them.

Amber was talking to some guy in a baseball cap. The two of them huddled close together and Amber passed him the note. Baseball cap read it, then scanned the set and waived over a young guy with a walkie-talkie.

"Do we have any new hires or locals working on set today?" Baseball cap acted like he was the guy in charge.

"No, I don't think so. Why? What's up?"

"Some freak's leaving Amber love notes under her door and it's creeping her out."

"Whoa. Can I see?"

Baseball cap passed the note. Amber grabbed it back.

"I don't need everyone knowing about this," she said. "I just want it taken care of. I don't need to be attacked while I'm trying to work."

"Why don't you station someone outside her trailer?"

"You got it, chief."

"You're sure there's no one new on the set. Someone maybe you didn't get the chance to check out?" she asked.

"I really don't think so."

Amber turned away from the lunkheads. She looked right at Jeffrey and Jeffrey peered at her through the strands of hair hanging in his face.

She turned back to walkie-talkie guy and baseball cap. She said something quietly that Jeffrey couldn't quite hear and motioned in his direction with her thumb. Baseball cap looked past Amber's shoulder and spotted Jeffrey. So did walkie-talkie guy. Baseball cap rubbed Amber's arm and he and walkie-talkie guy started walking toward the hydrant.

Jeffrey stayed absolutely still. If worse comes to worse, he could always turn on the fire hydrant and spray them with water to create a diversion. He reached down to the knob and tried to unscrew it, but it was dead shut.

"Hey! Hey you! Can I talk to you for a second?" baseball cap yelled.

Jeffrey stayed still.

"Hey, you on the hydrant!"

Jeffrey remained motionless. He wondered if Amber was watching. Fucking hypocrites. They don't know anything about her.

"Hey, I'm talking to you!"

Jeffrey moved before they got too close to him. They called out again and Jeffrey instinctively began to run. He didn't look back, but he was sure the two guys were chasing him. He ducked between two parked trucks and ran across Independence Avenue. Cars in four different lanes screeched and honked at him and Jeffrey fell down, tearing a hole in his jeans and scraping his lower leg. He made it back to his feet, ran down the escalator steps of the Smithsonian Metro station, and fed his farecard into the gate. As luck had it, a train pulled up right then and Jeffrey got on board and conveniently found a seat. His legs were shaking. He was sweaty and out of breath, but he was laughing on the inside. He wished they had followed him down here so he could wave good-bye to their sorry asses as the train pulled into the underground tube.

*

JEFFREY'S KNEE ACHED as he entered the hotel lobby. He had been walking on his injured leg all day, having ducked into the Museum of American History as a way to kill time and shake the goon squad off his trail. It was only one Metro stop from the movie set; they would never think of looking for him so close by. He had spent a good part of the afternoon watching the museum's giant pendulum swing back and forth and eventually knock over a little peg, thus indicating that the Earth was indeed rotating. Now that the sun was going down, he limped clumsily into his home away from home. The tear in his pants kept brushing against the raw part of his wound, stinging his skin. He wasn't sure if the desk clerk looked at him funny or not. He made a beeline for the elevator.

Once upstairs, Jeffrey staggered down the hall to the ice machine and filled up his wood-patterned plastic bucket. He clutched the fake walnut bucket to his middle and hobbled back to his room. As he fiddled with his keys, he heard someone's door opening. Jeffrey didn't want to see any of the guys from the movie set so he hastily unlocked his door, which caused the ice bucket to tumble out of his arms and crash to the floor, cubes asunder. He grabbed the bucket and shut himself inside.

He looked through the peephole to see who it was. No one. Whoever it was must've walked in the other direction. Jeffrey was worried about the ice cubes littering the carpet outside his door, but he didn't want to poke his head into the hall and risk being seen. He wondered how long the cubes would take to melt. He remembered hearing that a sharp icicle was supposed to be the best murder weapon because the evidence melted away. He forgot where exactly he heard that. Maybe he read it somewhere or saw it on TV.

Still, water stains on the floor might cause attention. He didn't want the janitor knocking on his door.

Jeffrey slowly, carefully, hoping it wouldn't squeak, opened his door. He squatted down and scraped the ice cubes into his room. There were a few he had to crawl out to get, but he was pretty sure he got them all. One ice cube sitting in the hallway wasn't going to send up a red flag. Before he shut the door, he hung the "Do Not Disturb" sign on the doorknob. Then he locked the door and latched the little gold chain in place.

Jeffrey popped a Valium. As the shakiness subsided, he realized he was hungry. He wandered over to the bed and picked up the phone. He deserved room service. He deserved an over-priced cheeseburger deluxe with fries and a piece of apple pie à la mode. A cup of coffee and a Coke.

A bellhop delivered a cart to his door and Jeffrey signed for it, feeling rather grown up that he was signing for things. Jeffrey turned on the TV for comfort as he ate. The six o'clock news. Brezhnev, Beirut, El Salvador, Iran versus Iraq. Same old, same old. And to wrap things up, here's a shot of a flamingo that escaped from a zoo in Florida and went for a walk down Main Street. When he was done eating, Jeffrey peeled himself off the bed to wheel the cart into the hallway. No one told him he was supposed to do that, he figured it out himself.

As he piled his dirty dishes back on the cart he noticed his room service check sticking out from underneath a silver domed lid. He pulled out the piece of paper. His order was handwritten followed by a stamp that said, "charged to room," and at the very bottom of the check, in different handwriting, was:

Thanks! —Bobby.

Bobby.

Bobby was probably the bellboy. He probably wrote that so when you check out you say, "Here's a bob for Bobby." Smart.

BobbyBobbyBobbyBobby.

He had something here.

Jeffrey picked up the phone and dialed the code for the front desk.

"Lobby desk, how may I help you?"

"Hi, this is Bobby with room service. I have a little problem. I was delivering some food and I guess I got the orders mixed up. Could you do me a favor and connect me with Miss Carrol in the penthouse so I can clarify the situation?"

"Sure, Bobby."

It was that easy. It couldn't be that easy.

In the silence during the connection, Jeffrey bit his bottom lip. It felt numb and his teeth slowly slid off, back into his mouth.

There was a click followed by a two-pulse ringing.

"Hello?"

It was her. She was six stories above him. They were connected. Ear to ear. She was probably sitting on the edge of her bed. Her bed was probably in the same position as Jeffrey's. Or she could be lying down. She might have been resting after her long day and simply rolled over onto her stomach to reach for the phone.

Jeffrey held his breath. He wasn't sure for how long.

"Hello??" she asked again.

He wasn't some freak. She had to know that.

"Miss Carrol?" He felt formal calling her that. It seemed stiff and old-fashioned. It was polite, though. The polite thing to do. Girls appreciate good manners. His mother was always saying that.

"Yes?"

"Hi."

There was a pause. She was probably rolling onto her back to make herself more comfortable.

"Who is this?"

"It's . . . we met in California."

"What?"

"At the Sunrise."

"The Sunrise?"

"Yeah. I'm in town. In DC, that is, and I was wondering if you'd like to go out to dinner sometime. Someplace nice, we could talk and . . . talk about your films and pick up where we left off."

"Where we left off?"

"Yeah. Are you free tomorrow by any chance?"

There was another pause and Jeffrey thought he could hear the rustling of sheets.

"I'm really sorry, I didn't quite hear you when you said your name."

"Oh."

"It's just that I meet so many people and I travel a lot and I'm so terrible with names."

"It's Je . . ." Jeffrey stopped himself. He remembered she had misunderstood the note he left under her trailer door. He had signed his name. He didn't want her to hold it against him. He'd rather start fresh.

"Jed?"

"No, it's Jay." He didn't particularly like the name Jay, but he couldn't think of any other J names on the spot. Better to stick with the letter. He could sign everything J. Hackney and she wouldn't know the difference.

She would think it was a silly mistake she'd made on her own and they would joke about it later when they were married.

"Jay, right."

"How's tomorrow?"

"Tomorrow?"

"For dinner."

"Oh, I'm sorry. They have me on this incredibly tight schedule, I really can't. Thanks for the invitation. I actually have to go now."

"What about . . . maybe later in the week?"

"I'm really booked solid the whole time I'm here. It's an exhausting schedule. I'm sorry. Maybe some other time back in California."

"How about . . ."

"Bye," she said in a sleepy, sexy voice and hung up.

He debated calling her right back, but then he thought she probably *was* tired and needed to sleep. She'd been on her feet dodging fake bullets all day.

Jeffrey forced himself to stay up until two a.m. He had concluded that this would be the best time to slip downstairs. The bar closed at midnight and the crew would have to get some sleep before their five a.m. donuts.

He was getting smarter. This time he took the stairs. He didn't want the elevator ding to call attention to himself.

The lobby was quiet. The lights in the bar and dining room were turned off, as were the overhead lights in the couch-lined waiting area. Only a few table lamps were still lit. It felt cozier this way.

If the desk clerk bothered him, Jeffrey's plan was to ask for an extra roll of toilet paper. That wouldn't raise any eyebrows. You need it when you need it.

The desk clerk was asleep with his head propped up against the wall and his mouth hanging open. Jeffrey reached into his pocket and pulled out the letter.

The desk clerk snored and woke himself up. He looked confused for a moment before snapping into action.

"I'm sorry, can I help you?"

"I need an extra roll of toilet paper."

"Oh sure." The guy hopped off his stool and disappeared around the back of the mailbox slots.

When he was gone, Jeffrey placed the letter in the inbox, face down. The guy came back and plunked two rolls on the desk.

"There you go. Sorry about that."

Jeffrey smiled. He headed for the stairs, but thought that might look suspicious and opted for the elevator instead. It was less suspicious to do the normal thing.

"HELLO?" HER VOICE was mushy with sleep.

"Amber?"

"Yeah?"

"Hi. It's me. It's J."

"Jay?"

"From California. We talked for a while yesterday."

"Ohh. Right."

"Were you asleep?" He imagined her lying there with her blonde hair twisting like vines along the pillowcase.

"Um, I don't know. I think so."

"I didn't mean to wake you."

"That's okay."

"I thought if you were up, maybe we could go out for breakfast. Or we could order room service."

"What?"

"I said, or we could order room service."

There was a pause. Jeffrey wondered if she was drifting back to sleep. He half hoped she would and he could stay on the line and sleep with her in his ear.

"Who is this?" she sounded more awake.

"It's me."

"Tell me your name."

"Jeff." It slipped out without him noticing it.

"Jeff?"

Her phone jostled and he heard her take a few steps and shake something in the background.

"Wait, is it Jeff or Jay?"

He wasn't quite sure what to say.

"It's Jeff, but sometimes I go by J. My father's name is Jeff too, so sometimes people call me J. to tell us apart." Good answer, he thought. Good answer. Good answer. Clap clap clap. *Survey says . . . !*

"Are you the guy who's been leaving me notes?"

"What?"

"Because I really don't appreciate it."

"No, I . . ."

"I don't like being followed and I don't like talking to strangers."

"No, I'm not a stranger. We met in California."

"Oh, yeah? Where?"

"At the Sunrise."

"Sunrise? Sunrise what?"

"The Sunrise Motel. Right before your movie came out. You were waiting for a ride."

"I don't know what the fuck you're talking about. I don't know you. I appreciate you being a fan and all, but maybe you want to contact my fan club."

"No, we met. I'm a writer and a songwriter. We both miss John Lennon. I'm working on some stories and songs, I think they'd be great for you."

"That kind of stuff has to go through my manager. I don't deal with people directly."

"I just want to talk to you, take you out. I think you really understand me and what I'm going through, and I think we could help each other. I'm not some crazy . . ."

"Okay, look. Number one, I don't go out with people I don't know. Number two, I would appreciate it if you would stop leaving me messages and stop calling me. If you don't leave me alone, I'm going to have to get the police involved. I don't know you. We never met. You probably have some problems of your own and you read some article about me in a magazine. Then you developed some idea about me, some fantasy in your head, and now you've gone and gotten yourself all worked up. But you don't know me and I don't know you. And I'm going to have to ask you to leave me alone and not talk to me. If I were you, I'd go back to my wife and try to patch things up."

"But, I'm not . . ."

"Look, I'm sorry, but I really mean it. Leave me the fuck alone."

She hung up.

Jeffrey thought about calling her right back. She had him confused with somebody else. She was probably the type of person who is cranky when she first wakes up in the morning. He decided to let her go back to sleep.

Jeffrey must've drifted off himself, because the next thing he knew, someone was knocking on his door.

In his sleepiness, he forgot to check the peephole. He just opened up.

Three men were standing in the hall: the morning desk clerk, one of the movie guys, and a large black man in a red blazer.

"Mr. Hackney?" the desk clerk asked.

"Yes."

"I'm sorry to say we've had complaints about you from some of our other guests."

Jeffrey didn't respond. It was always best to let the other guy go on talking, that way he would eventually reveal more than he wanted to and Jeffrey would be holding all the cards.

"I hate to do this Mr. Hackney, but we're going to have to ask you to leave the hotel."

Jeffrey stood perfectly still and let the guy sweat.

"We have to uphold certain safety measures here, especially for some of our more well-known guests who are entitled to their privacy."

Jeffrey blinked the perfect blink, perfectly expressionless.

"I don't know what your travel plans are, but we've taken the liberty of securing you a reservation at another hotel where we're sure you'll be quite comfortable. But I'm afraid we are going to have to ask you to leave immediately."

Jeffrey looked down at his feet and saw that he was barefoot.

"We have a shuttle service that can take you to the new hotel free of charge. But I do have to ask you to gather up your personal belongings and leave right now."

The guy said all of this with a smile on his face. It never once broke.

Jeffrey turned away from the door without saying anything. He walked over to his suitcase and flicked it open. He walked around the room and nonchalantly threw his things inside. No folding necessary.

The men took a few steps into his room. They probably think I'm going to steal something, Jeffrey thought. I'll probably get blamed for something the maid took. Or Bobby. All those people have keys.

Jeffrey went into the bathroom. He zipped his prescription bottles into his shaving bag and stuffed in a few bars of hotel soap. They would remind him of Amber.

As he was packing, he noticed the pad of hotel stationary sitting on the desk. He had only used a few sheets. He felt awkward about just grabbing it in front of these guys.

"Mind if I take this?" he asked.

"Please do," said the desk clerk. "It's complimentary."

Jeffrey placed it on top of his clothes and clicked the suitcase shut. The black man opened the door and Jeffrey walked out into the hallway followed by the other two. He felt like Jesus being escorted by his three wise men: two white guys and a Moor.

A taxi was waiting for him outside the lobby. Trouble gets you service, he thought.

Jeffrey climbed into the backseat and told the driver to take him to National Airport.

LAND OF THE LOST

* ❖ *

Before Tammy left for school she reminded her mother about the form she had brought home the week before. She was supposed to get a donation from her parents for a special fund that would go toward a memorial for Kirin. They were going to build a bench and plant a tree in front of the school and they needed to collect money for it. Tammy was the only girl in her class who hadn't turned in the form yet.

Tammy's mother set her coffee cup on the kitchen counter. She was dressed in her work outfit of a skirt and blouse.

"I don't think we can give money for that right now." She said that Steffi's class was having a bake sale to raise money and that Tammy and Steffi could make something for that if they wanted. She said they didn't have any money for extras at the moment.

"But it's not an extra," Tammy said. "We're not buying anything extra."

"It's still extra money," her mother said. "And we just bought the computer not too long ago. Then we gave what extra money we had to the Vietnam vets fund."

"Why?" Tammy said.

"Because the vets are building a memorial, and Nick wanted to contribute something to it. It was important to him. It was his birthday, remember?"

"Why can't we do both?"

"Because there's not enough money, Tammy. Why don't you make something for the bake sale?"

Tammy couldn't make something for the bake sale because that was what Steffi's class was doing. Tammy's class was supposed to collect donations. Tammy should've realized this was what her mother would say. Her mother didn't like collecting donations. She never went to PTA meetings. Sometimes she went to parent-teacher conferences, but sometimes she didn't. "You always bring home good grades," she said. "I'm not worried." She and Nick didn't go to the meeting about Kirin either. The night it was happening her mother and Nick sat on the couch watching the news. "I know a lot of people think it's important," her mother said, "but I just don't see how being in a room with a lot of other people talking about it all over again is going to help." Tammy said all her friends' parents were going. Nick said, "If all of your friends were jumping off a cliff, would you jump too?"

A FEW DAYS later, Tammy rode her bike down Bemis Street and turned onto 46th Street. She wanted to ride by Kirin's house. She knew Monique wasn't home because she said she was going shopping with her mother after school. And Gretchen had to go to the orthodontist. Tammy knew the block would be empty, and if Monique or Gretchen and their moms drove up, Tammy could say she was just riding by to see if they were back yet.

In front of Kirin's house Tammy squeezed her brakes to a full stop and kept her hands clasped around her handlebars. She didn't want to look right away. She didn't want to be too obvious. She kept her head down and fiddled with the black tape that was beginning to unwind from her handlebars. The brick walkway to Kirin's house led up to the front door. Tammy stared at the front door and thought about going up to it and ringing the bell and seeing what would happen, seeing if anyone was home. But if anyone was home, she wasn't sure what she would say. The white door stared back at her. It dared her to come toward it. It dared her to set one sneaker toe on the brick path. Tammy's eyes found the tiny white doorbell button surrounded by a ring of gold to the side of the door, but the door was saying, don't even think about it.

Tammy let go of her hand brakes and the metal levers pressed their way back into position beneath Tammy's thumbs. Through the downstairs window Tammy could see that the dining room table was still there. So were the chairs. Tammy could see almost all the way through to the kitchen and she thought she could see the round kitchen table still there too. But that was it. That was all she could see. She would need binoculars to see anything specific.

Tammy didn't know why she came here. She wanted to remember that Kirin was real and that she used to live here. Steffi had pictures and maybe something of Kirin's from school, but Tammy didn't have anything like that.

Tammy pushed her bike forward and walked toward Gretchen's house. A Century 21 For Sale sign was planted in the grass at the border of Kirin and Gretchen's house. Tammy was sure it was for Kirin's house. Gretchen hadn't mentioned anything about moving. Kirin's dad probably didn't want to live there anymore.

A car turned down the street causing Tammy to jump. She gave herself a few scoots to get her bike going and pedaled as fast as she could to the corner. She could've switched gears to make it easier to pedal, but she was too scared. She didn't feel like going home, so she rode to the park where she squeezed her brakes and skidded to a halt next to the swing sets. There were no kids in the park, even though it was a perfectly nice day. There was just one really little kid with his mother on the merry-go-round. That was it. It was like all the kids had disappeared from the neighborhood or moved away.

TAMMY KNEW STEFFI thought about dropping out of the chorus because she and Kirin used to stand next to each other and share a music book. Tammy figured it made Steffi sad to stand there by herself and not share her music book with anyone. Steffi stood all the way over at the end of the second row, the only one without a partner, wearing her Oz bib made out of green construction paper. Her class ended up having to make a second batch of bibs because they got messed up during practice.

Steffi didn't drop out. Probably the music teacher wouldn't let her because it was so close to play night.

The music teacher made the sixth graders rehearse almost every day during what was supposed to be the Language Arts period. Mrs. Perkins would write the schedule of the day on the blackboard. She was always erasing certain sections and writing "play rehearsal" instead. The word "rehearsal" was on the spelling test. The play was taking over the school.

Tammy waited for Hugh after school because it was her day to baby-sit him. Kindergartners were always the last to come out because it took them longer to clean up and get their coats on. By the time Hugh got outside, no one from Tammy's class was still hanging around.

After the crossing guard waved them through the first intersection, Tammy spotted Gretchen and Monique stopped halfway down the next block. When she caught up with them Gretchen was standing behind Monique trying to unzip her backpack, but the zipper was stuck. When Gretchen finally pulled it free she took a book out of her bag and tried to stuff it into Monique's backpack.

"Hurry up!" Monique said. "Someone's going to see it!"

Monique's backpack was packed full of her gymnastic leotards and sections of her big, aluminum foil–covered cardboard Tin Man costume and the book wouldn't go in all the way. Gretchen pushed it a couple more times, then gave up and pulled the book out. "I'll give it to you when we get home," she said.

"What is it?" Tammy asked. It was the first thing she said since she'd caught up with them and it felt dumb to say it. It felt like she had to remind Gretchen and Monique that she was there.

"It's *Forever*," Gretchen said. "You know, the sex book. It's about a girl whose boyfriend names his penis Ralph."

"Shhh! Someone could walk by here!" Monique said.

Forever was the only Judy Blume book Tammy hadn't read. It was hard to get because a preteen girl couldn't exactly ask her parents to buy her the Judy Blume sex book and she couldn't take it out of the library without parental permission.

"How'd you get it?" Tammy asked.

"Heather checked it out of the library for me. They believed her when she said she was fifteen."

Tammy had to admit that Gretchen was pretty smart, but she didn't say anything. She walked the rest of the way home with them, Hugh trailing a few steps behind, until they split up at the corner of 43rd Street.

*

IF YOU HAD a part in the play, you were in charge of making your own costume. Tammy's costume was a black turtleneck and a black skirt she borrowed from her mother. She made a cape out of a big piece of black fabric and cut a head hole in the middle. When she melted, she tucked her head inside the hole, hid under the cape, and disappeared into a black blob.

The only hard thing Tammy had to make was the special golden hat she used to call the winged monkeys. She had to ask her mother for help because she didn't know how to make a hat.

Tammy's mother started looking through boxes in her bedroom closet. Her idea was to decorate a hat they already had. She took down a long flat box with glossy roses painted on it. Everything inside the box was white. Her mother said this was her wedding dress when she married Tammy's dad. She didn't wear it when she married Nick because Tammy remembered she wore a pink sundress when they got married in her aunt's backyard.

Her mother pushed the dress aside and starting unwrapping stuff that was covered in white tissue paper. There was a pair of white shoes, a white purse, and a sprig of fake white flower buds. Then she found a white hat that was attached to a long flowing veil. She turned it over a couple of times, took a pair of little nail scissors, and began to snip off the veil until there was just a hat with a raggedy edge of netting.

She handed Tammy the hat and said, "I think this will work." She rewrapped the shoes and the purse in the crinkled tissue paper and put the box back in the closet.

Tammy wasn't sure what she was supposed to do with the hat, so she stood there waiting for instructions. Her mother shut the closet door, turned around, and squinted at Tammy.

"You can take it," she said.

"It's supposed to be a golden hat."

"You can color it in."

"I don't have to give it back?"

"No. Do what you want."

Tammy felt weird about it. It was as if suddenly a rule had been broken and they were both supposed to pretend the rule never existed.

"Would Dad be mad?" Tammy asked.

Her mother had her back to Tammy when she said that. Her shoulders drooped and Tammy could tell she was getting mad. She was probably going to say, "Enough!" which was what she said when she wanted to yell but didn't have the energy and didn't want to cause a scene. She didn't like Tammy mentioning Dad. She once told her not to talk about him in front of Nick. Tammy asked why and she said because it pushes his buttons.

Tammy didn't understand why it would push his buttons because she and Steffi only saw their dad on school vacations, and not all of them, only when he wasn't out of town. Maybe four or five times a year. But they weren't allowed to open the birthday and Christmas presents he sent in the mail at the same time as the rest of their presents. They had to go up to their rooms and open them in private. Tammy's mother made up this rule. She said otherwise it would hurt Hugh's feelings.

"Just take it, Tammy," she said.

So Tammy just took it. She felt awkward about it, but if her mother told her she could draw on it and glue things to it, then Tammy guessed it was okay and she wasn't pushing anyone's buttons or hurting anyone's feelings.

BEFORE DINNER, TAMMY asked Steffi to rehearse with her so she could practice memorizing her lines. Steffi read the Dorothy parts and Tammy melted on her bedroom floor. Tammy liked yelling the last part about how she couldn't believe a little girl like Dorothy could kill a Wicked Witch like her. And then she died.

Steffi read the whole part lying on her bed with the script pages sticking up out of her stomach. She wasn't really acting.

"I don't think you're doing it right," Steffi said.

"What do you mean?"

"I don't think you should yell this part."

"Why not? I'm mad. I'm supposed to yell."

"Yeah, but you're melting. I don't think melting people can yell."

"Yes they can. They can when they're mad that someone threw water on them and melted them. They're mad because they're dying and they don't want to die."

"I don't think the Witch is that mad. I think she's sad. I think she's trying to decide what to do."

"She can't *do* anything. She's melting."

"But maybe there's a magic spell to stop her from melting and bring her back to life. But she doesn't know what it is. This is her last chance. It's her last chance to be a good witch."

Tammy knew Steffi was wishing there was some kind of magic spell to bring Kirin back to life, but there wasn't. She was really dead. They had gone to her funeral and Tammy had worn her itchy pants suit and Steffi had worn a skirt. Kirin's dad cried the whole time and it was hard to look at him. When Tammy and Steffi left the church, he pulled Steffi toward him in a sideways hug. Then he let her go and walked into the parking lot still crying. Steffi thought she would get to see Kirin lying in a coffin, but there was only a little square box about the size of the jewelry box their mother kept on top of her dresser. Tammy's mother said that meant Kirin had been cremated and now she was just ashes. Tammy and Steffi never saw Kirin again, not even dead.

Tammy wasn't sure what Steffi meant about the Witch trying to be good. Tammy couldn't change the words in the script. Even if the Wicked Witch was going to decide to be a good witch, it's all the same in the end. She has to die and the nice girl has to win.

DINNER WAS SPAGHETTI and Tammy and Steffi and Hugh ate off of plastic TV trays in their kids' TV room. They used to not be allowed to do that, but a couple nights after Kirin died Steffi asked if they could, and since then they always ate in front of the TV.

Tammy didn't notice at first that Steffi had gotten up from her TV chair a while ago and had not come back. The clue that Steffi had been gone longer than a normal bathroom break was the change of the TV program at the half hour. *Bosom Buddies* had ended and *Dallas* was about to start, but Steffi hadn't come back.

Tammy took her ice cream dish to the sink and saw Steffi sitting in the living room on the couch. Tammy's mother was slumped against the cushions with her hand on Steffi's back and Nick was standing with his back to the kitchen leaning with his shoulder against the wall. Steffi was sitting up perfectly straight and answering questions from a man and woman who had dragged over chairs from the dinner table and were scribbling notes onto yellow pads.

The woman was leaning toward Steffi with her elbows on her knees, her hands clasped together, and her thumbs hooked behind her chin. She wore a suit like a man's except with a ruffly blouse underneath the jacket and a skinny ribbon bow tie. She was still dressed in her work clothes even though it was nine p.m. and Tammy's mother and Nick had changed into jeans a long time ago.

"Can you tell us," the woman asked, "what Kirin thought about her mother? What her feelings were when she talked about her?" When the woman spoke, her fingers came apart, but at the end of each sentence she clasped them back together. Steffi sniffed a few times to get a good breath so she could answer the question.

"Sometimes," Steffi whispered, "Kirin said she hated her mother." Steffi squeezed her eyes shut, as if not crying somehow excused her from telling this secret. Steffi looked worried, like she would get in trouble for something, like she should have already told someone this. If she had told the woman about it before, maybe Kirin wouldn't be dead. Maybe her parents would've gotten a divorce and she would've gone to live with her dad or her grandmother. But Tammy knew that when someone is crazy, that's it, they're crazy, and there's nothing you can do about it. They have to go live at a psychiatric hospital like old people who live in old folks' homes. They can't take care of themselves. Sometimes people are normal and then all of a sudden they go crazy and the police have to come and take them away. It just happens. That's probably what happened to Kirin's mom.

Everyone was so focused on Steffi that they hadn't noticed Tammy standing there eavesdropping. Tammy's mother eventually looked over at her and motioned to Nick who turned around. "This doesn't concern you," he said and he told her that she could go back and watch TV or go to her room. Tammy didn't say anything and headed up to her room.

In the shadows of the upstairs hallway, equidistant between her bedroom and the bathroom, Tammy could listen in on the living room conversation without anyone seeing her. If anyone did notice her, she could say she was going to the bathroom.

"One time," Steffi sniffled on, "her mom didn't talk to her for almost three days. Kirin thought maybe she had tonsillitis, but she didn't go to the doctor. She wouldn't even write notes or use sign language."

"Was Kirin afraid of her mother?" the woman asked.

"I don't know. But she did say the house was haunted. Her mother said it was."

The woman asked more questions that Tammy couldn't quite hear and Steffi answered only yes or no. When Tammy heard them all stand up, she darted back into her room and pretended to read a book.

A minute later, Steffi walked by Tammy and through the separator door. Steffi left the separator door open and Tammy got up off her bed and stood on the narrow piece of wood that marked the official border of their rooms. Steffi was curled up on her bed with her back to Tammy. Tammy asked her who the people in the living room were. Steffi said they were lawyers. She told them that sometimes Kirin said she hated her mother, but Steffi didn't think she really meant it. Everyone says that, right?

Tammy said it all the time about her mother, but usually when she said it she meant it.

Tammy asked Steffi if Kirin's mother was going to jail. Steffi said she didn't know.

Steffi didn't say anything for a few minutes. She lay there on her bed and Tammy watched her side move up and down as she breathed in and out. After several breaths Steffi said very quietly, "Do you think they found the wine? In the closet?"

Steffi seemed worried about this. Steffi never got into trouble, but the way she asked Tammy, it was like the wine was a big deal. She didn't want them to find it. Tammy told her they had probably already found it. Police usually search a house where a murder takes place. They have to look for clues. But would they look in her closet? Steffi asked. Tammy had read all the newspaper articles. She didn't remember them mentioning the wine.

"I wish we could go get it," Steffi said, "and pour it down the drain and wash it out."

Tammy said it didn't matter anymore. Kirin was dead. Kirin couldn't get in trouble anymore. It didn't matter if they found the wine or not. That made Steffi start to cry. Tammy said she was sorry. Don't cry, she said. It was mean of those lawyers to come and talk to you. Why did they do that? You don't know anything.

"It's not just that," Steffi said, squeezing her eyes shut, "I left something there."

Tammy tried to tell her that whatever it was, it was probably too late. Or the police took it. Gretchen said that no one went in the house anymore. Kirin's dad had moved away.

"Do you remember the photos we showed you?"

Tammy looked at the piece of Steffi's hair that was plastered with tears across her cheek. It looked like a dead worm that had drowned on the sidewalk after a rainstorm. Steffi had her face turned toward the wall and the blue pencil mark in her cheek still hadn't worked its way out. Tammy didn't know why Steffi was bringing up the photos, unless she was going to say that she knew they were taken with Tammy's Polaroid camera.

Tammy muttered, "Yeah," because she knew Steffi needed it to go on.

"We took Nick's gun that was in there. I let Kirin borrow it."

Tammy was shocked. Steffi was going to get in big trouble for that. Tammy was surprised Nick hadn't noticed it was missing. Kirin had been dead for a couple of weeks. Steffi would definitely get in trouble for that and she would most definitely get spanked. Tammy almost wanted to laugh at Steffi for so obviously breaking a rule. Stealing Nick's gun was such a stupid thing to do. If she wanted to use it she should have just used it at home, quietly in her room, and then put it back before Nick came home from work. She shouldn't have let Kirin take it to her house. Or if she and Kirin wanted to use it at Kirin's house, Steffi should've taken it there and brought it back home the same day, or the next morning if she was sleeping over. She shouldn't have let Kirin take it for a couple weeks and promise to bring it back like a library book.

Tammy felt herself beginning to get nervous. A prickly feeling was creeping across her hands and her skin was starting to itch. She was partly nervous that *she* would get blamed for losing the gun, because who would believe that Steffi would do such a thing? It was so un-Steffi. Hugh wouldn't do it. Tammy was the only logical choice. And telling the truth would be too farfetched. No one would ever believe that it was still at Kirin's house in her bedroom closet with a Tupperware container full of wine.

Tammy's stomach turned over and her mouth felt cold and mucusy from the ice cream she had eaten. This was serious. Now that Steffi had told her about it, Tammy was involved. If Nick found out, and eventually he would notice it was gone, even if Steffi confessed, Tammy doubted

Nick would believe that Steffi had taken the gun. He would probably think that Steffi was trying to do something nice for Tammy. That she was covering up for Tammy. And no one would ever punish Steffi now with Kirin dead. They all felt bad that her best friend was killed. And they really didn't want to think about how many times Steffi had slept over at Kirin's house.

"Why?" was all Tammy could put together in her brain to say.

"Because," Steffi said. The pink was draining from her face and she was breathing funny. "Kirin's mom said there were bad people living across the street who might come in and try to kidnap her. She was scared. She needed it."

It occurred to Tammy that Nick's gun could have been the one that killed Kirin. Maybe those lawyers already knew about it or they thought Nick had killed Kirin. After all, Nick wasn't home that night, and when the guy at the music place made the announcement, her mother didn't answer. Tammy really couldn't say for sure where they were that night. They hadn't written down the number. The guy who worked at the music place couldn't say for sure they were there. Tammy didn't know what time they came home. But why would Nick want to kill Kirin and injure her mom? That was the part that didn't make sense.

Tammy walked over to Steffi's little wooden desk. She had a manila folder their mother had given her from her office to make a file about Kirin. Steffi had cut out all the newspaper articles about Kirin and put them in the folder. Tammy read through one of the articles. She had read it before but she didn't really remember any of the details. This time when she read it, she saw that Kirin had been killed by a big, rifle-style gun and not a little gun. It also said that Kirin's mom said she did it. Tammy closed the folder and a piece of gray newspaper shot out trying to escape.

It was back to Tammy and Steffi. Nick was a dick, but he had nothing to do with it.

"We should go get it," Tammy said.

Steffi finally turned her head away from the wall and looked at Tammy. Her right cheek had zigzag marks pressed into it from her pillowcase. She had dark circles under eyes and her breath was getting the little whistle that meant she would soon begin to wheeze and need to take her asthma medicine. It was a capsule full of teeny brown and white balls that she took by opening it up, like the red capsule in the Contac cold medicine commercial, and mixing the balls with a spoonful of applesauce. Steffi didn't know how to swallow pills.

Tammy knew Steffi didn't want to go back there. She didn't want to go back into her dead best friend's bedroom and look at the spot where she got shot. That house was definitely haunted now.

Steffi's eyes were straining and she was starting to wheeze.

"Do you want me to get Mom?" Tammy asked.

Steffi shook her head.

Tammy tried not to look directly at Steffi. She stared down at the gray floorboards and glanced over to the closet where Steffi and Kirin used to stand on the dresser and sing songs to the radio. Kirin was the one who made up the deejay game.

"I'll get it," Tammy said. "I'll get it out of her house."

Steffi's face relaxed a little bit. "How are you going to do it?" she asked.

"I don't know," Tammy said. She didn't know how she would do it, but she knew it had to be done. Tammy had to be the one to do it. Steffi was too scared. If Tammy made Steffi go back in that house with her, Steffi would get asthma and give them away. Tammy and Steffi didn't say anything about what Nick would do if he found out. Tammy realized that she and Steffi never talked about Nick, just like they never talked about their dad. And soon, Tammy thought, they would never talk about Kirin and her mom, about the time all three of them had slept over there and could've been killed, shot to death in their sleeping bags on the floor of the guest TV room. It was the unspoken rule in Tammy's and Steffi's house not to talk about things that scared them.

"You should do it soon," Steffi said.

"Yeah," Tammy said. It had already been too long. Tammy was surprised they weren't in trouble already. But whenever someone dies things get stretched out longer. Like the extra time Mrs. Perkins gave Tammy's class for their book reports that were due the Monday after Kirin died. Sooner or later though, they'll remember, they'll think it's been long enough, and why did you think we didn't notice, or why did you think we had forgotten, or why did you think you could get away with it? Just because someone died doesn't mean you can get away with something.

ON THE ROAD

* * *

There was a moment at the airport when Jeffrey felt like one of those women in the supermarket checkout line. The cashier rings up the total and the woman digs through her big messy purse full of crumpled tissues and lipstick caps. She finds her wallet, but she doesn't have enough money. She writes a check instead and the cashier has to get it approved by the manager. The manager, some fat, bald guy in a white shirt with short sleeves, comes over and looks at the check. He won't accept it because she's bounced a check to the market before and now she's on the no-check list. The woman looks at her groceries that have been pushed off the conveyor belt and into the tin basin where they wait for some kid to bag them. What should she throw back? Now she's holding up the line and the cashier's got to get the key for the register in order to void out what doesn't make the cut. And you can tell the thought is going through her head that she hopes she's not on the no-check list at the gas station because she's almost out of gas. She can eat, but she might not be able to get home. By the time she's out of there no one feels sorry for her. Her kids are screaming. Everyone just wants her gone.

Jeffrey felt like that woman when he opened his wallet to pay the agent for his plane ticket back to Texas. He didn't have the cash and he didn't want to admit it. He thumbed through the bills in his wallet. He knew it wouldn't be enough. Jeffrey felt someone unscrew an opening in his body and pour corrosive battery juice directly into his veins. He felt it travel down his arms to his fingertips, down his legs, and finally, it grabbed onto his jaw. Jeffrey turned his head and looked back at the lines of people shoving their suitcases along with their feet as they waited to check in. No one else seemed to be having this problem. There was one guy who was loudly complaining about something, opening and closing his ticket envelope, but he was one of those guys who liked to be loud.

"Sir?" the ticket agent said, trying to get his attention. She had perfectly white teeth and perfectly hair-sprayed hair. Why wasn't she a stewardess?

Jeffrey could feel the people behind him becoming restless. Some whiner said, "What the heck is taking this idiot so long? I've got a plane to catch."

Jeffrey turned back to the ticket agent.

"I'm sorry. I have to make a telephone call."

Jeffrey picked up his bags and walked away from the counter. The ticket agent called after him. Jeffrey thought it best not to explain too much. Better to act like he was obsessed with important business matters.

For good measure, Jeffrey went to the nearest pay phone, picked up the receiver, and dropped in a dime. He waited a moment and then held down the coin release latch. The dime tumbled back to him. At least some things still work around here.

Jeffrey swallowed a few times to oil his tight jaw. Then he dialed zero for the operator and placed a collect call to his parents.

Jeffrey had the cab ride from the hotel to lay out his excuse. He had gone to the Columbia School of Broadcasting for orientation day, but he wasn't on their list of new students. They had lost his application. The lady in the registration office was nice enough about it; he must have caught her on a good day because she let him fill out an application form right there and said she was going to see if she could push it through. She understood that this was probably the school's fault, and she confided that this type of thing had happened before. She could probably get the whole mess straightened out and he would only have to miss the first few classes. It would be easy enough to catch up. But, she would need a copy of his high school diploma and his immunization records or a note from his doctor. He needed to come back home to get them.

Jeffrey thought this was an excellent story.

"I just don't understand why you need to come all the way back here for that," his mother said. Jeffrey knew she was standing very still in her sunny Texas kitchen. She was speaking very softly because she hadn't yet decided whether to involve Jeffrey's father. "I can easily mail it to you."

"I don't want to take a chance on it getting lost in the mail."

"I'll send it to you special delivery. Or certified. You have to sign for certified."

"Mom, I'm sure even special delivery stuff gets lost once in a while."

There were some muffled words exchanged on the other end of the line and somewhere in it he heard his mother say, "He needs his immunization records for Columbia and he says it's very dangerous to mail them."

Jeffrey's father got on the phone.

"We're not wiring you money for a plane ticket. You're not coming back here. We'll find your papers and send them to you, but you're not flying all the way back here to get them."

Jeffrey stared at his muddy reflection in the silver pay phone casing.

"You need to learn how to stand on your own two feet, be your own man, prove yourself to the world." Jeffrey could tell his father was angry because he was recycling his worst clichés.

"If you don't take a stand, Jeffrey, you're going to die and the world will never know who you are. You've had the same opportunities as your brother and sister. You don't need much to make it out in the world, just hard work and a good attitude. Quitting is not a good attitude. All you've shown your mother and I by calling us like this is that you're a quitter. Is that what you want us to think? That you're a quitter?"

Jeffrey was silent.

"I know it's hard out there," his father said, softening his tone. Perhaps Jeffrey's mother had left the room and he no longer needed to make a show of manly, fatherly power. "You've got to have faith, Jeffrey. Faith that something is planned for you, something is right out there for you to take if you have the balls to step up and take it." His father sighed, or maybe he was softening a belch by puffing his cheeks and then exhaling. "You want to know why I love Jesus? It's not because of some moralistic crap. And it's not because of anything historic or something that's in the Bible. Hell, I would love Jesus even if there wasn't a Bible. It's because he can help people have better lives. Do unto others. It doesn't take a rocket scientist or an MBA to figure that out. And if the roles were reversed, if you were the father and I were the son, I would want you to treat me the same way I'm treating you now. I'm sincere about that, Jeffrey. You can do it, Jeffrey, you know why?"

Jeffrey looked out across the ticket area. A man was pulling a suitcase on wheels, but it was too big or too full and he couldn't pull it in a straight line without it twisting to one side and pitching over.

"Because I love you and Jesus loves you. Now you just got to show us how much you love us back."

JEFFREY TOOK A cab to the bus station. It was his last bit of luxury.

He spent the next three days on busses. He wasn't going anywhere, he just needed time. He would've preferred to go back to his parents and be sick for about three days. If he couldn't do that, then he wanted to be nowhere. He needed a retreat to build up strength.

He took a roundabout route in case anyone was following him. It was for Amber's protection as well as his. If anyone asked he would say he was going to visit his grandma in Florida, or he was just coming from visiting his grandma in Florida, depending on which way the bus was headed. Every bus station looked the same: the same orange, yellow, or teal plastic seats stuck together in the waiting area, the same pay-a-quarter-to-watch-TV chairs, the same bleached menthol smell trying to mask the odor of stale Cheetos and the great unwashed. The drivers all went through the same routine of teasing people into thinking it was finally time to board the bus. The driver gets on first, then shuts the door and spends a good twenty minutes doing absolutely nothing. Sure, he's adjusting the seat and the rearview mirror and checking over some list. He's also probably taking one last swig for the road. Then finally he opens the door and punches your ticket.

Jeffrey discovered that the best way to get two seats to himself was to sit up front near the driver. People will always pass you by looking for something better. By the time they get to the back of the bus, they're too tired to back up and the aisle is too crowded. They missed their chance.

Jeffrey sent Amber a postcard from every town where the bus pulled in for a rest stop. He wrote her notes and poems and sent them care of her DC hotel. He thought it was romantic and it showed he was thinking about her all the time. *Wish you were here*, he wrote. *Forget about the phone calls. You've been working so hard on this film, and your second film really is more important than your first. You need to prove to people that you're not just a flash in the pan, and you will. Don't worry. I just want you to know that I'm here for you. Thinking of you.*

He felt closer to her this way. He wasn't very good on the phone. He was a writer, he felt more comfortable pen to paper. With the postcards, he wasn't interrupting her; she could enjoy him at her leisure. He would be a little voice waiting for her when she got home, reminding her of how much he loved her.

In South Carolina, he found what he was looking for. He saw it from his window seat as the bus wound its way into a station for a one-hour break. Jeffrey got off the bus and headed toward the dusty supermarket across the street. The windows were completely covered in signs advertising pork and beans for pennies a pound in big, cheap red letters.

Jeffrey passed through the narrow opening between the supermarket and a liquor store and emerged at the back of the building where trucks loaded in battered produce and broken shopping carts were put out to pasture. There were a few shops and offices back here, dingy ones that didn't care about storefronts and good parking. He walked over to the white, lit-up Coca-Cola sign flickering on its way to extinction. The neon sign next to it crackled a high-pitched hum and said, *Guns and Antiques Dealer*.

It was run by an unshaven, malnourished old-timer with Vaseline-slicked hair and cough-drop breath, the kind of guy most people wouldn't think still existed. Most people thought his types were all living in shacks out in the middle of nowhere waiting to die. But this guy was alive and well and called him son.

Jeffrey gave him his story. A stranger had started following his girlfriend home. He had gotten her number somehow and would call all the time, only to hang up when she answered. The guy wouldn't take no for an answer, thought he was her boyfriend. Jeffrey had told his girlfriend to start wearing her grandmother's engagement ring as a ploy to get rid of him. The old-timer thought that was a good idea. Yeah, Jeffrey said, but the guy still wouldn't let up. Broke into her house and went through her, you know, unmentionables drawer. Her slips, stockings, and things. Her private things. His girlfriend was scared. Jeffrey was staying over there all the time now, even though his mother didn't like it. She's old-fashioned. Anyway, Jeffrey wrapped it up, he thought this would be a good idea. He wasn't going to shoot anyone. He's not the type who could take somebody's life. It's just something to scare the guy off or keep him there while we call the police, get him locked up. Even if he stops and leaves her alone, who's to say he won't start up on some new girl?

"A lot of sick people in the world," the old-timer said.

Jeffrey thought this fellow had heard it all. A guns-and-antiques dealer was the type of guy people poured out their troubles to.

The old-timer gave him a good deal on a .22 blue-steel revolver. Smart-looking thing, not too small. It'll do the trick, the old-timer said, you're gonna want the sucker to see it.

Jeffrey tacked on a box of ammunition and paid in cash. The geezer was in a good mood and threw in a used shoulder holster, no extra charge, and showed him how to load the gun. Jeffrey walked out into the bright setting sun glaring down on the brick back lot. He emerged in front of the supermarket, his guitar case in one hand, brown paper bag in the other, and walked back across the street and reboarded the bus. No one had spotted him and he had erased all of his tracks.

In North Carolina, he missed a connection and was stuck in a dead-end town for twelve hours until four o'clock the next morning. Jeffrey wandered out along the two-lane highway and made his way to a run-down strip mall with a motel at the far end. Maybe that's what he needed: a shower in nowheresville.

The strip mall contained a bridal shop, a donut shop, and a pawnshop. That was it. Honeymoon at the motel.

Jeffrey walked into the pawnshop, just to look around. The place was full of TVs, some jewelry, mostly junk. Here he got his knife. It was a nice hunting knife in its own little sheath. He liked it that way. He didn't want to be bothered with having to flick something open, and a Swiss Army knife was too much trouble. A knife was a one-shot deal, Jeffrey thought. You need something hard and quick. Jump, stab, and make your getaway.

On his way out, he spotted a Radio Shack tape recorder under the glass cabinet. He paid another ten bucks for it. It was more than he wanted to spend, but it would be like a date. Even though Amber wasn't with him, he could still take her out.

After a donut and a shower, Jeffrey sat down on the scratchy poly-ester bedspread and picked up his guitar. He popped a cassette into the recorder, pressed down PLAY and RECORD together, and said, "Hello, testing, one, two, three." He played the tape back and his tinny voice trickled out of the speaker. He was now in his own private recording studio. Pretty cool.

He rewound and pressed PLAY and RECORD again. He whis-pered, "Two, three, four," to himself and then began to play his guitar. He sang "If I Fell" by the Beatles and almost made it through the first verse without screwing up. He was going to stop and start over, but he kept going. He made it through the rest of the song with only a few messed-up chord changes. When he finished, he was about to press the STOP button, but instead he leaned into the machine and put his mouth close to the special little dots of the mic square.

"Hi, Amber, it's me, Jeff. Or J. Whatever you want to call me. Either is fine. That was me just now, singing. And playing. I told you I was a writer and a songwriter. Although I didn't write that song, that was the Beatles. But you knew that. You're not even here and you're making me giddy. I'm all alone right now. I'm on the road. I'm staying in a hotel. Just took a shower. That's where I got the idea to make you a tape. People get all kinds of crazy ideas in the shower. Anyway, I thought it might be different. And I wanted to hear your voice so much so . . . I feel like I can hear your voice right now. You're right here with me. And we're just talking. I have a donut, do you want some? We could live here, you and I, in this little town. It's kind of a run-down town, but they have a donut shop and it's clean. There are woods nearby. It'd be away from all the dirty scum of Hollywood. Lots of actresses leave Hollywood and buy a ranch somewhere to get away from it all. That's what this place could be like. We could buy the motel and sleep in a different room every night. And we'd have a maid and room service. That'd be fun. I love you so much. You know that, right? I know someone was probably with you when you were talking to me on the phone so you had to say those things. I know you feel differently. That's why I keep writing, just to let you know I don't take it personally. I still love you. There's nothing you can do to make me stop loving you. I'll always love you. So here's another tune for you. I don't know, I guess I'm in *A Hard Day's Night* mood even though I like the John and Yoko stuff too. So here we go. I kinda feel like a deejay."

Jeffrey gave another, "Two, three, four," and plucked the four strings of George Harrison's intro to "And I Love Her." He was warmed up now. He was smooth. He was in the moment. He let the last chord ring out until all was quiet in the room again.

"That one's a lot easier to play. The first one I did was really hard. So many chords. Kinda complicated. I hope I didn't ruin it for you. I haven't played in about a week. I'm probably a little rusty. I probably need to tune it better too . . . Amber, Amber, Amber . . . I love you so much. Don't go back to California. It's so phony there. Nobody is real, they're all put on. You're not like that. You're real. Don't go back there. Please. They'll eat you up and spit you out and make you do nude scenes. They're just using you. They're all full of shit. Did you know the CIA uses movies to communicate with agents overseas? They send messages through the dialogue. It's not the kind of thing you read in the paper, but it happens. You just have to know the right people and they'll tell you it's true. Just look at Reagan. He knows. A Hollywood actor is president. Can you believe it? The world is ending. It is. Do you believe in Nostradamus? He predicted the end of the world. Listen to me, I want you to come here. I want you to live in this motel with me. Just come here and we'll be safe. If the world ends we'll be together. Or we can commit double suicide. That's what people who are really in love do. But don't worry, if I die before you, I won't cheat on you in Heaven. I'll wait for you."

A large drop of sweat fell onto the tape recorder.

"Hold on, technical difficulties," he said and pressed STOP.

Jeffrey stood up to get a towel. He caught sight of himself in the mirror and saw that his hair was pasted to his forehead with sweat. He looked pale. The white towel around his waist disappeared and became part of his body.

He heard someone outside his door and ran for his gun. He pulled it out of his jacket, cocked it, and aimed it at the door. The footsteps walked away and a car drove off. Jeffrey's hands were shaking.

He went back to the bed and pressed PLAY and RECORD.

"Okay, false alarm. But don't worry. I'm prepared in case of emergency."

Jeffrey curled up in a fetal position with the recorder cradled in the crook of his right arm.

"I wonder if I can shoot with my left hand. I'm right handed. Well, most people are. I have a gun. I might kill myself here. I might kill myself while this tape is going. That would mean something, wouldn't it? You'd know I loved you and I'd be waiting for you in Heaven. Then you could kill yourself too as soon as possible. But don't shoot yourself. Don't ruin your pretty face. Do something painless like the car in the garage. Or pills. Lots of sleeping pills and then it's just like you're falling asleep. I tried to kill myself that way once. I did it in the bathtub, hoping I'd drown. But I was stupid and left the tap running. The whole thing overflowed and it was a big mess and my mother found me. It's kind of a funny story now. Anyway, now I have a gun. Guns are messy, but hey, they work."

Jeffrey angled his left elbow up to the ceiling and pointed the gun down against his damp temple.

"I'm aiming the gun at my head. This could be it. Unless you say you love me. Unless you really don't want me to. 'Oh no! One more song! One more song, Jeffrey!' Oh, okay."

Jeffrey picked up his guitar and launched into "I'll Be Back." He sang louder than he usually did. His sweaty skin stuck to the back of the guitar. He shook the damp strands of hair out of his face. He belted out the bridge. On the record the song fades out, but Jeffrey didn't fade out. He extended the vamp and ended with a cadenza on the major chord, strumming as hard and as fast as he could. He went for it.

"That's the end of the album, Amber. I'll see you soon. And you'll see me. Don't worry."

PART THREE

THE NATIONAL

* * *

The Washington bus station was in a bad neighborhood. Jeffrey noticed Washington was like that. He could go from polished white government buildings to a sea of black faces in a few short blocks. It was no different from anywhere else in the country; bus stations were always on the wrong side of the tracks. Jeffrey never thought about taking the train. He didn't like trains. His brother went through a phase where he built an entire little town in the basement and laid down model train tracks. He even painted a sign that said, "Welcome to Hackneyville, a happy place to be." Jeffrey could hear the train motor from his bedroom. It seemed to him that train cars derailed a little too often, and he wouldn't want to be on a real train that derailed and be the sole survivor stranded in the middle of a cornfield.

The bus station's fluorescent lights made it seem like morning even though it was the middle of the night. The McDonald's attached to the station was closed, as was the ticket counter. Passengers were confined to a few benches while they waited for daybreak.

The sun came up around six a.m. McDonald's opened for breakfast at six thirty. By seven, Jeffrey was on his way. He walked a few blocks until he spotted the Capitol dome in the distance and headed toward it.

Jeffrey made his way to the National Hotel. It took him a while to find it since all he had was an address copied out of the phone book at the bus station and it didn't list the cross street. When he finally made it, he was disappointed. The owners of the National Hotel were letting the historic landmark go to pot. This was, after all, the hotel where John Wilkes Booth stayed the night before he shot Lincoln. Jeffrey thought history buffs would want to keep it in shape.

It was historical, all right; it was old. It had long blue-gray velvet curtains covered in dust. There was no need for the curtains because no natural light reached into the lobby. The stately striped wallpaper was fading into yellow and the furniture had obviously been acquired from a restaurant's going-out-of-business sale: green vinyl bar chairs and overly lacquered tables made of short stocky wood. There was no cafe, no bar, just beer lights nailed to the walls and a murk of smoke lingering along with skinny black girls in shorts whose skin stuck to the seat cushions.

The place was a dump. No one would bother him here.

Jeffrey checked in and the clerk slid him a key with a wooden number 7 attached by a gold chain. Lucky.

His room was narrow and dark. He thought about asking for the Booth room, but he didn't want to call attention to himself. Plus, they probably didn't rent it out. It was probably sectioned off by a rope and you had to be a museum worker to go in there, or some sicko senator with a thing for cheap call girls dressed up as Mary Todd Lincoln. Jeffrey wondered how much the clerk got under the table for arranging that sort of thing.

Jeffrey lay down on the bed and picked at the white nubbed blanket. Pigeons cooed outside his window. Jeffrey thought it was ironic that Booth was an actor and now an actor was president. He fell asleep.

When he woke up it was after noon. He needed to eat. He didn't want to go out, but there was no room service.

Jeffrey stepped out of his room into the blue-gray carpeted hallway. Everything in the National was the color of smoke.

Two black kids were standing at the end of the hall. One of them had a wine-colored umbrella, the kind with a button you press and it automatically extends out and opens up. The kid was using it as a gun, firing on the other kid who was trying to grab it away from him. When the kids saw Jeffrey they quieted down and started whispering to each other huddled against the last door at the end of the hall.

Jeffrey locked his door and headed to the elevator. When he reached out to press the button, an umbrella appeared out of nowhere and slammed down against his forearm.

"Chicken!" one of the boys said excitedly, the white parts of his eyes lighting up. "Chicken! You chicken!" he said again and then quickly withdrew his umbrella and ran down the hall to his friend.

Jeffrey was stunned. He was afraid of this boy. This boy saw right through Jeffrey. Jeffrey had a gun in his pocket, but he was a chicken. Jeffrey was chickening out. Jeffrey knew this, but the boy was broadcasting it, telling the whole world what it already knew: that Jeffrey was too powerless to ever accomplish anything, that he was too scared to demand anything of this world, that he desperately wanted to be seen, but was too timid to speak. Jeffrey was so saddled with truth, he could not perform a dare.

The elevator door suddenly dinged and opened. Jeffrey automatically stepped in as the boy ran back down the hall, this time shouting, "I'm not afraid of you, chicken!"

The boy lost the race with the elevator door. It closed in his face as he was laughing.

When the elevator arrived on the first floor, Jeffrey half expected to see the boy again, but there was no one except the clerk and an old black man sitting on one of the vinyl chairs with a brown paper bag on his lap.

After a quick Burger King meal, where he could at least have things his way, Jeffrey set out for Amber's hotel. The neighborhood cleaned up as he went.

He waited across the street from the hotel and tried to see who was in the lobby. It was hard to make out, but he thought he saw a female desk clerk. A good sign; Jeffrey didn't know her. He didn't see any of the fat fucks hanging out either. Jeffrey slipped his hand into his jacket pocket and felt the cool hard surface of his gun. He pressed it against his body and crossed the street.

The lobby was brightly lit and all the surfaces shiny and polished. It felt more akin to an airport than the dusty, dim, decrepit National. Jeffrey walked up to the desk, hand steady in his pocket. His finger wasn't on the trigger, he was just resting his hand there. Just resting his hand in his pocket. Just in case. The girl clerk had her head bent down and didn't see him. Jeffrey was tempted to ring the tin bell for service, but she looked up before he had the chance. She squinted at him and then launched into her automatic friendly routine. They probably taught her that in hospitality school—how to be bubbly and bright when you really don't want to.

"Can I help you, sir?" Smile.

"Yes, I was staying here about a week ago, and I think there might be some mail or messages for me."

"Hmm. We usually don't accept mail for guests after they've checked out unless they have a reservation to return. We usually forward everything along to your home address."

"Could you please check for me? I think some things may have been lost or held up."

"Sure. I'd be happy to."

Jeffrey gave her his name and she disappeared through a door behind the desk. He glanced up at the shelf of key nooks. The top row only had two slots. Penthouse suites A and B. There were no keys. She was probably here right now.

Jeffrey's heart started beating erratically and he decided to do something rash. He dashed over to the stairwell before the girl came out of the office.

He quickly bounded up two flights of stairs, entered the hallway, and waited for the elevator. He rode to the last floor before PH and found the stairwell. Jeffrey didn't know why he had never thought of this earlier. He ran up the last set of steps and pulled on the PH door, half expecting it to be locked, half expecting he would have to kick it down or blast off the doorknob.

It opened easily into his arms.

Jeffrey released the door and let it drift shut. He sat down on the stairs and dug around in his breast pocket. He came up with a stubby pencil and a Trailways ticket envelope. There wasn't much space to write except around the edges.

Amber,

I made it. I'm here. Want me, I'm yours. Believe in us. We'll be so happy together. Romeo and Juliet. I'll take the poison from your delicious lips. Kiss of death and the bad actors who try and take over the castle will die and we will live happily ever after in our perfect heaven. Imagine.

—J

He looked through the little rectangular window. No one was in the PH corridor. He still didn't know which room was hers, so he opted to leave the note on the floor halfway between penthouses A and B, and, just so she wouldn't miss it, he took the John Lennon button off of his lapel and pinned it to the envelope.

Jeffrey took the stairs back down to the first floor. When he got to the lobby he walked up to the reception desk as though nothing he had done was out of the ordinary.

This time the girl squinted and didn't smile. Bad girl. Go to hospitality detention.

Jeffrey excused himself for disappearing and said he had needed to use the facilities. The girl clerk told him there wasn't any mail. Jeffrey was a little confused. He should've received some mail from Amber. It should be waiting for him. The clerk apologized, politely and professionally, probably trying to make up for not smiling. Jeffrey felt lucky and he decided to press it.

"Actually, could you connect me to Miss Carrol?" Jeffrey asked, picking up the in-house phone.

"I'm sorry, who?"

"Miss Carrol. Penthouse suite."

"You mean the actress with the film crew?"

"Yes."

"I'm sorry, sir, they all moved on a few days ago. They've checked out."

Jeffrey wasn't quite sure whether or not to believe her. He had been gone less than a week. It took longer than a week to make a movie. There must be a secret code he had to give the clerk so she would know he wasn't some crazy fan. That was probably the routine for security purposes. But Jeffrey didn't have the secret code. He could whip out his gun and force the girl clerk to talk, but he was caught off guard. He didn't have time to think the scenario through. The gun hung heavy and awkwardly in his pocket, and he felt unable to touch it without drawing attention to himself.

"Could I write a message for her and you could forward it along?"

"Sir, we really—"

"I don't want her address, you can just include it with her regular mail."

"Sir, it's not our policy to—"

"It's very important. It's very important that she get this as soon as possible."

"Sir, if it was that important, you would probably already have Miss Carrol's address."

Jeffrey was shocked. This wasn't hospitable at all. He took the hotel pen he was holding and walked out.

Amber had his heart and she had left with no forwarding address. There was no way for him to protect her. He had to find her. She couldn't have gone far. She had a movie to make. She couldn't have gone far. Jeffrey could find her.

Jeffrey scudded down the street, away from the hotel. He bumped into someone with his shoulder and didn't bother with an "excuse me." He felt bad about it, but he had no time to be polite. He walked several blocks with his head down, looking at the sidewalk. He had no plan other than to find her and to find her quickly. He had to find her quickly. Time was not on his side, in fact, time was on the opposite team, taunting him, knowing that he was always the last one picked, always the last one up to bat, and always sure to strike out. Fuck you, fuck you, fuck *you*, time. Jeffrey weaved through office workers eating their bag lunches in Lafayette Park. He scanned the line of tourists waiting outside the White House gates. He thought about getting on a bus heading up Pennsylvania Avenue. On a bus he could cover more ground. But he wouldn't be in control. He might not get a window seat. He might not be able to get off where he wanted. The bell might not work. Some pregnant woman might go into labor and the bus would have to make a detour to the hospital. Jeffrey would walk. He stayed on Pennsylvania Avenue and walked.

Jeffrey started to sweat. He slowed down.

The air was humid and thick. It was making him tired. He looked up at the sky and it was only then that he realized it was a gray day.

Pennsylvania Avenue abruptly ended and Jeffrey was deposited onto M Street. He didn't like being on a street named after a random letter of the alphabet. Streets should have names. Things with just letters were never anything good—KGB, CIA, SDS, MIA, IBM, you name it. Wisconsin came to his rescue. Jeffrey hung a right onto Wisconsin Avenue. He felt a little better. He didn't see Amber or any movie crews. He kept walking.

He walked a long while.

He passed Garfield Street and thought, dead president, you get a side street. What a letdown. Give your life for your country and you get a fucking side street, or a faceless white tombstone in Arlington Cemetery identical to every other faceless white tombstone in Arlington Cemetery so no one can ever find you. That's it. Sorry. Oh, and here's a folded-up flag for your mom.

When he arrived at the border of Wisconsin and Massachusetts he wavered slightly and stayed on Wisconsin. At the intersection of Wisconsin and Nebraska, Jeffrey stuck with Wisconsin. Wisconsin turned out to be a long avenue. He didn't know how it earned its status as a major artery when it didn't seem like a major state. It wasn't New York or California or Texas. But for some reason Wisconsin was awarded a lot of traffic, an odd honor for a state specializing in cheese.

It began to rain. Jeffrey didn't know where he was or how far he had walked. He was wet, his search was foiled, he had nowhere to go. His tired legs arrived at a corner where a dinky local library stood across the street from a Sears department store, a little publicly funded David against the capitalist Goliath. The rain was beating on him. Jeffrey ducked into the library for cover.

The turnstile creaked loudly as it propelled Jeffrey into the quiet sanctum of books. Jeffrey looked around, embarrassed, and wondered if anyone noticed the film of water covering his face and dripping off the end of his nose like snot. It wasn't snot, but Jeffrey was disturbed that people might think it was. A handmade sign of puffy magic-marker letters spelled out *INFORMATION* beneath a cloudy layer of Scotch tape. Jeffrey walked up to the desk and asked for the men's room.

When Jeffrey opened the restroom door, he was so startled that his neck locked up like an Easter Island statue. A young girl was sitting on the toilet, her pants pushed down below her knees and the tiptoes of her sneakers touching the floor for balance. Jeffrey had bulldozed through the moment when she could've said, "Just a minute, please," and all she had left at her disposal was to move a forearm protectively over her lap. He didn't know how long he stood there staring at her, and she staring back at him. It was long enough for him to see that one of her sneakers was untied and the gray laces were lying flat on the floor getting wet. It was only when he realized he had blinked, and blinked a second time, that he looked away from the girl and quietly backed out.

A few moments later, Jeffrey heard the toilet flush and the girl came out. He watched her as she disappeared between the stacks of books.

In the bathroom, Jeffrey dried himself off with brown paper towels. He still felt the presence of the girl, as if this large beige closet were somehow hers, or as if he were a married businessman who had come home late one night and accidentally wandered into the wrong house, into the wrong bed, next to the wrong wife, and did not want to leave. Jeffrey stared at the white oval toilet seat and, against his better judgment, wanted to touch the surface.

After rubbing more paper towels over his damp head, Jeffrey emerged from the bathroom, walked over to the magazine rack, and picked up an outdated copy of *Time* magazine. The magazine rack was by the exit. He would wait there for the girl. Read a magazine. Wait. The *Time* magazine headline beamed. "The Peril Grows," it said. It was growing in Central America. He flipped open the crumpled pages to nowhere in particular.

The girl walked up to the checkout desk with a pile of books followed by a really little kid in overalls. At the bottom of the pile, the librarian paused her methodical stamping of index cards. She pushed her glasses up her nose and tapped the book with her finger. The library lady was not relinquishing the last tattered paperback. "I'm sorry, but we have certain restrictions with this book," the librarian said and continued on with some sort of official jargon. Jeffrey could tell the girl just wanted to let it go. Her eyes were shifting intermittently between the floor and her remaining pile of books. Jeffrey saw himself in the girl. She wasn't a fighter. She wasn't going to argue. If she couldn't get what she wanted then she just wanted to be left alone.

Being gallant was never part of Jeffrey's character, but this girl wanted her damn book and she should have her damn book. He could shoot the library lady, grab the book, the girl, her brother, and get the hell out. Maybe grab the drawer of loose change where they kept everyone's five-cents-a-day penance. They didn't have a getaway car. They would have to hope for a bus.

"Excuse me," Jeffrey said, surprised to hear words come out of his mouth. The library lady looked up at him with her too-large face on her too-large head with hair curled too tightly from a perm. She looked like a clown. "Could I be of some assistance?" He meant to say "help." "Could I be of some *help*?" But now that he said it, "assistance" sounded better.

The library lady looked at him, looked back at the girl, and looked at him again as though she detected a family resemblance. "I would need you to sign for this book," she said. Jeffrey hadn't given a story for the librarian to buy, but she had apparently invented her own. Jeffrey leaned over and signed the index card. He slid it back to the library lady. He was still too nervous to look the girl in the eye and instead glanced down at the metal fasteners on the boy's overalls. The book in question—it was called *Forever* and had an illustration of a gold locket on the cover—was stamped and shoved aside with the girl's other selections and the three of them were free to go.

Jeffrey followed the girl to the exit and held the glass door open for her. The girl paused on the sidewalk and looked at Jeffrey. Jeffrey was half expecting a "thank you" but then he remembered that he was the one who had walked in on her in the bathroom and she could still hate him for that.

"I'm sorry," Jeffrey said, "about before."

The girl half shrugged and gave him a barely audible, "It's okay." Her brother was looking at his reflection in the library glass.

Make it up to her, Jeffrey thought.

"I'm really sorry," Jeffrey said, repeating his last line to buy himself some time. "Could I . . . would you like to . . . I could take you out . . . if you want." I'm a loser, Jeffrey thought. I can't put two and two together. This is a kid. Think about what kids like.

"We could go get ice cream if you want."

The girl squinted at him suspiciously, but the boy turned around and his formerly lethargic limbs came to life. He clasped his hands together and for a moment looked like a miniature little old man. The girl wasn't so easily sold. She turned around and tugged on the hood of the boy's jacket. "Let's go," she said and was met with a round of "Noooo," from the boy. The boy went so far as to turn red and prepare to cry. The girl told him to shut up, but Jeffrey could tell she didn't mean it. She was just embarrassed.

"It's really no problem. It's my treat."

The girl paused at each intersection and reached for her brother's hand. Cute, Jeffrey thought. She takes care of him. He tried to remember if his sister did that sort of thing when they were kids, but it must be different growing up in DC. Any foreign thug could run you over and claim diplomatic immunity. As they waited for the light to change, Jeffrey noticed the letters on the building across the street—Washington Psychiatric Institute. The windows were tinted brown and behind them were brown vertical blinds and no one was entering or exiting through the sunglassed front doors. Jeffrey glanced up at the building's six stories and caught sight of a nurse passing by a window.

At the Swensen's ice cream parlor Please Wait to be Seated sign, the three of them were escorted to a booth in the back. The girl and boy ordered small matching sundaes called Mr. San Francisco, basically an upside-down ice cream cone with a little added fluff. Jeffrey thought they were being polite by ordering the cheapest sundae on the menu. Jeffrey ordered a milkshake because it seemed more adult.

As they waited for their ice cream, Jeffrey thought of all the different ways he and Amber could fall in love. He could invite her over to his apartment. He could ask for her help with something, like picking out curtains or deciding where a lamp should go. He could ask her to teach him how to cook a certain recipe. They could wear silly aprons, make a mess in the kitchen, start a food fight, and wash each other off. She could shake his hand good-night and he could hold on to it just a little too long. She would put her other hand on top of his and gaze up at him with her perfect eyes. And when she had looked at him long enough, she would close her eyes and wait there, wait in the atmospheric space beneath his shoulders. She would wait for him to land on her lonely planet.

Jeffrey thought these things as he stared across the white table that was damp from being freshly wiped clean. This is probably what Amber looked like at her age, he thought. This is what she was like when she was pure, before the Hollywood goons got to her. When she was just a kid, like this, carefully eating ice cream, methodically dissecting a candy snowman face. Everything in this ice cream place was cold and wet, everything except for Jeffrey and this girl.

The girl didn't like talking. Jeffrey was the same way.

But Jeffrey had to be the big guy here.

"So, what's the deal with the book?" he asked as nonchalantly as possible.

"It's just a book," she answered without looking up from her dish.

"Why weren't they letting you take it out?"

"It's a book for preteens, or for teens, but they say you need parental permission. It's stupid."

"What's the book about?"

"It's a Judy Blume book and sometimes people don't like her books because they talk about real life." The girl shrugged. "It's just a book."

"Yeah," Jeffrey said. "I get it." Jeffrey didn't know who Judy Blume was, but if she was someone who cut through all the crap, then this kid should be allowed to read whatever the lady writes.

"You like to read?" he asked.

"Yeah."

Jeffrey wrapped his hand around his glass. He attempted to lift it off the table, but the condensation around the base glued it down like a suction cup. He slid the milkshake across the table and the seal was released when it reached the edge. The airborne glass felt shaky in his hand and he tried to steady it with his lips. He felt awkward about the whole operation and thought, this girl probably thinks I'm a freak. Jeffrey set the glass back down on the table and curled his arm around it as if to say, it's the glass, not me, that's shaking.

The boy ate with a spoon too large for his face. He opened his mouth wide and clamped it down trying to get as much in one bite as possible. He hadn't yet learned how to ration like his sister.

"People who don't let you read," Jeffrey began slowly, not sure what he was going to say next, "don't understand." He felt himself forming a big idea in his head. It was so big, he wasn't sure if he understood it, and he knew that if he went to say it too quickly, the words might dart away never to be heard from again. "People who don't let you read are jealous. They just want to talk all the time, but they don't want to hear what you have to say. They don't want to let you read either, because then you're not paying attention to whatever stupid shit they're saying."

The girl looked at him, gently tapping her spoon against the side of her dish.

"I shouldn't have said 'shit,'" Jeffrey apologized.

The girl shrugged.

Jeffrey saw a few nurses being seated across the room. They were fat and didn't look good in white and didn't need the ice cream.

"The thing is," Jeffrey continued, lowering his voice, "these people sense that you're smarter than they are. And that pisses them off. They don't want anyone to be smarter than them. But look at what they've done: they've gone and fucked up the world. Telling people they can't read. That's the worst. They just want to keep you down. Then they complain that you're not pulling your own weight. They don't know anything."

Jeffrey was talking too much. The girl wasn't saying anything.

"Do you like your mom and dad?" he asked her. It was an idiotic question but he couldn't think of anything else to say.

The girl shrugged. "My parents are divorced," she said.

"Oh." Divorce was not a part of Jeffrey's world. His parents were hopelessly, helplessly married. The thought probably never occurred to them.

"I live with my mom and my stepfather. He's really my half brother," she said with a gesture in the boy's direction.

"Do you like your stepfather?"

"I guess," she said staring down into the soupy remains of her dessert. Jeffrey knew she didn't mean it. She was too polite to tell the truth. She probably hated the guy. He was probably a real bastard who didn't give a shit about her. Give her a few years and he'll probably kick her out of the house and say, you're on your own, kid. Go suck off guys for a living, I don't care. If she's lucky he'll wait until her eighteenth birthday, or maybe the day after.

"Have you ever thought about running away?" Jeffrey asked.

"Where would I go?"

"I don't know."

They said nothing for a moment.

"You could take a bus somewhere," Jeffrey said.

"Where?"

"I don't know." Now it was Jeffrey's turn to shrug.

"I'd probably need somewhere to stay where I could go to school."

Jeffrey wished he had a safe house to offer her. A place out in the woods near a one-room schoolhouse. A place where the backwoods schoolteacher would take her in like the black kid in *Sounder*, take a special liking to her and give her books to read while she waits for her real father to be freed from jail.

"Where would you go if you could go anywhere?" he asked.

The girl looked at him then. Before, she had looked at him only to satisfy some conversational rule and then quickly glanced away. This time she looked at him and allowed him to look at her. Their eyes locked and something, an energy or an ESP feeling, poured back and forth between them and Jeffrey couldn't tell who was really looking at whom. Her eyes had become his and he was looking at himself. The girl started to speak about a tree house, or a fort or something, someplace where she used to live where she could go back to her old school, but Jeffrey felt the whole time he was watching himself from outside his body. And with her eyes he was bathing himself in a blue watery glow. It was surrounding him and tugging at his throat. He felt strangely, peacefully, about to cry. Flood his face with tears like her little half brother. He felt like there was a hand clenching his throat, but he didn't feel pain. He knew what the invisible hand was doing. It was shushing the sob that was welling up. It was creating a dam with the back of his tongue. It was reminding him that she was the kid here, and he was the grown-up. He was the one who should save her. Just like he was the one who should save Amber. That is what men do.

"You should go there," he said. "Maybe today, even. I could take you to the bus station."

"I have to watch him," she said, gesturing to the boy.

"Where are we going?" the boy asked.

"Nowhere."

"Are we going to look at busses?"

"No."

"Can we?"

"No."

"Why not?"

"Shut up," she said softly. "You have chocolate on your face." She reached over and tried to wipe his mouth with a napkin.

"Stop it!" he said, turning away from her.

"You have to wipe it off."

"No I don't!"

He hid his face near the bench. The girl tugged on his shirt a couple times and then gave up.

"We should go," she said to Jeffrey.

"Do you want me to take you to the station?"

"No, I mean, we have to go home."

It wasn't that Jeffrey was disappointed in her response, it was that he understood this was not the moment when she needed him. She might need him in the future. She might not ever need him at all. She might need only the essence of Jeffrey, only the memory of him to remind her that she is not alone out there. He's out there too. And if she knows he is out there, she might begin to like his being there, she might begin to enjoy the presence of his existence, she might begin to love him. And all Jeffrey would have to do is telepath over to her, appear in her dreams, leave little bits of food outside her hideaway, light up the pebbles on her walk home from school as it's getting dark out. Because the girl was, without lifting a pinky, showing Jeffrey what to do next.

The girl scooted out from the table and uttered an awkwardly quiet good-bye as she passed Jeffrey on her way to the door. The boy slid off his seat until his feet touched the ground and followed her.

JEFFREY TOOK A bus back to the National Hotel.

He took a nap.

When he woke up it was raining. The gray day outside matched the smoky interior of his hotel room. Everything was merging into one color.

Jeffrey wondered if he had slept through the night and now it was morning. He didn't know. It was probably early evening, but he decided it was morning because he wanted it to be.

He didn't have to get dressed because he had never gotten undressed. He didn't look too shabby either. He could use an ironing, but that was about it. Somebody should invent a full-body iron, he thought, something you do without having to take your clothes off and set up an ironing board.

Jeffrey checked the peephole before opening the door a crack with the gold chain still latched in place. No kids. The coast was clear.

Jeffrey ducked through the rain to the little convenience store across the street. He bought a box of Frosted Flakes and a little package of Hostess powdered donuts. He bought a newspaper too because there was no *TV Guide* in his room.

Back at the National, Jeffrey ate cereal directly out of the box. He licked the powdered sugar that stuck to his fingers from the white donuts. He flipped through the paper, his moistened fingertips turning gray from the ink. He usually didn't read the newspaper. Maybe just the funnies or the movie reviews. Stuff like that. But today he read through the front page, Metro, Business, and Life. The Brits were shooting up the Falklands, people were still upset about the Chinese girl's design for the Vietnam memorial, Brezhnev had been missing for a month and everyone thinks he's dead, El Salvador, El Salvador, El Salvador, and someone made the Guinness Book of World Records for blowing the largest bubblegum bubble. Funny, Jeffrey thought. How do they measure the bubble before it bursts?

The TV listings page was at the very end of the Life section. They obviously didn't think it was that important. Right next to it was something called the District Diary, which listed special events: museum exhibitions, the cherry blossom festival, congressional goings-on, and where the president was going to be that day.

That was the funny part. Reagan would be attending a Kennedy Center gala celebrating "The Artistic Life of America." Amber was one of the celebrities doing a song-and-dance number. It would be broadcast live via satellite hookup. Amber was still in town.

But it wasn't funny. It was a cover-up. Was she here or not? It was either a big coincidence or a big scam. Or a big joke on him. Maybe that female desk clerk knew someone at the paper and called it in just to fuck with him.

Jeffrey picked up the phone and dialed Amber's hotel. His father always said, if you want to know something, pick up the phone and find out.

A male voice answered the line.

"Hi, could you please connect me to Miss Carrol in penthouse suite A?"

"One moment please."

Surprisingly, Jeffrey made the fifty-fifty guess correctly. He felt kinda proud of himself.

"Thank you for holding, could you please repeat the name of the guest you are trying to reach?"

"Miss Carrol, Amber Carrol." He said it in a low voice as if to say, don't let this get around. She's famous, you know.

"I'm sorry, sir, Miss Carrol checked out a few days ago."

Jeffrey hung up. He didn't need to go through the whole good-bye routine.

He flipped to the TV listings page and saw the long rectangular box graying out eight p.m. to eleven p.m. Had he not bought the paper today,

Amber would have slipped by him, her blonde buttery hair melting through his fingers, their chance at happiness forever blown into the wind. She was being inducted into a society of hate. A society of liars and users and phonies. They would do whatever it takes to get her on their side and keep her quiet. She was already being brainwashed. She was just a young girl out on her own trying to make it in Hollywood. All she ever wanted to do was be an actress and love people. They prey on girls like that, girls with big hearts and big dreams just off the bus from Smalltown, USA, where her dad smacked her around for letting a boy look at her tits and her mother was too nervous to do anything to stop him. She took the bus out to Hollywood to prove them wrong. She wasn't a worthless slut. She had talent. The feds knew that. They knew everything, that's why they picked her. Every one of those Hollywood girls has a secret: an abortion, an uncle who raped her, a cheerleading team who humiliated her. They get dirt on you as part of their insurance. They've got you trapped. You pay your debt to society by being a super-secret covert operative. When they're done with you, your body washes up somewhere, mysterious circumstances, drank too much at a yacht party, fell overboard, your secret life of drugs, an abusive boyfriend. I knew she was depressed, your fake friends tell the magazines, but I never dreamed she would, you know, commit suicide. Jeffrey had to step in. He had to be the cult deprogrammer she would fall in love with. He had to get her out of there. Jeffrey the hero. Jeffrey the savior. Jeffrey would inherit the Earth. Who wouldn't love him?

He supposed he needed a ticket to get in. A ticket and a tuxedo. Even if he couldn't get in, Amber would certainly notice him outside. It's like when you see someplace you know on the news. Hey isn't that . . . and the little black kids from the hall would be jumping up and down behind the reporter making funny faces, purposefully walking back and forth behind him several times and then giving him bunny ears with their fingers. She'd see him and she'd feel safe. She might get worried at first about how it would all go down, but when he needed her, she'd step in. She was on his side even if she didn't know it yet.

Jeffrey stared at the wallpaper peeling away from the corner at the foot of his bed. For a fugitive, solitary moment, he experienced a state of being without thought, without the burden of words. He was perfectly still, like the model he drew in art class. He didn't blink. He didn't sing songs in his head. His entire existence blended into the stillness.

A pigeon cooed outside his window, bringing him back to life.

Jeffrey looked around his room. Are we doing this or aren't we? What do you think? I don't know. What time is it? It's not far. What do you think'll happen? Maybe Amber will come over to the screaming fans and sign autographs. Then he'd be able to rescue her. The CIA was probably trying to get her to insert messages into the dialogue. She shouldn't do it. They'd ruin her in the end, even if she agreed to do it. That's how it works with them. You do what they want and they fuck you over anyway. Probably that soda fucker working on her crew was one of them. That whole soda conversation could've been some kind of code. Jeffrey could've received the messages and not even have known they were messages. The kids in the hall with the umbrella could have marked him, inserted some microscopic device into his arm to track his movements or to release some sort of poison at just the right time. They would force him to deliver the message he didn't know he was carrying and then he would die.

Fuck it, I should just kill myself, Jeffrey thought. Over and done. Beat them at their own game.

Jeffrey stared at his bed, at the grayness that enveloped the historic National Hotel. It was reminiscent of a vision he often had right before falling asleep. The hotel was out of focus. It was blurring away like an eraser rubbing out pencil marks, or a pen with erasable ink. Just enough markings are left behind so you know that something was erased. Something used to be there, but you can't make out exactly what it was, and something's fucking with your head so you can't remember either.

I can't die here, Jeffrey thought. Not alone, bleeding to death in this gray room. If I shot myself here, even my blood would run gray.

Better to go down in a blaze of glory. Better to let the world know I was here. Better to let Amber know I really loved her. Better to let everyone know that I was here and I existed and I had feelings. I had ideas. I had thoughts. I wanted things. And nobody listened to me and nobody cared. They just erased the parts of me they didn't like and didn't want to see. But they could only erase the parts they saw. I still saw the rest of me, the parts they didn't give a shit about. They hate me because even after the erasing, all the putrid parts grow back. My skin is rubbed raw from all the erasing and it stings every time it grows back, and then before it has time to heal, I get rubbed out again. Everyone wants me to be some normal all-American businessman, play ball, make a buck, chow down on a Big Mac, fuck some Playboy pinup girl, buy a house in the suburbs, and take out the garbage. All I want is Amber. All I want is for me and Amber to be together the way we should be, the way we're supposed to be. We would spend a year in bed like John and Yoko. We would be king and queen because we understand things, we would change things, we would make things right. Everything now is a mistake. The whole world is a mistake. It was all a mistake that I am where I am. I wasn't meant to wind up in a shithole like this. I should walk over to the White House right now and shoot myself on the pearly white steps, stain them up good with my blood. Or catch a bus up to New York, do it right where John fell. I'm just never given a chance. Nobody cares. My parents haven't even tried to find me. Good riddance to bad rubbish, they're probably thinking. Jesus is the one who saves. We don't have to worry.

Let's go. Let's do it.

Okay, but let's be smart about it.

Jeffrey straightened up his room. He tossed his clothes back into his suitcase and threw his food wrappers into the trashcan. He smoothed out the bed cover and tried to tuck it back over the pillows the way the maids did. He picked off the toothpaste glob in the sink and washed it down the drain.

He reloaded his gun. He wanted all fresh bullets. He wanted everything about it to be clean. He put the gun in his jacket pocket. He went into the bathroom and wiped off his hunting knife with a towel so it was all shiny. In the mirror, he noticed that his hair was full of static. He patted it down with water the way his mother had showed him how to do as a kid going to school picture day.

He did a few practice draws to make sure he could get everything out of his pockets. Gun right, knife left. Shoot forward, stab backward. Grab Amber's wrist. Then let go of the knife, and keep shooting forward. This will clear some space around you, and you'll have more of chance of making a dash. Best place to go is the Metro. Get lost in the crowd. Change trains. Change directions. Double back. Then get out and take a bus. No one will know anything on a bus. If none of that works, shoot four times and save the last bullets for you and Amber. She would want it that way.

There was nothing left to do but walk out the door. He thought he should do something ritualistic since he was going into battle, going to reclaim his Helen from Troy. He needed war paint or something, but he didn't have anything like that. Jeffrey put everything back into his pockets and felt the knife clack against something inside. He reached in and pulled out the little gumball machine bird. Jeffrey wound her up and set her down on the hotel dresser.

The bird wobbled and walked forward as the gears turned inside her plastic body. Jeffrey thought she was going to fall off the dresser, but her gears wound down and she stopped with one foot lifted up, balanced perfectly on the edge. She looked like a cartoon character about to walk off a cliff. Jeffrey was afraid that any movement he might make would send her over to meet her doom on the gray, carpeted floor. He walked sideways over to the door doing the grapevine step he learned in gym class right before they taught square dancing. Everyone hated square dancing, but they kept teaching it year after year.

He made it to the door and carefully turned the knob. The bird stared at him as he walked backward into the hallway.

"Good luck!" the little bird said.

Jeffrey smiled back.

Inside his head he said, "Thanks! I'll need it."

The little bird understood.

ON HIS WAY over to the Kennedy Center, Jeffrey orbited the rotary of Washington Circle three times, crossing Pennsylvania Avenue, K Street, New Hampshire Avenue, and 23rd Street over and over and over again. He had read somewhere that if you walk in a circle around your bride three times, you were married. He felt married, he felt bound to Amber, inexplicably intertwined with her honeyed braids.

Each crosswalk offered Jeffrey a different view of the future: the White House down Pennsylvania Avenue, the Lincoln Memorial down 23rd, and the Kennedy Center down New Hampshire. Jeffrey turned down New Hampshire and noticed the sounds of his footsteps echoing Amber's name: Am-ber, Am-ber, Am-ber. Left foot was Am, right foot was ber. This was a good sign. It was doubly good because Jeffrey had to pass the Watergate Hotel. Deep Throat could be on to him.

Jeffrey saw the action from a block away. The Kennedy Center was lit up with columns of light from the ground, just like the Metro. Extra lights flooded the entrance for the television crews. Jeffrey played it cool and watched from across the street. He noticed a traffic cop nearby and asked him what was going on.

"President's coming through here," he said. "Special award ceremony, lots of movie stars too."

"Oh really?" Jeffrey said. He sounded truly surprised. He was convincingly playing the part of a curious passerby.

Then, stroke of genius, he asked the cop if people were allowed to watch. The cop said, sure, you can go right over as long as you stay behind the barriers. It's crowded though. You might have to elbow your way in there if you want to see anything.

Gee, thanks, Officer Friendly. You sure are nice for a pig.

Jeffrey crossed the street against the light. He figured it was okay to jaywalk since the cop told him he could.

He made it to the crowd of fans and squeezed his way to the second row of people behind the barricades on the grassy knoll. He could see Secret Service men with their little wires going from their ears down into their suits. He wondered if they wore bulletproof vests. A little old lady was making her way along the red carpet that curved through the driveways. She wore a bright blue sequined dress and a white fur stole draped across her shoulders. On her head was a diamond tiara. Little old ladies liked to dress up and parade around this way thinking they were the Queen of England. Jeffrey didn't think she was anyone famous. Not anymore.

A limousine pulled up and Jeffrey's heart thumped wildly in his fragile chest. For a second he thought it might be Amber because he didn't think presidents took limousines, but he knew that movie stars did. He wondered what kind of car the president took. Something official. Some kind of bulletproof police car. But maybe some kind of limousine. It could be a limousine.

The people in the crowd behind him pushed forward and Jeffrey was pressed into a guy in the front row whose long hair brushed against his face. The president appeared out of a secret entrance near the Hall of Nations, having bypassed the red carpet runway. He posed for pics under the flags, giving cheery little waves. A posse of tuxedoed Secret Service men encircled him and Nancy. Good, Jeffrey thought, he's over there. That'll keep the Secret Service out of the way.

Jeffrey was pressed so hard against the long-haired guy, he wasn't sure how long it was before he turned his head back to the movie star gauntlet and noticed the second limousine. He wasn't sure if the limousine had just pulled up or if it had been there all along calmly waiting for the good parking spot.

A chauffeur stepped around and held his hand out to the passenger inside the shaded luxury vehicle. A small, delicate, white hand placed itself in his palm. Amber emerged out of the darkness, her bright hair flowing free in the evening air. The silky pink dress clinging to her skin looked more like a slip than formalwear. It invited people to look at her body. She smiled at everyone. She blushed a little. A single tuxedo followed her a few steps behind. She didn't have a date to the prom, it was just some hired thug.

Nancy and Ronnie waved like ruling emperors at the coliseum watching the virgin being sacrificed for fun. Then, not needing to see the carnage, they went inside.

Amber worked the crowd like a pro. She went over to people and shook their hands. She signed a few autographs. She accepted a teddy bear from a little girl and tousled her hair. She turned toward Jeffrey and started walking over to him. The movie screen that divided them, that kept her life separate from his, was melting away. The transparent fabric was vaporizing and Jeffrey could no longer tell if he was becoming a part of Amber's movie or if she was becoming part of his.

He stuck his right hand in his pocket so he could feel for his gun and reached out with his left. Amber was shaking hands, moving down the line. She touched Jeffrey's hand and gave it an awkward little squeeze. He was touching her. He wouldn't let go. He had her. He had her now. All they had to do was make a run for it. Amber reached out with her other arm to clasp another fan's hand, and she began to drift away with the crowd and dislodge from Jeffrey. Jeffrey pulled her back. She looked at him and smiled as she jerked her arm back. She wasn't getting the message. It could be too late.

Jeffrey let his eyes travel all over her. He had never been this close before. She tried to jerk her hand away again. Jeffrey's palms were clammy from nerves and he was afraid her slender hand would slip out. He wrapped his fingers around her wrist making a bracelet that snapped in place. In a barely audible whisper, he mouthed the words, "Let's go."

Amber turned her head away from Jeffrey and motioned to her male escort. The tuxedo started heading over. Amber gave one more ladylike jerk and Jeffrey released her wrist. It was too late. She was too far gone. Jeffrey had to step in or there would be no hope for either of them. He was going to have to save her. He was going to have to shoot. He had thought she might run away with him when she saw him, but that wasn't happening. She needed him to save her. That's what had to happen.

This was Jeffrey's movie. It would go down the way he wanted. He was the writer, director, and star.

Shoot forward, stab backward.

Six shots. Six chances. Good odds.

Jeffrey took a deep breath. He heard someone call, "Action!" inside his head.

Our hero draws his gun and locks his elbow in a straight line extending from his shoulder. His arm feels like part of the gun. It feels strong and made of steel. He pulls the trigger.

The first shot is loud and sends a jolt through his body. Women scream and everyone ducks down. Jeffrey feels better after the first shot. Things are in motion. There is no more worry about whether or not something is going to happen. He had jumped out of the airplane, the parachute had opened, and he was launched into a controlled free-fall. A pleasurable feeling of power sweeps across Jeffrey's arms, the same arms that would soon hold Amber close and tight. With the second shot people scatter on the ground like cockroaches bombed out of their lairs. The Secret Service men draw their weapons. The tuxedo pimp grabs Amber. Fucker. Let go of her. Number three. Bang! Jeffrey gets used to the sound. Flashes are going off, Jeffrey is stepping out onto the red carpet. His fans are cheering. Some fucker tries to push his arm down. With his free hand, Jeffrey pulls out his knife and stabs the guy in the gut. We'll see what you had for breakfast. Four. Pow! Amber is screaming, confused. She's breaking down. He's getting through to her. Jeffrey feels arms grab him around the waist. Jeffrey doesn't care. He doesn't care as long as he has that one arm. All he needs is that one arm. Someone kicks the back of his knees and makes him take a step forward.

There are two bullets left, one for each of them. He has to take her with him, even if he isn't getting out of here. That was the plan. Finish what you started. That's what his dad would say. Jeffrey tilts his head to the side and presses his cheek into the flesh of his upper arm. Make it a good one. Do it for her.

I'm sorry, Amber. I love you. This might hurt. I love you. I'm sorry.

Five.

Amber turned around and lurched like a duck trying to fly off the surface of a pond. She looked directly at Jeffrey and opened her mouth as her pink bodice became soaked with red, matching the carpet beneath her glass slippers. She stumbled to her knees and collapsed to the Earth, blonde locks cascading perfectly over her face as a golden shroud. She was an angel now. Jeffrey had made her one.

Jeffrey felt exhilarated. He felt all the color being restored to his body. He heard the crowd screaming for him. He felt alive, alive, alive. So alive, he must've been dead before. He forgot about the last bullet meant for him. He could do it, but he didn't need to. He didn't want to. He felt great. He felt high. He was walking on air even as someone wrenched his arm behind his back, kneed him in the stomach and shoved his face down to the uncarpeted concrete. He loved that concrete. All the tiny pebble dots making up a smooth, hard surface with little glints of sparkles. The first time he spoke to Amber she was sitting on concrete. If he was lying like this and she was sitting there again, he would be able to see the clean white surface of her underwear glowing beneath her skirt.

He would be allowed in.

TO SEE THE WIZARD

* * *

Dress rehearsal was held during recess on the day of the performance. Everyone had to be back at school by six p.m. because the show was at seven p.m. The music teacher suggested they eat a light dinner and drink a cup of tea with lemon for their singing voices. When Tammy and Steffi got home from school they made two glasses of Nestea from a scoop of powder mix. They didn't have any lemon so they put in honey instead. They had to keep stirring between sips because otherwise the honey would stick to the bottom.

Tammy's mother and Nick got home around five fifteen p.m. Tammy told them that she and Steffi had to eat a light dinner and be back at school by six. Her mother said to make a sandwich. Tammy said a sandwich wasn't dinner. A sandwich was lunch. Nick yelled, "Then I guess you don't want dinner!" Tammy didn't want them to yell anymore so she and Steffi made peanut butter sandwiches and ate them with their iced tea, side by side, at the table.

The red kitchen phone rang and Nick answered, "Mmm, hello?" He always answered the phone that way, and for the first year he lived with them, Tammy and Steffi thought he was saying "mellow," and they didn't understand what it meant. Nick talked in a smart-sounding voice, which Tammy knew meant it was something about work. After he hung up, he ran upstairs, and when he came down again, he had changed from his jeans back into the gray suit he had worn to work.

"How come you changed back?" Steffi asked.

"I have to go back to work," he said. "I'm sorry, but . . . I think I'm going to miss your play." He was about to say something else, but then looked down at the floor. "I'm really sorry," he said again.

Tammy really didn't care, but Steffi stared at her plate and the uneaten half of her sandwich. She put her hands in her lap and sat like that for a minute and Tammy thought she might lean down and try to eat her sandwich as if she had no arms. In order to do that, Steffi would have to get her face really close to the plate and try to scoop up the bread with her tongue. But of course, Steffi would never do anything like that. She had very good table manners. She kept her eyes on the jagged triangle of bread and peanut butter and didn't do anything weird. Then, without saying, "Excuse me," Steffi got up from the table and went upstairs. She didn't finish her sandwich and she didn't clear her plate.

A little while later, Tammy's mother came downstairs and told her that Steffi was sick and she couldn't be in the show tonight. Her mother said it would be all right because Steffi was in the chorus and they had lots of other people to sing. No one would mind, but could Tammy tell the music teacher when she got there?

There was one other thing—Tammy's mother couldn't come to the show either. Since Nick had to go back to work, her mother had to stay home with Steffi in case the asthma got worse and she had to go to the emergency room.

"So, basically, no one is coming to the play," Tammy said. She put her hands on her hips and mashed her lips together. This always happened. Whatever was important to Tammy was overlooked or not important enough to anyone else. She would have been madder about it, but it happened all the time.

"Hugh wants to come," her mother said.

It was the night of her play and Tammy was getting stuck watching her brother.

Tammy went up to her room to get ready. The separator door was open and she could see Steffi lying in bed, under her mustard blanket, curled up facing the wall.

"Are you really sick or are you faking it?" Tammy asked. She never asked Steffi this outright, but Steffi was being so obvious about it tonight.

Steffi slithered under the covers. She curled herself up tighter and her legs made an S shape under the blanket.

"I don't feel well," Steffi said.

"Do you have asthma?" Tammy asked, trying to trip her up and make her give herself away.

"I just don't feel well."

Tammy forgot that Steffi was the expert at being sick. If she wanted to, Steffi could probably make herself sick just by thinking about it. If Steffi were a superhero, that would be her special power.

"Oh well," Tammy said in an attempt to make Steffi feel guilty, "guess you're not going to be in the play." Tammy acted like she didn't care what Steffi did or didn't do and started to close the separator door.

"I think you should do it tonight," Steffi said quietly, a few decibels above a whisper, before Tammy could let go of the doorknob. She didn't turn away from the wall when she said it. Tammy was almost going to say, "Do what?" but she knew what Steffi meant. She wasn't 100 percent sure, but she was pretty sure. Tammy rested her hand into the square part of the separator door that was missing a windowpane and let her fingers creep across the official boundary and into Steffi's room.

"Tammy?"

"Yeah?"

"I think you should do it tonight. After the play."

Steffi's clock radio said 5:45. Tammy was 90 percent sure that Steffi was talking about going to Kirin's house and getting Nick's gun, but she wanted her to say it. She waited until the clock changed to 5:46, and then to 5:47, but Steffi didn't say anything more.

"I have to go," Tammy said.

Nick was on his way out the door and said he would give Tammy and Hugh a ride over, but they would have to walk home or get a ride from someone.

Nick dropped them off in front of school.

"Good luck," he said and gave Tammy's shoulder a little squeeze as she got out of the car. He was trying to be nice, but he didn't know it was bad luck to say good luck for a play.

Tammy told Hugh to find a seat in the auditorium while she went to put on her costume. The girls' bathroom was packed with everyone changing. Mrs. Perkins was helping them with makeup. Tammy put on her costume and covered her face with green eye shadow. She had to buy it with her allowance, but it was only ninety-nine cents and she could keep it afterward.

When the girls were finished getting dressed, they were told to go backstage. Tammy took her broom, which she brought from home, and her special hat, which she had decorated with gold glitter, and made her way through the audience to the stage door. Some mother with a little kid said, "Oh look, there's the Witch!"

The show started with the narrator standing off to the side. The narrator was an easy part because he didn't have to memorize his lines; he could just read them off the script at the podium. He was lit by a slide projector without a slide in it that made a square of light around his head.

Gretchen wasn't very good as Dorothy. She sang very softly and very high, but she was loud enough when she was talking. She had her hair done in two braids and was wearing a blue dress with a checkered apron and ballet slippers covered with red glitter. Toto was a wind-up toy dog. Gretchen was supposed to be able to clap her hands to make him start and stop. When she set off down the yellow brick road, she put Toto in her picnic basket, but he didn't exactly fit and had to be stuck in nose first. He fell out once, landed on his back, and turned himself on with his feet moving in the air. Gretchen had to clap four times before it would stop. Someone in the audience yelled out, "Toto's dead!" Everyone laughed.

Tammy's first scene was with Kenny. She put on her golden hat and called him and the other flying monkeys to the castle. The boys flapped around in a circle, acting more like superheroes than winged monkeys. Tammy told them to go get Dorothy and bring her to the castle. The boys flapped away and the narrator explained how they find Dorothy, kidnap her, and fly her to the Witch's castle. Tammy was onstage during this and she was supposed to look out at the audience and rub her hands together like she was watching what was going on in her crystal ball. Tammy looked out and saw the music teacher sitting in the front row. She held up a card from her lap that said, "Good Job!" Tammy didn't think the music teacher was supposed to do that because now Tammy was looking at her instead of looking out at the audience and rubbing her hands together. The music teacher sorted through the cards on her lap

to his mouth and took a long slurp. When Heather's mom was gone, he opened his mouth wide, showed her his orange tongue, and said, "Ahhhh!"

"Let's get out of here," Gretchen said.

"Who's gonna drive us?" Josh asked.

"No one. Let's walk. It'll be cool," Gretchen said.

It was agreed that this was a cool idea. They were too old for this kind of stupid kids' party. After all, they were going to be in junior high next year. In a year, they would be teenagers. And it wasn't that late. It was maybe eight thirty or nine p.m. and it wasn't a school night.

No one noticed the group of sixth graders leave out the back door. If they had, some mother probably would have said she had to drive them. Heather had to stay because it was her house and her mother was there, but Monique, Kenny, Colin, and Josh came along. When they were on the back stoop, Gretchen said to Tammy, "What about your brother?"

"Shit." She had forgotten him inside. Tammy walked back in the house and saw him licking the icing off a tinfoil cupcake wrapper. She grabbed his wrist.

"We have to go."

"No."

"Come on, we're going."

"No."

"Do you want another cupcake?"

"Yes."

"If we leave right now, you can take one with you."

Hugh climbed off the couch and walked over to the food table. He took another cupcake even though some mother gave the two of them a mean look. Tammy scooted him toward the kitchen and out the back door.

"Are you the baby?" Kenny asked.

"No," Hugh said.

"You have a baby-sitter."

"I'm not a baby."

"But you have a *baby*-sitter."

Hugh stood on the back porch and refused to move.

"Come on," Tammy said as she pulled his sleeve and tugged him down the steps. She yanked on him a little too hard and his cupcake fell to the ground. He whimpered and asked if he could go back inside and get another one, but Tammy said, no, they had to go. He started breathing funny like he might start bawling really loud. Tammy whispered to him, "Just pick it up and see how dirty it is."

When he picked it up the icing stuck to the ground and peeled off, but the cake part looked fine and he ate it.

"Gross!" Monique said.

"Let's go before they come out here," Gretchen said.

They walked through Heather's backyard, ducked under the fence that ran along the school playground, and started what was the normal route home. As they walked down the street, Monique started to sing, "We're Off to See the Wizard." Everyone joined in, even though the chorus sang this song in the play. Everyone knew the words from the movie and as they skipped down the street, they looked like they *were* in the movie. Dorothy, the Scarecrow, the Tin Man, the Lion. Tammy and Kenny were a little out of place since, in the movie, they weren't in the yellow brick road scenes, but they were still in the movie.

When the song ended, everyone was quiet and the only sound was seven pairs of feet thumping along the sidewalk. They arrived at 43rd Street on the corner across from Tammy's house. They were on the edge of the nice neighborhood.

Tammy had been so caught up in the play, she had completely forgotten about Steffi. It wasn't until she saw her house that she put it all together. This was the best time for her to go to Kirin's house, get the gun, and pour the wine down the sink. It was dark out so no one would see her at Kirin's. Her mother and Nick hadn't given her a specific time to be home. They didn't know how long the play was or what time the party ended. And the party was still going on. Her mother and Nick might not be home. Nick could still be at work, and her mother could have taken Steffi to the emergency room because of an asthma attack.

"See ya," Gretchen said as the group turned down Bemis Street and continued on.

Hugh had chocolate cupcake crumbs stuck to his face. Tammy had to get rid of him. She wanted to go to Kirin's house and walk a little bit behind Gretchen and the gang so she wouldn't feel so alone walking in the dark, and if anything happened, if someone tried to jump out and kidnap her, she could try and catch up with them. Or she could scream and Gretchen would probably recognize her voice.

"Look," Tammy said to Hugh, "go inside and tell them I had to go to Gretchen's house to pick something up."

"What do you have to pick up?"

"Nothing. . . . My book bag, I left my book bag at school and Gretchen's mom accidentally took it home."

This was too confusing for him, although it was a good excuse.

"I don't want to go by myself," he said.

"You're not going anywhere by yourself. Our house is right there. Just go in."

"I don't have a key."

"You don't need a key. Just knock on the door and they'll let you in."

"I want to go with you."

Tammy was worried that if she argued with him anymore he would start to cry and someone would hear them. And in a weird way, even though he was six years younger, Tammy felt safer with him around.

"Come on," Tammy said.

And so the two of them crossed 43rd Street and entered the dark, forested neighborhood. And at night, the interior of Friendship Heights felt far more unfriendly than its shady borders.

Tammy didn't want to run into Gretchen and Monique, so she opted to walk through the alleyways that ran behind the houses, parallel to Bemis Street. The alley pavement was broken in places and full of pebbles and broken glass and other stuff that had erupted from the street. Hugh bent down every now and then to pick up bottle caps, checking to see if someone accidentally threw one away that could be turned in for a prize. Once he won a free soda and made Tammy take him to the grocery store to redeem it.

When she got to 46th Street, Tammy crouched down between two parked cars and held on to Hugh's sleeve so he wouldn't walk out into the street and give them away. Tammy had to make sure no one was around and that Gretchen and Monique had already gone inside their houses. She looked both ways, grabbed Hugh's wrist, dashed across the street, and entered the alley that ran behind Gretchen's and Kirin's houses.

Tammy wasn't sure what she was supposed to do next. She had never broken into someone's house before. She had never done something that was against the law. She might have to break a window. If she did, she would do it with a rock so she wouldn't cut herself.

"Is this Gretchen's house?" Hugh asked in his little voice. He wasn't curious as to why they were going in the back way because he and Tammy were used to it. They only had a key to the back door of their own house and they rarely used the front.

"No, this is Kirin's house," Tammy said. She lifted the latch and pulled the gate open.

"What are you doing?"

Tammy spun around. Gretchen was peeking through the cracks of the tall wooden fence from her backyard. More than one pair of eyeballs blinked at her between the cracks. Gretchen's gate swung into the alley and Monique, Colin, Kenny, and Josh spilled out.

If it had been just Gretchen, Tammy might have told her what she was really doing at Kirin's house. But she couldn't tell all of them. She had to think of something fast.

"I thought this was your house," Tammy said. "I was trying to catch up with you."

Tammy wasn't sure if anyone bought that explanation or not. No one said anything for a minute and then Kenny blurted, "Shit, she almost went in there!" He laughed out loud as Tammy stepped away from the gate. Tammy forced herself to laugh a little bit so she blended in with the group.

"Let's go in," Gretchen said. "Let's check it out."

"What's there to see?" Josh asked.

"Ghosts," Gretchen said, "and blood."

"There's not still blood."

"Yes there is. It's hard to get bloodstains out. My mother had to throw out all her bloody clothes."

"I don't know," Monique said.

"Let's do it," Josh said. "We're here anyway."

"Yeah," Colin said.

The boys moved in toward Kirin's gate, but Gretchen pushed ahead of them. She obviously wanted to be the boss since she lived next door. Tammy thought the best thing to do was to go along with them. Then she could either stay behind and get the gun, or leave with them and sneak back after everyone else had gone home. Either way she was stuck with them for now.

Monique said she didn't think this was a good idea.

"So don't come," Gretchen said and she opened the gate like she owned the place. Monique came along. Monique was always saying she didn't like things, or that they were going to get in trouble, but then always going along anyway.

The white pebble path glowed in the dark; it stretched out in front of them leading up to the back porch. Colin took a couple steps on the path making big crunching sounds with his feet. Josh stopped him and motioned for them all to walk on the grass.

They tiptoed up to the back door. Gretchen tried to open it, but it was locked.

"It's locked?" Josh asked.

"Of course it's locked, dumb ass!" Kenny said.

"You don't have a key?" Colin asked. "Great plan, Gretchen."

"Shut up. Let's look around."

They looked in all the usual places, under the doormat and under the flowerpots, but they didn't find anything. Monique said that her mom used to hide a key in the dirt. Not under the flowerpot, but inside the dirt, covered up.

They dug around in a couple of pots.

"Hey! I found it," Hugh said holding up the dirt-covered key in his stubby little fingers.

"Thanks, Toto!" Gretchen said.

"Hey, yeah. He can be Toto! Good boy!" Kenny said and patted him on the head.

Gretchen wiped the key off on her Dorothy apron. She put it in the lock and took a deep breath. Then she turned the knob and the door popped open.

Inside it was dark. Kenny reached over and flipped on the light. Gretchen whipped around and hissed at him. Josh made a face.

"What?" Kenny asked.

"Don't turn on the light, dumb ass! People are going to know we're here!" Josh said.

"Okay, dumb ass, I'll turn it off!" Kenny turned off the light and shut the door.

"Don't shut the door!" Josh said.

"Oh, what now, dumb ass? You don't think people are going to know we're here if they see the door open?"

"We may need to get out fast."

"Oh, so now you're a dumb ass and a cowardly lion."

"Shut up!"

"SHHHH!" Monique said, raising her Tin Man axe at them.

They moved through the kitchen and into the living room. The only thing in there was the couch. Other than that it was empty.

"We should go upstairs," Gretchen said. "That's where it happened."

No one said anything, but inside they all agreed. They walked around to the front of the house where the stairs stood opposite the front door.

"Where is everybody?" Hugh asked.

"They're not home," Tammy said.

"Where are they?"

"They don't live here anymore."

"Why not?"

"Because, Kirin died, remember? And her mom's in the crazy hospital and her dad moved away."

"So we won't sleep over here anymore?"

"Shut up!" Tammy said and pushed him up the stairs.

Kenny was the last one in line going up the stairs. He kept leaning into Tammy's ear, flapping his monkey wings, and saying, "Caw!"

Upstairs in the hallway, everything looked normal. They didn't see any blood.

"We should go in her room," Colin said. "That's where she got shot. I read it in the newspaper."

All the bedroom doors were closed. Everyone looked around to think of which way to go.

"It's down that way," Tammy said.

"Witchy witch knows! Witchy witch knows which way to go!" Kenny said.

Tammy turned around and gave him a look, which meant, shut up. He grinned at her and said, "Caw!"

Kirin's door made a long creaking sound as Colin pushed it open with Monique's Tin Man axe. Someone shoved Tammy in the back and she tripped on her long skirt and stumbled into Kirin's room.

"You're the witch. Witchy witches live in haunted castles," Kenny said.

Tammy ignored Kenny because she couldn't think of anything good to say back.

"That's right, Wicked Witch," Gretchen said. "This is your house and you've kidnapped us here."

Gretchen took a step into the room with a smirk on her face and switched on the light. She wasn't acting scared. Maybe she'd been here before.

There wasn't any blood. The room looked like a normal kid's room, but some things seemed to be missing. Kirin used to have her swimming ribbons hanging up and they were all gone. She used to have all of her stuffed animals in a perfect line on a shelf and they were gone too. There was nothing on the walls. Tammy couldn't remember what used to be there, pictures or posters or a map of the world maybe, but now the walls were blank. There were no books on the bookshelf and probably if they pulled open one of her dresser drawers there would be no clothes inside. There was still a lamp on her desk and an empty corkboard. A bunch of empty cardboard boxes were stacked one inside another. One box had all of Kirin's board games in it, but the rest were empty. Her bed was missing the top mattress. Just the bottom box spring was there with no sheets and it looked too close to the ground.

Tammy stared at the bed. That was where it happened. Kirin was asleep. Tammy couldn't look away. She had never seen a spot where someone had died.

"That's where she was shot," Colin said. "On the bed."

Gretchen sat down on the corner of the box spring.

"Don't sit there. You shouldn't do that," Monique said.

"Why? Are you going to kill me?"

They suddenly heard adult voices coming from the hall. Or maybe it was from right next door, or outside a window. But it sounded close. Gretchen made a motion with her hand at Kenny and he turned off the light. They stood in the dark and listened. People were talking. It was definitely coming from the hall.

Tammy realized she didn't know where Hugh was. He wasn't in the room. At least she didn't think he was and now the lights were out and she couldn't tell.

"Witchy witch," Kenny whispered loud enough so that everyone could hear, "it's your house. Go see who it is."

"No way."

"You have to. It's your haunted house."

"Where's my brother?"

"I ate him. Monkeys eat babies."

"Shut up."

"Just go quick and check it out and come right back," Monique piped in.

Tammy went into the hall because she knew they wouldn't leave her alone unless she did. The voices were coming from the guest room. Tammy didn't have to turn the knob because she could see the guest room door was already open a crack. She tapped it open with her broom, very slowly, so whoever was in there wouldn't notice.

Hugh was sitting on the floor watching TV in the dark.

"You're not supposed to be in here," Tammy whispered and switched off the TV.

"I can watch TV. The ghost said I could."

"What ghost?"

"Angel ghost. Remember?"

"There's no such thing."

"Kirin said there was. She said they lived here."

"Well Kirin is dead and all the angels moved out."

"Why did they leave the TV?"

"I don't know."

"Can we keep it? Can we take it home?"

"No," Tammy said and pulled him to his feet.

When Tammy and Hugh walked into the hallway, the door to Kirin's room slammed shut. Tammy saw the light switch back on through the slit where the door met the carpet. She could hear everyone moving around in there. Tammy didn't want them poking around in the room without her.

She tried to turn the knob but it was locked.

"Let me in."

Magically, the door opened by itself. Kirin's room looked empty and Tammy guessed everyone was hiding somewhere as a joke. She walked inside and Hugh followed her.

Kenny and Josh grabbed hold of Tammy and pulled her arms behind her back.

"Gotcha, witchy witch! You're our prisoner now."

"Let me go! You're not funny!"

"Let me go, you're not funny!" Kenny said in high-pitched voice like he was trying to imitate her.

"Stop it! Let go!"

"Shut up, witchy bitch. Shut the hell up or we'll lock you in this room and leave you here."

"Stop it. You're just fooling around."

"No we're not, bitch witch. We're serious."

The closet door opened and Gretchen poked her head out. "Yeah," she said, "we're dead serious." Gretchen, Monique, and Colin had been hiding in the closet.

Tammy stopped wriggling because it just made Kenny and Josh hold on tighter and it made her arms hurt.

Gretchen walked over to the bed, held her arms out to Hugh, and said, "Come here." He didn't move at first. Gretchen said she would let him keep the TV if he came over and sat with her on the bed for a minute.

"Good boy. Good Toto. You're still Toto the dog, remember?"

He nodded as he carefully sat down on the bed.

"Gimme a bark, Toto. Pretend you're a dog."

He barked.

"Good boy. Good doggie, Toto. Now lie down here. Lie down on the bed and go to sleep. You can pretend. You don't really have to go to sleep."

He leaned back on the bed and curled up in a ball. He even stuck his thumb in his mouth and made snoring sounds.

"Good boy. Go to sleep now." Gretchen got up and walked over to Tammy with a know-it-all smile on her face.

"Okay, Wicked Witch, first of all I'm taking your broomstick and I'm keeping it." She picked up Tammy's broom, which Tammy had dropped when Kenny grabbed her arms. Tammy couldn't tell if Gretchen was playing around or if she was really going to keep it. If Gretchen didn't give it back, Tammy would get in trouble because she had taken the broom from home to use in the play.

"Now you have no power and you have to do what I say. Are you going to do what I say?"

"I don't know."

"That's not an answer. Yes or no?"

"Okay, just let me go."

Gretchen looked at Tammy long and hard.

"Let her go, monkey, but guard the door."

Gretchen opened the closet door and pulled out a Tupperware container. It was the wine container that Kirin had kept in her room.

"We found this container of pee. You have to drink it."

"That's not pee."

"It looks like pee and it smells like pee. Therefore, it is pee."

Tammy knew it was the wine, but Gretchen could have had one of the boys pee into the container while the door was shut.

Gretchen peeled off the lid and passed the container to Tammy.

"Drink up," she said.

Tammy held the container with both hands and lifted it to her mouth. It smelled bad, but it didn't smell like pee. She put her mouth around the edge and let a tiny sip of liquid enter her mouth and flow back into the container. It was the wine. It tasted like apple juice that had gone bad.

Gretchen crossed her arms over her chest.

"You have to drink the whole thing."

Tammy didn't want to drink it, but then she thought, if she did, it would be gone and no one would find it. Steffi wouldn't have to worry about it. No one would dust an empty Tupperware container for fingerprints. They would think it had just been forgotten and left behind by accident. People forgot Tupperware containers all the time.

Tammy held the container to her mouth. She drank the first gulps quickly, trying to block her nose inside her mouth so she wouldn't have to taste it. She felt herself start to throw up a little bit, but she managed to swallow it back down. She drank a couple more gulps, came up for air, and wiped her mouth with the cuff of her black witch's turtleneck. There was only a little bit left for Tammy to finish, but Gretchen took the container from her, set it on the floor, and pretended to wake Hugh up.

"Come here, come here, boy. Take a drink from your bowl," Gretchen said. Hugh got down from the bed on all fours like a dog and crawled over to the plastic bowl. He gave a bark and stuck his head in the Tupperware to drink. He took one slurp with his tongue and spat it out.

"You have to drink it. You have to drink it, doggie. I know it tastes bad. Just drink it really fast. Be a good dog and you'll get the TV."

Hugh stuck his head back in the dish and started slurping. He was slurping and spitting and giving a cough or two. Tammy was a little worried about him, but she decided not to say anything and let the wine disappear down his throat. Just let it go. Let it get swallowed up. Then she could cross the wine off Steffi's list. Hugh managed to lick up most of what was left in the container. He lifted his head out of the bowl and let his tongue hang out of his mouth.

"Good boy!" Gretchen said and gave him a few pats on the head. "Now come here and go back to sleep."

Hugh jumped back up on the bed, and instead of staying near the edge, he crawled all around acting like a dog. Hugh usually didn't show off like this in front of Tammy's friends. Tammy had to drag him along sometimes, but usually he was quiet. Finally, he collapsed and curled up with his back to them. Tammy watched his side move up and down and she started to feel sleepy herself.

Gretchen stood in front of Tammy, right in front of her face.

"You've got some explaining to do, young lady," Gretchen said. She looked older when she said that. It sounded like something a mom would say. She went around to the other side of the bed and Tammy noticed that someone had knocked over the box with board games and all the Monopoly money was scattered everywhere. Gretchen squatted down by the game Sorry! and lifted up the lid to the box at an angle so Tammy couldn't see what she was looking for inside, then she closed the box and held something behind her back. She started to laugh and had to scrunch her lips together so she could talk.

"Would you mind explaining *these* to us?" she said. She took her hands from behind her back and shoved something in front of Tammy's face. Gretchen held it too close to Tammy's eyes so all she saw was a square of dark shapes. Gretchen pulled back and the picture came into focus. They were the Polaroid photos of Tammy's mother and Nick. Gretchen held them in front of Tammy's face and, one by one, went through them like flash cards for a vocabulary test. They were the naked photos taken with her camera. Tammy's chest started to feel funny and her cheeks felt limp. Her arms were hanging loosely at her sides and she could feel them start to shiver. She tried not to look at the photos, but past them and at the floor.

"Well?" Gretchen said. She bent down and put her head in line with Tammy's vision and forced Tammy to look at her.

"I don't know," Tammy said. She said it very lightly. She didn't want to say anything and she didn't want to look at anything. Anything, at this point, could make her cry.

"It's your mom, right? And your stepfather." Gretchen knew that it was and she wasn't going to let it go. She flipped through the photos again. When Tammy tried to move her head Gretchen held them closer and forced her to look at the naked bodies sprawled against the rainbow bedspread and the one of Nick taking a picture of himself in the mirror wearing only a pair of brown socks. Tammy didn't know what those pictures were doing here. The only thing she could think of was that Steffi and Kirin must've borrowed them along with the gun, hidden them in the Sorry! box, and nobody found them. It was strange that the police didn't look in every nook and cranny, but if Kirin was shot on top of the bed and her mom said she did it, maybe they figured they didn't need to. And maybe when Kirin's dad moved her stuff out, he was trying to do it quickly and forgot about the board games.

"Your mom's a hooker," Kenny said.

Tammy didn't say anything back.

"What does she charge? Probably not a lot. She's not that pretty."

Tammy wanted to tell him to shut up, but she couldn't say anything. If she said a single word, she would start crying really hard. She had never once seen Gretchen or Monique cry. The only girl who ever cried in school was Olga, the Russian girl, when everyone made fun of her for being Russian, and one time Heather cried at school because her dog died the night before. Tammy didn't cry at school about Kirin. No one did. Except Steffi.

"Does your mom teach you how to be a hooker? Do you run around naked all the time and have sex and take pictures? Where are the naked pictures of you? Huh? We want to see them," Kenny said.

Gretchen finally took the pictures away and put them in the pocket of her costume apron.

"How much do *you* charge?" Josh piped in.

"Hey, Lion here wants to know how much you charge," Kenny said. "It probably depends on what you want her to do."

"What if she shows us her tits?"

"She doesn't have any tits! You'd be wasting your money."

"How much if she gets completely naked?"

"Will you two shut up?" Gretchen said. She bent back down to the Sorry! box and lifted the lid again. This time when she stood back up she was holding a gun. It was black and Tammy was pretty sure it was

Nick's gun. Kirin and Steffi must have hidden it with the pictures in the Sorry! box.

"Let's play Truth or Dare," Gretchen said. "Tammy's going first."

Gretchen pointed the gun at Tammy and said, "Truth or dare?" It was Nick's gun and Gretchen knew it.

"Pick one. Truth or dare."

"I don't know."

"Just pick one. Just say one of the words."

Tammy had never played Truth or Dare before, but she had heard what it was like. Heather had told them her older sister had played it once and as a dare she had to stick a cookie down her pants, rub it around her vagina, and then eat it. Tammy thought truth would be a better option.

"Truth."

"Okay, truth." Gretchen stopped pointing the gun at Tammy and twirled it around one of her Dorothy braids. "Which boy in our class do you like enough to have sex with?"

"None."

"That's not an answer."

"I don't like any of them."

"She's a faggot!" Josh said.

"Okay, since you didn't answer my question, you automatically have to do a dare."

Monique said that's not how it works. She said you ask a question *or* do a dare and then you have to move onto the next person. You don't get to do both to one person in one go-round. Gretchen didn't like Monique butting in and telling her what's what. She pointed the gun at Tammy again and told her she had to do the dare anyway. Tammy was afraid Gretchen was going to make her take off all her clothes in front of the boys, or something like that. Some sex thing. If Gretchen made her get naked, Tammy wasn't sure what she would do. She guessed she could do it. She knew Gretchen had sucked face with Josh and Kenny in her basement rec room after school and Heather had let boys feel her up. If Gretchen made Tammy have sex with one of the boys, she guessed she could do it. Tammy hadn't gotten her period yet, so she knew she couldn't get pregnant. Tammy would do it to shut Gretchen up and get her out of there. She didn't think Gretchen had it in her to actually steal the gun. Gretchen liked to make a big deal about following the rules when they were at school. She liked to misbehave, but only when the teacher was out of the room.

"You'll do it?" Gretchen asked.

"Yeah, I mean, I don't care. I'll have sex."

Tammy didn't mean to say the last part. She didn't know what made her say it. It slipped out of her mouth like the little bit of vomit that bubbled up her throat when she drank the wine. Gretchen's eyes grew wide and she kind of coughed and laughed at the same time.

"You *are* a faggot!"

Tammy held her breath because otherwise she was going to sob. She knew Gretchen had been acting like she was older than she was ever since sixth grade started. But Tammy was loyal. Tammy hadn't told anyone when Gretchen started wearing a bra last month, and when the boys went around recess one day feeling girls' backs to see if they were wearing a bra that they could snap, Tammy stood behind Gretchen and backed her up against a wall so they couldn't get to her. But Gretchen had forgotten about all of that now. She had forgotten that she used to like to hang out at Tammy's house because there were no parents around after school. She had forgotten that she and Tammy's favorite game was pretending to be Q107 deejays. She didn't care that she was embarrassing Tammy with the naked pictures and she didn't seem to care if Tammy had to get naked in front of everyone.

"Are you going to do the dare?" Gretchen asked.

Tammy nodded. She concentrated on trying to breathe through her nose. She felt like all the parts of her body were coming apart and she had to think really hard to keep them together. She managed to whisper, "Okay."

"Everyone wants to know what happened here," Gretchen said. "We want to know what it was like. You have to take this gun and pretend to be Kirin's mom. That's your dare."

Gretchen held out the gun and Tammy took it with two hands. It was heavier than she thought it would be. It was black and matched her costume. She had it now. She could leave now. Kenny was standing by the door. There were three boys here. If she tried to make a run for it they would probably grab the gun from her. And then there was Hugh sleeping in the bed. She would have to do the dare and then somehow keep the gun. Or sneak back in when it was all over and get it. Tammy didn't think this dare was so bad. She didn't have to take her clothes off. She didn't have to have sex with Kenny. Gretchen explained that Tammy was supposed to use the gun just like Kirin's mom did. Everyone else would be silent observers and they would judge what really happened. Tammy was supposed to go out into the hall and come back in pretending to be Kirin's mom. It was like being in a play.

Tammy went out into the hall alone and Gretchen shut the door. She felt dizzy, but she thought she could do it and get it over with. She raised her hand to knock on the door, but, she thought, if Kirin was asleep, her mother probably didn't want to wake her. She probably just wanted to check on her or kiss her good-bye. She probably didn't knock. Tammy reached down and opened the door.

Hugh was still lying there curled up on the bed. Gretchen, Monique, and the boys were lined up by the window like an audience watching a show. Tammy took a few steps into the room, not sure what she was supposed to do next. She didn't have a script. She didn't know what she was supposed to say.

"You're supposed to aim the gun," Colin said. Tammy was holding the gun down by her side, the same way she would carry a book. She lifted up the gun and held it parallel to the floor. She took a few steps closer to the bed and veered a little to one side. Every time she moved, her head moved a little farther than the rest of her body and made her feel off balance. She saw her brother lying there like a sleeping lump. She sorted it out in her brain that he wasn't playing Toto anymore, he was playing Kirin. Usually kindergartners don't get two parts.

"Get closer," Gretchen said.

Tammy took a couple of steps toward the bed.

"Really close," Gretchen said.

Tammy shuffled forward until her shins were touching the side of the box spring and the gun was a few inches from her brother's back.

"Now shoot her," Gretchen said. Tammy took a deep breath and waited for Hugh's breath to catch up with hers. She used to do the same thing with her dad when he fell asleep in his armchair watching Saturday-afternoon sports on TV. Tammy didn't like to watch sports, but she would climb into his big chair and match her breath to his. It was the only time she ever liked taking naps.

Tammy tilted the gun up to the ceiling. "Pow," she said quietly in an annunciated whisper.

"That was lame," Gretchen said. "No one believed that. You have to really do it. Do it better."

It was agreed that Tammy would have to pull the trigger to make it real. She hadn't thought about it, but they were right. She should be serious. After all, it was a real gun. She should do everything real.

Tammy got back into position. She held her arms straight out and pointed the gun at her brother's back. It was easier to get her finger in the trigger hole if she held the gun with two hands. She looked down at her black sleeves merging into the black gun. The end of the gun was splitting in two. Her arms were wavy. There were lots of wrinkles on her sleeves because it was her mother's turtleneck and it was too big for her.

She looked at Hugh sleeping in front of her. He often fell asleep watching TV if Tammy and Steffi let him stay up late when their mother and Nick were out. For a second Tammy thought she might fall asleep and softly float down onto the bed like a person who was fainting. Tammy had never fainted, passed out, or had her lights knocked out. That happened all the time on TV. A person passes out and then wakes up in their bed the next morning. They can't remember how they got there, but everything is okay again.

Tammy didn't know how long she stood there, waiting to faint, about to shoot her brother, but it was long enough for Gretchen to say, "Okay, we're waiting." Tammy knew this was Nick's gun. She knew it was real. She knew that if she pulled the trigger, a bullet would go into her brother's back and probably into his aorta and his heart. His heart would stop beating and he would bleed a lot. And then Tammy wouldn't have a brother anymore. She wouldn't have to walk him to school or baby-sit him at night. She might be able to move into his room and not have Steffi walk through her room all the time. Nick and her mom might get a divorce since they didn't have a kid together anymore. Nick would move all of his stuff out. They wouldn't have his shit-green coffee table anymore or any of his stupid stuff. Nick would be out of their lives and they wouldn't have to see him on school vacations since they weren't related. He would be gone and he wouldn't come back.

It would be sad that Hugh died. Everyone would cry a lot. He would have a funeral. Maybe he would be cremated and put into a little box.

But then everyone would get over it and move on and stop talking about it. People would even say, you shouldn't talk about that anymore. That's what happened with Kirin.

If she did it fast, she thought, she could shoot the gun and not kill her brother. She could shoot it into the wall or into the air. Tammy was trying to stay in character, but she wasn't sure which character she was anymore. She didn't know if she was Kirin's mom, or the Witch, or Tammy. Or if she was some other character. Some person who couldn't talk. Some girl who was raised by wolves. Some Indian girl who was left behind on the *Island of the Blue Dolphins* for so long that she forgot how to speak because there wasn't anyone to talk to for years and years. She was alone for all that time. Her tribe had left her and her brother on the island to fend for themselves. They had left her brother by accident and she had jumped overboard from the white man's ship so that her brother wouldn't be alone. But the tribe never came back to look for them. Her brother died a few days later and she lived there by herself with only her pet wolf as a friend until she was an old woman and there were no more real Indians left in the world.

Tammy lifted the gun up and pointed it at the wall and squeezed her fingers against the trigger. She didn't think about it. She did it the way a person has to jump into a swimming pool they know is full of freezing cold water. You have to not think about it and just jump in. Almost surprise yourself that you are doing it. If you try to ease yourself in bit by bit, the water will be even colder. And it will be freezing by the time you finally get your bathing suit wet. You will never get used to it that way and you will probably back out before you are all the way in.

The gun went off with a loud crack and spat out a little flash of fire. Tammy lurched backward, tripped on her skirt, and fell down on her butt. Her head spun to the floor and for a moment she didn't know where she was, whose room she was in, or what furry, carpeted planet she had crash-landed on. She heard Monique say, "Oh my God," and Kenny say, "Holy shit!" and she heard them all race out of the room and down the stairs. Hugh was making high-pitched screams with his lungs, which meant he wasn't dead.

Tammy's head hurt. She felt hollow inside. She lay on the floor with the gun in her hand, her eyes closed, her arms spread wide over the plush. She wondered if she had missed the wall and maybe Hugh had a bullet wound and needed to go to the hospital, but she didn't get up to check. She felt heavy lying on the carpet and had no desire to move. The carpet was nice and cushiony and it felt good under her body. She felt warm and comfortable and the rectangle of skin exposed between her turtleneck and her skirt felt good. She wanted to stay like that a long time.

Tammy opened her eyes and stared up at the ceiling. It was the kind of ceiling made up of little stucco bumps. They looked like distant stars in a galaxy far, far away. If she closed her eyes halfway, her eyelashes made purple waves and a flashing rainbow of light. She wondered if they had rainbows in outer space. She slowly opened and closed her eyes a bunch of times, making flashing rainbows of different pastel colors. No one could see them but her.

A laser beam shot through the night stucco sky. In her extraterrestrial world, Tammy thought it was a spaceship coming to rescue her and take her home. As it got louder, she knew it wasn't a laser beam, but something else. She rolled onto her hands and knees and crawled over to the window to peek out from behind the shade. Swirling red police lights turned down 46th Street a couple blocks away.

Tammy bolted upright. She had to get out of there. Her brother was still on the bed. Tammy didn't see any blood, but Hugh was still crying. He was curled up with his eyes closed and he didn't notice Tammy until she grabbed his arm. Then he let out a scream and tried to pull his arm back.

"We have to go," Tammy said and dragged him off the bed. She saw the naked photos lying on the carpet near the bedroom door. Gretchen had probably dumped them on her way out. Tammy grabbed them, but she didn't have any pockets in her costume so she stuck them down the front of her underpants and hoped they wouldn't fall out.

Hugh moved slowly because he was still breathing heavy from crying. Tammy told him to hurry up, but after all, his legs were much shorter than hers. At the bottom of the staircase the two of them saw the red police lights shine through the window next to the front door. The laser siren stopped and Tammy could hear a car door slam.

"Run!" Tammy said to Hugh giving him a little push on his back. She turned him in the direction of the back door and he ran out into the backyard. Tammy didn't tell him not to run on the pebble path because she figured the police might find them if she said something out loud. She lifted the latch on the gate and the two of them ran into the alley. They ran as fast as Hugh could to where the alley emptied out onto the street. Tammy thought they would get caught if they walked on the sidewalk so she took Hugh's hand, crossed to the other side, and continued running through the alley. Hugh was dragging behind her, slowing her down. She pulled his arm until it almost stretched out of its socket and Hugh was running on his tiptoes. He stumbled over his loose shoelaces and fell down to the pavement. His pants ripped at the knee and his pink skin showed through the hole and started to bleed in tiny dots. Hugh began to cry.

"Shut up!" Tammy said, but it didn't help. Hugh shook his hand free from hers and acted like he wanted to sit on his butt in the alley for the rest of his life.

"Come on!"

"Nooooo!" Hugh wailed. He looked at his bare knee as if it didn't belong to him, as if a small pink worm had inched across his body and taken over his leg.

"Come on," Tammy said. "I'll give you a piggy-back ride." It was all she could think of to get him up. She squatted down with her back to him and he wrapped his arms around her neck and buried his snot-drippy nose in her hair. Tammy hooked her hands under his thighs. She had the gun in her right hand and it made it hard for her to hold his legs, but she managed to hoist him up and start running again although she was slow and clunky. After another block she turned and took the alley that ran in the direction of their house. She was tired, Hugh was heavy, but she ran all the way. She ran until the alley dumped them out onto 43rd Street and she only stopped to let Hugh slide off her back when they crossed to the corner where their house stood.

Tammy thought it would be better to go in the back door. That way maybe her mother and Nick wouldn't hear them and they could sneak in and pretend to be watching TV with Steffi. She could pretend they got home a while ago and everything was normal. That was her plan. To act normal like nothing had happened and the police weren't after them. But Hugh was a problem. He couldn't be trusted to tell a lie.

"Look," Tammy said. She wasn't quite sure what to do with him. She thought it would be better to see who was home and then sneak Hugh in. "I have an idea. Sit on the steps and count to one hundred and then come inside."

"Like hide-and-go-seek?"

"Yeah."

Hugh sat down, put his hands over his eyes, and started counting in a soft voice. Tammy pulled her cape around to the side and wrapped the gun by winding it in the fabric until it was twisted up into her armpit. She would wait until her mother and Nick were at work and then put the gun back in their room. She fished her key out from underneath her shirt and pulled it up through the turtleneck opening.

When she unlocked the door, Steffi wasn't watching TV. No one was in the kids' TV room. Tammy decided it was still a good idea and walked over to the TV. She reached for the channel dial when Nick grabbed her elbow and whipped her around. She didn't even hear him walk in.

"Where have you been?" he asked. "Do you know what time it is?"

Tammy tried to think of something. She needed an excuse, a good one. She thought about saying she got lost walking home in the dark, but she knew he wouldn't believe her. Even if she told him the truth he wouldn't believe her.

"Where's your brother?"

Tammy wasn't really scared before, she was just kind of confused. As soon as Nick said, "Where's your brother?" a thousand ants were crawling over her skin. She had forgotten what her plan was, and whatever it was, it was already not working out. She knew if she said Hugh was outside it would be followed by something like, what is he doing out there? And it's possible that Hugh could get spanked for something Tammy told him to do.

"I don't know," she said. It was barely a whisper.

"You don't know?"

"Nope." Everything she said got quieter and quieter and she hoped she was slowly falling asleep.

"Well, think!"

Tammy thought she was going to fall over and crash into the shelf. The only thing holding her upright was Nick's big hand wrapped around her arm.

"I don't know . . . outside somewhere," Tammy said.

Nick pulled her wrist forward and stepped behind her. With his other hand he spanked her hard across the butt over and over again. Really hard and it hurt.

Tammy wanted to tell him to stop it, but she was scared that if she did, he would spank her harder. She usually didn't yell when she got spanked. She just took it and cried to herself.

Nick spun her around to face him. "Where is your brother? You left a little boy somewhere late at night and forgot about him! Where is he?" He grabbed her wrist tighter. It was swelling up and he was cutting off the circulation.

"I don't know!"

"Yes, you do!"

"I don't know! He's probably outside playing somewhere."

"Where?"

"I don't know!"

Nick turned her around again and took off one of his shoes. This time he spanked her over and over again with his shoe across her butt. A couple times he missed and got her shoulders or her legs. Tammy's mother wandered into the kitchen to see what was going on. She stood in the doorway to the kids' TV room. Tammy could see her watching. Her mother didn't come in to stop Nick. She watched for a little bit and then walked away.

"Stop it!" Tammy yelled and tried to get away from him. She took a step forward, tripped over one of her brother's toy trucks, and fell down. The gun slipped out from her armpit and unraveled to the floor. She tried to reach for it, but Nick yanked her back up and grabbed it.

"Where did you get this?" he yelled. He clicked something and took a piece of it apart saying, "Jesus fucking Christ." Then he screamed at her, "WHAT THE HELL ARE YOU DOING WITH THIS? DID YOU TAKE THIS OUT OF MY ROOM?"

Tammy didn't take it out of his room, so she said, "No." Nick punched her in the face with his hand. It made Tammy's head turn and it knocked her off balance. She took a step to keep from crashing into the toy shelf and tripped over the truck again. She fell down to her hands and knees with her butt facing Nick. Her head hurt. Her teeth hurt. Her nose hurt. She tasted blood inside her mouth. The photos hung in her underwear and slowly peeled away from her skin. She squished her eyes closed, not sure if she was crying or not, and wondered if Steffi was upstairs, directly above where she was now, listening with her ear to the floor.

Tammy couldn't move. She waited on her hands and knees for Nick to start spanking her again.

"Go to your room," Nick said.

Tammy picked herself off the linoleum and walked inside to the living room. Her mother was sitting on the shit-brown couch watching TV, pretending like she didn't know what was going on. Nick grabbed a jacket and said that Tammy was a liar and a thief. She was irresponsible and had left her brother behind at school all by himself. Nick was going to go find him. They would decide her punishment when he got back. When he opened the door to go out, Tammy yelled at him, "I HATE YOU! YOU SHITHEAD!" He turned around, pointed his long finger at her and told her to go to her room. And Tammy's mother repeated, go to your room. Tammy told her she hated her too. Her mother said too bad.

Tammy heard a squeaking sound from the kids' TV room. She looked over and Hugh popped out from behind the back door.

"He's right there," Tammy said as Hugh walked into the kitchen. Nick turned around and her mother got up off the couch. Nick put his hands on Hugh's shoulders and asked, "Are you okay?" like he was all of a sudden trying to pretend he was such a nice guy who really cared. Everyone was such a fake. Everyone pretended. Everyone was really mean. Everyone would kill people if they thought they could get away with it.

Hugh was sent upstairs to bed. He tried to say, "Good night, Tammy," as he walked up the stairs, but Tammy's mother said, "Hugh, just go to bed," in a mean voice and he ran up the rest of the way.

"Sit down," Nick said when Hugh was gone. "We have something to tell you."

Tammy sat down on the shit-brown couch. The TV was still on. It was some boring detective show that her mother liked. Nick saw her looking at it and turned it off. Her mother and Nick went through the usual stuff about how they were disappointed in Tammy and how she was going to have to learn about *responsibility*. She was *responsible* for her brother. She was *responsible* for making sure nothing happened to him, for making sure he got home safe, and for making sure someone was around in case of an emergency. Playing with a gun was not responsible.

She could've seriously hurt someone or even killed someone. They'd tell Tammy what her punishment was tomorrow. Tammy only half-listened because they always said the same thing. They were like a commercial she had to sit through in order to watch what she wanted on TV.

"Was there something else?" Tammy asked because she was bored.

"Watch it," her mother said. This was usually supposed to scare Tammy, but Tammy didn't care. She thought, you can't punch someone in the face and beat them up with a shoe and then expect them to be afraid of a "watch it."

Her mother and Nick were quiet for a minute and then they both sat down. Nick had gotten a new job, her mother said. Well, not exactly a new job, but a promotion and a transfer. And a raise. We didn't want to tell you until we knew for sure, they said. The new job was in Topeka. They were going to move there a few weeks after school ended in June. Tammy asked where Topeka was. They said Kansas.

Kansas.

Kansas was in the middle of nowhere. It wasn't near any oceans. They have tornados there. Tammy didn't know anyone there. It seemed very far away from everything. She didn't want to move to a new place and not know anyone and have only her family who didn't understand her.

"I'm not going," Tammy said.

Her mother said it would be the easiest for Tammy since next year she would start junior high and would be going to a new school anyway.

"I'm not going," Tammy said again. Her mother said she knew it would be a big change, but they moved here and that was a big change and everything turned out fine. Her mother said that Tammy was in a mood and they would talk about it in the morning. She told Tammy to go wash off her makeup and go to bed.

"No, I'm not going. I'm not moving. I'm staying here."

"What exactly do you think you're going to do?" her mother asked.

"I'll go live with Dad."

Nick stood up. Tammy thought he was going to yell or punch her out again, but he slowly walked to the kitchen and didn't say anything.

"I don't think that's a good idea," her mother said.

"Why not?"

"What about your brother and sister? They would miss you."

"Not really."

"Look, it's not going to happen."

"Why not?"

"Your dad has to travel a lot for his job. He's out of town a lot."

"That's okay. I have friends here I can stay with when he goes away."

"Tammy, it's not going to happen."

"I'm not moving away with you and Nick. I'll move in with Dad."

"Tammy, he doesn't want you." She said it in her half-mad voice. Her too-tired-to-yell voice. Her voice that meant just shut up. Just shut up, shut up, shut up, Tammy. Enough, Tammy. I don't want to hear it, Tammy.

Tammy looked right in her mother's face. "You don't want me either," she said. Her mother didn't say anything back for a minute, so Tammy knew it was true.

Tammy stared into her mother's eyes and dared her to blink. "You don't want me either," she said again.

"Tammy—"

"Why don't you put me up for adoption? Then you would be rid of me altogether."

There was a pause while her mother looked at her and Tammy got the feeling that her mother had thought of it before. If not adoption, something else like it. Some other way to get rid of her. Then her mother took the same kind of saggy breath as when she was going to say no to something and didn't want to give a reason.

"We're all you've got, Tammy. This is your family. Not Dad. This is it."

Something inside Tammy took over then. Usually she wasn't this bully-like with her mother when Nick was around because she was afraid of him. Tonight she felt different. Maybe Kirin's house was haunted and there was a spell put on her. Maybe she was the Wicked Witch come back to life. Maybe she realized her mother had lost the ability to love her and Tammy had nothing left to lose. She stared at her mother and she spoke very slowly and didn't yell.

"I fucking hate you, and I fucking hate Nick. I wish you would kill yourself like Kirin's mom and I hope you don't miss."

Her mother was shocked. Tammy could tell. Tammy couldn't stay in this house with them anymore. She opened the front door and walked outside. When she got to the sidewalk she heard Nick say something like, "She'll come back when she's tired." Tammy didn't look back. She kept walking. She walked all the way down Bemis Street, past 46th Street,

47th Street, 48th Street, and 49th Street, until she got to Western Avenue, which was the official marker of the city limits. If she crossed that street, she would be in Maryland.

Tammy waited until no cars were coming and ran across the avenue. There were no sidewalks on the other side and the streets were curvy. In the distance, a gas station glowed under bright white lights. It looked like a satellite glittering in outer space. Tammy walked toward it because she didn't have anywhere else to go.

Tammy didn't realize she was crying until she walked into the square of gas station light and a man filling up his tank looked at her funny. When she wiped her nose, blood and green stuff came off on the back of her hand.

Tammy found a dime in the pay phone coin return. She dropped it into the change slot and tried to hide behind the scratched-up Plexiglas. She dialed her dad's number, but the operator came on and told her it would cost more money because it was a long-distance call. Maryland to Virginia. State to state. The operator asked Tammy what she wanted to do and Tammy couldn't say anything. She asked her again and Tammy started crying. The operator said, if Tammy wanted, she could put it through as a collect call. Tammy said okay.

The phone rang six times. Tammy's dad picked up and she could hear him talk to the operator for a second.

"Hello?"

"Dad?"

"Why are you calling this late, Tam?"

"I just wanted to know . . ." It was hard for her to talk because her lip was swollen like when she got a novocaine shot from the dentist. Her face had turned to stone and it wasn't letting her talk.

"I just wanted to know . . . if I could come live with you?"

"What, hon?"

"Can I come live with you?"

"Tammy, where are you?"

"At a gas station."

"Why aren't you at home? Isn't it kinda late?"

"I just wanted to talk to you."

"You can talk to me the next time I see you. Okay?"

"Can I come stay with you?"

"You'll stay with me the next time I see you."

"But can I come live with you?"

"What do you mean?"

"Can I come live with you instead of Mom?"

"No, hon. You have to live with your mom. I'll see you when school's out."

"But I don't want to live with her. I want to live with you."

"Honey, you have to live with your mom."

"But she doesn't want me . . ." and here Tammy's voice trailed off and bloody snot bubbled out of her nose. She thought her dad said something back, but she couldn't hear what it was. He went on about how they probably had a fight and she was just upset and that she should go home. Tammy told him it wasn't about a fight. Her mother and Nick hated her and she hated them. Tammy's dad didn't believe her. She asked again if she could live with him and he said her mother wasn't going to allow it. So Tammy asked him why he wouldn't allow it.

Her dad was quiet. Then he took a big breath and let it out.

"Look, honey, I'm just not at a place in my life where I can have a bunch of kids all the time. Okay?"

Tammy didn't understand what he meant. It sounded like he was saying she could live there part of the time, which would be okay because she was in school most of the day. She said over the summer he could send her to sleep-away camp and then she wouldn't be around much. She said he could even send her to boarding school if he wanted and then she would only be home on holidays, so it really wouldn't be much different than it was now. He said he couldn't send Tammy to all of those places. He didn't have that kind of money. Tammy said she could probably get a scholarship because she got mostly As on her report card. He said he didn't think they had scholarships for places like that.

"Your dad's not a rich man. This is all just not going to happen."

Tammy said she would stay at school all day and be very quiet when she was at home. She thought it could work out. It would just be her and not Steffi.

"Look, hon, do you remember Cindy? Well, Cindy and I are getting married this summer. Cindy's going to have a baby. So it looks like you're going to have another brother or sister."

That made Tammy stop crying. The phone hung in her fingers as if the black plastic receiver were the last autumn leaf clinging to a tree. She felt like a tree with skinny branches in the winter that just snap off. Her dad had said he was marrying Cindy and having a baby like those were happy things, but Tammy felt her branches crack and splinter away. Her dad was her one last hope and now he was gone. He was closing the door to his house in her face.

As she stood in the transparent gas station phone booth, Tammy could see into the future, like someone in a special time machine or a *Land of the Lost* magic pylon. She could see what it was all going to be like. Steffi would be the flower girl at the wedding and Tammy would be in the pictures wearing a pants suit that itched. And there Cindy would be taking extra-slow steps on Steffi's petals. Cindy would marry Tammy's dad and then she would have the same last name as them. She would have a baby and name it after someone in her family whom Tammy and Steffi never met or someone they met at the wedding who smiled at Tammy and Steffi as if to say, "It's too bad you exist. You make things awkward." Tammy would be shut out. Tammy realized that's partly why people like Cindy and her mother have babies when they get remarried, to cut the other kids off. Like some kind of insurance. Tammy's dad would love that baby more than Tammy, just like her mother and Nick loved Hugh more than Tammy. And everyone automatically loved Steffi because she was cute and sweet and a pleasure to have in class. Steffi made a point of being good so that everyone would love her. Steffi ignored all the bad things and pretended like they didn't matter. But Tammy couldn't do that. All the bad things were tied up in Tammy. They used to be good things, but then overnight, and Tammy couldn't remember when, they had turned bad. It was easy for people to ignore Tammy and assume she was old enough to take care of herself. She thought, that's what people tell themselves to feel better when they realize they've forgotten about you. Or when they don't want to think about you at all. When they'd rather pretend you didn't exist. Or when they wished you were dead.

Tammy realized that if she were killed in an accident everyone would be much happier. They would be rid of her. They didn't like her being around because she reminded them of all the mistakes they had made in their lives. All the stuff they wished they could undo. And Tammy couldn't let go of the mistakes and pretend they weren't there. She knew that's what everyone wanted her to do, but she couldn't do it.

Tammy didn't say anything for a long time and her dad asked if she was still there. He said they couldn't talk too long because it was expensive. He asked where she was and Tammy said she didn't know exactly. He said that if she knew how to get home by herself, then that's what she should do. He said, "Bye, hon," when he hung up. He usually said, "Bye, hon, love you," but he didn't say the "love you" part this time. Tammy didn't say anything. She just hung up.

She walked around to the side of the gas station, went into the bathroom, and locked the door behind her. She pulled the Polaroids out from under her skirt and threw them in the trashcan. She looked at herself in the mirror. Her skin looked extra green under the half-burned-out fluorescent light. Her eyes were puffy from crying so much and her lips were swollen. Blood was caked around her nostrils and her green makeup was smudged. She looked like a witch. She was ugly.

She gathered up her witch's skirt, pulled down her pants, and sat on the toilet.

The inside of her underwear was stained with blood.

THE VISIT

✳   ✳   ✳

Josie went on a Saturday when Gretchen was off with friends and her husband was parked on a golf course. When she got to the hospital she accidentally got on the Sabbath elevator. It stopped on every floor because today was Saturday, the day Jews can't touch any buttons. Josie wished she had something like that, a small ancient rule that actually provided you with a sense of relief.

Josie was buzzed into the ward and then buzzed through a second door into the women's wing. Because Valerie was on suicide watch, Josie was told to leave her bag with the nurse at the desk. Another nurse led her down the hall, squishing along in her white rubber shoes and white polyester pants that stretched too tightly across her hips. She dictated to Josie a list of rules and said she'd be back to check on her in fifteen minutes.

"Don't tire her out," the nurse said.

The door was already propped open waiting for her.

Valerie was lying on her bed in a hospital gown with a second gown wrapped around her shoulders like a cardigan sweater. One arm was bandaged in a sling. Normally Josie would have brought flowers and put a smile on her face. Today she was empty-handed. She couldn't fake it anymore.

Josie sat gingerly on the edge of the hospital bed. Valerie's head was turned toward the window; she hadn't noticed Josie enter the room.

Josie thought about getting up and leaving, telling the nurse Valerie was asleep and she didn't want to disturb her. What was she doing here anyway? What did she want to say? Fuck you? How could you do what you did? Or, we cleaned up the house for you. You don't have to worry. I'm sure everything will be all right. You'll get some help. You'll be all right. Things usually work out for the best. That's what a good friend would say. She would say all those things and then change the conversation to this-and-that anecdotes, throw in a joke, something funny she'd seen on TV, or some new ethnic food she'd tried at a restaurant.

She didn't know where to begin.

Josie remembered when she and her husband moved to the block; Valerie was the first person they met. It was summer and Josie was six months pregnant with Gretchen. She wore a kerchief in her hair, a light green peasant blouse flowing over her belly, and tan shorts with an elastic waist. Valerie waved to her from her porch, walked over to shake her hand, and invited Josie and her husband over for a barbecue that night. I know you'll be too tired to cook, she had said. Valerie helped Josie hang curtains in her new house and pick out sunflower wallpaper for the kitchen. Valerie hosted a baby shower for Josie. Two years later, Josie gave Valerie all her maternity clothes. It was over ten years ago, Josie thought. It was 1970.

In the here and now, in the humid summer of 1982, Josie's eyes rested on Valerie's luminous cheek shining up toward the ceiling. Josie was waiting for instructions. She felt like a plane circling the airport waiting for permission to land. In her airy orbit, she wondered what she should do now, now that she was ten or twelve years older, now that she had a sensible haircut and widening thighs, now that she was seated on Valerie's hospital bed in a psychiatric ward. She didn't know how to make things better. She had no clue as to how to be a mother or a friend. Is that what she should do? Act like she was Valerie's mother? When was someone going to take care of Josie? Where was her fairy godmother? I'm the one who's stuck here, Josie thought. My husband's cheating on me. My daughter hates me. I'm doing nothing with my life. No one wants to talk to me about any of this. I'm getting painted over along with the rest of the bloody mess. I'm the one who's alone. All I have is Val.

Josie and her husband hadn't made love since it happened. All they did at night was watch TV in bed until one or both of them woke up an hour later and switched off the set. Josie realized the last person she kissed, fully kissed on the lips, was Kirin. And it was a futile kiss, one unable to waken the sleeping princess.

Josie scrunched her eyes closed to keep the tears from falling down her face. She let out one gasping sob and quickly covered her mouth with her palm. She felt something brush against her skin. She looked over and saw Valerie gently stroking her arm with two fingers.

"It's okay, baby," Valerie said. "It's okay to cry."

Josie clenched her stomach in a desperate effort to keep control over her body. Tears spilled over onto her cheeks and flowed uncontrollably down her face. Her mouth torqued into a sad grimace and she cried out in agony. She couldn't bear sitting upright and collapsed forward into Valerie's chest. She buried her face in Valerie's long hair and felt her body embraced by Valerie's twiggy good arm. Valerie ran a gentle hand up and down her spine and Josie occasionally heard through her own wails a quiet "There, there." Josie cried until all the water in her body was dried up and her sobs were reduced to a series of convulsive inhalations. Finally, her breath softened, and the two of them lay there together, wet and rumpled and exhausted, like a pair of spent lovers.

The nurse came back and said that Valerie had an appointment. Josie peeled herself off the bed and wiped her eyes with her fingertips. Valerie smiled at her and waved good-bye with her good hand.

The nurse at the desk handed her back her purse. It's good you came today, she said. She's being transferred to St. Elizabeths tomorrow. Court order.

Josie stepped into the elevator's shiny metal box and glided down to the first floor without stopping, without anyone bothering her or asking if she was all right. She walked through the lobby and into the sunny Saturday afternoon of the parking lot. The vinyl of her car seat stung her skin. She shut the door and sat in her sealed automobile breathing in the hot stale air. She hadn't spoken a single word to Valerie, but there was nothing left to say. It was then that she realized she would never see Valerie again.

Josie rested in the sun-drenched quiet of her parked car until sweat started to drip under her arms and trickle down the inside of her blouse.

She cranked open the window and started the engine. As she slowly drove up to the stop sign at the parking lot exit, she thought to herself, I could go anywhere. I've got the car and the checkbook. I could drive off anywhere.

A car behind Josie honked a short beep, startling her back to life. Josie looked both ways and instinctively turned toward home.

THE GARDEN

They were having a Halloween party in the middle of June. They probably figured we wouldn't notice, Jeffrey thought. Or they're trying to pull some sick joke over on us, make the crazy people crazier by telling them Halloween is in June and acting like it's normal. They probably want to keep us crazy. After all, Jeffrey thought, we pay the rent.

They made their own costumes in Art Therapy. Or Occupational Therapy. Or Industrial Therapy. One of those. They had a therapy for every day of the week. Jeffrey wanted to be a pirate, but the therapist wouldn't let him have a hook hand. Too dangerous. Nothing dangerous allowed in the C ward. For the longest time, Jeffrey thought they were saying "sea" ward because the halls were painted aquamarine blue. Someone finally clued him in and said, "The *letter* C, man. C for criminal. We're doing time."

Jeffrey was a pirate without a hook or a sword. He wore a black cowboy hat and a white shirt that was too big for him. The therapist allowed him to wear an eye patch.

They lined up in the sunlit hallway between rows of rocking chairs. Jeffrey avoided this hallway when he took certain medication. All the bobbing chairs made him nauseous.

"Let me ask you this, let me ask you this . . ." Jeffrey was standing behind the skinny kid who always asked questions and never retained the answers. He was the type who was in constant motion. Not a rocker. The rockers sat in rocking chairs all day. When they weren't in rocking chairs, they sat in regular chairs and rocked side to side grinding their teeth. This kid never sat. An attendant once made the mistake of ordering him to sit. The kid sat on the couch in the day room, counted to ten, then got up and started slamming his head into the wall. Today he was wearing an orange cape. Jeffrey wasn't sure what he was supposed to be.

The doors buzzed open and they shuffled down the corridor, a motley crew of freaks.

After they passed the cafeteria, they were buzzed into the garden. When the door opened, their ward supervisor turned around to face them and reminded them of their manners.

"Remember, we're guests here."

Yeah, right.

Their line stayed more or less intact as they walked along a path through the manicured sloping lawns, past the little driveways named after innocuous trees: Spruce, Birch, Willow, Ash, past the sweeping vista of the Anacostia River with the Washington Monument poking up in the distant skyline saying its own private little fuck you. Fuck you, I'm the tallest. No one can be taller than me, so sayeth Thomas Jefferson and the Frenchies who designed this town.

The kid in the orange cape broke away from the group and ran streaming down a hill with an orderly chasing him. He looped back up to the group and got back in line, a huge grin on his face. He did it a couple more times, but didn't run as far. He was getting a kick out of it.

They arrived at the Square Garden. The correct name for it was the English Garden, but everyone just called it the Square Garden. Some ladies' horticultural do-gooder society had donated it and paid for its weekly pruning. It had rose bushes and walls made of four-foot-high green shrubs. The women's ward had decorated it for the party, an idiotic idea. Why decorate flowers? Paper chains drooped from the hedges. They had set up card tables with paper tablecloths, a bowl of Kool-Aid punch, and paper cups. Everything in this place was made of paper.

A nurse got things going by turning on the record player. They played lousy music and everyone bopped up and down together in the middle of the square. Some people sat on benches off to the side.

One girl refused to leave the Kool-Aid table. A lot of guys grabbed whatever piece of ass they could. The girls were forced to sell themselves for good socialization points. Jeffrey wondered what kind of therapy this was.

Jeffrey sat on one of the benches and looked down at his feet with one eye. I'm the most famous guy in here, he thought, and I can't get a date to the party. Not that there's anyone in here who I would actually date. You can't go from being involved with Oscar-caliber actresses to dating mentally ill trash.

Jeffrey's shoes had no shoelaces. They were a step up from the paper slippers he wore when he first arrived.

Valerie didn't want to comb her hair, but the angels made her. Just because you're in here is no reason to let yourself go, they said. Valerie let them help her. They would get so testy if she didn't. Now that she lived in their red brick castle they thought they could boss her around all the time. Valerie tried to ignore them at first, but they woke her up in the middle of the night and slapped her around. She only had one good arm. It was hard to defend herself.

She made her costume with the other ladies on her hall, meticulously cutting fabric with school safety scissors. It took Valerie a few tries to get the hang of it, jamming her adult fingers into the child-size holes. She wasn't exactly sure what she was making; she let the rounded scissor tips lead the way through the white sheet. She crawled across the white ocean and followed the dull blades to the opposite shore. When she arrived she had two white triangles and a handful of pipe cleaners.

The angels helped her slip her arms into the linen wings. They didn't stick up the way the angels' did. They drooped toward the floor and dragged along behind her picking up dust.

A nurse pulled out an old Christmas wreath made of golden tinsel and placed it on Valerie's head.

"Am I one of you now?" she asked the angels.

Not yet, but you're in training. Study hard and do good deeds. And most importantly, keep your mouth shut.

"Why?"

There are those around here who wouldn't understand.

Valerie waited on a bench in the garden with the other ladies: an assortment of princesses, animals, and nurses.

When the music started, Valerie was snapped back into reality. This wasn't an enchanted castle. She wasn't an apprentice angel. She was a bad person wearing a dirty sheet. She didn't understand how any of this was supposed to make her feel better.

A pirate was staring at her from across the square with one eye.

Valerie looked away. She would wait it out. She didn't belong here. But it was her fault. She had failed at death. She wouldn't try again unless she had a foolproof plan.

"I don't dance."

Valerie looked up. The pirate was standing beside her.

"Do you?" he asked.

Valerie shook her head.

"Good."

The pirate sat down on the edge of her left wing anchoring her to the bench. Valerie thought about tugging it free, but decided the pirate might think it rude. She stared across the square at the girl who had started crying because she had spilt Kool-Aid on her costume. She was transfixed by the cherry-red stain running down the girl's front. A nurse was trying to calm the girl. The image didn't upset Valerie. She simply stared at it, blankly wondering what it was that attracted her eyes to the girl's sticky chest.

"Did you know that the average length of stay for a staff member is longer than the average length of stay for a patient?"

Valerie shook her head.

"Do you know why?"

Valerie looked into his one blue eye.

"Government job. They get all these pension benefits and then retire early on your tax dollars."

She wondered if it was a joke. She didn't get it.

"My name is Jeffrey. I'm a poet. This is a famous place for poets, you know?"

She nodded.

"Are you supposed to be an angel?"

She leaned over and whispered in his ear, "I'm in training."

As she slowly pulled away from his ear, he turned his head toward hers and his cheek accidentally brushed her lips. The sun was setting, lighting up the sky in a glorious pink and turning the Washington Monument into a silhouette.

AMERICA (THE FRONTIER)

THERE IS NO HOME-LIKE PLACE

*   *   *

Moving day was exactly one week after sixth-grade graduation. There was a pool party at the Promenade Swim Club, but Tammy wasn't allowed to go as part of her punishment. She wasn't allowed to do anything after school until the school year was over. She tried to argue the night before that technically school was over when the bell rang that day at three o'clock, but her mother and Nick weren't buying it. They said they were sorry she would miss the party, but even the last day of school was a school day. She had to come straight home from school after they played the *Chariots of Fire* theme song for the sixth-grade class in the auditorium.

Tammy couldn't even do much of anything the first week of summer break because they had to pack. Her mother made the kids pack two boxes a day of stuff from their rooms and two boxes of things from the living room or kitchen. Clothes that didn't fit anymore or toys they didn't play with anymore were put in a pile for the Vietnam vets charity.

On moving day, they rented an orange U-Haul truck. The plan was for Nick to drive the truck to Kansas and the rest of them were going to follow in the car with Tammy's mother driving. It took all morning to pack up the truck and the car. Tammy's mother kept rearranging things so she could see out the rearview mirror. When they were all packed up, Nick locked the door to the house. He dropped the keys into an envelope and licked it shut. Then he went up to the next-door neighbor's house and knocked on the door. He gave the guy the envelope and shook his hand.

When he walked back out to the curb he said, "We're going to make one stop downtown, and then we'll go."

Tammy's mother said it was out of the way and she wasn't sure if there was time, but Nick was already in the truck and didn't hear her.

They drove to the Mall where all the monuments and museums were. Nick pulled over and walked back to the station wagon. "I don't think we can park here," he said to Tammy's mother. "So, can you watch the truck?"

"Where are you going?" Steffi asked.

Nick had already started walking across the grass. "Come on," he said without looking back.

Tammy, Steffi, and Hugh got out of the car. Don't take too long, their mother said, we don't want to get a ticket.

They walked along a fence looking for a spot to see in. They didn't see where Nick had gone. They stopped next to a big gate where a bulldozer was parked.

"What's this place?" asked Hugh.

"The vets memorial," Tammy said.

It didn't look like much. It was all muddy and still under construction. There was a cement wall with sticks poking out of it in the shape of a wide V and a sidewalk that wasn't finished. The sidewalk ended on the far side in a pile of rubble. It was a big mess. Tammy didn't know what it was supposed to look like when it was done.

"What's a vet?" Hugh asked.

"Someone who was in Vietnam," Tammy said. "They're building this place because a lot of people died."

"Do we know anyone who died?"

Tammy looked at Steffi, but she had spotted Nick and was running over to him.

Nick didn't say anything when Tammy and Hugh caught up with him. He just looked at the construction site and the bulldozers and the men in hard hats smoothing out cement.

"Guess I won't be able to see it," Nick finally said. Then he started walking back to the curb and said, "Let's go."

They climbed back into the station wagon and Tammy's mother started the car. Steffi waved her hand and said, "Good-bye, Washington,

DC!" Hugh chimed in too. As they curled around the Lincoln Memorial, Tammy pulled her Polaroid camera from her backpack and aimed it out the car window. She had a new pack of film. She took nine photos and laid them on her lap to develop. She knew the pictures would come out blurry because they were in a moving car, but she knew she couldn't count on her family to remember anything.

For the last picture, she turned her camera around and aimed it at herself.

They crossed the Potomac River and headed west.

Printed in the United States
by Baker & Taylor Publisher Services